BOUNDLESS

ERIN ENTRADA KELLY • JASMINE WARGA • VEERA HIRANANDANI

MÉLINA MANGAL

AKEMI DAWN BOWMAN • ANIKA FAJARDO • SHANNON GIBNEY

I.W. GREGORIO • TORREY MALDONADO • ADI ALSAID • ERIC SMITH • LORIEL RYON

BOUNDLESS

NASUĠRAQ RAINEY HOPSON

EDITED BY
ISMÉE WILLIAMS AND
REBECCA BALCÁRCEL

EMIKO JEAN • GOLDY MOLDAVSKY • RANDY RIBAY • TARA SIM • KAREN YIN

ISBN-13: 978-1-335-42861-5

For questions and comments about the quality of this book, please contact us at CustomerService@Harlequin.com.

Inkyard Press
22 Adelaide St. West, 41st Floor
Toronto, Ontario M5H 4E3, Canada
www.InkyardPress.com

Printed in U.S.A.

CONTENTS

To all whose identities cross boundaries
And to love that knows no bounds

A FOREWORD FROM
THE EDITORS

We all struggle to figure out who we are and where we belong. We try to find our place and our people. It's a lot harder if we don't even fit in with our own family. Some of us don't have the skin color of either of our parents; some of us don't speak the languages of our grandparents; some of us have siblings who look like one race while we look like another. Meanwhile, outsiders puzzle over which box to put us in.

The authors in this anthology are all multiracial and/or multicultural. We have all faced challenges with our identity. At times, we have felt alone and without connection to either of our parents' communities, like islands set apart. However, because we have lived in two or more cultures, we also have developed extraordinary empathy and resilience. We recognize multiple ways of living, multiple lenses on the world, and various sides of conversations because we live, speak, and breathe these different sides. We can bring together distinct groups, improving communication and understanding between them. We can be bridges.

When we look in the mirror, in our pantries, in our hearts, or in the eyes of someone who says, "What are you?" we know we don't fit into one category. At times, this is awkward, even painful. But we hope readers will see what it means to transcend categories, to be uncontained by a checkmark in a single box, to be boundless.

Our stories are nuanced and as varied as our own experiences. We hope you enjoy them.

THE CHAIR FAR AWAY FROM THE TABLE

By Akemi Dawn Bowman

SPRING

When Aunty Fei opens the door, the smell of chicken katsu, barbecued ribs, and potato curry tumbles out of the house like an explosion of contradiction—sweet and spicy, old and new, Asian and not Asian.

Well, maybe the last part is just me. *Projecting*, as Hannah says.

My older sister beams beside me and holds up a paper bag. "We brought sweet rolls!"

"I told you on the phone not to bring anything but yourselves," Aunty Fei scolds, even though her eyes are sparkling. She glances at Dad, who inhales the intoxicating scents from the doorway. "Save your money, Hiroichi. We have enough food to feed an army."

Dad laughs. "I'll remember that for next time."

He says that every week, but we *never* show up to karaoke night empty-handed. Aunty Fei may pretend like it's not necessary, but it's one of the unspoken rules Dad's side of the family seems to have. You're supposed to make an effort, even when everyone tells you not to.

Aunty Fei waves us all in. "I hope you folks are hungry."

"Starving," Dad replies, and Hannah and I follow him inside.

There's a row of aunties already waiting to greet us. They make all their usual comments—they ask how we've been managing since Mom left, they ask Hannah what she's planning to study at college, and they tell me I'm getting "so tall, just like your dad," even though me and Dad aren't exactly being recruited for a basketball team anytime soon.

And then they shuffle us toward the enormous table packed to the edges with Crock-Pots, glass bowls, and ceramic dishes. All the usual potluck favorites are here, plus a few new ones from the extended aunties and uncles.

Technically they're not *all* relatives, but my family is from Hawaii. Every friend of the family is considered an aunty, uncle, or cousin.

Someone shoves a plate in my hand, and Hannah nudges me forward, hurrying to get to the dish wedged between the potato mac salad and the spam musubi.

"They have the Jell-O," she whispers over my shoulder.

It's the most out of place dish on the whole buffet table. Half emerald-green, half milky-white, Aunty Fei has been making the half-and-half Jell-O squares for as long as I can remember.

I put two pieces on my plate and surround them with rice and chicken skewers.

One of the aunties sees my choices and looks personally offended, but then brightens when she sees everything on Hannah's plate.

Hannah tries *everything*—even the smoked tako—and everyone in the family seems to love her for it.

I don't have my sister's people skills, *or* her palate for octopus.

I don't even have her features, which are unmistakably similar to Dad's.

She never wonders if she's Asian enough to be a part of this family. But me?

I'm more like the puzzle piece that accidentally ended up in the wrong box. I don't fit.

Hannah disappears with everyone else into the dining room where the Big Table is set up for all the grown-ups. My sister is only just eighteen, but she stopped sitting at the kids' table years ago.

I'm not sure if I was ready for her to leave me behind, but Mom used to come to karaoke nights back then, and she never sat at the Big Table. She said she preferred sitting with the kids.

Maybe she never felt like she fit in, either.

But Mom is on the other side of the country now, chasing dreams that were too big to find in Las Vegas. And I'm too old for the kids' table.

I take my plate and find a spot in the corner of the living room, where Uncle Albert is sitting in his favorite red chair. I plop down a few feet away, eating in awkward silence while Uncle Albert rests his eyes.

He doesn't like socializing with the other aunties and uncles. I'm not sure he likes people coming to the house at all.

But I've been gravitating toward Uncle Albert and his chair ever since I was little, and he never tells me to leave. He just lets me sit with him in the quiet, and occasionally offers me candy.

Out of everyone in my family, I think I relate to him the most.

After dinner, my relatives flock to the TV in the big living room, where me and Uncle Albert are still sitting in the corner. There are over a dozen aunties and uncles, all gathered on footstools, cushions, armchairs, and patches of carpet.

When the blue karaoke image appears on the screen, one of my oldest uncles moves for the microphone and bursts into a very animated rendition of "Nagasaki Wa Kyou Mo Ame Datta."

And then Hannah leaps to her feet, rushing for the next turn while everyone offers words of encouragement.

Hannah doesn't even speak Japanese, but she knows all these old songs by heart. She's been singing them since Aunty Fei *started* karaoke nights.

I watch from the back of the room, like I'm on the outside looking in.

It's easy for Hannah. She looks more the part than I do; she has Dad's black hair and dark eyes, and skin that tans impeccably well in the sun. I inherited Mom's freckles and mousy brown hair and a face that is neither Asian nor white. It's racially ambiguous. The kind of face that confuses people, and they end up asking the same question over and over again. The question I dread most.

What are you?

Nobody on my dad's side of the family ever asks me that. But sometimes they look at me like they're waiting for me to figure it out.

Uncle Albert leans forward and grunts, interrupting my thoughts. He's holding a koa box full of See's lollipops: chocolate, coffee, vanilla, and butterscotch.

I take one of the butterscotch ones because they're my favorite, and pull off the wrapper. "Thanks," I mumble.

Uncle Albert twists his mouth and sinks back into his chair, setting the box beside him while Hannah finishes singing the last note in her song.

Aunty Fei's gaze immediately seeks me out like a spotlight. "Come, Nina," she calls, waving her hand toward the television. "You try next!"

I shake my head and point to the candy in my mouth like I'm apologizing, even though singing in front of my relatives—in front of *anyone*—is a genuine, recurring nightmare. I think I might even prefer the smoked tako.

Hannah stares at me for a second too long before handing

the mic to one of our cousins. She takes a seat next to Dad, but she's still watching me with the kind of urgency that makes me nervous and embarrassed all at once.

We've never had a secret sister language. We're not even really close.

But ever since Mom left, Hannah has been acting weird. Like she thinks she needs to fix me before she leaves for college and she's out of time.

I tug at my sleeve, cheeks burning when Hannah shakes her head at me from across the room. She doesn't have to say anything—I can read the message in her eyes.

You have to try, Nina.

Not about karaoke—she wants me to try harder to be a part of this family.

But she doesn't get it. Belonging comes naturally to her. She's never *had* to try.

I wish being myself were already enough.

I stare at the carpet, thinking of Mom on the other side of the country, and wonder why loving me wasn't enough to make her stay.

SUMMER

I sit in the living room, wedged between the floor fan and Uncle Albert. I forgot to bring a scrunchie, so I grab my hair with a fist and hold it off my neck.

Uncle Albert's snores grow and grow until he startles himself awake. He jolts, searching the room for all its familiarities, and then drifts back into a nap.

Hannah appears with her hands on her hips. "The buffet is outside," she says, using that weird Mom-like voice that's only gotten more obnoxious over the months. "Aren't you coming?"

"It's July," I reply with a blank face. "In Las Vegas."

She lifts her shoulders like she doesn't understand my point.

"It's like a hundred and twenty degrees."

"So? They have misters. Just put on some sunscreen—you'll be fine."

"I'm fine in here."

"Seriously, Nina," Hannah says, and now her arms are crossed, so I guess she's really upping the Mom impersonation. "You can't just keep avoiding everyone all the time. You need to be around other people."

I twist my mouth. "Nobody *needs* to be around other people."

"Yes they do," she snaps back. "Social isolation is *literally* a form of torture. You're just weird."

Her last word stings like salt in a wound that won't heal.

Hannah purses her lips. "I know Mom is gone, but—"

"This isn't about Mom," I say, bristling. Even though I mean it, Mom is always going to be a sore subject. It doesn't matter that she left months ago; there isn't a time limit on when I should be okay with one of our parents abandoning us.

I will never be okay with it.

Hannah sighs like she's tired, and maybe she is. But maybe I am, too. "She hated karaoke nights. And I think she made *you* hate them."

"She didn't make me do anything."

"Really? Because you were basically her shadow for fifteen years, Nina. You never left her side. You would've done anything to make her happy, even when she constantly asked for too much."

A scowl tears across my face. "What's that supposed to mean?"

Hannah's hands shoot up in desperation. "You didn't even yell at her when she left! She told you to understand, and you just...*did*. And now she's gone and it's like you're this lost puppy. I'm *worried*."

I flatten my mouth, holding back the words I want to say but wouldn't dare in front of Uncle Albert, sleeping or otherwise.

It was always me and Mom on one side, and Hannah and Dad on the other. Two different sides of a coin. Two contradictions.

Mom didn't abandon them the same way she abandoned me. She left them—but she left me *behind*.

I wasn't supposed to have to be a teenager without her. I wasn't supposed to feel this alone.

Of *course* I'm angry. Of *course* I'm sad. But what good would it do to say it out loud?

Nobody here would understand.

I don't want my mom to be the villain. But she was the person who felt most like family, and she didn't choose me.

"I'm not talking about this with you." My voice is stiff, and maybe a little cold.

But Hannah pushes anyway. "Family is important. Please try to make an effort. For Dad."

"What does Dad have to do with this?"

She eyes Uncle Albert, still asleep in his chair. "I think he needs karaoke nights more than you realize," Hannah says solemnly. "And I think... I think it's good for him to have a reason to leave the house. I think it's good for both of you."

"If you're worried about Dad, fine," I reply sourly. "But leave me out of it."

Hannah sighs. In a voice that's barely audible, she adds, "I just don't want you to always feel disconnected from the people who care about you. Mom liked to make her problems your problems. If she couldn't fit in, she didn't want you to, either. She didn't want to be alone—but she had no problem leaving *us* alone." She shakes her head. "You always deserved more than being Mom's shadow. You can just be *you*. I hope someday you'll believe it."

My mind spins too fast to reply, and then Hannah is gone and it's just me, Uncle Albert, and the buzzing fan.

When he speaks, his voice croaks like a bullfrog. "You're angry at the wrong person. Your sister is just trying to help."

I sit up, slightly alarmed. "I—I thought you were asleep."

"You woke me up."

My cheeks flush. "Sorry."

Uncle Albert folds his hands over his stomach. "How come you're always sitting here instead of hanging out with everybody else?"

"It's not like anyone cares." When I hear the words out loud, my eyes open wide. "I don't mean it in a bad way—I just mean that I'm not good at being around people the way Hannah is. So it doesn't really matter if I'm here or outside, you know? I'm like...invisible, I guess."

"Why do you have to be like your sister to spend time with your family?"

I blink. "Hannah is likable. She fits in. She sings karaoke and eats all the spicy food. She knows what to say to make everyone smile."

"You think eating spicy food gives you permission to sit at the table with everybody else?"

My jaw tenses, but I don't respond. I don't really know how to. Maybe it sounds silly, but Hannah never questions whether she belongs. She just *does*.

I guess I'm still trying to figure out what the difference between us is.

Uncle Albert stares up at the ceiling like he's searching for a memory. And then he lifts the koa box from the side table, removes the lid, and holds it toward me.

I take a butterscotch lollipop. He takes a coffee one.

We sit in the silence for a long, long time, listening to laughter in the distance. And I think maybe Uncle Albert understands me more than he wants to admit.

Maybe deep down, he doesn't feel like he belongs, either.

FALL

It's strange not seeing Hannah at karaoke nights. She still calls once a week to catch up with Dad and tell him about college. But there's an empty space she left behind that's even more noticeable than the one Mom left. She was a constant in our family—like the North Star. A nearly ever fixed source of light that everyone was drawn to. Dad most of all.

All Dad and I really share is the quiet.

And sometimes the quiet is the loudest thing of all.

I sit in the corner of the living room with my head down, drawing shapes in the carpet.

When the koa box appears in front of me, I take a piece of candy and look up at Uncle Albert. His brown eyes are thoughtful, watching me with a calm recognition.

He doesn't take the box away. "Give one to your dad," he says curtly. "He used to like the butterscotch ones when he was little, too."

I hold it in my hand, rolling the lollipop stick between my fingers. "I know what you're trying to do."

"What's that?"

"You're trying to fix me and Dad."

The corners of Uncle Albert's eyes wrinkle, but he doesn't smile. "I must be a clever guy if I'm doing all that just sitting here."

"Well, it's not going to work. He needs Hannah, not me."

"Who do *you* need?" When I don't answer, he leans his head back. "Go talk to your dad. And if you forgot how, just open your mouth and say words."

"It's not that easy."

Uncle Albert clicks his tongue. "That's because you need to practice more."

"You sound like my sister," I say but stand up anyway.

Dad's sitting on the couch in the far room, eating red bean mochi with Aunty April, Aunty May, and Aunty June. They're all named after their respective birth months, which seemed pretty unoriginal until I realized Dad and his brothers— Hiroichi, Hironi, and Hirosan—were basically named Hiro One, Hiro Two, and Hiro Three.

When I hand Dad the See's lollipop, he raises an eyebrow. "I haven't had one of these in years."

"Uncle Albert said you liked butterscotch the best."

"I do. Something you and me have in common." For a moment, he almost sounds relieved. "How about a trade?" he offers, holding up the container of mochi.

I take one of the round off-white pieces covered in rice flour.

Dad's entire face brightens. "Remember that time Grandma made you eat a whole bowl of poi because you'd gotten it confused with mochi and told her poi was your favorite?"

"Yeah. It tasted like glue," I say, chewing. "I think I cried at the table for two hours straight."

Aunty May makes a noise of surprise. "Did you mix it with sugar? It's real ono like that, you know."

"Grandma didn't say anything about sugar." I shrug. "She just said I wasn't leaving the table until I ate all of it because it was expensive."

Aunty April turns to Dad, laughing. "Your mom was so strict, yeah?"

Aunty June scoffs. "You and your brothers were always making humbug. She *had* to be strict."

Dad rubs the back of his neck sheepishly. "We weren't *that* bad. Although, there was the time we almost set the house on fire playing with toy soldiers..."

He spends the next few minutes reminiscing about his childhood in Hawaii, where Hannah and I probably would've grown up if Mom hadn't been in such a hurry to move. We have aunties and uncles in Vegas, but nowhere *near* as many as on Oahu.

Sometimes I wonder if karaoke nights would've felt different if I'd grown up where Dad did, around more people who looked like me. So many people in Hawaii are multiracial. It isn't weird or different or *exotic*, like I've been called most of my life. People in Hawaii share a similar cultural influence— there are pieces of Polynesian culture, with lots of love and respect for the Indigenous people of Hawaii, and a blend of Asian countries, including Japan and China where Dad's side of the family lived over five generations ago.

Dad calls it *chop suey*. All mixed up. And everyone in his family is considered kamaʻāina—a child of the land. Like they *belong*.

I wish it were that easy for me. But I didn't grow up in a land that wanted me.

I grew up with a Mom who decided she didn't.

When Dad finishes his story, all three aunties are laughing, and I realize he's no longer paying attention to me. They jump to the next story, and the next, and pretty soon I feel like I'm listening in on a conversation I'm no longer a part of. So I slip back out of the room and return to the corner of the house where Uncle Albert is asleep on his red chair.

I sit on the floor, folding my legs like a pretzel.

Sensing me, he shifts. His white socks are pulled halfway up his calves, and he's still wearing a pair of therapeutic flip-flops. *Slippers*, as my dad calls them.

"Go talk story with your cousins," he growls abruptly, the bags under his eyes darker than usual. "Play cards with your aunties. Anything except sit in this room all by yourself."

"I'm not by myself," I argue.

He waves a hand. "You're not here to talk to me. You're here because you don't know how to talk to anyone else."

My heart pinches, defensive. "Well, why are you here, then?"

For a long time, he's quiet. "Because," he says seriously, "I didn't practice enough when I was younger."

We sit together when the room fills back up with relatives ready to sing karaoke. The music starts, but I don't move from my spot. Every time I glance at Uncle Albert, his eyes are closed like he's asleep again.

But I don't think he's sleeping.

I think he's so used to feeling alone that he wants to convince himself that he really is.

WINTER

The house feels emptier than usual, even when there's twice the amount of people.

Not for karaoke night—for Uncle Albert's memorial.

It happened without any warning at all. He had a heart attack, and then he was gone.

There was no choice to leave or stay. Not like Mom, who packed her bags and planned her exit and recited her goodbyes like an essay she'd prepared again and again.

I'm not sure it matters how people go. All that matters is the hole they leave behind.

Mom is gone, and Hannah is gone, and now Uncle Albert is gone, too.

And I don't just feel alone—I feel lost.

Dad finds me in the laundry room, where Aunty Fei's chubby dachshund Mele Kalikimaka—Mele for short—is asleep in his bed.

"He sure does enjoy his naps," Dad remarks, shutting the door and sitting on the tile beside me.

"He doesn't like the noise." I don't know why I'm defending Mele. He *barely* tolerates me when he's awake.

"Is that why you're hiding in here?" Dad asks gently. "Because it's too loud?"

I flatten my mouth. "I'm not hiding. I just don't want to be out there."

"I know you and Uncle Albert were close. And if you want to talk about it…" His voice trails off, and I can't tell if it's because he doesn't know what to say, or if he's hoping I won't take him up on the offer.

It's awkward between us. It has been for a long time. But I'm holding too much in, and I don't know how much more my heart can take before it bursts.

I try to ignore the salt-sting in my eyes when I look at Dad. "What is so wrong with me that I can't get anyone to stay?"

"What?" Dad pulls his face back. "Honey, Uncle Albert passing was not your fault. Nobody could've controlled that."

I smear my tears with the heel of my palm. "Mom left. Hannah only talks to me when she's trying to boss me around. And you—you have more fun at karaoke nights than you've ever had with me."

Dad looks like his heart might burst, too. "That's not how I feel at all, Nina." He clenches his teeth, blinking too many times. "I can't defend or explain what your mom did. If I'm being honest, I still have questions, too. But I know Hannah loves you. *I* love you."

I sniff into my sleeve, shutting my eyes tight.

Dad hesitates, swallowing. "I'm not going anywhere, you know. I'm here—and I will be, anytime you need me."

I study his face for a moment, sensing the sadness in his eyes.

Hannah said it's always been there. Maybe even for as long as I've been holding on to my own hurt.

My chest tightens. "I'm mad that Mom left."

Dad's eyes crack like glass. "Yeah, kiddo. I'm mad about that, too."

"And I'm—I'm mad that she always made me feel like it was her and me, and you and Hannah." My cheeks darken. "And I'm mad that you always seemed okay with it. Like it was totally normal to love Hannah more."

He sits up then, eyes big and glistening. "I didn't know you felt that way, Nina. I love you both the same, and I always have. I guess I just assumed that you didn't always want to talk to me or hang out." He rubs his forehead, trying to find the right words. "That's my fault, not yours. I'm the dad—I should've told you more often that I wanted you around. And I'm sorry for that." He leans in, face serious. "But you are *not* my second choice. Ever, ever, ever, okay? Hannah being gone, your mom being gone, even Uncle Albert being gone... You and I are family forever. And there will never be a moment in my life where I don't want you in it."

"Okay" is all I can think to say.

Dad offers a sad smile. "That's your family out there, you know. And they love you, too."

"Sometimes I feel like Hannah matches this family better than I do. She's more like you—I'm more like Mom." My voice scratches. "Sometimes I feel like I'm not very good at being Asian."

Dad barks a laugh so loud it makes me jump. "Sorry," he says, holding up his hands. "But that is impossible. You *are* Asian. That's it. That's the prerequisite. It doesn't matter the language you speak or that your hair isn't as dark as mine or how much you know about the culture. You just *are*."

I press my lips tight to stop myself from crying.

Dad leans in, voice softening. "I'll tell you a secret. I couldn't figure out how to use chopsticks until I was fifteen. Everyone at school used to make fun of me. Grandma used to make me practice with the training kind. I can't tell you how many jokes my friends made about me not being a *real Asian*."

I wrinkle my nose. "Is that true?"

He holds up a hand. "I am dead serious." And then he stiffens. "Maybe that's an inappropriate thing to say today, with the memorial and all."

"Uncle Albert wouldn't mind." I motion toward the door. "He would've been more upset about all the people in his house."

Dad chuckles. I stare at my feet.

"I know he didn't talk a lot, but I miss him," I say, tears building in the corners of my eyes.

Dad tilts his face and nudges me with his shoulder. "That's another good thing about having family. We can all miss him together."

SPRING

Uncle Albert's red chair sits in the corner of the living room. It hasn't moved in months, even though nobody uses it.

I don't know why I do it—maybe because it's been so many

weeks since Aunty Fei has had karaoke nights again, or maybe because I just want to know what he saw when he watched all of us from his corner of the room—but I sit down in Uncle Albert's chair, lean into the worn cushion, and look around.

It feels like...

It feels like being on the outside looking in.

I swallow the knot in my throat, eyes drifting to the koa box nearby, full of See's lollipops.

My heart tugs, straining against my rib cage. He was here when nobody else was. He heard me, even when I wasn't trying to be heard.

Uncle Albert spent most of his life sitting far away from the people who loved him. Maybe he wasn't good at saying all the things he was thinking. Maybe being quiet became a habit that was too hard to break.

He'll never know all the people who came to his memorial, who told stories about his life and ached at the thought of never seeing him again.

He deserved so much more than a corner of the room. He deserved to know how deeply he was loved, from the very beginning.

And maybe I do, too. Maybe the only real difference between me and Hannah is that I'm still waiting for my family to give me permission to join them, when all I've ever really had to do was give permission to myself.

I sit in Uncle Albert's chair for a long time, listening to the noise on the other side of the wall, where everyone is busy eating at the Big Table.

With a quiet breath, I stand up, make my way into the dining room, and take a seat beside my family.

★ ★ ★ ★ ★

HISPANIC JEWISH BINGO

By Goldy Moldavsky

There are two old adages that pop into Amalia Lipski's mind as she stands in the sparkly decorated event space of her synagogue.

Un arbol torcido jamas su tronco endereza. And *Al tiftach pe l'satan.*

The one in Spanish literally translates to "a twisted tree will never grow untwisted" (meaning you can't change something that's already set in its ways). The one in Hebrew translates to "don't open your mouth to the devil" (aka, don't speak it into existence 'cause the devil might be listening and take you up on it). Amalia loves these sayings because she's pretty sure a version of the former exists in every culture and language in the world, and the latter casually confirms the existence of Satan when people who didn't know better tried to eradicate him from Jewish lore.

Amalia doesn't know why she is thinking of devils and tree trunks upon meeting Javier Ackerman, but the thoughts make her feel dirty, and she wants to banish them from her mind before they show up on her face.

Javier and Amalia are introduced to each other by a gaggle of

little old ladies who belong to the synagogue's sisterhood committee. Everything the two learn about each other comes from
the lilting voices of the sisterhood's chorus.

"Javier's father is Berto Poskolowitz's college friend. Visiting
from out of tow—"

"—Amalia planned this entire function. Casino Night. Isn't
it classy—"

"—Javier is a star soccer player. The shul doesn't have a sports
league, but maybe we should make one? You'll join. Also, he's
top of hi—"

"—Amalia is also top of her class *and* she's on the tzedakah
committee here. Charity is so impor—"

"—Javier is from Argentina—that's why we're introducing
you two—"

"Amalia is from Argentina, too! How marvelous is that? Two
exceptional young Jewish Argentines! Both at our shul! And
look how cute they are—"

"—Cute? They're gorgeous!"

Amalia stops listening. Mostly because she wants to hide under
a rock anytime she hears anything remotely like praise, but also
because that last part is definitely a lie. Gorgeous? No. Though
the way some of the girls here ogle Javier, it is only half a lie.
But the sisterhood's statements have other inaccuracies (Amalia
is from Peru, not Argentina). All in all, it makes her question
the validity of the rest of the proclamations. Already Amalia
finds herself doubting that Javier is both a star athlete and star
student, or even from Argentina.

But Amalia nods politely because she understands that the
million little old ladies who make up the sisterhood of the Beit
Ahava synagogue have never in their lives encountered other
(multiple) Latino Jews in their midst. They are clearly hoping
that Amalia and Javier—both high school seniors (or "Señores!"
as Mrs. Rubenstein exclaimed in full flamenco pose)—hit it
off tonight so that they can discuss among each other which

of them was responsible for the shidduch (the match) and get a seat at the wedding.

"You have to hear Amalia say something in Spanish."

"Do you speak Spanish, Javier?"

"Of course he does."

"Amalia, say something in Spanish."

Javier looks at her expectantly. There is a sardonic pinch at the corners of his lips. A condescension in their plumpness. A holier-than-thou, on-the-burst-of-laughing twitchy mirth. Doesn't he know how this goes? They must be respectful of the older women, endure their statements and questions, and perform when asked.

Amalia takes offense at his cavalier attitude. And she's not all that pleased to be introduced to him, either. Why should they be matched up simply because they both understand when Dora the Explorer needs help finding her backpack or whatever? But Spanish is the ace up Amalia's sleeve. It's a beautiful, important language to know, and it's also a party trick that shocks and amazes both the Jewish and Latino people she meets. No one ever expects it from her, the white-looking girl. It could be used to great effect. A glamour. A secret weapon.

Amalia holds up her cup as though in a welcoming toast but what she says is, "Mi vaso tiene agua." (My cup has water.)

Javier's smile deepens. "Me pica la rodilla," he says. (My knee itches.)

Upon hearing the romantic language, the million little ladies swoon. Then they leave so that Amalia and Javier can get to know each other better. When they are alone among the partygoers, Amalia and Javier look at each other for a beat. Then, at the same moment, they walk away in opposite directions.

Tonight is the annual Beit Ahava Tzedakah Function. Every year the synagogue throws a social event that masquerades as a charity event (or vice versa). It's like prom—with decorations and music and refreshments—but all ages, no dancing, and much less fun.

Amalia, as youth ambassador, was put in charge of the planning committee and chose Casino Night as the theme, a decision she now regrets. It's too weird. Too fulsome. It's a charity event (good, wholesome) but there's gambling (definitely not the most upstanding pastime). It isn't age-appropriate for anybody (too much dress-up and fake fancy cocktails for the children, too many games and fake fancy cocktails for the grown-ups). This whole party is like a manifestation of when you say something stupid and innocuous to somebody once but rethink it for the rest of your life. Amalia practically grows hives just standing there.

But she picked Casino Night because the only other option was an auction, and she definitely didn't want to cold-call local businesses begging them to donate gift baskets full of lotions or bath bombs or deli meats for people to bid on. Plus, Amalia didn't need to know anything about gambling to know one thing for sure: the house always wins. In this case, the synagogue was the house. Everyone would have fun while giving to charity, the shul would make a lot of money, and Amalia would prove that she was a capable—nay, *perfect*—youth ambassador. There wouldn't be any doubt about—

"This is the luckiest night of everyone's life!"

Amalia turns to find Mrs. Aaronson at her side, clutching a plastic take-out container nearly overflowing with tokens and poker chips.

"What?" Amalia says.

"I'm making a killing! G-d forbid, but you know what I mean. Gladys Shmueleki just won five hundred dollars at roulette and Shimi Cohn only started with five dollars in chips and he's up a thousand!"

A thousand? The claws of panic start grazing Amalia's neck. "But...but the house always wins."

"Not tonight, hon. Tonight we take back the house."

"But the shul is the house."

Mrs. Aaronson appears not to hear her. Instead, her eyes dart over Amalia's shoulder until she spots who she is looking for. "That boy over there, he's winning the most. Javier Ackerman, have you met him? Hey, you both speak Spanish, isn't that something?"

In terms of the two of them having anything to do with each other, it amounts to less than nothing, but Amalia doesn't say that. She only watches Javier at the craps table (which she painstakingly made with cardboard, green felt, and fabric paint, thank you very much), where three things happen in quick succession: he shakes the dice, he tosses them, and the crowd around him goes wild with cheers.

And then there's the fourth thing, which seems unrelated to the other three: Javier finds Amalia's eyes over shoulders and heads and makes a face like, *Can you believe my luck?*

The claws of panic abandon their romantic grazing and opt to full-on choke. Amalia scratches her neck and tries not to think of how much money the shul might be losing. Tries not to think of how much research she did not do about gambling. Tries not to think about Javier Ackerman and how he's looking at her.

She needs a fancy fake cocktail.

Javier finds her at the drinks table.

"Hola," he says cheekily.

Actually, Amalia isn't sure if it is cheeky or not. Maybe he really truly is only saying hello, and not trying to make a *thing* out of it. Maybe she's just used to people greeting her with "hola" just to be cheeky.

"You don't have to talk to me just because we both speak Spanish," she says. "I mean, you don't have to go out of your way."

"Not out of my way. Tengo sed."

Well, he must be very parched because Javier Ackerman grabs three different bottles, necks tucked between his knuckles, and pours from them all into one single cup. Sodas and a juice, once individually brightly colored, swirling together to produce something you'd see if you turned the tap on a rusty sink in an abandoned house. He hands the concoction to Amalia. Gentlemanly and gross.

"No gracias."

"It's really good. Trust me, I know what I'm doing."

Amalia especially doesn't want to drink it now that she knows that he *knows what he's doing,* but she also doesn't want to seem like a no-fun stick-in-the-mud (though she suspects that train has already left the station). She takes the drink but does not drink it. A compromise. Javier makes an identical cocktail for himself, using the last of the cups. Amalia makes a mental note to get more from the supply closet.

Javier sips and watches Amalia over the rim. She can see the Jewish and Latino instincts warring within him to both boldly check her out from head to toe and to not overtly check her out at all. Either way, it makes Amalia's ears and cheeks and neck tingly. She knows very well that she doesn't know how to dress for anything fancier than a Shabbos dinner. When she looked in her closet tonight, trying to find something that an extra might wear in a scene from *Casino Royale,* she came out with this: a maroon button-down blouse and an A-line black skirt. Anyone could easily mistake her for a cater-waiter.

"And I know I don't have to talk to you," Javier says, his eyes coming back up to meet hers. "I know how this goes. Hispanic Jewish Bingo."

The words bounce around in her mind like a neighbor's wayward ball over a backyard fence, surprising yet inevitable. And though she obviously understands the words individually, she has no idea how they work together. But before she can ask Javier to elaborate, something not much taller than a five-drawer dresser comes barreling toward her and knocks into her side. It makes the muddy mocktail swish over the brim of her cup and spill onto her Shabbos shoes.

"Hit me!" the dresser-sized thing says. He is a bar mitzvah–aged boy with the clammy sheen and wild eyes of someone who amped his power trip with a sugar high. And Amalia can't even be mad at the bumping-into or the ruined shoes because in a small way (okay, a pretty big way) this boy is her fault. He's got tokens weighing down his pockets and clamped in sweaty fists, and he is clearly making a speedy return trip to the candy table and Amalia should have had the foresight to know that a casino night in which children are invited to gamble and have unlimited access to a *candy table* was a deliriously bad idea.

"Hit me!" the boy demands, coupling it with a raucous snort-laugh. Turns out kids love to take blackjack phrases and turn them naughty. Who knew. "HitmeHitMehItmE—HIT ME!"

Javier slaps the kid upside the head.

The boy is shocked silent, but he's no longer asking to be hit. He walks away.

"You just hit a kid," Amalia says, if only to get her jaw up and moving again.

"Barely."

"He's a *kid*, Javier."

"He was wearing a hat. And call me Javi."

She will *not* call him Javi, and this is not simply a commentary on headwear. In their Jewish world, boys can start wearing their wide-brimmed hats when they turn thirteen, an age that marks them as men, so Amalia knows what Javier means but, "Still!"

Javier shrugs. "You can't say he wasn't asking for it. Plus, he got your shoes dirty."

Amalia looks down at her black suede oxfords that come to a sharp point. "These shoes pinch, anyway."

Javier chuckles. Amalia doesn't know what it means, but it means *something* and it can't be anything good since he won't elaborate. Suddenly, Amalia doesn't want to be in these pinchy shoes or in her ho-hum outfit, talking to this borderline rude guy who hits barely-men boys and is apparently draining the shul of all its money. "You should get back to your games," she says. "Seems like you're quite...winsome."

"'Kay, ciao."

When Javier is out of sight, Amalia finally takes a sip of his juice/soda mix.

Dammit, it's delicious.

Mrs. Lebowitz is looking for a cup. Mr. Arnold mentions this while also asking if there will be better refreshments coming anytime soon. Amalia says no, there won't be, while she speeds toward the precariously stacked supply closet with the cups on the first floor.

Amalia sees Mrs. Lebowitz just outside the closet, reaching for the knob, and it is a frightful sight because anytime Amalia has ever opened the supply closet door, something unwanted has tumbled out.

"Mrs. Lebowitz, can I help you?" Amalia says when she reaches the woman.

"Oh, thank you, dear, but I found someone else to help me."

The closet door opens from the inside, and things topple onto the floor as expected, but one thing doesn't tumble out—it saunters. Javier Ackerman steps over the mess of decorations and paper towel rolls at his feet. His arms are overflowing with disposable cups. "Did you say you need one cup or five hundred?"

Mrs. Lebowitz laughs and actually touches Javier's arm, though maybe that's for balance. Amalia gives her the benefit of the doubt because the shmaltzy joke was not that funny.

"Amalia, have you met Javier Ackerman? He's from Venezuela. Javier, this is Amalia. She's from Brazil. Isn't that nice? You both speak Spanish."

Amalia was born in Peru, and they speak Portuguese in Brazil, but she does not correct Mrs. Lebowitz because her Latina mother taught her better. Mrs. Lebowitz plucks a cup out of Javier's arms and says, "Well, I'll let you two get to know each other," before shuffling off.

When Amalia bends to pick stuff up, Javier helps. To make things not so quiet and awkward (and also because it's been nagging her since he brought it up), Amalia asks him a question. "So, what's Hispanic Jewish Bingo?"

Javier puts a bundle of decorative twigs back on a shelf and smiles. "You know. *Can't tell if you're a Hispanic Jew? Play Hispanic Jewish Bingo!* It's the stuff that only happens to us."

"Like what?"

"Like the sisterhood ladies thinking we'd hit it off because we're from the same hemisphere."

Amalia gets it instantly. She realizes she's been playing Hispanic Jewish Bingo her whole life. "I once went to a Hispanic-owned salon and they thought I was in the wrong place because I was wearing my school uniform and no Jewish girl had ever walked in there before, so I spent my entire haircut talking to them in Spanish and explaining that Hispanic Jews do, in fact, exist."

It all comes out in one breathless burst but is cushioned by Javier's knowing smile.

"This kid in school used to tease me every day because my name wasn't Jewish enough," he responds.

"Did people ever think your mom was your babysitter?"

"Of course. When you visit your cousins, do you have to always explain that you can't eat their food because it isn't kosher?"

That one is specific, yet relatable. "How about when you volunteer to make food for your school's chesed program and everyone just expects you to bring nachos even though you are not Mexican, but you do bring papa a la Huancaina anyway because you're a dweeb and it's your favorite dish?"

The smile on Javier's face widens. "Mine is ropa vieja. How

about when you're asked for your family's entire genealogical history to explain just what in the world makes you Jewish?"

"Or truly Hispanic."

"So you have to educate them."

"Tell them your entire life story."

"And then they want to set you up with the only other person they know with a similar one."

It's nice, talking to Javier—Javi—like this. It feels familiar, even though they just met. In the time they talked, they have managed to tidy up the closet and their understanding of one another. No longer is Javier the smug guy from earlier. Maybe it's the fact that Amalia walked in on him helping out a little old lady, but it's something else, too. Where once she thought they had nothing in common except their heritage, now Amalia knows that that's something. Their shared experience means they understand each other on a level other people wouldn't have.

And now that she's found this connection, she wants to share more, see how far she can take it.

"Do you also find it hard to...exist in both worlds?"

Javier considers her question. "What do you mean?"

"The Jewish world and the Hispanic world," Amalia says. "I've always wanted to be as Latina as I could be in my Jewish world and as Jewish as I could be in my Hispanic world. All at once."

Javier doesn't say anything, just continues to watch Amalia. And the quiet attention is almost like standing on hot coals. She needs to fill up the small space with more words. "I don't know, it's just hard. By trying to hold on to those two identities, I feel like I'm doing a disservice to both. Like, I'm trying to find the right balance, but I want to be more than just fifty percent Judía and fifty percent Latina. I want to be two hundred percent everything. I want to be more than what everybody expects me to be. I want to be...perfect."

He still watches her silently, taking in what she's saying, and it only makes Amalia doubt her words more. *Perfect?* She sounds egomaniacal—crazed! And two hundred percent? What even is that? It's impossible math is what it is. She pushes off the shelf she's been leaning on and reaches for the door. If this were a sitcom, she'd discover that the door is stuck, damning her to an evening in a confined space with her greatest (most intriguing?) sudden foil. But this isn't a sitcom and the knob turns no problem.

"Why do you want to be perfect so bad?" Javi asks.

Amalia shrugs, though she knows the answer all too well. "To show them I belong here."

For the first time that night, Javi looks kind of sad. "You're a teenager who spends her free time volunteering at a synagogue," he tells her. "The people here love you."

"Love is a strong word."

Javi cuts right through the wall she's putting up. "They accept you," he says firmly.

He's just being nice, Amalia is sure. She'd found common ground with him and then made things too weird and now he's just being nice.

"It doesn't matter anyway," she says. "The night's a bust. The shul's probably going to lose more money than it's taking in. It's all my fault."

"The night is young," Javi says. "Como nosotros."

Amalia can appreciate his optimism, but it isn't going to rub off on her. There is one last thing on the supply room floor left to pick up. A playing card, the ace of hearts. "You drop this?"

"Yes," Javi says. "Thank you."

He takes the card from Amalia's hand and she feels something pass between them, an ephemeral buzz that shoots right through her gut and fills her up.

That ephemeral buzz, which was nice at first, has transformed into a deep burning ire. Incredulity. Disgust!

She finds him outside the men's bathroom.

"You're cheating!" She has to whisper-shriek this because the bathroom opens directly into the event space and as big as her anger may be, it still feels like something that needs to be kept under wraps. What will they think if they see the Only Two Hispanic Jews arguing?

Javier does not exactly balk at the accusation. He doesn't even deny it. "*Cheating* sounds like such a...mala palabra."

Amalia's first instinct is to frisk him (no, too touchy). Maybe better to alert security. The synagogue has security because it is a synagogue in the year 2021. But her second instinct is to protect him. She can't let everyone know there's a thief in their midst. And especially not him. Because...

Because just being who he is means he has something to prove. Because he is like her.

Amalia holds her hand out, palm up. "Give me your cards."

Javier sighs—still so infuriatingly at ease—and feels around in his breast pocket like he can't remember exactly where his cards are. He pulls out a deck—a full deck!—and places it in Amalia's hand. As if the thing were ablaze, she flings it out the open window directly behind Javier's head.

"Amalia!"

She startles at the sound of her name, called by a deep male voice that does not belong to Javier. She turns to find Mr. Katz, on his way to the bathroom. He's smiling, so chances are good he didn't see her violently hurl something out the window.

"Casino Night is mamash a hatzlacha."

It's nice hearing that the party is a success, even as she's trying to put out this Javi-shaped fire. "Thank you, Mr. Katz."

"I told you, call me Morty."

Amalia will never not use an older person's title to address them but she nods anyway. Mr. Katz notices Javier. "Amalia, have you met this young man? He's from Bolivia, aren't you?"

"Sure," Javier says.

"Amalia here is from Cuba. Amalia, say something in Spanish," Mr. Katz prompts.

So Amalia dutifully turns to Javier and tells him in simple, clear Spanish that she can't believe he has the chutzpah to cheat. That he should be ashamed of himself. That he is playing right into dangerous stereotypes of both *Jews* and *Latinos* and how dare he!

"Like music to the ears, isn't it?" Mr. Katz says.

"A symphony," Javier agrees, smiling.

Mr. Katz slips into the bathroom, leaving Javier and Amalia alone in the crowded fake casino.

Even though she's just accused him of doing something awful, it rolls right off Javier's shoulders. And as Amalia looks at him now, her hands balled up in unsatisfying fists while his own hands lie limp and relaxed, she finally understands what it was she didn't like about him since the moment she met him.

Javier Ackerman is *comfortable.*

He's comfortable in his tailored suit, and with his devilish smile, and in a room full of people he doesn't know. He's comfortable breaking rules and charming old folks and slapping man-kids. And most of all, he's comfortable living in two worlds.

Amalia has lived her entire life trying to straddle the line between her two worlds. She's read enough to know that other people who come from two cultures sometimes try to bury one away, or fully assimilate to the one they prefer, but not Amalia. When she's in Jewish spaces, it's like she can't let herself forget that she is also a Latina. And when she's in Hispanic spaces, she is stringent in presenting a Jewish exterior. It is an impossible balancing act, and it doesn't even take into account the regular old American culture, which is a completely different spinning plate that she can't get into right now.

She's careful all the time. Javier can't even be careful enough to not get caught. It was so easy for him to have it both ways. Even his name. His infuriatingly perfect name is both equally

Hispanic and Jewish all at once, and not in a glaring way that makes you scratch your head. In a way that rolls off your tongue and makes you appreciate the beauty in the whispery bits between the consonants.

"Javier Ackerman."

"Llamame Jota."

Amalia will *not* call him J, and how could he *still* be so comfortable even after being caught *cheating*? Amalia was constantly aware of what she did, of how she presented herself, of doing everything right and trying to be the best version—no, the best *versions*—of herself that she could be. But here was Javier, not caring about any of that.

Amalia's eyes canvas the room until she spots a man in uniform standing by the double doors and heads straight for him. His badge says Mendoza and she hopes this means he speaks Spanish.

"Séño, me ayudas, porfa?"

She catches herself using slang when she talks to fellow Hispanics, all to telegraph that she is one of them. This isn't your basic AP Spanish—there are no proper nouns or conjunctions here. She shaves off the ends of words to show Mendoza that this is the Spanish of her gente. Nuestra gente.

But Mendoza only looks at her funny. Maybe he doesn't speak Spanish, after all?

"No hay problema, güey," Javier says. He is suddenly at Amalia's side once again, talking to Mendoza, too, only difference being that Mendoza actually seems to understand him.

"Los Judios aqui hablan español?" he asks, confused but intrigued.

"No, just us," Javier says. He abruptly does a one-eighty and wades back into the party, and Amalia is surprised to find that she has done the same. She looks down at her hand and realizes why. Javier is holding it.

"I have a proposition for you," he says, staring straight ahead.

"You're holding my hand."

"You're too strung up on being perfect. What if I can help you let go of all of that?"

They wade through the party, and while before Amalia was worried about drawing attention by arguing with Javier in public, he's found a loophole around that. They can talk openly, without having to whisper if they talk in Spanish. So he does.

"Help me cheat," he says. "It'll free you."

He keeps saying things that don't make sense. Even his words are dichotomies. But Amalia sees him now for what he is. Her yetzer hara personified. The devil on her shoulder. She poured her heart out to him and now he dares to confront her with a totally outrageous not-solution to her problems. She drops Jota's—Javi's—*Javier's*—hand.

"You said it yourself," he says. "You aren't comfortable living in two worlds, and all I'm saying is that that's because you're living according to other people's expectations of you."

"No I'm not."

"You kind of are. You want to be the perfect Latina and the perfect Jew, but perfect according to who? You already are perfect. Just by being you."

His hand is no longer holding hers but it still feels like it. Or, it feels like he's holding more than that. At the same time, the cynical part of Amalia's brain couldn't help but think, *Is this pendejo for real?*

"Seriously," he continues. "I don't care what everybody's expectations of me are. And look how good I turned out."

"Conceited."

That infuriating smile of his again, the definition of rolling with every punch. "Maybe. But I'm cool with that."

"Of course you are."

"Do one bad thing that no one is expecting from you," he says. "It won't even be that bad. We can give all our winnings to the synagogue."

"What?"

"We can both publicly donate everything we make back to the shul. You'd be doing a mitzvah, the shul won't lose all its money, Casino Night will be a rousing success, you'd give us—the Jewish Latinos—a good name, and the big, beautiful cherry on top—you can let your hair down and live a little.

"You won't believe how good it feels on the other side of everything that's holding you back."

It is a simple conceit. Communicate in Spanish, tell each other what cards they have, bet accordingly. They stand at the poker table, three other players marking the space between them. As luck would have it, they are all people Javier and Amalia have interacted with tonight. One of the sisterhood ladies, Mr. Katz, and Hit Me Kid.

Javier looks at his cards, and when he locks eyes with Amalia, he has a sparkle in them. "Dos jotas," he says.

Amalia imagines winning, giving the money right back to the synagogue instead of letting Hit Me Kid take it and spend it on video games or stickers or whatever younger kids are into. She lets her mind wander, imagines herself and Javier as Bonnie and Clyde, but instead of bank robberies, it's games of Hispanic Jewish Bingo. Run amok. Un laberinto. Meshugas.

"Apuesta mas," Javier says.

"Uhh, what's he saying?" Hit Me asks the table. "Shouldn't we not be talk—?"

"Shhhh," Mr. Katz tells him. "Do you know how special it is to know another language?"

"Spanish is so beautiful," the sisterhood lady says.

"Like music to the ears," Mr. Katz says.

"That's what I always say," the old lady agrees.

The English is background noise, as are the other people there. For Amalia, there are just her cluttered thoughts, her racing heart, and the cards in her hand. She looks down at them, then back at Javier.

"Lo apuestas todo?" he asks. *All in?*

She wonders if she can cheat and still be a righteous, good person. Can she have it both ways?

All she has to do is change.

"Wait up!"

It's Javier, come to find her in the shul parking lot. She's a few paces from her car, keys in hand, but she turns at the sound of his voice. She expected him to come find her. He is, as always, smiling.

"Thank you," he says. "I had fun tonight."

After everything, Amalia is still not sure what Javier's idea of fun is, but she accepts this as the compliment it's meant to be. "I'm glad."

"You surprised me there," Javier goes on, "at the poker table."

"That's me. Unpredictable Amalia."

"Why didn't you cheat?" He is not mad as he asks this, does not lament all the money he put down that was eventually swept up by the little old sisterhood lady. He's more curious than anything.

So, why didn't she help him cheat? "Because a twisted tree will never grow straight."

The smile stays on his face, even as it morphs into something more bemused.

"Cheating is stealing," Amalia explains. "And that's a big no-no. Ten Commandments big."

"But it was going to go to charity."

"Didn't you ever learn that Halacha, that you can't do a bad deed, even if it's for the greater good?"

"I did learn that," Javier says.

"Well, there you go. I was never going to cheat. That's just not who I am."

Javier cocks his head, his jaw catching the glare of a streetlamp. This seems like the part of the conversation where their strange paths come uncrossed. But before they can go their separate ways, there is something Amalia needs to say to him.

"I may not have cheated, but I still took your advice."

"How so?" Javier asks.

"I could have saved Casino Night, but I let it fail. The shul probably lost a lot of money. It will be a fiasco that I will not be able to live down anytime soon."

"You let yourself not be perfect," Javier says appreciatively. "How does it feel?"

Amalia takes a deep breath and lets it go. She smiles. "Good."

★ ★ ★ ★ ★

THE PERILS OF BEIGE

By Nasuġraq Rainey Hopson

The van hit a bump, the jolt pushing me into the seat belt. The bounce cleared some of the cobwebs of tiredness from my brain. From my spot at the very back, I could see Helen and Luke, two blond-headed kids, in the next set of seats. Their hair glowed from the dim light of the streetlights as we drove on the dark concrete roads. Helen and Luke were the teachers' kids and were not impressed by the city, having seen them in multitudes I'm sure, since they were from the Lower 48 somewhere. They both bowed their heads over their phones. I stared out the window, clearing a bit of fog on the glass with my hand. The city for me was foreign, so different from the dusty village where I lived. Downtown Anchorage was filled with intimidating storefronts filled with expensive-looking items and tall shimmering glass buildings. Concrete was everywhere, making the world seem flat and monochromatic in the warm glow of the streetlights. It was only the third time I had even been here. The other times I had only been to the Alaska Native hospital to take care of my grandmother. We had never even left the hospital grounds, as they had small housing dorms for village patients. All I had gotten from those trips were sore feet and legs, as the concrete was painful for bodies used to a more forgiving terrain.

Beyond Helen and Luke sat Edith and Frances, first cousins who looked like twins. Or Eddy and Franky, as they liked to be called. Long dark hair, straight as nails down their backs. Same slim shoulders. Even with the more masculine nicknames, they were too pretty to be mistaken for boys. Unless you looked closely, it was hard to tell them apart. Eddy had canines that stuck out, making her look like a wolf. Franky had a rounder face and deep dimples that showed even when she wasn't smiling. They liked it when people thought they were sisters. Indigenous girls. Exactly what you would picture if you imagined a modern Inuit girl from the Arctic. Just enough glam and just enough fur clothing and Native Power T-shirts. They giggled with each other over Franky's phone.

Every once in a while, they would flick away their hair from their faces like you would see girls do in the movies. It was stupidly feminine, and they probably practiced for days so that it would look natural. I envied them for that. I avoided looking at my own reflection in the dark glass of the van, knowing I would see the unruly halo that was my own hair. It was too curly to properly flick away from my face. In the corner of my eyes, I saw my dark-skinned reflection staring away from me, hardly much difference in color than the night sky.

I wondered if I zoomed in to my DNA, like they do in the films they showed during biology class, if there would be a normal helix strand. Or would it be cut in half from top to bottom? I could picture in my mind a vibrant-colored helix of 3D string with ladder spokes suddenly ending in midair as it turned slowly to give the audience a full view of its missing half. No. Not quite missing… It would be ghostly and dark.

Geez, Jen. Even when you are being dramatic and sad, you are still a nerd, I said to myself.

★ ★ ★

Mr. Gertery's voice droned on in tired annoyance. We stood around the front desk of the hotel, ignoring the desk clerk with the tired eyes. "Your room phones are disabled for phone calls. Any food delivery you order, you will have to pay at the door. After 9:00 p.m., you are not allowed to leave your rooms, and we will do a room check. You know the rules, guys—no visitors unless they are cleared with us, no leaving the hotel at all unless you are with us. Wake-up call at 7:00 a.m.…." He paused so we all could groan like the well-trained zombies we were. "Breakfast is at 7:30 till 8:30 a.m., registration downstairs at 8:45. Then we break for half an hour, and then meet at the lobby and hit the malls for clothes for the competition."

Mrs. Gertery's head perked up, and she waved at us for some reason, probably trying to look enthusiastic about having to do clothes-shopping for a bunch of annoyed sub-adults. Our sturdy jeans, T-shirts, and dirt-stained shoes, though normal in rural Alaska, would stick out like a lump of ice in the sea of formal wear that was encouraged for the Debate and Speech competition. Our isolated village had no clothing stores, so it was decided early on that it would be easiest to buy clothes when we got here.

"Jennifer, you are rooming with Helen," Mr. Gertery said while handing us each a key card. Helen smiled a tired smile in my direction that I tried to match. "Eddy and Franky, you're together. Luke, you get a room to yourself." *Lucky Luke*, I thought as I made my way to stand next to my roommate. She waved her card in the direction of the elevators as everyone else walked down the hall to where the vending machines were. We dragged our luggage over to the doors to stand in front of their shiny surfaces with our hands clasped in front of us like some weird sort of meditation or prayer. Helen was a senior, so we hadn't really interacted with each other even though our school was small. *Hopefully she doesn't snore.*

I did know that Helen was the reason we had a Debate and Speech team at all this year. She was really good at debate apparently, and her parents wanted her to have the competition hours for her college applications. Those hours would look good on my application, too, and maybe in a couple years I could make it out of the village and get into a good school somewhere far away. She was a teacher's kid and had moved into the village only a couple months ago, so no one had really taken the time to get to know her from what I could tell. She seemed to mostly keep to herself. *Why put in the effort?* Jen thought. Teachers were mostly pretty flaky about teaching in rural Alaska. You never knew if they were going to make it through the first year, let alone if they were going to be there for your whole school career. Once, we had a teacher get off the plane, turn around, and get back on after taking a one-minute look at our humble village.

The elevator dinged, and like dutiful priests we jumped on, retreating to our separate corners, placing our luggage between us like another barrier. We pretended to look at our phones and avoided having to make small talk.

Luckily, our room was pretty close to the elevator, so we didn't have to walk very far. Helen swiped the card across the panel, and the lock echoed in the quiet hallway. The room was a pretty good size with two large queen beds, a small desk with a chair, a loveseat, a large wall-mounted TV, and a door that led to a bathroom with a sink, a wall mirror, and even a tub. The decor was outdated in shades of earthy orange and mottled brown, but it looked and smelled clean. It felt *bare*. My home back in the village was full from top to bottom with *things*— things on shelves, things hanging on the walls, things we might need, things we got from family and friends, pictures, souvenirs, drawings, art, every award I ever got at school, trinkets and decorations of every kind. These sparse walls and blank spaces felt so *empty*.

Shrugging the feeling off, I walked over to the bed farthest from the door. "Mind if I take this bed?" I asked. As an answer, she flopped down on the other bed, taking off her heavy coat and boots. I did the same, taking the time to throw my ski pants, boots, and sheepskin parka into the small closet next to the door. Shedding all of the weight of my village winter gear made me feel lighter. I closed the closet door, and the scent of fur and earth disappeared from the room.

I emerged from the JCPenney's dressing room, tugging at the clothes I had put on. The long-sleeved dress shirt in a lackluster beige tucked into my pants wasn't too horrible to look at, but it felt foreign to me. The polyester scratched at my skin and clung to me a little too tight, making it so that I could *feel* the shirt every time I moved. It felt like I was wearing an octopus that kept panicking every time I shifted. The black straight-legged pants were no better and made my skin clammy. Mrs. Gertery frowned behind me, as she noticed the visible panty lines showing through the annoying fabric. I waited to see if she would say something. There was no way I was going to wear a G-string or go bare. She dove into the pile of clothing she'd picked out for me to try on and came up with a dark gray thigh-length cardigan. I put it on and was happy to at least feel a little bit less exposed. I guess I would have to get used to being sweaty and warm.

Eddy and Franky sat nearby on a bench, rolling their eyes and giggling at their phones again. They, of course, found clothes quickly enough with their slim and more socially acceptable-sized bodies. It took more time to find clothes that fit my wider frame. They had both picked clothes in muted shades of pink and green that looked good with their complexion. Mrs. Gertery had tried to get me to wear brighter colors that I must admit did look good next to my darker skin, clothes in shades of bright yellow and tropical blue. But they made me feel like I stood out too much. I had always stood out too much as is, dark skin and textured hair, so no bright clothes for me.

I stared at my short form in the mirror and tried to smooth down my hair a bit again, the movement practiced. I liked how the pants made me look taller, but I wondered if I would even have a chance to wear these clothes again after this. My mom had given me some of my college funds to buy these clothes, and I hoped it wasn't a waste. Staring at the clothes made my stomach swirl with beige-colored anxiety.

The next day, my name showed up in the 8:00 a.m. slot. Seeing my name in stark black ink on white paper made my heart crash against my rib cage like ocean waves on the beach during a fall storm. *No getting out of this now, Jen. Just get past the first round and it will be cake.* But even my inner voice sounded wimpy next to the pounding waves. The rest of my team left soon after finding out the competition lineup to review and prepare for their competitions with Coach and his wife, so I would be doing my speech alone.

It was Eddy and Franky's first competition, too. They teamed up for a try at Debate and were also doing individual speeches. Eddy had a pretty good dramatic interpretation performance, and Franky was giving it a go with a persuasive piece. Helen and Luke were focused only on Debate. This was a state competition, so most of the teams were from on-the-road systems and the bigger schools. Only a couple of the teams were from smaller villages. All of the out-of-town teams stayed in the same hotel, and a nearby school was used for the actual competitions.

Five rooms of competitions would be going on at the same time, each round lasting about two hours. Teams and individuals would be eliminated after each round. One room for Debate with two people per team, one room for Informational speeches, Dramatic Interpretation speeches, Persuasive speeches, and the like. This was my first time competing, and I had chosen to do an Informative speech. Everyone else thought they were boring and dry, but I liked them because the focus was mostly on the information and not the speaker.

The halls of the school were only half lit on the weekends to save on energy costs, even during competition, making them dim and eerie. The air in the halls was cool and smelled like heavy-duty cleaner and industrial floor wax. I found the classroom where I was competing, and taking a deep breath, I swung open the heavy door and entered the room. Without looking around, I immediately walked all the way to the back and took a seat.

There weren't that many kids here, six total. Two adults sat in the front, facing the small podium with the logo of the school and the words *INFO round 1* taped crookedly to its front. The judges, a youngish man in jeans and an older woman in a matching blue pantsuit set, looked bored as they sipped coffee from cheap paper cups. Three boys sat closer to the front of the room in a group, whispering quietly to each other. Their perfectly fitting jackets in a dark blue color all had a school patch sewn to the front. Some private school, then. The other three were girls whose eyes flicked toward me with mild curiosity. One of the girls openly stared at me with a raised eyebrow till I looked away, pretending to smooth the wrinkles of my clingy pants. It was then I realized that everyone in the room was white. I felt the darkness of my skin and wished I had convinced someone to come and sit with me.

I nervously flipped through the three index cards in my hands. I had worked hard at memorizing my speech and had it down pat. But this was competition, and I had yet to actually do this speech in front of an audience other than my own team.

I could feel the sweat on my palms staining the cards I was holding. The sound of a bell from the hallway announced the time. The older woman glanced around the room and waved her papers at the podium, her voice papery thin and dry.

"There is no order, so anyone can go first." I immediately shot my hand up, and she motioned me to the front of the room. I preferred to get the speech over with as soon as possible—the waiting for my turn was more painful than giving the speech itself. I walked up to the podium and arranged my cards carefully on the small surface.

"Jennifer Akalik, Tikigaq High School," I said. The judges nodded and wrote my info down on their pads, and the woman picked up a timer.

Most would say that giving speeches in front of people was terrifying, but for me it was the opposite. For a few minutes, I would know exactly what was expected of me, and I knew exactly what was going to happen, and that was comforting in a way. Predictable. I took a deep breath...and began singing in Inupiaq. It was a quick simple tune, a couple of lines in a lullaby singsong melody. I wasn't that great of a singer, but it did what it was designed to do; all eyes turned toward me. Vague interest was at least some interest. I then poured myself into the speech, relying on the hours of practice I had done at home in front of my mirror, making sure to step in the predetermined pattern I was supposed to around the podium as I moved through the different topic points.

"My name is Jen, and I am from Tikigaq, also known as Point Hope, Alaska. I am Inupiaq and, in our culture, we still rely on hunting whales to feed our village for the whole year. My speech today will be about my experiences growing up in this tradition and what that looks like day to day..."

Once I had started the speech, I thought I did fairly well. No one looked bored at least. When I finished, I thanked the judges. They nodded at me as they finished writing notes before the next contestant got up, and I made my escape out the door.

The blood was pounding through my veins in delayed reaction as I walked through the dim halls. That always happened when I was in intense situations. Once I didn't have something to focus all my energy on, my body caught up to me. It was fine in this circumstance, as long as I could make my escape before embarrassing myself. My fingertips were becoming numb, so I concentrated on taking deep breaths through my nose as I made my way back to the room my team was practicing in.

The next morning, we all raced to the huge corkboard wall at the front of the school building where they posted the results from the day before. Trying not to look too anxious, I made my way to the board and skimmed quickly through the pages, searching for the Informative speech group. *There...* My name sat at the top of the list; I was going straight to finals. *FINALS.*

"Cool, you made it into finals," said a voice behind me. I turned to see one of the boys from yesterday's round. The private school boys. Another boy stood behind him.

"Thanks," I replied, trying hard not to smooth down hair that probably needed to be tucked behind my ear again. He was cute in a nerdy kind of way, dark-haired with freckles that stood out on his light skin.

"Everyone on our team thought your speech was sick. You know judges these days, though. They love that type of stuff. It's almost a guaranteed pass. It's so...cultural...you know?" He flashed his perfect white teeth in an odd smile.

I blinked a bit and smiled hesitantly. *Did he just insult me?* He was talking faster than I was used to. His expression didn't match his words.

"You can speak well for being rural, though. You must not have grown up there. My name is Tim, and this is Chance." He gestured to the other guy before I could respond, who nodded. "We usually get together between rounds and work on our speeches. We can give you some tips if you like. Coaches like that type of thing. Your coach would be impressed." I glanced at the rest of my team as they searched for rankings a few feet away, trying to hide the clenching of my jaws.

"The rest of my team, too?" I asked, trying to buy myself some time, not wanting to reject him outright. He didn't seem the type to take something like that lightly by the way he liked the sound of his own voice. Tim exchanged a quick glance with Chance who smirked and shrugged, and then turned to me again with that smile. He sighed and stepped back a bit from me, tucking his hands in his trouser pockets.

"They would probably be a little *too* much, you know? But anyways, we got to run." He did a little salute, and turned, and walked away before I could answer. I watched him for a moment.

Slim hands reached around the crook of my elbows from either side. Eddy was on my left and Franky on my right. I could feel their freshly manicured nails scrape across the fabric of my cardigan.

"Got a nalagumiu boyfriend, Jen?" asked Franky. Eddy made a *hmm?* noise in my other ear. I felt my ears heat up as I blushed. "The dark-haired one is cute. He looks expensive." They giggled.

I reached up with both my hands and smoothed my hair behind my ears, using the movement to dislodge the girls from my arms. If only they knew what he just said, they probably wouldn't think he was so cute.

"Atchu, I don't know," I said and shrugged my shoulders as I stepped away from them, hoping they wouldn't ask me any more questions. The brief conversation with the expensive cute boy left me feeling like I needed a shower.

Later that night, I sat at the desk, staring at the door to our hotel room, a twenty-dollar bill gripped in my hand. I glanced at my phone and confirmed that the pizza was now fifteen minutes late. My stomach grumbled. Helen was reading on her bed. It had been a long day, and I had been too nervous from competition to eat much till now. I debated whether or not I should go back down to the lobby and grab something from the vending machines before our curfew.

"Those private school boys, they are jerks," she said as she looked at me over her book.

"What?" I said, caught off guard. We rarely spoke to each other unless it was about the competition.

"Those boys that talked to you at the rankings board? I know them, or at least I've seen them at events. They tried talking to me a few times, till they found out I didn't have the same... opinions...as them." She frowned. "They are pretty stuck up. They think that Speech and Debate should be, you know... like a club. For certain people." My hand tightened around the twenty-dollar bill. What was she getting at?

"Huh. Yeah, they seemed a bit sketchy. I don't know why they talked to me," I said.

She shrugged, a frown on her face. "They like to get under people's skin, try and get them rattled. Plus, they probably think you're...you know... African-American." I glanced at her face, trying to figure out her motives. Most people don't just straight out say that. She didn't look like she was trolling, though.

"I am, though," I said, raising my eyebrows at her boldness.

"I mean, they probably can't *tell* you're Native. Till they heard your speech. I mean, you didn't grow up Black, though, right?" I blinked a bit. Again, usually people don't say that part out loud. Yeah, it was true I wasn't part of that scene, and my relationship with my birth dad was sparse and rocky to say the least, but it didn't negate the parts of me that were curlier, darker, and rounder than others.

"There aren't many POC in Debate in Alaska," she said quickly before I could form a reply. And she was right. I sat there and tried to think of how many non-white faces I had seen during competition. At least obvious ones. I didn't really wonder why till now. Maybe one other person came to mind. Besides me and...

"What about Eddy and Franky? They count. Why didn't the guys talk to them?" Again, that little shrug.

"They are...you know..." she waved a hand in the air like she was trying to flick at mosquitoes "...*too* Native. Kind of over-the-top. I don't think they see them as a threat."

"Too Native?" I repeated, like a parrot learning new words.

Two pink spots appeared on her cheeks. "Just be careful, Jen," she said and shrugged, raising her book back up, stopping the conversation. I rubbed a finger on the bill I was holding, trying to figure out what she meant by *too Native*. Eddy and Franky were a bit much sometimes. They weren't shy, and the giggling could get annoying. But I had known them my whole life. I tried to see them how a stranger would see them. They were definitely Indigenous-looking and Indigenous-sounding. Their speeches were peppered with emotive Inupiaq words, and they already had that "aunty" confidence that intimidated a lot of people. But *too* Native? And what did that say about me?

Did the boys see me as someone they could easily eliminate as competition?

Informative speech finals were one of the first events of the morning on the last day of competition. This time when I walked into the room, it was more than half filled with kids and a few coaches along with the judges. The judges were an older dark-skinned woman with gray hair and thick glasses, and a middle-aged man wearing a bulky red sweater. The paper pads that sat in front of them were wrinkled with notes from the multitudes of rounds they'd judged before.

Senior judges, then.

I could feel my heartbeat in my chest again, thundering against my rib cage. I took a few deep breaths, trying to calm myself. *Easy as cake, Jen. CAKE.* I took a seat in the back once again and looked around. Besides me and the one judge, the room was filled with curious white faces. I had asked Eddy and Franky to come and sit in the audience this time, but they weren't here yet. We weren't that close, but they didn't even bat an eye when I asked them. It made me feel a little less anxious knowing that there would be at least a couple people there not staring at me like I was a unicorn.

I saw the private school boys at the front. Tim turned in his chair and gave me a little wave. I waved back. I don't know why I waved back. *Geez, Jen, get yourself together.* A few of the other kids turned in their chairs and looked at me with curiosity.

Where were Eddy and Franky?

The bell rang, and again the judges asked for volunteers to start off the competition. I raised my hand as quick as I could, but this time another girl was picked to go first. She had bright red hair that looked just vivid enough to come from a box. I leaned back into my chair and twisted my hair between my fingers. Coach hated it when I did that, but he wasn't here to frown at me. He was busy helping Helen and Luke prep for a round in Debate.

The judge signaled that the timer had begun, and the red-haired girl moved her hands in the air in fluid graceful movements. It was instantly captivating. She didn't speak at all for a full minute, the silence working to grab her audience immediately as everyone tried to work out what was happening. It was beautiful. Her speech was about learning sign language and her experience growing up deaf. It took me a minute to adjust to her speech pattern. I was impressed. She was articulate and friendly and even got the audience to laugh a few times. I don't remember if I even got a chuckle during my speech. Of course, I didn't write any funny stuff in there, but still. *Maybe I should have? Am I funny, though? Geez, Jen, concentrate.*

When she was done, she even got a few brief claps. I raised my hand even before the woman turned for more volunteers. She nodded in my direction, and I got up and walked to the front of the room. I smoothed the suffocating clothes around my body. As I stepped up to the podium, Eddy and Franky walked into the room, giving everyone a little wave and big apologetic smiles as they found some seats in the back. I sighed in relief and the nervous smoothing-of-clothes ritual stopped.

I concentrated on relaxing the rest of my body as I sang, and once again the world slipped into that oh-so-comfortable, predictable zone. This time I focused on projecting my voice more, trying to make sure the people in the back could hear me. When I got nervous, I tended to grow quieter. The audience blurred into vague figures as I paced myself through the speech.

Once I was done, I heard a few enthusiastic claps, mostly from the back where Eddy and Franky sat. I didn't care that a few of the other kids turned to frown at them. I thanked the judges and made my way out the door, not wanting to wait around and watch the rest of the speeches. The adrenaline rush I was expecting was building. Eddy and Franky followed right behind me.

"Jen! That was so goooood, holy! Kinaaq, *crazy*, even better than practice," Eddy said, giving me a quick awkward hug once we were in the hallway and away from the door so no one could hear us. Franky added an enthusiastic, "Yeah!" and a giggle. I smiled at them, a genuine one, and mumbled, "Thanks."

Oddly enough, one of the most boring parts of the whole competition was the awards ceremony. I mean, sure, we might win and get a trophy and have to grab it from the stage, but really it was a few hours of sitting at a table, trying our best not to fall asleep to the droning speeches of the school thanking sponsors and trying their best to "inspire" kids.

We sat at a round dining table in the back of a dark conference room at the hotel, struggling not to nod off. We had already checked out of our rooms early that morning and had our luggage and most of our winter gear piled into our rented van. We would be heading to the airport after the awards ceremony to make our way back to the village, a trip that would take a couple flights and all day to get back home.

The actual announcing of the results seemed to go by pretty fast. Eddy placed third in Dramatic Interpretation, and both Eddy and Franky placed fourth in Team Debate, which was pretty good for the first time they had ever tried it. Luke and Helen placed high in their own events, of course, winning second place in Team Debate.

"And now for the top awards for Informative speeches," said the man on stage. I froze in my seat, trying not to look too eager to hear the lineup. *Don't be disappointed, Jen. Don't embarrass yourself. It's your first time. Don't expect too much.* He unfolded a piece of paper and leaned down to speak closer to the microphone. "Third place goes to Andrew Parker, West Valley High School. Second place goes to Tim Klein, Monroe Central School," he said, pausing between each name for the smattering of applause and to give time for the winners to make their way to the front of the room to receive their awards from a table on stage. "And first place goes to Jennifer Akalik, Tikigaq High School." Everyone at my table looked at me. I blinked and froze, not too sure I had heard it right. Eddy reached over and pulled on my arm, lifting me out of my seat, letting out a loud howl and laugh.

I won. What?

They mispronounced my last name and school name, of course, but nothing could dull the warm feeling in my chest. I floated to the stage and took the small plastic trophy and certificate from the hand of the dark-skinned older woman. She smiled at me and shook my hand. As I walked back to my team, I heard a smattering of clapping. Of course, Eddy and Franky were whistling and stomping their feet in enthusiasm, causing some other kids to look askance in our direction.

My head buzzed with success. I texted my mom back home. She promised to make a big pot of my favorite caribou soup when I got back, complete with deep-fried doughnuts. We found a section of floor space out of the way of normal hotel traffic near the conference rooms and piled our heavy coats so we could sit comfortably. We had about two hours before we needed to head to the airport, and since the Wi-Fi and coffee were free here, the Gerterys decided to take advantage of it.

Coach, his wife, and Luke had wandered back to the vending machines. Franky was leaning over, and we were watching a video together. Her uncle had posted a couple of Kivgiq dances online. The drums sounded tinny and small coming out of her old phone.

I heard footsteps approaching me on the carpet and looked up to see Tim and his friend Chance. It took me a moment to recognize them without their matching school coats. Their clothes looked new and expensive, and I suddenly became aware of my worn-out Alaska Grown T-shirt. I stood up quickly and kicked my heavy jacket over my feet, hoping they would not notice that I had my heavy winter boots on.

"Just wanted to come over and congratulate you on your win, Jennifer," Tim said. I nodded and shrugged, not too sure what to say. "Of course, it was almost a for-sure thing, right? I mean Judge Mathison was guaranteed to enjoy your speech."

"Judge Mathison?" I tried to remember if I had met someone by that name. I didn't like how off-balance I felt when I talked to him.

"She was the Black woman judging Finals. I mean, you guys seem to stick together." *You. Guys.* Something hardened in the pit of my stomach. "We were about to go and get some coffee around the corner if you want to hang out before you go? I'm sure your coach would be okay with it." I looked at Franky who sat wide-eyed and quiet for a second. I watched as the realization of what type of guy he was dawned on her face. She looked at me with raised eyebrows and crossed her arms. Something passed between us. There weren't any crashing waves in my chest this time. She waited.

Time to stop being beige, Jen.

"No. *Heck* no," I said loudly, forcefully, startling everyone around. "You can take your coffee and shove it." I stared him down, daring him to make a scene. I heard noises behind me as Franky and Eddy and Helen moved to stand beside me.

Tim paused, his face hardened, and all traces of fake friendliness disappeared in an instant. His jaw tightened as he looked at Chance. With stiff fingers, he plucked his phone out of the breast pocket of his jacket. I hadn't heard it vibrate. With an exaggerated frown on his face, he looked at the screen.

"Aw, well, we will have to hang out some other time. Looks like I got to get back to my parents' house. It was nice to meet you, Jennifer," he said and flashed that unnatural smile at me again. He did that little salute and walked toward the front of the hotel lobby.

Franky stood closer to my shoulder and snorted indelicately. "The weirdo never even looked at me the whole time. What's his deal? Rude." I nodded. Rude, indeed. She stared at me for a moment. "Want me to French braid your hair, Jen? I watched a couple videos on how to braid your texture of hair. I think it would look nice. You won't have to tuck it behind your ears anymore."

I nodded, grateful for an excuse to sit back down on the pile of jackets. I could feel the wave of adrenaline flooding my body. I took a few deep breaths, telling my body to relax. Franky sat behind me and pulled out a comb from somewhere, Helen sat back down nearby, and Eddy grabbed her gear and sat closer to watch as Franky worked the comb through my hair.

I wondered if I zoomed in to my DNA, like they do in the films they showed during biology class, if it would be braided like Franky was braiding my hair? Thin strands being woven over and over by Indigenous hands?

★ ★ ★ ★ ★

INVISIBLE

By Emiko Jean

Your office smells like a combination of disinfectant and clove oil. I google *weird odor orthodontist* on my phone as you lead Dad and me to the room with your desk. Tooth dust, it's called.

Dad nudges me as you shut the door. "You almost ran into the wall back there," he says. I look up, and he is grinning. He likes to tease me about walking and staring at my phone. His face blanks, and he mimics a stiff walking zombie.

I knock his arms down. "Please, don't," I say, stuffing my phone in my pocket. Dad has the worst sense of humor.

You laugh, flashing some teeth of your own as you slide an open folder across the desk. The front page is an invoice. Twenty minutes ago, you examined my teeth. Asked me to smile, then pressed pieces of crinkly graphite paper between my molars. Dad whistles low, seeing the bottom figure. "The price of a beautiful smile," he remarks.

You reassure him that there is little work to be done. I'll only need braces for a year and eight months if everything goes exceptionally well. It is my bite that concerns you. "It needs to be addressed," you say.

Dad nods and studies the figures. While he does, your gaze bounces between the two of us. You have that look in your eyes—a curious squint. One I have seen before. Your whole face is a question mark. *How?* How does Dad have sandy blond hair? How do I have black? How are the shapes of our eyes and faces, the shades of our skin so different? How do we fit together as daughter and father? Maybe you think I'm adopted. *Where did you get her from?* a woman asked at the grocery store when I was eight.

Behind your desk is a file cabinet, and on it sits a picture of your family. Two girls and two boys with fair skin and fair smiles. They match you. Your wife. If Mom were here, I might make more sense to you. You would see me in her. But she left when I was seven. And I am more my father's daughter than my mother's.

Dad signs the paperwork. On our way out, he pays the deposit, and we make the first appointment. Two weeks later, I am back in your office. My friends are texting me GIFs. Pictures of girls with mouths full of metal, headgear, and even a couple stuck together by hooked wires in their mouths. I text them back a thumbs-down. I am the last of the group to have braces. I shouldn't have waited so long. But I was too scared in middle school. And Dad wouldn't make me. He's no good at tough love.

"All right, let's get started," you say, rounding the dental chair. You slap on a pair of blue latex gloves. "Cool shoes," you say. I glance down at yours. Nike Air Force 1's tucked into khaki pants. Mine are Converse, with two holes in the corner of each where my pinkie toe has rubbed away the fabric. You roll toward me on your stool and pick through gleaming tools set on a tray with a blue napkin. "Ready, Tammy?"

"Tami," I say, pronouncing my name correctly, emphasizing the phonics—*Tah-mi.*

You pause, place the tools down. "Tah-mi? Like the boy's name?"

No, not like the boy's name. Like my grandmother's name on my mom's side. It means pearl. I nod mutely. You switch to a keyboard, click, and open my chart. Next to my name, you type out *Tommy*. You hand me a pair of sunglasses and recline the chair. A hygienist arrives to help you. I close my eyes as you shift the overhead light closer. You get to work. I zone out while you clean and dry my teeth. While you glue on brackets and shine a blue light on them. While you slide on the bands and archwires.

An hour passes before you say, "Nearly done." You tighten a wire, ask me to open and close. I do, and one minute later, you say, "Looks good." You peel the gloves from your hands, rattle off aftercare instructions, and hand me a sheet with printed directions. The hygienist holds up a mirror and tells me to take a look. I smile, but it's more of a grimace, and my mouth gleams with metal. My God, it's worse than I thought. I run my tongue over the braces, then curl my lips inward, trying to adjust to the feel.

The hygienist lays the mirror down and pats my shoulder. "You'll get used to it," she says before leaving.

"Where are you from?" you ask, pushing a button. The seat rises, and suddenly I am upright.

I blink, startled. This is not the first time I have been asked this question. In fact, I have lost count of how many times I have been asked this question. But it's always surprising. There is a drop in my stomach as if I am teetering on the edge of a minefield. "Oh, um." I'm flustered, and my jaw is sore. I touch my lip. A little blood comes away on my fingers. You hand me a napkin, and I dab the corner of my mouth. You're waiting for me to answer. "I am Japanese. Half, I mean. My dad is white, Jewish." I cringe at my words while you nod thoughtfully. I swore I wouldn't do that, wouldn't divide myself up. Not after a teacher called me half-and-half in elementary school, like coffee creamer or as if to measure me like one does a recipe, segmenting me into parts. Am I too much of something? Not enough of another? I know what I am not—*whole*.

"Were you born here?" you ask, writing some notes into my chart.

"Yes," I rasp.

"That's cool," you say. But it doesn't feel that way unless you mean cool as in cold. As in exiled, left out in the darkness of space. I shouldn't be surprised. There are thousands of years of history of people expelling what they don't understand, what doesn't conform, what doesn't fit. You stand, and I have to crane my neck to find you. The light obstructs your face. "Give us a call if the tenderness lasts more than a few days."

As I walk out, I see you with your next patient, hear you through the open door. "You play sports?" you ask him. I can't see his face, but I can see his hands loosely gripping the armrest of the dental chair. He's white.

I drive myself home, and when I get there, Dad's special tennis shoes (that I wish he wouldn't wear out in public) are by the door. They're black with at least three-inch soles that help with his plantar fasciitis. Enya blasts through the house. We drove six hours one summer to see her in concert. The only thing Dad loves more than Enya is magic. If Enya ever put on a show with David Copperfield, my dad might actually die. I laugh with my friends about it.

Dad is in the kitchen. "Hey, you," he says. A towel is thrown over his shoulder. His sleeves are rolled up and in his hands is a mixer, which he's using to whip mashed potatoes. The whole space reeks of garlic. "How was your appointment?" he asks, then in the same breath says, "Let me see." He clicks the mixer off and wipes his hands on the towel, waiting for me to show him.

"Fine," I say, then pulling my lips into a smile, which quickly deflates into a frown.

"You okay?"

I think about you. Your words. *Where are you from?* It's hard to process right now how I feel, so I focus on the physical. "My mouth is sore," is all I say.

He gives me a sympathetic look. "I figured. That's why we're eating like Great-Grandma Rose tonight," he announces. The table is set with green Jell-O, oatmeal, mashed avocado, and applesauce. "In fact," he says, spooning mashed potatoes into a bowl, "I figured we'd have an old-lady night—early dinner and bedtime, maybe a puzzle in between."

I hold up my hands and say, "Woo-hoo."

When I go to bed, my mouth is numb from ice cream. I don't sleep very well—I toss and turn and think about you, your question and how I wished I'd answered differently.

Four weeks later, I am sitting in the chair again. As I wait for you, I stare at my name in my patient chart. The letters blur together—Tommy, like the boy's name. Just like last time, you start right away. Probing my mouth, tightening wires. But you're done quicker. Just a check-up. "All looks good," you say. You write something in my chart. "Where are you from?" you ask, finger perched above the keyboard. The glow of the monitor highlights your cheeks.

It takes me a moment to understand your question. That you are asking me the same thing again. Don't you remember? Clearly, you do not. You wait for me. I mumble out an answer. A little better than last time. "I'm Japanese and white." *Whasian* is what some of my friends call it.

"Have you ever been to Japan?" you ask, turning to me, hands braced on your knees.

I shake my head.

"I've heard it's beautiful, the country and the culture," you say. "My brother has been. Do you speak Japanese?"

You are not the first to ask me to downplay my whiteness, to play up my Japaneseness. I feel a tug-of-war inside me. Between you and the articles I read online on how to lighten my hair and make my eyes appear larger. "Some," I say. More than some. But I keep it to myself. I don't feel like pleasing you in this way. Proving myself.

In the car, I text Dad I am on my way home. He asks how my appointment was. I tell him fine, because all I want to do is forget about you.

The month goes by too fast. Soon I am back in your office, dread settling like a pit in my stomach. It grows as the minutes tick by. You are running late.

"He'll just be another minute," the dental hygienist assures me and pats my arm. I am already reclined. Sunglasses on and bib pinned to my shirt, ready for you. My toes curl in my sneakers, and my heartbeat increases. You are in your glass office with another parent and child, sliding the open folder across your desk. I watch you stand and shake the mother's hand. Squeeze the kid's shoulder.

Then you walk toward me and start without much preamble. While you tighten my braces and finger my mouth, I think about you. What you have asked me before, what you will probably ask me again soon. Somewhere you learned that it was okay. To say what is on your mind. To speak without considering the consequences.

I flex my hands and cycle through responses.

What if you ask me again? What will I tell you? These questions—*where are you from? What are you mixed with? What are you?*—are like bombs with timers. They detonate later inside me. Why can't you see the fallout? Why can't you see that I belong here, too? I want to say that you make me feel unnatural having so many cultures living inside me. Like Frankenstein, I am made up of spare parts.

Or maybe I'll make it more personal. Maybe I'll say, *Your daughters, your sons, do you think they have ever been asked a question like this? Where are you from? Sweden? I hear that's a beautiful coun-*

try. Wonderful culture. Were you born here? Do you speak Swedish? It is your privilege not to have been asked such things.

You finish up. Withdraw from me and strip off your gloves, leaving them crumpled on the tray. Someone else will clean them up. "Where are you from?" you ask, as I predicted you would.

I swallow. Feel the blood in my mouth not from your ministrations this time but from biting my tongue. "I'm Japanese and white," I say, and that is all because somewhere I have learned to be silent. If I point it out, you might deny it. Would you be angry? Offended? Defiant? Open? Hostile? It is the uncertainty that keeps me quiet. Somewhere deep down, I know. You want to talk about race. But you are not ready to talk about race.

I schedule my next appointment with you.

Dad is there when I get home. He is in the kitchen. He is holding a pan, and the house stinks of burned food. "Well, my risotto didn't turn out," he says with a frown. I pause in the entryway of the kitchen. Dad turns, sees me. "Honey?" he says. "What's wrong?" I wonder if you know your children so well. If you can read their faces like maps. Dad's eyes climb the hills of my cheeks, settle in the pools in my eyes.

I swallow. The words I could not speak to you bubble up in my throat and block it, threatening to choke me. But then there is a tiny pinprick in the dam—my dad stepping toward me, hand outstretched, ready to swim in the flood. I inhale a deep breath. In the acrid smell of our kitchen, I tell him about you. When I am done, Dad declares, "This calls for the very best of Enya." He switches on the music and plays "A Day Without Rain." Then he announces, "I am going to defrost some matzah ball soup."

He directs me to sit and wait on the couch—because he says I need to be somewhere it feels as if I am being held. He brings me a steaming bowl of hot soup. Placing it in my hands, he asks me to tell him again about you, about how I feel. So I do. I recount how you saw me—my dark hair, my roundish eyes that flared at the corners, how you made my body feel not like my own.

It is agonizing, pulling this shrapnel from my skin. But I do. I let the wound bleed. Then, at last, it clots just as I finish telling my father how you saw me and how I have never felt less seen.

★ ★ ★ ★ ★

MARIACHIS VS. BLUEGRASS

By Loriel Ryon

The blast of trumpets startles me. I lock eyes with my sisters, Vero and Paola, through the misty hair-sprayed dressing room.

There's no way.

Vero gives me a panicked oh-no-she-didn't look.

The trumpets echo down the hall, and then there's a guitar strum. Paola cringes.

"She did," Vero says, her voice rising in panic. She pushes up from her seat and rushes to the door, her wedding dress swishing around her.

I knew it. Mom hired a mariachi band for the wedding. After we all begged her not to.

Dad is going to freak out.

Vero peeks through the crack.

"What if Matt sees you?" I run and push the door shut. "It's bad luck!"

Vero closes her eyes and takes a deep breath. She's rather lovely, all done up with fancy makeup and long dark curls. Though I've drawn at least a dozen portraits of her, she looks different on her wedding day, older somehow. Like she's really ready to begin her new life with Matt, and leave me and Paola behind.

One stern look from her and I step aside.

She pulls the door open again.

A guitarrón player strums the rhythm and the reedy sounds of an accordion echo as an all-woman mariachi band wearing matching gold suits and sombreros marches by. Their ornamented trousers tinkle as their boots thump on the ground, the hearty voice of the lead singer crooning the opening lines of "Cielito Lindo."

Mom went all out.

How did she even find a mariachi band willing to come all the way to the beach?

Vero shuts the door and leans against it. "Dad's going to be furious, and then Mom will threaten to leave, and this whole wedding was a terrible idea."

A few months ago, there was an argument about the bands. Dad wanted bluegrass. Mom wanted mariachis. Vero didn't want either because choosing one would mean not choosing the other. Matt finally stepped in and said they knew a DJ who would do them a favor.

We thought that had been the end of it. But apparently not.

"Let's leave," Paola says, wrapping a strand of her own dark hair around the curling iron. She adjusts the small silver hoop in her nose while she waits for the iron to heat her hair. "Call Matt. He said he'd be thrilled to elope."

Vero rolls her eyes at Paola.

Vero is our oldest sister and a typical first-born. She hates disappointing people. She didn't want a huge wedding, but to keep from making waves, she relented. Paola, our middle sister, is a bit of a rebel. She doesn't care what most people think of her, though I know deep down she cares what Vero and I think. They are both always there when I need them.

In their own ways.

Like when I got dumped by my first boyfriend last summer, Vero cuddled up in bed with me and handed me tissues while I cried, and Paola came into my room with an armload full of toilet paper rolls and asked for his address.

And then there's me. Irene (EE-reh-neh) to my mom's side of the family (the Mexican side); Irene (Eye-reen) to my dad's side of the family (the Irish side). I'm the baby. I'm fifteen, and I love to draw. My goal in life is usually to keep my head down.

But today, I just want our parents to get along, for Vero's sake. She deserves to not have to be the mature stand-in parent for once.

Vero shakes her head and then starts hiccupping. It's what happens when she's nervous. Sometimes, it'll get so bad she can't breathe.

I guide Vero back to the seat in front of the mirror and then open the window to the dressing room, letting the salty beach air fill the room.

Vero's face is red.

"Breathe, Vero," Paola says, fanning her and smacking her chewing gum. "I already did your makeup."

Vero squints and grabs Paola's arm, bringing it close to examine it. "When did you get this?"

Paola got a new tattoo last week, a giant calavera I drew for her that covers her entire upper arm. She took me to the tattoo shop so I could watch them do the outlining. Paola wrestles away and covers her arm with her shawl.

"Mom's going to be mad," Vero says.

"And?" Paola scoops some ointment out of a jar and rubs it over the tattoo. "Maybe it'll distract her from Dad."

I get a bottle of water from the cooler and give it to Vero. "It's going to be okay."

Vero takes the tiniest sips between hiccups. She looks unconvinced.

This will be the first time our parents have seen each other in over six years. Since their less-than-amicable divorce (to put it nicely), my sisters and I have kept them from ever having to be near each other at the same time.

The divorce is one of the reasons I stopped playing the cello and started drawing. No more concerts where they might run into each other. It's easier to stagger entry times to an art show.

Dodging parent collisions has been the plan for years. From across-the-stadium seats at graduations to separate birthday parties and holidays. We've become experts in keeping them apart.

But six months ago, Vero wanted both of them to meet Matt's parents at a small dinner. Disaster.

I (stupidly) let it slip that Dad and Davis (Dad's new husband and Mom's ex-assistant) were both going to be at the dinner, and Mom freaked out and refused to come. Dad heard Mom wasn't coming because of Davis. He got upset and turned his car around in the driveway, leaving Vero parentless at the meet-the-parents dinner. I'll never forget her calling me from the bathroom, her voice shaking. And then the hiccupping started.

Paola and I hopped in the car and sped all the way there, making a quick stop at the grocery store to pick up a gigantic CONGRATULATIONS cake.

So *today* will be the first time they (hopefully) make it into the same room.

"They are going to ruin everything," Vero says, taking another sip. "What if they can't get it together to walk me down the aisle?"

I bite my thumbnail and look to Paola. Paola tried to convince Vero to elope months ago, but after Grandma threw a fit about not being able to see her eldest granddaughter get married, and threatened to *probably die soon*, Vero relented.

The mariachis start up "Volver, Volver," and Paola sways to the music and pops her gum. "I'm glad the mariachis are here." She twists a strand of Vero's hair around the barrel of the curling iron. "Volveeeeeeer," she sings.

Vero glares at her.

"I just mean for the live music, not for our parents."

"They are going to get along," I say. "They can't keep doing this."

Paola blinks at me in the mirror. She's skeptical. She doesn't believe our parents are capable of being adults. But I think they can do it.

They have to.

"When does Mom's flight get in?" Paola asks.

"Shooting for the season finale ended last night." I check my phone. "Fifteen minutes."

And I feel like throwing up.

"You aren't going to miss us one bit, are you?" Paola mists Vero's hair with hairspray.

I'm surprised to hear Paola say it because I didn't think she cared like I did. It's been a growing lump in my throat for months. After the wedding, Vero and Matt are moving to Washington State so Vero can get her master's in social work.

"Of course, I'll miss you both." Vero's eyes water. "I'll visit. And besides, you're going to be in Spain all summer. Irene's the one who will be all alone."

Both of my sisters are leaving. My throat tightens. It's something I don't like to think about, so I change the subject.

"Were our parents ever happy together?" I ask.

Vero pats my hand. "Yes. But you were a baby."

"They loved to dance," Paola says.

Vero nods. "Remember when they used to dance salsa in the kitchen?"

"Dad danced salsa?" That's not something I remember. Everything about who they once were together is so far away now; it's a vast canyon dividing them. Like it never even happened.

I don't remember fights or yelling like my sisters do. I remember a feeling. An icy dread that crept its way into the walls of our home, settling in the bones of the family and refusing to leave. Everything was quieter. Life felt breakable, and if I made one wrong move, it could shatter at any moment.

During the divorce, things were bad. It was painful to play the cello in the elementary school cafeteria while they sat at opposite sides of the room. I didn't make it through the first piece without sweating through my itchy white button-down shirt. Then, I had to pick which parent to see first after it was over. Instead, I ran to the back and hid. Paola eventually found me curled up in a closet and took me home. Vero tried to get me to keep playing cello, but after that, I was done. No more events where they had to be in the same room at the same time.

It was Vero who decided that we wouldn't choose one parent over the other, even when the court said we had to pick. She stood up, all of sixteen years old, and said, "Fifty-fifty. No matter what." I remember the dread of thinking we'd have to choose one of them.

How do you pick one when you love them both?

Even when they are imperfect and full of pain.

"We won't choose," Vero said, her pointy chin so sure as she addressed the judge. But she started to hiccup, and her hands shook while she spoke, so I took hers in mine to steady her.

Vero kept it together. Vero kept us together when our family fell apart.

And it's only fair that I try to repay her.

"It was only bad toward the end, I guess. But now we get to see them play it out over Vero's big night," Paola says, half joking.

Vero and I both shoot her a look. "No. They will not ruin this," I say. "It's time for them to grow up already." My voice comes out louder than I expect.

Paola raises an eyebrow, surprised to hear me say such things. My cheeks burn.

The door to the dressing room slams open and two of our

cousins, Marisol and Linda, walk in. They are dressed up for the wedding, but I can see the hangover from last night's rehearsal dinner written all over their faces. They shuffle past us to the toilets.

"You look gorgeous, Vero," Marisol says in a singsong voice.

Vero smiles and looks down shyly. "Thank you."

Linda gives Marisol a side-eye glance, and they each go into a bathroom stall and shut the doors.

Marisol and I used to be close.

When everything went bad with our parents, things changed with our extended families as well.

When I was with my dad and his side of the family, no one ever asked about my mother. It was almost as if I had never had a mother at all. Like my sisters and I had miraculously emerged from a crack in the earth all by ourselves and our father had been the only one to ever care for us.

They quietly followed the latest news of her movies and TV shows, though they didn't openly talk about it. But I'd find stacks of entertainment magazines with her pictures in the bathroom under the box of tissues.

And when I was with Marisol and my mom's side of the family, we never spoke of my dad. At least they never talked with *me* about him. Which was for the best, because the one time I slipped up and mentioned him, my aunt said something in Spanish under her breath to my grandma about him and Davis. I know they didn't understand him marrying a man, and I'd be lying if I said it hadn't taken me and my sisters some time to get used to it, too. But he and Davis are happy together. It's hard to imagine there was a time when they weren't together.

I didn't understand the word my aunt used, but Marisol did. She gave me a sheepish look, and I could tell whatever it meant, it embarrassed her.

They do that a lot.

Switch to Spanish when they want to talk about us.

It's not like I expected Marisol to tell her mother to stop. She was just a kid, like me, at the mercy of our parents' world.

Marisol and Linda speak Spanish, and it echoes in the dressing room.

They did it at the rehearsal dinner last night. Speaking Spanish around us, *about* us, so sure that we won't understand a word.

And Paola and Vero don't have a clue what they are saying.

Our mother never taught us Spanish.

But I've been taking it in school, and I've gotten pretty good.

They laugh loudly, and Linda says something so fast I almost miss it.

Blanquita.

Last night they called me Blanquita at dinner. Grandma calls me that because I have the lightest skin on her side of the family. But when Grandma says it, she does so with love. When Marisol and Linda say it, it's with a pinch of condescension. They like to make fun of us for being half Mexican and half white.

I held my tongue last night even though my insides were sparking like firecrackers. I ignored them, like I always try to do, but the stress of the wedding and our parents seeing each other are too much.

Then Marisol says something about the mariachis and Vero being an imposter Latina.

I hate that they are talking about my sister, and she can't even defend herself. I stand up, my jaw tight, and Vero touches my arm to try to stop me.

The words slip out in a flurry. "Yo entiendo. Son pendejas. No te metas!"

The bathroom falls silent, and Vero stares at me wide-eyed. My hands are shaking, and my ears burn with rage. I lost my cool.

Marisol and Linda don't say anything else. The toilets flush one after another, and the locks to the stalls click open. Marisol's cheeks are bright pink, and they both wash their hands, not looking at us. They leave quickly.

"What did you say?" Paola applies dark red lipstick in the mirror, carefully lining the bow of her lips.

"I told them to mind their business." I press my lips in the reflection and my stomach tumbles over on itself. I don't want to tell Vero what they said about her.

Paola raises an eyebrow at me. "I heard...pendejas."

I bite my lip and spin around. My sisters may not know much Spanish, but they know that word. "And I called them pendejas."

Paola busts out laughing, and Vero hits me on the arm with her water bottle.

There's a knock at the door, and then it opens.

Matt stands in the doorway, wearing a navy suit and looking very handsome with his dark hair styled into a swoop. He covers his eyes with his hand. "I won't peek. Promise."

"Matt!" Vero yells.

I run to close the door on him, but he squeezes through before I can.

"I'm just here to talk about the bands—"

"My mom hired the mariachis," Vero says, exasperation in her voice. "I'm so sorry. I didn't know she was going to do that."

Matt nods in understanding. "So, she hired both bands?"

"What do you mean *both bands*?" I ask.

Matt chews his lip. "Well—"

I open the door to the dressing room, and three men walk by in jeans, carrying what looks like a guitar case, a banjo case, a fiddle case...and yep, there goes the bass.

I shut the door; my eyes widen with shock. How do I tell her?

"What?" Vero says, not taking her eyes off me. "What is it?"

"Um..." Matt says, his hand still covering his eyes.

I take a deep breath and wring my hands. "So...it appears Dad hired the bluegrass band."

Vero's mouth drops open. "No."

Paola collapses into a fit of laughter again. "Wow. They really are trying to ruin everything, aren't they?"

Matt clears his throat and feels around the room with his free hand, searching for Vero. Vero steadies him and interlaces her fingers with his.

"It's not a big deal. We'll have one band play before the ceremony and one after, and keep the DJ for the reception. People love live music," he says.

"Told you," Paola says, tilting her head back and forth.

"I just need someone who speaks enough Spanish to talk to the mariachi band, because mine is really bad," Matt admits.

"I'll do it," I say.

Vero leans in and kisses Matt on the lips. "I'm so glad I'm marrying you," she says.

Matt kisses her back, and his hand slips a little from his eyes. "Me, too."

"Now, now, now." Paola moves in and covers Matt's eyes with her shawl. "There will be plenty of time for *that* later."

She steers Matt toward the door and shoos me out with him. "Go fix the mess," Paola says. "I'll be out in a minute." She shuts the door behind us.

Matt uncovers his eyes.

I'm happy for Vero. Matt is cool. He's kind and really cares about her. And us. He doesn't hold all the dumb stuff our parents do against her.

He looks at me. "I can't wait to marry your sister and get out of here."

I give him a sad look. "I'll have to come visit." My voice catches.

He wraps an arm around my shoulder and squeezes. "Of course. We'll fly you out anytime."

Vero is leaving, and it hurts, but I'm glad that at least she'll be with Matt.

"It's time for my parents to figure their stuff out and stop acting like this."

Matt laughs and we head toward the back of the venue where the doors open to the beachside ceremony. "I don't know if your parents are ever going to figure their stuff out."

"No. They will," I say. "I'm going to make them."

Matt looks at me with sympathy. "I know you want to, but don't expect too much. There's a lot of hurt there."

His words sting. Part of me knows he's right. "Vero deserves to not have to be the parent for once. She deserves to have her parents support her and not make it all about themselves."

Matt puts a hand on my shoulder and squeezes it. "She has me. And she has you and Paola."

"True." I rub at a dark charcoal stain on my palm. I stayed up late finishing Vero's wedding present. "But...she deserves to have her parents, too."

Matt nods and lets go of my shoulder.

The mariachi and bluegrass bands are both unloading their equipment next to the bar where the cocktail hour will be. Matt and I walk over to them.

The warm salty breeze and the sound of waves crashing relaxes me a little.

In my rudimentary Spanish, I let the head of the mariachi band know that they will be playing the pre-ceremony music while Matt talks to the banjo player and lets them know they will play the cocktail hour. The bands are a little confused to see each other, but they don't seem to mind too much. The bluegrass band takes their equipment up to the gardens to warm up. The mariachi band starts to play.

There's a small crowd of wedding guests—some of my mom's side, my dad's side, and some strangers who I imagine belong to Matt's family—who have gathered around the stage. Matt goes to talk to someone near the bar.

"Interesting choice for wedding music," Aunt Ginnie says,

raising an overly penciled eyebrow at me and then toward the mariachi band.

I give her a small fake smile, like I always do when Aunt Ginnie says not-so-nice things.

And then, thankfully, Paola is there. She tsks at Aunt Ginnie and rolls her eyes, but Aunt Ginnie doesn't hear her.

Paola gives me a playful look.

"Don't," I warn.

The mariachis near the end of the song, and when they finish, Paola takes in a huge deep breath and leans in close to Aunt Ginnie.

I shut my eyes and brace myself.

"Brrrrrrrrrrrrrrrryeeeeeeeeeeeeeeyieyieyieyowwwwww," Paola yells. Her grito rings down the beach and Aunt Ginnie looks at her with a mix of amusement and disgust. She stirs her drink and walks off.

"That's almost as good as Aunt Loretta's," I say.

"No one is as good as Aunt Loretta," Paola admits.

My phone buzzes. "Hi, Mom."

"Hi, sweetie. I just got in the limo. Be there soon."

Limo? Of course, she's in a limo. "Okay."

"Did my surprise make it?" The mariachis start up again and Mom laughs on the other end. "Oooh, yep, I hear them."

Paola takes in a deep breath and yells again. This time louder and Uncle Sylvester follows with one of his own gritos.

I cover the phone and walk away from the crowd.

"Loretta is there? I thought she wasn't going to make it."

"No, Mom. It's Paola doing gritos for Aunt Ginnie."

"Oh, I bet your Aunt Ginnie is having an absolute fit over the mariachis. She used to say some really awful things about—"

I interrupt before she gets too far. "It's hard to hear you. I'll just see you when you get here." I pause. "We need to talk."

"What, sweetie? You're breaking up. Is your father there?"

"I think so."

"With Davis?"

I gulp. "Yes, he's here, too, Mom. They're married."

"Hmm. Okay, sweetie, see you soon!"

I head toward the entrance to wait for Mom. Dad is getting out of his car, wearing the gray suit Davis and I picked out a month ago. It makes his silvery hair really pop.

"Dad?"

"Hi, baby." He hugs me and cranes his neck to look through the glass doors. "I need to see if the band is here—"

"They're here," I say. My knees start to jump. I don't want to explain the mariachi band. Or Mom.

Dad pulls a garment bag out of the back of his car and closes the trunk. "Yeah?"

"Yeah. And, Dad, I don't think you should've gone behind Vero's back—"

The door opens and a wave of mariachi music escapes. My dad's bright blue eyes slightly widen. "She didn't." He heads toward the music.

"Dad!" I chase after him.

His eyes flash. "I can't believe she went ahead and..." His jaw twitches.

"Dad. You did it, too." I look at him for a while, hoping he'll see his own role in this, but he just keeps standing there with his hands on his hips and shaking his head.

"I just cannot believe—"

"The mariachis will play before the ceremony, and the bluegrass band can play the cocktail hour."

"She's unbelievable," he says.

"Dad." I put my hands on his arms. "Not today. This isn't fair to Vero."

His eyes soften and he holds his hands up in defeat. "I'm not... I wasn't..." Dad clears his throat. "Your mom on her way?"

"Yeah," I say.

★ ★ ★

It's been almost eight weeks since I've seen Mom. She's been in New Mexico shooting the latest season for her hit detective show, so I've been staying at Dad's. She tries to be home as much as she can, and I'll get to go visit her on set this summer, which I'm really excited about.

Mom's acting career took off in the midst of the divorce, and Dad fell in love with and married her old assistant. It wasn't obvious to me that our parents came from vastly different backgrounds until the divorce happened. Our family life was a meld of southern traditions and Mexican American ones. My sisters and I never noticed that we were the only house on the block making paper bags full of sand and candles for Christmas or cascarones for Easter. We always had southern fried chicken and greasy green beans for Sunday dinners. We sort of knew which pieces went with Mom and which went with Dad.

But it didn't matter which traditions belonged to who…until it did.

After the divorce, we no longer ate tamales for Christmas when we were at Dad's. And Mom never made grits again, even though I think she really likes them.

Traditions and parts of our lives that seemed like they'd been perfectly melded were pulled apart and divided.

But how do you pull yourself apart? What pieces go where? Does my straight hair belong to my dad's side? And my dark eyes to my mom's? What about my artistic ability? There is no way to divide myself and put the pieces into nice little boxes.

After what feels like an eternity, Mom's limousine pulls up. The driver gets out and rushes around the side of the car to open her door, and my mother is out in one elegant swoop. She's wearing oversized sunglasses and her hair is very, very big today.

I run to hug her.

"Aye, Irene, I've missed you. Let me see you," she says, pulling back to look at me.

The driver unloads two massive suitcases and a long garment bag.

I raise an eyebrow at Mom.

"What?" she says, shrugging. "I need options."

"You're here for two days!"

Mom pushes her sunglasses up on top of her hair and digs into her expensive bag, letting me grab the suitcases. She tips the driver and starts for the door.

I walk behind her.

"Shooting got pushed back a couple weeks. I'll be here longer than just the two days."

"Really?" That makes me happy.

"Yeah. How are things going with all of this?" She waves her hand toward the venue.

"Fine," I say. *No thanks to you and Dad*, I think.

"Did your father throw a fit over the mariachis?" She says it with breathless anticipation and anger flashes inside of me.

I keep my eyes forward and pull the suitcase behind me. "None of that," I say in a warning tone.

Mom suppresses a smile and shrugs it off, like I am ridiculous for even suggesting such a thing.

But I know better.

Dad is coming down the hall and my stomach drops. This is it. I have to do this now.

I wait until Dad spots us, and then I pull Mom into the ballroom. No one needs to see this out in the open.

"I want to show you the ballroom," I say, leaving the door ajar behind us.

The ballroom is stunning, the tables glitter with silver and gold formal settings. Davis helped Vero pick color schemes and flowers while Mom was gone, and they'd gone with classic white with touches of gold and silver. It's a bit formal for a beach wedding, but gorgeous.

"Wow," Mom says, picking up a polished fork. "Davis did a nice job."

Through the corner of my eye, I catch Dad walk by the doors. *Come on. Come on.*

Dad stops.

His eyes fall on my mother, who leans in to smell the flower centerpieces.

"Peonies." She stands. "My favorite. White roses remind me of a funeral, so I don't love that, but the eucalyptus is a nice touch."

Dad walks into the ballroom.

I take a deep breath and steel myself.

They look at each other.

"Ed," my mother says.

"Maria."

They don't say anything else for what feels like forever and hope bubbles up in my heart. Maybe it won't be bad. Maybe they can be grown-ups. Maybe we've been worried all this time for nothing.

Dad speaks first. "You shouldn't have scheduled the mariachi—"

Mom interrupts. "You always think you know everything—not everyone wants to hear bluegrass."

Oh, no. Here they go.

Their voices get louder and louder as they talk over each other. Neither one cares what the other is saying. Mom starts yelling about Davis and betrayal, and Dad shakes his head and says their marriage was over years before Davis showed up.

"Hey!" I shout, holding my hands up. My voice echoes in the ballroom. Aunt Ginnie's face appears in the window. Mom and Dad stop and look at me.

"Enough," I say, searching for an escape. "You two need to figure out how to get along. We can't live like this, always tiptoeing around, hoping one of you doesn't get so mad you storm off and ruin everything."

Mom crosses her arms and raises an eyebrow at me. It's her way of trying to get me to back down, but I'm not backing down today.

"Irene," Dad warns.

"Well, I'll just go, then," Mom says, slinging her purse over her shoulder and starting for the door. "I know when I'm not wanted."

"Mom. That's not what we want. We want for you and Dad to be able to be in the same room together and not make it weird. I want you to be able to get along and be—grown-ups."

Now Dad crosses his arms and shakes his head, thoroughly insulted that I've suggested he's not acting like an adult.

This was a terrible idea.

They aren't listening to me.

A crowd has gathered by the doors to the ballroom. Linda holds her phone up to record the scene.

Oh, great. It'll be livestreamed and viral before the wedding even starts.

"Davis did a nice job." Mom adjusts a fork on one of the tables.

Dad fixes the lapels on his jacket. "He worked very hard."

They share a congenial look.

But it's short-lived.

"Wow, was that a compliment from you, Maria?" Dad says feigning surprise.

Mom narrows her eyes. "Really, Ed?"

And then they start talking over each other again.

I don't even know what it's about, but it doesn't matter. More faces appear in the windows.

Marisol.

Grandma.

Then Davis's face pops in and out of view.

I want to leave and let them have at it.

Why am I trying to protect them from themselves? This is their own fault. I feel stupid and heartbroken for thinking I could reason with them. There is still so much anger between them.

Paola was right. We should've kept them apart for as long as possible.

I walk across the ballroom and open the doors to the lush gardens outside. The bluegrass band is in the lower garden warming up and I recognize the song "Hey, Hey, Della Mae." The distant bass thumping echoes on the warm salty breeze, and a riff from the fiddle fills the air.

I turn back to my arguing parents, their arms flailing, brows furrowed, and steer them outside.

Their voices dampen as I close the door. I pull the curtains closed, so no one can see them.

Their echoing voices (and a few curse words) murmur faintly through the heavy door.

Maybe this is what they needed all along.

When I turn around Matt, Paola, and Vero are there.

"Hey, you aren't supposed to see each other," I say. "It's bad luck."

Vero holds out her arms. "I'm not sure much else can go wrong at this rate."

Paola looks at me with a sad, understanding smile, and Matt anxiously peeks through the curtains.

"Here comes your mom," he says, taking a step back.

The door crashes open and Mom rushes into the ballroom, fury all over her face. She beelines for her suitcases and struggles to right them both at the same time. She looks up. "I'm sorry, Vero." Mom's eyes are pained. "I just can't do this." The suitcases thunder behind her as she leaves.

I rest my head on Vero's shoulder. "I'm sorry I couldn't get them to figure it out." My chin quivers.

"This is not on you," Vero says, stroking my cheek.

Paola walks onto the patio. "Dad! Where are you going?" she yells.

The lump in my throat takes hold as the ending of the bluegrass song disappears on the breeze. Paola runs to the parking lot, and a car engine roars loudly and then fades away. Paola walks back in, shaking her head. "Dad left. And Mom just got in a cab." Her eyes water as she leans on Vero's other shoulder. "Pendejos."

I laugh and wipe the tears from my eyes.

My worst fear happened. And yet, my sisters and I are still here.

Together.

Vero sniffs and stands up straight.

Then a realization hits me.

"If you still want to get married today—" I say, grabbing Vero's and Paola's hands "—Paola and I will walk you down the aisle."

"Oh, it's happening today!" Paola says matter-of-factly.

Vero tilts her head and looks at Matt. "You good for that, Mr. Rosewater?"

Matt looks at Vero with so much love in his eyes, and I know she picked a good one. "I can't wait to marry you."

Vero smiles and squeezes our hands. "This should've been the plan all along."

★ ★ ★ ★ ★

I AM NOT A PAPAYA

By Veera Hiranandani

Rani and Asher sat on the old green couch in his basement, an open bag of kettle corn between them. His house had better food, so they had spent many years on this couch doing exactly what they were doing now—eating snacks and telling each other secrets.

Rani grabbed a piece of popcorn and held it up. Asher opened his mouth and she threw. He caught it like she expected he would. This relaxed her, because she knew what she was about to tell him might complicate things. Their friendship, ever since they fiercely bonded four years ago at a local theater camp, had been one of the least complicated things in Rani's life.

"I know you're going to think I'm nuts," she said, taking a deep breath. "But I want to ask Reed to Homecoming."

Asher gave her a small nod and wiped the crumbs from his mouth.

"That's it? Don't we hate Reed? Doesn't this make me a traitor?" She felt her heart speeding up as she waited for his response.

"No, Rani," Asher said after a second, then flicked his dyed black hair out of his eyes. As she waited for him to explain, he started twisting one of his chunky silver rings round and round, the one with a cross on it even though he was Jewish. It was another thing that connected them, though she always felt like she was a different kind of Jewish than Asher. Both his parents were Jewish and only her father was. Her mother was Hindu.

As she watched him play with the ring, she was struck by his large bony man hands. She could remember when his hands were delicate, and he wore striped T-shirts from The Children's Place. They had both changed so much in these few years.

"We only *pretend* to hate him. Everyone likes Reed, even people like us who are supposed to hate him. You don't think I've noticed those shoulders?" Asher said.

"Yeah, but you notice lots of, um, shoulders," she said, grinning and stuffing a huge handful of sweet-salty popcorn into her mouth.

Reed did have nice shoulders. He was on varsity basketball and lacrosse. He was tall, though not too tall, but it was his eyes she liked the most. They were blue and surprising against his dark hair, which was almost as dark as hers.

He walked the school hallways surrounded by a group of jocky boys—though, these boys did not call themselves boys. They preferred guys or bros or dudes—never boys. But they were boys, *such* boys. Reed seemed a little separate somehow, calmer. It was as if he were stuck in some kind of "bro" orbit, trapped in the fate of his broad square shoulders.

Still, she felt a little disgusted with herself that every time he looked her way, she caught her breath. It was all so boring and predictable—artsy biracial girl catches the white jock's attention. They would fall in love, dismantle stereotypes, and not only would *he* realize she was an actual person, she'd realize he was, too. She was a step ahead of it all. Yet, she had to admit she loved the color of his eyes. She was proud of her own large brown eyes and the inviting depth they offered, but his eyes

were the color of blue that didn't seem to have an end to it—
the kind of blue, she wondered, even with all she knew, if she
had access to.

"The thing is, though, I don't think boys like Reed get asked
to dances. Aren't they the askers?"

"And what about boys like you?" she asked him.

"Homecoming is for losers," Asher said, winking, but Rani
knew if Leon hadn't just broken up with him, he'd be owning
the dance with a vengeance.

"Gee, thanks."

"Anytime," he replied.

"Do you think Leon will go?"

"Leon will definitely go. Probably with Layla," he said, not
meeting her eye, suddenly very interested in examining a hole
in his jeans. Did Asher think that she was abandoning him?
Even though Asher was only into guys, they had an unspoken
contract. If one of them got hurt out in the world, they always
had each other.

"Well if Leon goes with Layla, maybe we should just go
together, too," she said, hoping he'd be glad she offered, but
wouldn't take her up on it.

"Don't compare us to Leon and Layla," Asher said, his voice
a little smaller. "No one is like us."

She smiled and tossed a piece of popcorn in the air again. He
caught it, but this time with his hand and threw it back at her.
She tried to catch it in her mouth but missed.

"You're right, I'm sorry," she said and rested her head on his
shoulder.

"If you want to ask Reed, then you should, but are you sure
you want to put yourself out there like this?" he said. "What if
he says no?"

"He probably *will* say no. According to my calculations," she
said as she pretended to press buttons on an imagined calculator,
"there's only a 6.7 percent chance of him saying yes."

"Well then why ask him?" he said, lifting her off him, facing her.

"I can't explain it."

"Rani, my queen," he said. "I'm worried you're going to regret it," he said with an edge of scolding in his voice.

"You know my name means *queen*," she said.

"Yes, you've told me that a million times."

"So every time you say my name, you're calling me a queen. You don't need to say it twice," she said, her own sudden irritation surprising her.

"Jeez," he said and started cleaning up the popcorn crumbs on the floor. "Didn't know it bothered you."

She just shrugged. It hadn't before, but somehow at this moment, it all felt like too much to hold.

"Hey, wait," she said, trying to move the focus off her. "I don't think I've ever asked you what your name means." He looked up, a handful of dirty popcorn in his palm.

"Honestly," he said, "I have no idea."

A few hours later, when she got home, she looked up his name as she procrastinated doing her homework. The name Asher meant *happy*. It sort of fit. Asher did wish everyone was happier, including himself.

His words rang in her head. *Rani, my queen, I'm worried you're going to regret it.* What was the point of being named a queen if she didn't have any queen-like powers? His words only made her want to ask Reed to the dance even more. She had this feeling often lately, an irresistible pull toward disrupting the order and doing the opposite of what was expected of her.

It's why she was on the bowling team instead of playing tennis or soccer or lacrosse like most of the girls she knew. It's why, every once in a while, she put her black clothes and ripped jeans aside, and wore flowered dresses to school all week. She wouldn't be forced into a box. It's also why she wanted to ask a guy like Reed to a dance. She hated dances. They were awkward spectacles filled with bad music and the popular kids getting drunk and making out in dark corners, but they were places where she could make people think harder, wonder about her, but also wonder about themselves, things she wished people did more of in general.

Also, she liked him.

"Dinner," her mother called, and Rani burst out of her room. She was suddenly starving.

They sat on the end of the long table meant for a bigger family—she and her father always across from each other and her mother on the end. She bit into one of the vegan cauliflower tacos, another new recipe her father made because he was on a healthy cooking kick. As she chewed, she studied her parents.

Her parents were like business partners. She rarely saw them being romantic or flirty. They were so organized and ran the house like a well-oiled machine. They alternated cooking and cleaning up. They both worked full-time, her mother as a high school English teacher and her father as a graphic designer. They seemed happy, she guessed, but they were always talking about work, or what was coming up for Rani in school, or other planning-for-the-future type things.

"Don't forget," her father said, "we have to drop off the Subaru for service next week."

"On the calendar," her mother said. "Rani, can you get a ride home from bowling next Wednesday?"

"Sure," she said and nodded.

"How are the tacos?" her father asked.

"Weird. And by weird, I mean really good," she said and smiled.

"Ha, ha," her father replied. "But you're right, maybe more salt. Red onions could be nice."

She observed them as they started talking about the grocery list and the plumber coming on Friday. What had they been like when they first fell in love? Had her mother ever felt about her dad what she felt about Reed? Her parents had met in college. Her mother was born in Mumbai but came to Connecticut with her family when she was five. Her father was Jewish and grew up in Westchester where he had mostly Jewish friends. He was used to fitting in. She was used to feeling like an outsider. Rani wondered if that's what attracted her mother to her father, a way in. Was that what she was doing with Reed? The lines felt blurry, like they usually did—her sense of fitting in or being an outsider.

The next day, she watched Reed closely at lunch, waiting for some kind of sign. She took a big bite of her kaiser roll spread unevenly with little pats of butter, the only thing she could stomach in the cafeteria, and poked Asher who was absorbed in tying the laces of his left black boot. He once told her he hadn't learned how to tie his shoelaces until a year ago. It was still hard for him.

"Look," she said. "He's talking to Claire McDonnell."

She saw Claire lean closer to Reed. She flipped her hair from one side of her shoulder to the other and laughed, flashing her straight white teeth. Then she touched his arm. As Rani and Asher watched, Reed looked right at Rani and shrugged. Then he went back to focusing on Claire.

"Did he just *shrug* at me?" Rani said, her face heating up.

"Shrug, he did," said Asher. "You weren't kidding. I'm getting some major vibes."

Rani decided if she were a girl like Claire, she would look away, pretend she and Asher were in an extremely important conversation, and make Reed feel both seen and ignored. So she forced herself to keep staring right at him and took another huge bite of roll.

"I'm not sure if having a face full of bread crumbs counts as flirting," Asher said.

"What? Oh," she said and wiped her face with the back of her hand. "I'm not flirting."

"Well, maybe you should be," he said.

"I'm still deciding," she said, "on whether or not to do it."

"Well if you don't, I think Claire will beat you to it. Okay, off to History." He started packing up his stuff.

"You seem annoyed."

He looked up. "Me? I never get annoyed. Or I'm always annoyed, not sure which."

"So should I ask him?"

"Whatever you want, Rani. Gotta go."

She swallowed. Asher wrestled with his overstuffed backpack, papers falling out through the openings. His bootlaces were still untied. So maybe Asher wasn't actually on board with the Reed thing? Was he really worried for her or just jealous about the fact that she had a new crush since he had just gotten dumped? Maybe both? She wanted to say something, but then decided to let it go and watched him walk down the long hallway and out through the swinging cafeteria doors. She had a study hall close by, so she sat, finishing her roll. As she saw the last of Asher disappear down the hallway, she heard a voice on her other side.

"Hey," he said.

She looked to her right and there was Reed, standing over her.

"Whoa, that was quick," she said. "You were just over there," she said, pointing to where he had just been. Then she laughed nervously and flipped her hair from one side of her shoulder to the other. Dammit. She hadn't even meant to.

"I'm actually a shape-shifter," he said.

"So what did you shift into?" she said, laughing a little again.

"Hmm, maybe I've got my supernatural powers confused."

"Maybe," she said. If anyone was a shape-shifter, she was.

"Uh, so. Do you have the notes for Precalc? Ms. Granger?" he said.

"Oh, you have Granger, too?" she asked.

"Yeah."

"How did you know I did?" She really wanted to know. They weren't in the same class.

"Because I saw you come out of her room once."

"And why don't you have the notes?" she said, squinting.

"You ask a lot of questions," he said.

She wasn't sure what to say. Did he not like girls who asked questions? She bit her lip. Then the bell rang.

"Oh no, I'm late," she said, startled by the noise, and grabbed her backpack.

"So can I get the notes?"

"Sure, now?" she said, not wanting to go through her backpack.

"I'll come by your locker after school," he said and then turned and walked off.

She stood there alone and nodded even though he wasn't there anymore. Her eyes fixed on his solid shoulders ahead of her. She hoisted up her backpack and started toward the same swinging doors, not even sure of what had just happened. She noticed Claire McDonnell give her some side-eye as she walked past, and felt a jolt of excited energy travel through her body.

She couldn't concentrate for the rest of the day and kept thinking of Reed, just standing right there, talking to her like it was no big deal. Had they ever even spoken before? At her locker, she started packing up her stuff extra slow, using her peripheral vision to look out for Reed so she wouldn't look like she was actually waiting for him, but he never came. Then she had to run to make her bus.

She texted Asher that night.

Did you know your name means happy?

I had kind of hoped it meant something else, he replied.

Like what?

I don't know, maybe Mysterious Handsome Genius. Happy is a silly word.

Why? she asked.

Is anyone really happy?

Oh, don't be such a cynic. But also, Reed sucks, she texted.

Uh-oh. What happened?

She told him about the encounter and then the missed locker appearance.
Well maybe he had a good reason, Asher said.

Whose side are you on?

Mine, lol, he texted back.
She texted him a rolling-eye emoji and told him she had to run for dinner, though she didn't have to just yet. Did Asher really see Reed as a threat to their friendship? Or was it just that if he didn't have a boyfriend, she couldn't, either?
She sat cross-legged on her bed for a long time, wondering what she had done to scare Reed off so soon. Maybe what she feared was correct, that her lines were too blurry for him. Perhaps he did want someone who fit more clearly into whatever box he was looking for, someone who flirted properly, someone who didn't ask so many questions, someone who actually wanted to flip her hair for him, someone as clear as Claire.
Another day went by, but Reed was nowhere to be found. She decided when she did see him again, she would be extremely friendly and then dismiss him as fast as she could. But she didn't see him for the rest of the week.
"Should I call him?" she asked Asher as they sat on the green

couch and plowed through a box of Triscuits and hunks of ched-
dar cheese.

"Call him? What is this, 1992? Do you even have his number?"

"No, but I'm worried. He's been out for days. I could DM him."

"Let it go, Rani. If you want to go to Homecoming so bad,
we'll go together."

"That's not the point," she said, stung.

"I'm sorry. I just hate the way these dances stir up drama.
It's stupid."

"Yeah, I know," she said, but she wasn't sure what drama he
meant exactly. Maybe the friendship she and Asher had wasn't
so special after all, just two outcasts clinging to each other.

That Monday, as she tried to stuff too many books in her
locker while placing her coffee mug on the floor, a sneakered
foot crossed her line of sight.

"I was sick. Strep throat," a voice said. She looked up, knowing it was Reed before she saw him. Her eyes traveled up his
body and landed on his eyes, which almost made her gasp. She
stood up and promptly kicked her drink over. The top popped
off, and it spilled everywhere.

"Oh, man, my coffee!" she called out. It was her mother's
fault. She made the best French press coffee in the mornings
and had turned Rani into an addict. Reed left and she wondered if she really scared him off now, but after a few seconds
he returned with a wad of paper towels. They mopped up the
coffee together.

"Thank you," she said, blowing a long strand of hair out of
her face.

"Sure. Now I won't feel bad asking you again for the
Precalc notes."

"You know, I'm not a math wizard. Like *my* notes are maybe
not the notes you want."

"You're probably better than me. I'm carrying a perfect
seventy-five."

"Oh, well, then I guess so," she said and smiled.

"Want to study for the test together this weekend?" he asked her.

She stared at him. "Is this all a ploy to get me to tutor you for free?"

"No, I'll pay you. In fresh coffee," he said, grinning.

Stay strong, she thought. "I'll think about it."

She did think about it and when he asked again later in the day, she said yes before he could finish the question. They studied at her house, and he brought coffee just like he'd promised. They sat at her desk, an extra chair pulled over for him. After an hour of pretending to study, he reached over and closed her book, very slowly. Then she watched his hand gently touch her wrist, and she let him slide the pencil out of her fingers. She looked up into his eyes and moved closer. They fell into each other easily as if they had kissed many times before. The door was halfway open, as her parents requested, but Rani knew they were absorbed in their weekend gardening, bill paying, emailing, or whatever they were doing.

It was only Rani's second kiss, but miles better than her first, a bumbled attempt with Asher's cousin at a party last summer. She told Asher how awkward it was, and they had laughed about it. But Reed had a confidence that thrilled her. His arms were even stronger and more comforting than she had imagined. He said that she was unique. She didn't even ask him how or why, just moved in for another kiss.

Oh boy, Asher said when she texted him later that day. You're toast.

I am.

Toast, she thought, *light and crispy*. Was that what she wanted to be?

She came down to breakfast that Sunday to a huge bowl of fruit salad her father made.

"All your favorites," he said and pointed to the bowl overflowing with cubed papayas, mangoes, pineapple, watermelon, and starfruit. She had a taste for tropical fruits, inspired by her mother's love for her childhood favorites. Her grandparents had given them a gift of a fruit club subscription for her mother's birthday, and each month they received a bounty that had to be eaten quickly. Usually it was apples, pears, bananas, or oranges. In the summer, there had been peaches, apricots, and cherries, but this one was her favorite haul.

"Yum," she said and piled several heaping spoonfuls onto her plate. She sank her teeth into a large piece of ripe sunset-colored papaya, her favorite of them all.

"Can I see the chart?" she asked. Her father pointed at the printed description on the counter that every fruit box came with. It was labeled *Our Exotic Fruit Collection*. She thought it was an odd title for a box of fruit, as she scanned the facts about each fruit's origin while she took bite after bite, losing herself in the tangy sweetness and thoughts of kissing Reed. *This is what it's like to be happy*, she thought, and made a mental note to tell Asher.

It was only two weeks before the dance. Now that Reed was hanging around her locker every morning and they walked down the hall together, even stealing a kiss every now and then, she didn't want to ask him. She wanted him to ask her. Somehow, in this releasing of her power, she felt more powerful. Asher had said boys like Reed were the askers, meaning popular boys. She noticed people watching them in the hallways and couldn't help feeling like she wanted to turn and yell out, "Ha! See?" but she wasn't sure exactly to whom.

Two days went by and still no ask.

"At this point, it would be insulting to me if I asked him," Rani said to Asher, this time at her house, eating more fruit.

"I was worried about this," he said, picking at his piece of pineapple. He didn't really like raw fruit, something she couldn't comprehend.

"About what exactly, though?"

"About him. Hurting you."

"Or maybe you were worried that he wouldn't," she said. "I just think you could be happier for me."

He opened his mouth to say something, but didn't. He got up and tossed his plate of fruit in the garbage. "I'm not sure why Reed is messing with us, but ever since you've been hanging out with him, you seem to think you're better than me," he finally said.

She looked at the fruit in the garbage and then back at him, surprised that he was confronting her so directly. "That's not what I think at all. I think you're jealous that I'm with a hot guy and you're not."

A moment of hurt flashed in his eyes, but then he just shook his head, mumbling something about homework, and left before she could say anything else. She had worried from the beginning that Reed might alter something between them, but it seemed like the truth wasn't either of those things, her thinking she was better, Asher being jealous. Perhaps it was just what people like Reed did, directed the energy toward them until everyone else felt left out. But was that Reed's fault?

Reed asked her the next day, by her locker. He whispered it in her ear.

"Will you go to Homecoming with me?"

She took in his blue eyes, his lips near her neck, the warmth of a sunbeam from the nearest window falling on them, and dove.

"Sure," she whispered back, pulling him close.

At the dance, she wore a wine-colored sleeveless sheath with an armful of silver bangles from her Aunty Meena, black boots, her hair loose and wavy—a look she knew would be different from most of the girls there in their pastel mini-dresses. Asher didn't even help her get ready or at least text her to have a good time. They hadn't spoken in days.

She caught Claire staring at them during a slow dance, whispering to her friends. Reed wore his dark blue suit well. It was everything she had imagined it would be and she wondered if anything had ever felt quite that way for her.

After dancing, they sat together in the back of the gym, drinking punch, playing with each other's fingers, kissing a little. Then he pulled her back on the dance floor when another slow song came on. She pressed her head against his chest as they swayed to the music.

"I wanted to ask you out for so long, but I was afraid," he said after a minute. She looked up.

"Why?" she asked. "Am I so scary?" she joked and made a claw out of her hand.

"No," he said, "but you know, you're different."

She remembered how he said she was unique before, and her heart started beating faster, like she had lived this exact moment in a previous life and her body knew the future. She looked up at the huge disco ball on the gym ceiling, the fractured light spinning everywhere. "Watermelon Sugar" by Harry Styles played in the background.

"How am I different?" she said, moving away, just an inch.

"You're exotic," he said.

She stiffened and stopped dancing.

"It's a good thing. I like it," he said and tried to pull her back to him.

Exotic, she thought. Did that mean different in a good way? Wasn't he just saying she was hot? But then the shiny list of fruits from the gift box popped into her mind—*Our Exotic Fruit Collection*. Fruits were meant to be consumed and easily replaced. Fruits didn't have feelings. There was a whooshing sound in her ears. She knew she was supposed to be okay with this and yet, or perhaps because of it, she couldn't stop herself.

"I am not a papaya, Reed," she told him.

"A what?" he asked, his face becoming serious.

"A papaya, you know, a fruit. An *exotic* fruit."

"Oh, hey, I didn't mean it like that. I meant it as a compliment."

"I know," she said, but she let go of him and dropped her arms by her side. "But I think..." and then she trailed off.

"Tell me," he said.

She forced herself to say it. "I think I should go home."

"Rani, no. You're taking it the wrong way. I really didn't mean to upset you," he said and looked truly confused, like a little boy. But he wasn't a little boy.

They stood for a second, looking at each other. Her feet felt stuck to the gym floor. She knew if she walked out, she would be giving up a certain kind of power she might have had as Reed's girlfriend. All she had to do was tell him it was okay and take his hand.

"I'm going to go," she said, wincing a little, like she was ripping off a Band-Aid. "I can walk. I live close by. I'm sorry."

Reed didn't say anything else and she turned, leaving him like a runaway bride. She didn't look back until she walked through the gym doors. She expected him to already be surrounded by his group of bros, nudging their arms, saying horrible things about her, or maybe with Claire, ready to fill in her space. But he still stood alone on the dance floor, looking frozen, like the dance was a movie and she had just pressed the pause button.

She walked faster, her boots suddenly deafening on the vinyl floor and headed out the front door of the high school. When she found herself in the parking lot, she took out her phone from her tiny purse and started texting Asher, ready to tell him the whole story, ready to repair things, but then she stopped.

She would text him tomorrow. Asher might understand, he might not, and she couldn't risk it now. Her shoulders relaxed. She was more familiar with this solitary feeling than she even realized. It brought a certain kind of comfort with its terror. Maybe this was actually how it felt to be a queen.

She shivered as the cool fall air chilled her bare arms. Looking up, she squinted past the light from the tall street lamps and gazed at the sky, hoping for a massive amount of stars spread out before her. It was a foggy night, though, with not a glimmer in sight. Still, she knew the stars sparkled behind the clouds even if she couldn't see them and continued walking toward home, not minding the sound of her boots anymore.

★ ★ ★ ★ ★

BETWEEN VISIBILITIES

By Adi Alsaid

It wasn't that Eitan was born invisible; it was that he was born between visibilities. You couldn't really tell where he was if you weren't looking at him. He was like a ghost, shrouded in fog. A reflection in a steamed-up bathroom mirror: that was Eitan. Only people who really tried to look could see him fully formed, and even then they had to squint, he had to hold still.

Sometimes people looked at him and thought they saw him clearly. His lanky outline, his sandy hair (both in color and in the fact that he spent so much time at the beach there were permanent grains falling from his scalp, trailing behind him like crumbs in a fairy tale). They thought they knew what Eitan looked like. They believed they did, would swear they had a complete picture in their heads. But most of these people didn't notice that he wore the same pair of doodled-on shoes every day, or that he always had a food stain in the exact same spot on his shirt (it was a curse, Eitan believed; no matter how many napkins he tucked into his collar at lunchtime—his friends had stopped making fun of him for it since they'd long ago run out of jokes—when the bell rang and it was time to return to class, the stain was back). Most of these people could only see one of his passports, the one granted to him because of his physical location at time of birth.

But there was more to him that they couldn't see, parts visible to a few others. His buck teeth, his smudged glasses that had lost an arm months ago, but he hadn't had it replaced because he lied to his parents and said he wore contact lenses to school (though he just wore the broken glasses most of the time). These other people could see his tan lines, but not the sand trailing behind him. They saw his skinny limbs running up and down the basketball court but would never describe him as lanky. His outline seemed to blur when he ran, so they thought he was just kind of skinny and really fast. This group of people, for whatever reason, could only ever seem to acknowledge his other passport, even though it was given to him by a country he'd never lived in. He looked more Israeli, though, so that was how they saw him. The truth was that he simply didn't look like what these people thought Mexicans could look like.

Eitan was used to all this. To people seeing a part of him and assuming it was whole. To people seeing something out of focus and assuming it was clear.

Truth be told, Eitan was often out of focus to himself, too. He'd wipe at his bathroom mirror as if he'd just stepped out of the shower, even when it was the middle of the day and he'd simply washed his hands.

When people argued with him that one or the other of his passports were the only one that counted, he didn't know exactly how to push back against the notion. Was a person more defined by where they were born or where their parents were born? If some government or the other decided to take away either one of his nationalities, he would still be Eitan. He would still have the beach, and the basketball court, and the food stains, probably. So what did it matter?

It didn't.

Well. It did.

Because everywhere around him, Eitan saw people that felt fully visible. Like Sandra Dominguez, who was in three of Eitan's classes. She wore her hair in a Natalia Lafourcade crown (which was really a Frida Kahlo crown, but Eitan didn't know that yet), and was a photographer. That was an inarguable fact, even if she was also fifteen and fifteen-year-olds didn't have professions. People could see Sandra's camera draped around her neck even when she wasn't carrying it; that's how clearly they could see her. When kids from school saw braids turned into a crown, they didn't think Natalia Lafourcade or Frida Kahlo. They thought: Sandra Dominguez.

Or there was Salo Maya, from his basketball team. Salo, who played with the tzitziyot hanging from beneath his jersey and a kippah clipped to his hair. Salo, who at the team taquizas never ordered the al pastor, or the alambres with cheese. He wasn't strictly kosher, but everyone knew when they saw cheese on a meat taco that Salo wouldn't be coming anywhere near it. They also knew that Salo had a penchant for saying "Shema Israel" at the slightest little thing, like someone missing a free throw in practice, or Sandra Dominguez coming to sit in the bleachers to watch them play. That was Salo. There was no mistaking him.

Did Eitan do anything that made people say, "That's Eitan, no doubt about it?" Even he didn't know.

On the first day of sophomore year, Eitan decided he was going to shave his head. He liked his hair and everything, but he thought maybe it would give him a Thing to be recognized for. He could be Shaved-Head Guy for a while, even if his mom cried when he told her the plan.

When he climbed onto the bus, he couldn't keep himself from grinning, waiting to see everyone's reactions. He made eye contact with the kids who sat at the front. But Eitan went to an international K–12 school, and the only ones at the front were the elementary kids who didn't know him, anyway. So, he continued down the aisle, waiting to see recognition on someone's face. Maybe Ana Kline—who everyone knew was The Nicest—would smile at him the way she always did, even doing a double take before returning to the novel she was reading.

Nope. An Ana Kline smile, to be sure, but just one of her regular smiles. No double take, no recognition. He walked past a few more rows, hoping to catch *someone's* eye. It was too early in the morning, though. Fernanda Reyes was asleep with her head resting against the window; Diego Prieto had earphones in and his eyes were glued to his phone.

Not wanting to make it all the way to the back of the bus with the seniors (who were mostly nice and just as sleepy as everyone else, but just more intimidating by sheer age), Eitan slunk into an empty row, a little bummed out. He looked out the window, at the city just starting to wake up. The ocean, only visible in glimpses from the bus route, taking on the colors of the sunrise. At the first few stops, he sat up straight, a smile still sneaking onto his face despite how dorky he felt as people passed by. Nothing, though. No one reacted. So Eitan tried to rest his head against the window and sleep until school, but the window was cool to the touch, and without the padding of his sandy curls, the rumble of the bus was too intense to sleep through.

When he finally arrived at school, sleepy and with a sore skull, Eitan thought, *Alright, here we go.* He got off the bus and saw Salo Maya get off his at the same time. Eitan walked toward him, raising a hand to wave.

Salo just walked right past, though.

The whole day, this happened. People looked right past Eitan, not even squinting in his direction, trying to make out his outline. It was as if cutting his hair off made Eitan less visible, not more. It took all the way until third period for one of his friends to even notice that Eitan had been at school throughout the day. So, okay, Shaved-Head Guy was a bad idea.

The next week he decided to try out something else. Like Salo, Eitan was Jewish. So maybe that could be his Thing, too. His family wasn't quite as religious as Salo's, though, so instead of wearing a tzitzit, which he didn't own, Eitan fashioned some out of an old white towel that had been in the linen closet for who knows how long. He ripped it into strips, then taped them onto a plain white T-shirt, which he wore beneath another T-shirt.

It seemed to work right away. People noticed the tzitziyot and made comments like, "I didn't know you were Jewish!" But then they started asking him about what was or wasn't kosher, and he only knew the big no-no's, which the people asking him already knew, anyway. When they were running a mile during PE, one of the other kids kept trying to yank on the tzitziyot. Then, after school was over, when they all rushed outside to Don Beto and Doña Gloria's puesto before basketball practice started, Eitan realized he wouldn't be able to fit the good Jewish image and still order the sincronizada he wanted to eat so badly. He watched as Gloria served one to Ben from the basketball team, dripping with cheese and smothered in that great avocado salsa she made. "Shema Israel," Eitan said, but it didn't feel right at all. Even Ben was like, "Dude, that's not your thing."

"Yeah, you're right," Eitan said. He looked down at his fake tzitziyot, and at Ben going to town on his sincro. Eitan was Jewish, but he wasn't Jewish like this. It felt like he was trying to put on Salo's skin. But he didn't need someone else's skin. What he needed was a sincronizada. "Me da una, porfa?" he said to Gloria.

A few days later, Eitan came up with a new plan. He was going to be a dunker. The Dunker. People would be able to see him, finally. Granted, he was only five foot seven, which was tall vis-à-vis other basketball players his age in Mexico, but not exactly close enough to the rim to make it easy. It was going to be an uphill battle (ha!), but he'd be thrilled to be known as The Dunker at school. He loved basketball and wanted to dunk anyway, so this was a pretty convenient plan.

A quick internet search recommended some plyometric workouts, which Eitan started doing one weekend morning. It was a terrible experience, so he quit the video halfway through and decided that on Monday he'd go to the gym at lunch and just try to dunk. Over and over again until he could.

Come Monday morning, Eitan had pictured himself dunking so many times in his head that he was eager to get to it. Even though he knew that the last time he'd tried to touch the rim he hadn't even come close, he felt like he'd already done a lot of the work, and surely he'd come much closer than ever before just from wanting it. Taking advantage of his limited visibility, Eitan decided to skip his first period Philosophy class and go to the gym right away.

He knew from experience that there was no PE class first period (an almost unheard-of mercy on behalf of the administration), so when he arrived, he calmly dribbled his basketball a few times. The echo would probably reverberate and be heard in the classrooms closest to the gym, as well as the Athletics Department offices. But he also knew from experience that the classrooms didn't have a direct line of sight to the basketball court. And even if the people in the offices glanced out their windows down, they wouldn't be able to see him, just the hardwood.

He shot a few free throws, performed some half-hearted stretches that didn't loosen him up all that much but felt necessary, anyway. Then he jogged up and down the court until he felt that warmed-up feeling in his legs. He went to the half-court and stared down one of the rims. When he had properly psyched himself up, he started running toward the hoop, imagining himself as LeBron James, Michael Jordan, Kobe Bryant.

Right foot down, left foot down, and a superman-jump up to the orange rim. He focused all his energy on taking off, fighting gravity. It was working. He could feel it. He was jumping higher than he ever had before.

That may have been true, but it was not enough to turn him into a dunker. The ball slipped from his hand on his way up and hit the rim at a stark angle, sending it bouncing back toward his face and knocking his glasses off mid-flight. The hand that had been holding the ball reached out for it, instead snagging itself on the bottom of the net.

Half a second after he went up, Eitan came tumbling back down to the ground. The ball bounced, then rolled somewhere behind him.

Okay, maybe it would take some time to become The Dunker. Eitan looked at his hand, at first to examine the rope burn–like scrapes the net had caused, and then to kind of blame it for everything that had gone wrong during the dunk attempt.

"Nice try," someone said from behind him.

Eitan whirled around, and saw a girl standing on the opposite end of the court with a foot on his ball. He was really good with names—it was the easiest way to make others feel visible—but for some reason he couldn't recall hers. What was more, he couldn't even tell if he'd seen her before. He didn't know how to describe her face either, couldn't say what any of her features were, specifically. She was like someone in a dream, familiar, but completely nondescript.

"I think I need to keep practicing," he said, pinching his shirt to wipe sweat from his face, though he wasn't even sweating yet. Hopefully she didn't know anything about basketball and wouldn't be able to tell just how sad his attempt had been.

"Maybe you should stick to layups until you grow a few inches." She leaned over and picked up the ball. But instead of tossing it back to him like he expected, she started dribbling. It was clear that this wasn't her first time handling a basketball, which made Eitan wonder if she was on the girls' team. If so, why didn't he recognize her?

"I don't know if I want to wait that long," he said, cleaning off the smudge from his lopsided glasses.

"What's the rush? Aren't you a sophomore?"

"Plenty of sophomores dunk."

"In Mexico?"

Eitan thought about it. "Well, no. But…" He wondered if he should just stop there. He didn't know this girl; he owed her no explanations for his ambitions.

She didn't seem on the edge of her seat waiting for him to go on. Instead, she dribbled past him, a waft of her lemongrassy shampoo smell in her wake as she shot a layup. Almost as soon as Eitan caught the whiff of her, it was gone. He watched her grab her own rebound, only now noticing he still couldn't tell what her features were. Her hair, even, was a color he couldn't exactly name. It wasn't a strange color or anything; it looked normal. But he didn't know what to call it.

"But what?" she said now, dribbling back toward the free throw line.

She dribbled twice, the echo of the ball in the empty gym such a satisfying sound, part of why he loved coming during class hours. Then she rested the ball at her hip, took two breaths, and shot.

"But I want dunking to be my Thing, is what I was going to say. I don't have a Thing."

He was still standing by the rim when the ball fell through the net, and out of habit he caught it before it hit the ground and passed it back to her. "What do you mean you don't have a thing?" she asked.

"You know, like Sandra Dominguez's camera and her hair. Ana Kline being The Nicest. A Thing."

The girl repeated her free throw routine. She clearly played all the time; how did he not know who she was? "Why do you need one?"

He could only blink at her as she shot again. It bounced on the rim a couple of times before falling through. "People can't see me," he said. "They don't know who I am, what my whole... you know, deal is."

She chuckled as she caught his bounce pass. "What's my name?"

Eitan scratched his head, grains of sand falling to the floor. He kicked them away. His hair had grown back a little quicker than he'd expected, but his head still felt strangely light. "I don't know."

"We're in four classes together."

"Oh."

She missed for the first time, and Eitan was thankful to have the excuse to go chase after the ball. When he caught up to it, she had moved to under the hoop, offering up the free throw line for him. He stepped to it. "Really?"

"Really. And that's just this year."

He spun the ball in his hands, the free throw routine his coach had insisted he find. "Wow. I'm sorry."

"It's okay."

He shot the ball. "Wait. That means..." He watched her rebound his miss. She bounce-passed the ball back to him, and now her face came into focus a little more. Were those freckles? "You're like me."

There was a long pause as they both weighed the statement. Or she was waiting for him to shoot. He looked up at the Athletic Department office windows. Inside, he could see that guy who wasn't a teacher but always wore a suit and coached the swim team. He was clicking around on his computer, looking bored. Eitan dribbled the ball once and waited for the man to turn. Nothing.

"People don't see you, either," Eitan said, wanting her to confirm it.

"Some of them do." She nodded her head at the ball, so Eitan shot a free throw. Another miss. The girl took the rebound and walked to the free throw line again, so Eitan moved away.

"Doesn't it bother you? People not knowing they've met you? Not remembering you?"

She shrugged, took her two dribbles. "Again, some people do remember me. The ones who take the time to." Swish. "It's Elena, by the way. My name."

She came a little more into focus. He could remember her now, sitting just behind him in his Geometry class. One time he had thrown his arm back behind him, trying to crack his back, and had accidentally brushed her knee. He was embarrassed that he'd forgotten about her, that he didn't know what space she occupied at the school, what circles she moved in.

"I don't remember your name, either, if it helps you feel better."

"Kinda. It's Eitan."

She missed a shot after about five or six makes in a row, and they switched spots again. He didn't feel any competition with her, and he'd forgotten all about his plan to try to dunk. Somehow it felt better to just stand and shoot free throws with her, even when silence fell between them and Eitan started wondering if he was being awkward or weird somehow. Or, rather, he knew he was probably being awkward or weird. It was just hard to see in what ways.

Then she passed him the ball again and said she should probably go.

"You're already so late for class, though."

"I have study hall right now," she said, and went to gather a backpack that she had set down by the bleachers. It was maroon, with a couple of pins on it that were too small to read. She slung it over her shoulder, then turned back to Eitan. "By the way, you have a stain on your shirt."

Over the next few weeks, Eitan kept returning to the gym to practice his dunking. He rotated through the classes he would skip (a perk of being between visibilities was that hardly any teacher noticed), but he found himself making excuses for why first period was the right time to do it. Second period was Russian Lit, which he liked too much to skip. Third period was right after lunch, so not the best time to run around. And fourth period was too close to basketball practice.

It didn't have anything to do with Elena, he insisted to himself—the way people for some reason feel the need to do, arguing with their own brains as if they're other entities. She hadn't shown up at the gym again, but he'd started seeing glimpses of her around school. At lunch, she sat with three friends in the corner of the soccer field, which was out of bounds but still in the sun. He still couldn't see her in all of his classes. In Geometry, he only caught whiffs of her shampoo, but when he craned his neck looking for her, it was like he couldn't get an angle around other kids in class. Sometimes he would just catch sight of her maroon backpack as she left the room.

He tried asking around about her but wasn't quite sure how to broach the subject with his friends without having them turn it into a whole thing about him liking her or whatever. The guys on the basketball team would be even worse. But from social media and a few of the more gossipy classmates, who needed only to hear a name before they gushed out everything they knew about the person, Eitan learned this about Elena:

Before moving to Puerto Vallarta, she had lived in Mexico City, and before that Buenos Aires. Both her parents were Mexican, though he wasn't sure where she'd been born or how many passports she held. She had been at the school since eighth grade, and was friends with some of the Mormons, though she herself wasn't. She had taken part in the open mic night once, though Eitan wasn't able to find out in what way. He pictured a guitar. Or maybe a poem. But it could have been five minutes of stand-up, too. No one had been able to confirm.

Then one day he was in art class, focused on a pastel portrait he was sketching of a random guy in a magazine ad, when he heard her speak beside him. "Do you have anything that looks like lavender?"

He blinked. "Elena," he said. He could see now she had curly hair, which she wore in a loose bun, and she wore braces, too. "Dammit, you've been here all along, haven't you?"

"To be fair, I just saw you, too." She reached over to his little bin of chalk and grabbed the closest thing to lavender he had. He looked at what she was working on—an underwater scene, the kind that could be found while snorkeling. She was shading in a coral reef. Her strokes were purposeful, caring. When he looked up at her face, he could see her even more clearly than before.

She noticed him looking and raised her eyebrows.

"Sorry," he said, and tried to go back to his drawing.

"How's the dunking going?"

He bit his lip, holding back a smile. "I think right now I've got a better chance of being known as The Guy Who Tries to Dunk But Obviously Can't. I was doing it for a whole PE class because I thought no one could see me, but by the end of it everyone was staring and shaking their heads like they were disappointed in me."

She snorted. "It's a shame that embarrassing things make us visible quicker than who we actually are."

Eitan laughed, but couldn't think of anything funny to counteract with, so he fell quiet, turning to his drawing instead, and thinking about what she'd said. After a minute of not adding a single stroke or finger smudge, he turned back to look at Elena. To try to *really* look at her and see the whole person sitting beside him.

"You asked me at the gym that day why I need to have a Thing," he said, after trying to see her for an appropriate amount of time.

"Mmm-hmm?"

"Don't you...have one? Want one?"

Elena kept drawing for a moment. She used her thumb to blend some purples together. "People don't really have Things.

There's the Things people assign to them. The Things people latch onto because we need to fit everyone into an easily understood box. But people aren't easily understood boxes. They're people. Sandra Dominguez's hair and her camera. They're all you see of her, but that's not her. They're not Things. They're just things. If you started being able to dunk, that's what people would see of you. But they'd still be missing the food stain. The glasses with only one arm—which, what happened there?"

Eitan shrugged. "Wore them playing basketball. Not that first time in the gym when you saw," he clarified. "Another time."

"The glasses, the sand falling from your hair all the time, your love of sincronizadas. That stuff makes you up, just as much as the countries listed on your passports do. More so, probably. Sandra Dominguez has an American passport."

"She does?"

"It's an international school. Lots of people here have multiple passports, not just you."

Eitan scratched the back of his neck, wondering how he hadn't even thought of that.

"We're fifteen," Elena continued. "We're still forming who we are. Not that it ever really cements, I don't think. People will always see your capital *T* things first. When those are hard to spot, they'll make them up. Because that's human nature, and it's easier."

"So, what, we stay hidden until we're older?"

"Nope. Some people will always be a little hidden. Everyone's a little bit hidden, actually. Some more so, though." It looked like she was done speaking, like she was just gonna keep drawing, and the most meaningful conversation in Eitan's life was just going to stop, just like that. Then Elena looked back at him. "Eventually, people will see more of your things. They'll get there. You have to give them time. You probably haven't even found all your things yet, anyway. Or your Things."

Now she turned back to her painting, pointedly, the gesture

almost an exclamation mark to her speech. Before she added anything to the canvas, though, she looked at him again. Actually, she wasn't looking at his face, but at his shirt. At his stain. "Seriously, the exact same spot?"

Eitan blushed and tried to scratch the dried salsa stain away. "I had chilaquiles for breakfast," he said.

Eitan stopped skipping class to try to go dunk, though he went back to the plyometric workout, because he still really wanted to dunk one day. He grew his hair out. He never again tried to say *Shema Israel* for no other reason than it just wasn't in him to do it, like saying *cool beans* with any bit of earnestness.

He grew comfortable with the notion that not everyone could see him, that he existed in a foggy state for those around him. After all, he existed in a foggy state for himself. Maybe that was it; he would learn to become comfortable in a fog. He knew that eventually, as he grew older, as he discovered his Things and his things, most of the fog would clear. He wasn't, after all, invisible. He was simply between visibilities, and those he wanted to surround himself with would learn to see him, too.

★ ★ ★ ★ ★

ENOUGH TO BE A REAL THING

By I.W. Gregorio

True story: it's taken twelve years, and a global pandemic, for some of my classmates at Utica Area School District to realize I'm Chinese.

With a name like Madison Rabottini, it's not like people are exactly programmed to think of me as Asian. But I have straight dark hair, and my eyes sorta look similar enough to my mom's that when I was a baby, my Amah praised me for looking "very pretty, sixty percent Asian, forty percent white," as if I had reached some kind of optimal grade in the Halfsie Appearance Index.

If I am honest, though, it kind of took COVID-19 for *me* to realize that I'm biracial, too. There is nothing quite like doing a Zoom party with the Italian side of the family to realize how out of place my brother and I look in box after box of curly hair and hazel eyes. Then we flip to a Skype with my mom's side, and suddenly Dad is the outsider.

What I'm saying is, I don't exactly look white. Plus, I'm sure my friends have seen my mom during pickup, or at my orchestra concerts. She even came in to help with a craft station at my school's Lunar New Year celebration one year.

So there's no excusing Jenna Thompson's TikTok video complaining about how her family's summer trip to France is being canceled because of the #ChinaVirus.

I'm scrolling through my feed while brushing my teeth when I come across Jenna's video, which is basically ten seconds of her face with artfully runny mascara cut with stock photos of the Eiffel Tower and the Louvre:

OMG I'm LITERALLY CRYING

FU #ChinaVirus

I've seen the hashtag before, of course, usually in the context of someone talking about how ignorant it is, but each time it's like a slap in the face. A reminder that there are people out there who think that my mom doesn't belong.

As venomous as it is to know that there are deplorables out there who use the hashtag regularly, it's something else entirely to see it plastered in bold white over the angry-crying face of someone who's too popular to be my BFF, but who I'd definitely maybe invite to my Sweet Sixteen birthday party.

My chest tightens as I drop my toothbrush to tap open the comments section.

that totally sux, I'm so sorry

noooooooooooooooo

freaking kung flu

The last comment is from Stacy Wilkerson, whose dad used to come to our first-grade soccer games wearing a I've Got

1776 Reasons Why You're Not Taking My Guns Away T-shirt. I click through her profile and scroll through post after post of her hanging out maskless and indoors with friends. I then think about my mom spending twelve hours a day double-masked with a face shield to keep her patients and our family safe, and how at the beginning of the pandemic she'd strip off her scrubs in our foyer and shower before hugging me and my dad hello.

"Madison? You almost ready? You've gotta leave in ten!" I realize that the faucet's been running for more than a minute and hurry to swish and spit.

Downstairs, my mom is chugging her coffee while shrugging on her white coat.

"Love you," she says, brushing an almost-but-not-quite-rote kiss on my head as she rushes into the foyer to slip on her clogs and strap on her N95 mask. "Don't forget to drop off the library books, and remember Mads needs an extra mask for PE day," she yells in the direction of my dad.

She doesn't wait for either of us to respond before the door slams shut.

My father grabs his own coffee and strikes his Dad pose, fanning out the actual physical newspaper he subscribes to, even though my brother read him the riot act for killing trees. It's something new that he's been doing since the pandemic made everything virtual; since he's an IT guy and doesn't have to commute anymore, he has an extra hour every day to do things like cook, drive me to school, and do a sudoku.

"Numbers are finally going down." He nods approvingly.

"Great, does that mean you'll let me start taking the bus again?"

"What? And give up the precious time to bond with my child? What would I do if I weren't chauffeuring you around while you ignore me to watch a YouTube video on how to get more followers on Instagram?"

"Dad!" That's just libel. I talk to him in the car. Sometimes.

"I'm kidding, I'm kidding." He gets up and pats me on the shoulder as he grabs his keys. "You know that's something your mom and I are going to have to talk about. We need to know you're safe."

"You just said that the numbers are going down!"

"Well, the coronavirus isn't the only danger out there," he sighs.

My eyes roll so far back into my head I can see my brain. But then I remember the email my Pop-Pop sent the other week after reading an article about hate crimes against Asians, telling me how worried he was about me and my mom, and that if we ever needed someone to escort us anywhere to give him a call. I grab my mask, a paisley one that my Mom-Mom Mary made me, and zip up my backpack.

"You know, you can't keep me in Bubble Wrap for the rest of my life," I tell my dad as we get into our Prius.

"I know, sweetie," he says. "I wasn't actually kidding, though. I like driving you to school. Is it that bad hanging with your out-of-touch dad?"

"You're not *that* out of touch," I mumble. And it's the truth—my dad is one of the most woke white guys you'll ever meet. It's just that sometimes things would be easier if he were more clueless, a little more hands-off. Bubble Wrap doesn't just protect things; sometimes it suffocates them, too. At some point, a girl needs to learn how to take risks and manage on her own.

My phone chimes, and I open the message from my bestie, Takiyah.

Ugh I hate 1st day of school after spring break

IKR, I could barely get up this AM

My hair look like:

I smile at the GIF she sends of a llama with bed head.

LOL, me too

Nah I don't believe you. Your hair couldn't kink if your life depended on it.

Unfair

Remember that time your mom curled your hair for picture day and there wasn't a single wave there by lunch???

Rude

It's okay girl, I love you just the way you are

Awwwww. ♥ ♥ ♥ At least someone does. CY soon

Up in the driver's seat, my dad clears his throat. "So, Maddie, if you really feel strongly about taking the bus again, I can discuss it with your mom. It's just funny to me. I hated riding the bus when I was a kid. It took half an hour to go two miles!"

"I know. I just feel babyish, getting dropped off by my parents like a little princess. But hey, maybe next year I can start driving myself!"

"Only if you let me teach you, not your mom."

"Burn!" It's a running joke in my family that my mom is, shall we say, not the most focused driver on the planet. She herself calls the little dents and scrapes she's accumulated on our car over the years *Driving-While-Asian Detailing.* Is it still a microaggression if it's directed against yourself? Or a gentle ribbing with someone you love?

I'm still thinking about it as I walk up to the school entrance, where Takiyah's waiting for me on a bench with a giant red taped *X* on the seat next to her. I hate the constant reminders to social distance from my BFF. "You know that you can tell me if I ever accidentally say something that's racist, right?" I ask her. "And that I wouldn't get mad?"

"Um, yeah?" She raises her eyebrows.

"Just making sure. I mean, I know nothing's ever come up, but sometimes I wonder. Like, I'm not perfect, right? I must've said something stupid about being Black at some point since fifth grade."

"Girl, if I took the time to call people out when they said stupid racist shit, I would never stop talking."

"Yeah, that's my point!" I say. "How do you know when to say something, and when to let it slide?"

Takiyah grimaces. "I dunno. It's personal, right? It all depends on how much BS you can stand to deal with. Also, like, the intention."

I'm about to ask her how the heck I'm supposed to suss out someone's intention on a TikTok post when the first bell rings. We hoof it upstairs.

"To be continued, okay, T?" I yell as we run to our respective homerooms.

It's a brand-new semester, so we're starting another unit in English. *Animal Farm* is required, but this semester, Mrs. Morgan passes out the choice reading list, too. From the little author pictures, I notice that five of the ten authors are people of color, and that Maxine Hong Kingston, author of *The Woman Warrior: Memoirs of a Childhood Among Ghosts*, is Asian, which I wouldn't have necessarily known from her name. I wonder if she's a halfsie, too.

Part of me wants to deliberately not choose that book, the same way I balked when my mom *suggested* that I have playdates with Chloe Chan or Linda Nguyen when I was in elementary school. When I was little, my mother packed my shelves with books by Grace Lin, Susan Tan, and Erin Entrada Kelly. Then when I entered my tween years, it was Stacey Lee or Kat Cho or Kelly Loy Gilbert or Abigail Hing Wen. My mom likes to talk about making *intentional choices* like it's a good thing, but I definitely never saw my dad's side of the family give me books by Italian writers. And don't get me wrong, I know why—I know that white is, like, the default, and my mom just wanted me to see myself in books that didn't have awful Asian stereotypes like *Tikki Tikki Tembo* and *The Five Chinese Brothers*.

Still. No one likes having their identity pushed on them.

I put away the choice reading list. I don't have to make my decision for a week, anyway.

Takiyah and I meet up for lunch with our friends, Julie and Maria. Julie shares pictures of the trip she and her moms took to the Maryland shore, while Maria and I moan about our parents' decision not to do any pandemic traveling. The highlight of the staycation that my mom planned was literally a trip to Ikea; Maria at least had been able to go to a cousin's outdoor masked quinceañera party.

"Was Tim around?" Julie asks. She had a crush on my brother in junior high and cried literal tears when he came out the summer before he left for college.

"Just for the first weekend, then he had to go back to campus." I don't envy him having a mostly virtual college, but he's making the most of it, quaranTEAMing with his boyfriend and bingeing our parents' streaming services. I'm totally jealous. "I so need to get out of this place. My mom says that we might be able to do a beach week this summer when I get vaxxed after my birthday."

"Nice, you know where?" Julie asks.

"Probably Ocean City." That's where my dad's family have been going for literal decades. "You guys think you're going to North Carolina again?" I ask Takiyah. She has family down there.

"Probs."

"Oh, Jenna Thompson's going there, too," Julie pipes in. "Did you hear that her family canceled their trip to France?" As editor of the school newspaper, Julie always had an eye on what the Cool Kids did on social.

"Let me guess," says Maria. "She's throwing herself a pity party that she has to settle for a trip to the Outer Banks." Always the actress, she pouts and wipes away invisible tears from her cheeks.

"Yes, she made an actual TikTok," says Julie.

"Oh, this I've got to see!" Maria pulls out her phone. She searches for Jenna's page and groans. "Okay, like, those are *not* real tears."

"Lemme see," says Takiyah. In a second, she's chortling, brown hand covering her mouth and nose. "Lord have mercy, that girl has issues…"

She stops laughing.

"What the fuck?" Takiyah says sharply. "What bullshit is this?" She grabs Maria's phone, pauses the video, and flips it around for the others to see.

FU #ChinaVirus

"Ooh, boy," Maria grimaces.

Julie looks guilt-stricken. "Oh, my God, I'm so sorry, Maddie, I totally missed that the first time I saw it. I feel so bad if it's triggering you."

Suddenly, the sandwich I'm chewing feels too dry, like sawdust in my throat. I take a sip of water and pick at the peeling Beach Patrol sticker on my Hydro Flask. "It's okay," I say, feeling kind of far away, like I'm looking down at myself from a security camera. "I saw it earlier. It's fine."

Takiyah gapes at me. "You saw this. Earlier. Is that what that convo was about this morning?"

I'm shaking my head before she's even done with her sentence. In the morning, I'd been wondering if it was racist of my family to make fun of my mom's driving. "No, that was about something else…"

"There's something else?" Takiyah presses. "Something worse?"

"No, there's nothing worse, it's just different." I mean, none of us mean anything by it, right? Not my family, and most likely, not Jenna, either. She was my lab partner in eighth-grade Chemistry, and she'd been totally nice. "The TikTok's not that bad."

"Maddie, it's awful. It's a racist slur," says Maria. She takes her phone back and starts keying in a response furiously.

My eyes widen. "Wait, what are you doing?" I say, reaching the table to grab at Maria's cell. She leans away from me to keep her phone out of my reach.

"'It's called coronavirus, Jenna,'" she says out loud as she types.

They never call HIV the San Francisco Virus, do they? Super disappointed that you would use that anti-Asian slur. How do you think @maddierab would feel?

"OMG don't bring me into it!" My face immediately starts to burn. Frantically, I look across at the cafeteria where Jenna's sitting with her friends. She looks down at her phone. "Delete it right now before she sees it! Please!"

"No, Maddie, no," Maria insists. "The only way she's gonna learn that these words are wrong is if we make her think of the people that they hurt."

"She barely knows who I am," I groan. I turn my back toward Jenna's table and hunch down to make myself look smaller. I feel a sense of confused panic rising in my chest, a whirling of emotions that I can't quite get a handle on. Sure, Jenna's TikTok upset me in the morning, but I shook it off. My friends' reactions, it's too much. Why are they more upset about it than I am?

"Guys, please," I beg. "It's not going to make her feel bad.

They're just going to think that I'm a special snowflake or something. Don't make this a big deal."

"It kind of *is* a big deal," Julie insists. "It's when all this rhetoric started that all the anti-Asian attacks happened. And, oh, look at Stacy's comment, too. What is wrong with these people?"

"Guys," I plead, grabbing her phone away from her so she wouldn't pile on with the comments. "Let's not make a mountain out of a molehill."

My phone buzzes, and I'm super grateful for the distraction. Until I see that the text is from Jenna.

I'm sorry if you were offended by my TikTok. I hope you know that I don't really think of you as Chinese. My parents taught me not to see color.

I'm literally speechless. I can't figure out whether to find Jenna's text funny or be offended. Truth be told, there are like a dozen different emotions running through my head: outrage, yes, but also hurt, and also…guilt. Because I *can* pass as not being Chinese, and let's be honest, with the anti-Asian violence going around these days, that's not a bad thing.

After about ten seconds of not being able to think of what to say, I flip my phone around and let Jenna's text speak for itself.

Julie face-palms.

Maria says, "That girl is the most clueless person I've ever met."

Takiyah's eyebrows are furrowed so tight she's a dead ringer for the red angry-face emoji. She takes a few deep breaths to collect herself before saying anything. "I mean, this here's wrong on so many levels I don't even know what to get pissed about. Should you be mad that she's apologizing that you felt bad, instead of apologizing for saying something racist? Or should you be upset that she thinks that if she's not insulting you directly, it's okay?"

"Or that being color-blind and, like, totally ignoring a person's race and background is a good thing, or even really possible?" Maria adds.

"I know, right?" says Takiyah. "Like, there's no looking at this and not thinking, that's one *fine* Black girl there." She waves her hand in front of her face, and then tilts her head toward my phone. "What you gonna say to her, Maddie?"

What *am* I going to say? I lay my phone on the table and fiddle with my neon-pink PopSocket phone grip, letting it accordion in and out over and over, like an ASMR video.

I don't tell my friends that my first impulse is to text Jenna back:

Yeah, you're right, I'm not really Chinese, am I?

The first time I felt Not Asian Enough was when I was ten, and my parents took us to Taiwan for the first time. We were half-dead with jet lag when we dragged ourselves off the plane, but I still remember the wide-eyed delight of our cab driver when he saw us, like we were some kind of exotic animal sighting that he couldn't wait to tell his friends about. He couldn't stop staring at us and seemed terribly disappointed when we only stared at him blankly when he started to speak Mandarin.

"Wo men shi mei guo ren," my mom said in her halting Chinese. She says herself that she basically speaks at the second-grade level.

Then my Amah took over the whole conversation, grabbing shotgun for the trip to her house and jabbering away in Mandarin so fast the only words I could understand were the occasional accented *A-B-C* when she turned around to look at my mom to label her an American-born Chinese.

After we got back to the US, though, I kind of forgot about that weird in-between feeling, until that awkward moment where I had to choose my foreign language, and I chose French.

"Don't you want to learn Mandarin?" wheedled my mom.

"Wouldn't it be great if you could talk to your grandmother in her native language? You'd be able to get so much fun stuff at the night markets next time we go!"

Since eating and shopping were the obvious highlights of any trip to Taiwan, I was seriously considering my mom's last line of argument when my brother chimed in. "Of course she wants to speak French, Mom. It's the language of love, macarons, and the Eiffel Tower. Not to mention Daveed Diggs when he plays the Marquis de Lafayette."

My dad's parents were both one hundred percent Italian going back to the mother country. Strange that I never worried about being Not Italian Enough.

I don't text Jenna back at all.

I tell myself it was probably just a text she sent as a cover because my friends called her out in public. I figure she doesn't really want a response, anyway.

But, of course, I'm wrong. Just as I'm about to step into Social Studies, my phone chimes again.

R we okay? I hope I didn't make you feel bad.

I close my eyes. I just…can't deal with this. I can't spend time holding Jenna's hand and reassuring her that she's a nice person, when I'm still trying to sort out my own crap.

NP. We're cool.

I've never felt more gross about a set of emojis in my life.

After I get home, I text my brother Jenna's TikTok video and a screenshot of her message.

Help me. What am I supposed to say to this????

LOL. I would be okay if people called it the China Virus if they also talked about and actually implemented the Taiwan Solution, which was for people to freaking wear masks and distance to get things under control. ELEVEN Taiwanese deaths the entire pandemic. 😲

Not helpful 😣

Should I actually call her out, though? I mean, she's kind of right. We're not really Chinese. Not like Mom. And it's not like she called *me* a virus. She just used the hashtag—it wasn't directed against anyone.

Right then, my brother actually calls me, via cellular phone, which is either a sign of the apocalypse or an indication that he's dead serious.

"Look, Maddie, just because I'm not Black doesn't mean I can't call it out when a white person uses the *N* word."

"But it wasn't targeting a person! It was just a general complaint about a virus that's causing a global pandemic."

Tim makes the little breath huff that means he's rolling his eyes at his stupid kid sister. "So what? It's still hate speech. Remember when Felix gege came to visit that one time, and he saw a pair of Dad's shoes, and he said, *Those are ugly. They're so gay.* Remember what you said?"

I had only been twelve years old, but I still remember my outrage at my cousin on behalf of my big brother, who had come out only months before: "Take that back! The word *gay* is not an insult."

After his initial shock, my Felix gege had just laughed uproariously, like it was hilarious that his younger cousin was getting all politically correct on him. My chin went up, and I would've said something more, but my mother took me aside to help with cutting fruit, and I remembered how my brother and parents had decided on a Don't Ask, Don't Tell approach to that side of the family for the time being.

"So where's my Social Justice Warrior sis now?" Tim asks.

"She's trying to survive high school, that's where she is," I respond defensively. "You do know that calling one of the most popular girls in school a racist would basically make me social roadkill?" Though I guess Maria already took a bullet for me by calling it out on Jenna's TikTok. I wonder if she's gotten any flak for it. Maybe she did but she just didn't care. She has all her theater friends watching her back.

I wonder if that's how it is, that it's easier to stick up for people than to stick up for yourself.

"Listen," Tim says. "You don't have to, like, drag her in public. You can just say, hey, this is how I feel, and this is why it's bad."

"But...sometimes I wonder, *why* is it so bad? Didn't they name West Nile Virus and Ebola after where they came from?" I lean back in my chair and do some neck rolls to get rid of the soreness in my neck. All this language stuff is exhausting to untangle.

"Yeah, they used to, but then they realized that these kinds of names caused targeting and backlash against the countries and locations they were named after. Basically, created bad juju. So the World Health Organization actually stopped naming diseases by place. It's a real thing."

"Oh." It's a lot to take in. "Who told you about all that stuff?" It doesn't seem like something people learned in freshman college classes, even at Stanford.

"Mom posted it on Facebook one time when she was trying to re-educate Uncle Rick at the beginning of the pandemic," says Tim.

I groan, both at the idea that my brother was officially an old person if he had a Facebook profile, and at the mention of my Uncle Rick. He's the type of guy who was all up in arms to support the PTO of my high school when it challenged a book about abortion, but got upset when three Dr. Seuss books got pulled for being racist.

After Tim and I hang up, I go downstairs to help my dad with dinner.

"Do you know when Mom's coming home?" I ask.

"It's her OR day, and she said her last case is running a little late, but hopefully soon."

I throw together a salad while my dad makes spaghetti. We keep it simple in our house—mostly pasta, frozen pizza, and grilled chicken and rice—both for my father's sanity and because my mom has to skip lunch a lot and half of the time is so hungry she doesn't care what's put down in front of her. Whenever we order out, though, she always wants something Asian. Only now, thinking of the things that my family does and doesn't do to reinforce my heritages, do I realize that my mom's choice of restaurants is a way to go back to her roots.

"Dad, do you think Mom would like it if I did some Skype sessions with Amah to learn how to cook Chinese food?"

My dad puts down his wooden spoon and turns to me, smiling. "Maddie, I think she'd love it."

"I'll send Amah an email," I say.

"It'd be a great Mother's Day surprise. What gave you the idea?"

I peel a cucumber into our compost bin. "I dunno. We're just sitting here making dinner, and Mom never has time to cook the kind of foods she had growing up, so."

"Hey, I boil dumplings once in a while!" my dad says in mock indignation.

"You know what I mean. The kind of foods that require more than heating up and dumping them into a dish."

"So that's it," my dad says darkly. "That's what my children think of me. All the hours I've spent slaving over hot dogs and Kraft mac 'n' cheese, and this is the thanks I get?" He puts his hands on his hips in an attempt to look stern. "Do you know how many years it took to figure out how to mix in that cheese powder without it ending up lumpy? Ungrateful, I tell you."

He's still riffing on his gifts to the culinary world when I hear our garage door open.

"Hi, Mom!" I yell as she comes into the mudroom. "How was your day?"

"Fine," she says, letting out a long sigh. "It was a day. Cases went well, except for the patient who had a positive on his COVID screening test."

My dad winces. "Yikes. Thank God for Pfizer."

"Yeah," says my mom. "I still double-masked and wore eye protection." She shrugs off her white coat, and the small #IAm-NotAVirus pin she put on her lapel the day after the Atlanta spa shooting flashes in our recessed lights.

As we eat dinner, my dad updates us on a call he had with my uncles in California. I tell my parents about my school day.

"Did they give you your reading lists?" my mom asks.

"Yeah." I pull it out, and she nods as she goes down the page.

"Ooh, *Invisible Man*. That's a good one. And *The House of the Spirits*."

"Actually," I say, "I was thinking of choosing *The Woman Warrior*."

"What, Maxine Hong Kingston?" The delighted look on my mom's face makes me sad, as if she didn't expect me to choose the Asian author. "That's a good one. It's not perfect, but it's important." My mom's smile turns fierce. "Kingston was one of the original Angry Asian Women."

After we finish eating and cleaning up the dishes, my mom and dad watch a movie on Netflix. As I grab my backpack and go up to my room to start homework, I catch a glimpse from the stairway of their two heads together: one curly, one straight. My dad's hand strokes down my mom's silky hair gently, over and over.

Up in my room, I unpack all my books and pin the reading list on my corkboard so I can scan it one more time. Is it too on the nose for me to pick Kingston? Like I'm a self-fulfilling prophecy? On the other hand, if I ignore her, am I turning my back on that half of my culture?

Maybe just this once, this pandemic year, I need to be intentional.

It's early, but I email Mrs. Morgan my book choice. Then I hop on my bed, thinking about battles, and what it means to be an Asian warrior.

As the baby of the family, it's not in my nature to fight on behalf of myself. I've always had my big brother to protect me from bullies on the school bus, and my parents at the ready to battle with the school if I wasn't getting what I needed. I know that I've been well taken care of for most of my life. That's why it bugs me when homophobes throw shade on Tim and why now I'm beginning to realize that, as much as I want to, I can't just let that hashtag go.

I might not want to do it for myself, but I've got to do it for my mom.

So I straighten my shoulders and take a deep breath. My thumb only wavers a bit as I swipe on my phone and open up a message to Jenna.

I lied. We're not cool. Can we talk?

★ ★ ★ ★ ★

THICKER THAN WATER

By Ismée Williams

I saw him the first time at brunch. My favorite Christmas song—
the one from *Love Actually*—was playing and I couldn't help
thinking, *Yes, that is all I want.* Red, green, and white lights
twinkled behind his broad shoulders as he waited patiently beside
the Belgian waffle station. He walked right by me and grinned
when my eyes dropped to the gummy bears studding the mound
of whipped cream on his plate. I'd wanted gummy bears, too,
but was afraid it would out me as an American. Looking back,
that was odd. I loved traveling. No one expects tourists to fit
in, so it was the only time I felt like I ever did.

His name was Miguel. I overheard others call him that at
the pool. I was straddling two lounge chairs pushed together,
my back to the water, playing PIG with Julia and Jordan. My
three jacks and I were convinced I would win. My hands were
sticky with virgin piña colada and the cards damp with humid-
ity. I flicked an ace I didn't need, trying to separate it from my

skin. It sailed up toward a towering palm, lifted by a salt-laced breeze. With a soft plop, it settled onto the surface of the pool.

Julia snorted.

"Pause the game," I muttered.

Only they both had their tongues out already.

"Jeez Louise!" I tossed down my now useless jacks.

Julia released a tinkling peal of laughter. The sound was similar to the wind chime at the far end of the swim-up bar. Her eyes were greener than before. The left one especially. A blue more Caribbean than Pacific. Could that happen? Could college not only mold you into a self-assured grown person but also make you more beautiful? We looked even less like sisters now, but I was happy for her and a little bit in awe. Who knew? Maybe two and half years from now college would do that for me, too.

"I love it when you shake your tiny fist up at the scudding clouds," Julia called out. "One of these days, they're going to listen to you and stop their scudding."

"Gotta stop scudding now, gotta stop scudding now!" Jordan crooned and Julia joined in. Their shoulders bumped as giggles burst from their wide white-toothed grins.

"Yeah, yeah," I grumbled, but as I slid into the water, I shook my fist up at the sky again. I smiled at their renewed fit of laughter.

I rescued the ace, careful not to look at Miguel, and returned dripping.

"Come. You look cold." Julia peeled herself off Jordan, making room between them. I climbed up, pausing to sprinkle them with drops from my wet hair. They shrieked. Jordan, still grinning, wrapped a towel around me.

"So many goose bumps." Julia rubbed my arms. "You're always sensitive to the cold."

"Must be Papi's hot Latin blood." She rolled her eyes before I could finish. It was my usual response. She didn't like that I made fun of how different I looked from her and the rest of our family. I was darker even than Papi.

I snuggled between them. My big sister and her best friend leaned against me, lending me their warmth. They worked hard to include me. I loved them for it, only sometimes it made me feel even more like a third wheel.

"You know, those boys are looking at you." Julia tipped her chin toward Miguel and his friends.

"They're looking at you. And Jordan." No one ever looked at me.

"Nuh-uh," Julia hummed. She picked up my piña colada and beamed, her gaze shifting to Jordan.

"They are totally looking at you, Frankie." Jordan unfolded a long arm, reaching for my drink to take it from Julia.

The guys sipped Coke with lime through tiny red straws. Two had thick black hair gelled up and away from their faces in a way that was totally not American. Miguel's hair grazed the tops of his ears, free from product. I wondered what they thought of us—the stunning blonde with turquoise eyes, statuesque Jordan with her glowing umber skin, and me, in the middle, looking like a muddied mixture of the two. If we told them a pair of us were sisters, would they believe us? Would they guess the correct two?

"So, what brings you to Ixtapa?" He spoke like he was from California. No accent. Carlos and Enrique had stumbled through introductions—Carlos was a sophomore, Enrique and Miguel seniors—while Miguel contemplated the terracotta tiles, the hint of a smile curving his mouth. Julia had transitioned to Spanish to spare them. I'd nodded and laughed when they laughed. I was used to pretending. Julia noticed me still shivering and suggested the hot tub. Miguel had followed, claiming his shoulder ached from his swim that morning. I didn't understand why he did that, why he didn't want to stay near Julia and Jordan, why he chose me instead.

Forced air rumbled through the water between us as he waited for my response.

I traced the ring of metal that jutted from the pearlescent tile. I pressed my palm against the jet, then let the current push my hand away. Was I going with the truth? Or would I shelter inside one of the tales I spun to make sense of me and my family?

"My parents love Mexico. We come at least once a year." The truth didn't sound bad.

"And you don't? Love Mexico, that is?" He was taller than me—much taller. His lashes were uncommonly thick. Tiny black flecks studded the brown of his irises.

I swallowed. "No, um... I like Mexico. Only, we come here because we can't go to my papi's country." Partial truth. We couldn't go to the island nation that was Papi's home thanks to political maneuverings that had nothing to do with us. If by some miracle we could, I'd bet Papi would nonetheless opt for Mexico.

Miguel nodded. "Cuba."

I started, then shifted as if I'd fallen off the underwater ledge. It was better than him recognizing my surprise. I almost asked how he knew. Had he heard it in Julia's accent? Maybe he was just an avid consumer of *The Economist* and confident about his guess. I wanted to stare into those eyes that were just as dark as mine and ferret out the answer. That would have been risky.

He switched out of English then. The only word I caught was guajira.

"Actually, my papi is from Havana. Not the countryside."

Miguel tilted his head. "You don't speak Spanish, do you?"

I pressed my lips together, staving off a frown. "I understand a little." This always bothered people. That the sister who looked half Cuban was the one who didn't speak the language. They never considered it was purposeful.

"Very little," he corrected. "I was paying you a compliment."

My cheeks flamed. I pushed off the ledge into the center of

the small pool. I sunk through the steam until my chin touched the froth. The burn of chlorine made my eyes water.

"Do you always travel for Christmas?" Miguel handed me a drink as Juan Gabriel crooned softly from speakers tucked into the thatched roof above us. He waited for me to sip before he sipped his. Agua quina con limón. That's what he'd asked for at the bar. I would remember.

"For the past eight years or so we have."

"I thought Americans liked to spend the holidays with their extended families?" he asked.

"Yup." I tipped the cup to my mouth again. "Mexicans, too," I pointed out.

He chuckled. "My family is all here. Carlos and Enrique are my cousins. We have the two villas down by the beach."

I pretended not to be impressed. By the size of his family and the two villas thing. "Yeah, well, my parents don't really get along with their families."

He pretended not to be shocked. I gave him points for not asking me more about it. I would have told him. It's not like I was embarrassed that my mom's family didn't respect my papi's family and vice versa. It was what it was. At least in Mexico, Christmas dinner came without a side of backhanded compliments about my dark eyes. No one called me exotic or lucky because I didn't have to worry about sunburn. No one called me too American because I talked back to grown-ups or dangled sticks of cinnamon gum to entice me to roll my r's—which only made me resist speaking Spanish even more. No parent excused themself from the table to hide in the bathroom or went for walks in the snow but really just sat in the car, waiting. I didn't miss those rides home where hurt and anger billowed from the front seats, more pungent than Papi's cologne and the smoke from Mom's cigarettes.

I drained my cup and shook the ice. I placed it on the counter and gave it a push. The bartender caught it before it went off the other edge.

"Sorry!" I cried out at the same time Miguel said, "Ay, perdón."

Miguel asked for another agua quina. I told the bartender "Gracias" and "Lo siento" when he handed it to me.

Miguel turned to face the ocean. He leaned back against the bar. He folded his arms in front of his bare chest and squinted out at the setting sun. "Did I mention my mom's from Atlanta?"

He chased me down the beach. I'd wanted him to. I'd thrown seaweed at him, hoping. My heart thundered, as loud as the galloping hooves of the horses Jordan, Julia, and I had ridden that morning along a neighboring stretch of ocean. Sand spread my toes wide, warm at the top, then frigid as I pushed deeper.

The shoreline curved, the resort disappearing behind us. I slowed to dodge the person-sized rocks jutting from the earth and splashed into the shallows. Broken shells bit at my feet but I ignored them. I ducked behind another rock and spun to face him.

He stopped, not ten feet away. His chest rose and fell but he was otherwise still, watching me. He was grinning, too.

He took a step forward. And then another. Horses galloped faster inside me. I didn't back away, but I kept that rock between us. Until he was leaning over it, reaching for me, pressing his mouth to mine.

I'd wanted him to do that, too.

"Where have you been?" Jordan's eyebrow quirked as I shut the door to our room.

Julia set down the curling iron and tossed a throw pillow at her. "You know where." She regarded me in the mirror as she separated another thick section of her sun-bleached hair. "Have fun, Frankie-boo?" she asked, one corner of her mouth arcing up.

I covered my smile with a cough and stared at the bits of sand still stuck between my toes. "I've got to shower." I slipped into the bathroom. Julia followed, bringing the hot iron with her. She knew I'd reveal more with the curtain between us. It was easier to talk when no one was looking at you. I've always had a thing about being judged by my appearance.

I told her about Miguel's mom being from the US, how he was basically my Mexican counterpart. As I rinsed out suds of guava-scented shampoo, I told her about our plans to meet before dinner. And after.

"He's not like the boys at school. He doesn't see me as someone different from him." Julia had it easy. She hadn't stuck out in the rural New England public high school my parents chose because of the local former Olympian equestrian trainer—for us, well, really for Julia—and the college with the vibrant art program—for Mom, so she could teach. Julia fit in wherever she was. "And he's not like the typical Mexican guys, either. Remember last year?"

"José?" Julia's snort made me laugh. Soap got in my mouth. It did not taste like guava.

"He was a presumptuous one," she added. That was one way to call it. Julia caught him bragging to his friends about his plans for *the loose American*.

"What are you going to wear?" she asked as I turned off the water. She heard the panic in my silence and slid out to confer with Jordan. They returned with a white spaghetti-strap sundress swinging from a hanger.

"It'll set off your tan," Jordan said.

"Want me to do your makeup?" Julia offered.

"I'll do your hair." Jordan plugged the curling iron back in.

He was waiting in the lobby, by the fountain that glowed lagoon-blue from underwater lights. We stared at one another, each of us gnawing on our lips to beat back our grins. I thought he might kiss my cheek in the standard Mexican greeting. Instead, his warm hand closed around mine and he pulled me to the stairwell. He somehow knew I wouldn't want to be kissed—even on the cheek—in such a public space.

Geckos darted from our path, scaling the stucco as if they had wings. I scrambled after him, teetering in Julia's strappy sandals. He tugged me into a shadowed alcove, lifting the wide frond of a banana plant out of my way. We stepped off the stone into the resort's jungle-like landscape. We were hidden, mostly.

Night creatures whirred and chirped in time with the uneven clip of my pulse. The heady tropical scent of plumeria and jasmine faded as I breathed in the clean soap smell of him.

"You're beautiful," he murmured.

I laughed, amazed the sound didn't shake. "You can't see me."

"I remember." He described my dress, the waves in my hair, Julia's shoes, even the tiny amethyst earrings Mom—I mean, *Santa*—had given me that morning.

"When is your reservation?" he asked.

It took me a moment to find my voice. "I have to meet my family at the restaurant in fifteen."

"What would you like to do?"

I thought I heard a smile in his question. I touched my fingers to his mouth and traced it to be sure.

I pulled away from him, gasping as singing grew louder. The slow clop of heels descending steps accompanied it.

"Jeez Louise," I muttered.

"¿Perdón?" He'd forgotten what language we were speaking. I liked that.

I parted the leaves that concealed us and stepped into the light. Miguel followed, his hand a soft weight at the small of my back.

The singing stopped, but Papi did not lift his face from Mom's hair. They were disgusting like that sometimes.

"Frankie?" Mom at least had the grace to blush. They hadn't seen us creeping from the foliage. But we'd seen them. She batted Papi away and smiled bashfully up at Miguel.

Papi tucked his thumb back under the edge of her blouse. "And who is your friend, Francesca?" He appraised the tall boy standing beside me.

I introduced them. Miguel delivered a "Mucho gusto" to Papi and a "It's a pleasure to meet you. I see where your daughters inherited their beauty" to Mom. She blushed again, of course. I did, too, that time, but no one was looking at me.

Papi asked Miguel a few things in Spanish. I prayed it wasn't anything embarrassing. I understood Miguel's Distrito Federal. He'd already told me he was from Mexico City. When Miguel mentioned Atlanta, Papi lowered his head and studied me.

Mom, also left out of the conversation, followed his gaze. "Wow, Frankie, you look so...so...pretty tonight." Her genuine surprise made me deflate, just a little. Miguel's fingers, unseen by my parents, grazed the crest of my hip, reminding me not to care. He'd chosen *me*.

"We'll see you inside? Your father requested a table by the water." She took Papi's arm and he kissed the top of her head.

"Oh, and here, Miguel." She opened her clutch and fished out a tissue. "You have something white on your face. Sunscreen, I think?"

I held onto my bland smile, commanding the horror from my expression. Julia was profligate when it came to powder. Not really her fault. My skin was pretty oily.

Miguel accepted the tissue and murmured his thanks. He wasn't as deft at concealing his confusion.

Papi led Mom away. "Don't be long," he warned. His narrowed eyes swung from Miguel to me.

That night, as the host led us to our table, I didn't notice the stares of the other guests. I was still walking the garden path with Miguel, laughing.

"Your friends are so lucky," the server commented as he handed Julia a menu. He passed me one that was in Spanish. Wordlessly, Julia and I switched.

She cocked her head at him, a small intelligent bird examining a bead on a string. "Disculpa, no entiendo."

He gave her a nod of appreciation but stubbornly stuck to English. "You invited them on this trip. Lucky friends." He gestured to Jordan and me.

Julia's smile sharpened. If it had been a mustache, she would have twisted the ends. "Pues, claro, es mi mejor amiga." She threaded her arm through Jordan's and kissed her full on the lips. "Pero, esa es mi hermana." She pressed her cheek to mine. "¿No nos parecemos?"

Papi uttered something in Spanish I assumed was, "Leave the poor guy alone." Julia fluttered her eyes at the server, who cleared his throat and recited the specials. I shrugged it all off. What did it matter? Miguel was waiting for me.

We ordered. We ate. It wasn't until Julia took out the brochure for the fancy riding camp in Spain—her big Christmas gift— that I focused on the conversation. I kept watching for Miguel, wondering when his family was coming to eat. They never did.

Mom and Papi excused themselves after the flan and café were cleared. Papi hummed under his breath, serenading her before they were even out of the restaurant.

Julia looked up from the glossy images of stallions, muscled necks curved under flowing manes. Her fingers rubbed her temple. "*Die Hard* or *Miracle on 34th Street*?" The green in her eyes had paled. They looked gray now.

"I think I might go for a walk along the beach. Want to come?"

Jordan glanced from the brochure and met Julia's gaze. Her forehead puckered but she patted my arm and smiled.

"We're good," she said. "Have fun."

Music pumped from one of the villas, loud enough to drown out the pound of the surf. It sounded like a live band. Blue and purple strobes of light flashed from the windows. Inside, people danced. I'd thought most Mexicans celebrated on Christmas Eve or Three Kings' Day, but what did I know? Miguel must not have been able to get away. I was jealous of him, of his family. He so clearly had a place where he belonged.

Back in the room, John McClane mused to himself from an air vent. On the bed, Jordan scooched away from Julia and lifted a bowl toward me. "Popcorn?"

I slid off Julia's sandals and dampened a washcloth. I didn't join them until I'd wiped every speck of sand away.

He found me the next day, tucked under an ocean-side palapa, wide-brimmed hat pulled low, sunglasses on, towel wrapped around my legs. It was overcast and breezy. Though I admit it, I'd been hiding.

"What's your favorite food and why?" He didn't apologize for yesterday but he sat on the very edge of the lounge chair, careful of my legs. "I love molletes but I also love bacon cheeseburgers. Only the ones in the States. Burgers in Mexico aren't the same."

When I didn't speak, he continued, "How about clothing? You have different sets? I have a closet of pants and shirts—and shoes that I only wear in the US."

That wouldn't apply to me since I couldn't visit Cuba. Maybe he wasn't as big a fan of *The Economist* as I'd thought.

He dug out my flip-flop and nudged it next to its pair. "Do people ever think your family isn't your family? We used to pretend my mom was the au pair hired to teach us English. She'd act as if she didn't know Spanish and say the most outrageous things." He chuckled to himself. "Hola, yo me llama Stephanie. Estoy calor. Porque no air conditioning?" He pantomimed taking off a sweater and fanning his face. His American tourist accent was dead on. I almost smiled. I almost told him that's one of the reasons I loved riding so much as a kid. Nobody at the barn ever asked Mom if I was adopted. Maybe it was because Julia and I always were hidden under those helmets.

A seagull cried out. Miguel craned his neck to watch its flight.

When the bird disappeared over the shimmering waves, the Mexican boy with the shaggy American haircut bent his head to the dough-colored sand. "My parents, when they argue, they're so different. My papá, he talks and talks. And shouts. My mom? She mostly ignores him. She just doesn't engage. It makes him furious." He whispered the last word.

I slid my foot, still under the towel, closer to him. "Mine, too," I whispered back. Only usually Papi kept at it, harping until Mom gave in and shouted, too. They always made up, though, as loudly as they fought. Disgusting.

"Does it work?" I asked. "Your mom's strategy?"

He glanced at me. "Yeah. It does. She most always gets what she wants."

I moved my leg again, until it was resting against him. His warm hand circled my toes.

He bought me lunch. He ordered a burger and fries for himself, just so he could prove to me how inferior it was. He told me about his annual trips to Colorado at Easter, for his papá's medical conference and to visit his mom's family and ski. We discovered we both loved New York City—the energy, its sheer size, and the people. Anybody could fit in there. Not to mention they had John McClane.

"Have you ever been to Rio?" He dipped his fry in my pico de gallo.

"I saw the animated film. Great soundtrack."

He laughed and snatched up a few more fries. "Rio's like New York but with tropical beaches and a rainforest. And the people?" He shook his head, smiling. "Super diverse."

The waiter came for our dishes. I marveled how easily Miguel switched to his other self. Miguel seemed purely American when he was with me, his mannerisms, the cadence of his speech. Mexican Miguel was a different person. And yet he wholly occupied them both. Julia did it, too, changing languages like a jacket. I envied them. Their ability to inhabit any space they chose. I'd never been able to do that. No matter where I was, I always felt like I was wearing someone else's clothes.

Miguel murmured something as he handed the waiter the last plate. The waiter hid his grin with his forearm and laughed. Miguel laughed alongside him. I could have laughed, too. It would have been the socially acceptable thing to do, even though I had no idea what was funny.

Miguel's hand was on my foot again. His fingers slid up to massage the muscles of my calf. I lay back, not moving my leg, and closed my eyes. What my body wanted him to do scared me.

I wondered what would happen if I stayed in Mexico, if I made a life with someone like Miguel. Could I belong here? Would the Latina within me step forward? I'd spent so long pushing her away, not wanting that to be all people saw when they looked at me. It would almost be a relief.

Miguel made his way up to my knee and stopped. He shifted, taking hold of the lounger, arms braced on either side of me. "You like dancing?" He hovered over me, so close I could feel his heat.

My phone vibrated. Ready?

At the pool, Miguel had downloaded a messaging app for me, then added his number. He wasn't going to let last night happen again. My parents had agreed to let him take me to a club. A true Christmas miracle! Only it wasn't a miracle. It was Julia. She'd said she and Jordan would go, too.

Yes, I typed back. "Meet you downstairs?" I called out. Jordan was dressed but Julia was just getting out of the shower.

"Yup. Be there soon." Jordan shook a small bag of pills. "Hey, do you have any Motrin?"

"Backpack. Inside pocket." I was out the door.

A low whistle stopped me before I got to the elevator. Miguel was down the hall behind me, leaning out over the open veranda.

"I want to show you something."

He positioned me in the spot he'd been standing. "Look." He pointed. Through the bougainvillea, peeking around the cut of the mountains, the half-moon shone, waxy and yellow, and so close it seemed I could touch it. Miguel's legs pressed against the backs of mine. His arm slid around my waist, hand coming to rest over the exact spot where my stomach quivered. I tipped against him, his heart drumming at my ear. I wove my fingers through his and brought his palm to my mouth. I stuck out my tongue to taste him. He inhaled sharply. And then he had me up against the wall, hands raking my hair back. His lips were gentle, almost too gentle, on mine. Until I whispered, "Por favor," and his name.

In the taxi, Jordan handed me a lipstick and then a brush. On her other side, Julia sat with her arms tucked in front of her. Miguel conversed with the driver as we inched toward the club. Miguel's arm, out the window, lifted again and again.

"¡Oye, güey!"

He seemed to know everyone.

When we finally arrived, Julia sprang from the car.

"You okay?" She sometimes got carsick.

"I'm fine," she said but her eyes slipped to Jordan.

"Excited?" Jordan squeezed my hand.

There was a line, but Miguel motioned us to the front. Four young women, dresses sparkling like they'd walked out of a Kanye music video, passed us.

"Ay, pero, ¡no se vayan!" Miguel turned to call after them. It was the first time I truly recognized the subjunctive. Or was it the imperative? Was he wishing they wouldn't go, or commanding them not to?

Miguel clasped hands with the guy at the door. Their faces dipped close to hear each other over the music. He was Mexican Miguel again.

Julia pressed a hand to her forehead as he ushered us inside.

★ ★ ★

Miguel got us a table and then drinks.

"I see some friends. I'll be back." He disappeared into the mass of bodies on the dance floor.

Blue and purple lights pulsed off streams of fog that billowed from the ceiling. I sipped my agua quina con limón and shivered.

"Would you like to dance?" It was not Miguel but Carlos.

I looked to Julia and she shrugged.

I followed Carlos because I was cold and tired of just watching. I hoped to find Miguel.

Julia and Jordan joined us. They were good, timing their dramatic moves with the strobe lights as KWS begged them not to go. I swayed, side to side, like an uncool American in a gymnasium. I hated that I felt so out of place. Vacation was supposed to be a vacation from all that. I searched the crowd, certain I'd recognize the slope of his shoulder, the jagged sweep of his hair. He promised he'd come back.

When a Luis Miguel remix came on, Julia stilled, fingers squeezing the bridge of her nose.

Jordan drew an arm around my shoulder. "We gotta go. Your sister has a headache again."

My unease shifted to concern for Julia and then to full-on anxiety about Miguel. I stood on my toes and peered through the throngs of people. I slipped out my phone to text him.

Julia pressed her sweaty forehead to mine. "Sorry, sis. I hate ruining your party."

My phone vibrated. I squeaked and showed her my screen.

Tell her I can take you home.

She snorted at what must have been my look of utter elation.

Jordan frowned. "Where is he?" she asked.

"I also can bring her back," Carlos said. He said some other things in Spanish.

Julia pushed some cash into my hand. "Just in case," she said. "Be careful. You better not get me in trouble."

I hugged and kissed her. My squeals made her wince. She waved as Jordan led her away.

Carlos took my hips, spinning me to face him. I threw my head back and pretended I was in a Kanye music video. I hoped Miguel was watching.

At the next song, I twirled, looking for Miguel again. "Where is your cousin?" I asked Carlos.

"What?"

"Where is Miguel?" I shouted.

Carlos shook his head. His hands circled my waist as Ozuna murmured mamacita. He pulled me closer. Everyone else was dancing just as close. I didn't want to be close to Carlos.

"Excuse me." I headed for the table.

Where are you? I texted Miguel.

I stared at the blinking cursor. I could still feel him, the weight of him, his body against mine. No one had ever made me feel so alive and so…hopeful. No one had ever made me feel like maybe I could belong.

The song changed to something even slower.

Carlos offered his hand. "¿Quieres bailar?"

"I'm going home."

"What?" He followed me out. "¡Espere!" He caught up to me at the cab. "I take you home. I promise Julia." He said her name the way Papi does. Who-lia.

I leaned against the window. I couldn't look at Carlos. My fingers clutched my silent phone.

The lone guard at the front desk nodded at me as I scurried across the dim empty lobby. The elevator dinged for my floor. As I stepped off, Mom and Papi's raised voices traveled down the hallway. Dang it. I'd gotten Julia in trouble.

The door to our room was open. That was odd.

Jordan crouched in the corner. Her hands covered her mouth. My chest tightened.

Julia's feet, I could just see them on the bed. They twisted, toes flexed, as if grabbing at something. Her skin was a mottled blue.

"What's going on?" I don't know how I got the words out. My throat felt stretched by handfuls of hot marbles. Mom was shrieking Julia's name. She kept trying to hold her hand, though it was stiff and shaking. Papi kneeled beside Julia's pillow. He spoke softly to her, holding her head to the side, protecting her from the hard angle of the table.

"Did you call for help?" I rasped. They didn't hear me. Julia was making horrible gurgling sounds.

"Did anyone call for help?"

Jordan glanced at me, eyes glassy with terror.

I ran. Not for the elevator but for the stairs. I kicked off my shoes and flew down the three flights. I slid to a stop at the front desk and told the night guard to call for an ambulance. I'm not sure he understood me.

"Frankie?" Carlos rose from a chair beside the fountain.

"Help! We need help!" I pleaded.

He shouted to the guard and took out his own phone.

I was running again. Out toward the beach. Miguel's papá was a doctor. He could help.

I didn't know which villa was his. I banged on the first door I found. It wasn't locked. The knob turned and I stumbled in, roaring.

Miguel leaped off the couch. He rushed toward me, arms wide. "¿Qué pasa?" The whites of his eyes were stark against the brown.

I wanted to fall into him. I wanted those arms to hold me together. I wanted him to tell me everything would be all right.

"Julia," I gasped. "Your papá," another gasp.

"Miguel?" a voice trilled from the sofa. A woman rose, tugging a tiny silver dress back down her thighs. She didn't look like she'd stepped off the set of a music video anymore.

Miguel shrugged the hair out of his face. "Ya voy." That's what he told her.

She said some things I'm sure were unfavorable. I'm sure they were about me. It didn't matter. I didn't care.

Miguel buttoned his shirt and tucked it in. He wouldn't look at me.

"Frankie!" Carlos called from the door. "¡Vamos!" An older version of Miguel pushed past Carlos. He jogged for the path to the main hotel, a black bag swinging in his hand.

Julia slept against me, a navy fleece airline blanket around her. Mom and Papi, in the row ahead, kept turning around to check on her. Jordan never let go of her hand. In the lull after John McClane had blown up the bad guys' plane and rescued Dulles, Jordan leaned over Julia's sleeping form and asked what happened with Miguel.

"Nothing," I whispered back. I hadn't seen him again. I'd deleted the app. I didn't want to read excuses or apologies. I didn't want to wait for messages that might never come. Carlos had explained Veronica—music video girl—went to their school. She and Miguel had been on again, off again. As if that made it better.

"I thought you had something nice going with him?"

I shook my head. I held my breath, desperate to keep away tears. I fiddled with the shade, determined to keep out the light. I didn't want Julia to wake. She was fine. She was going to be fine. She had to be. Mom said there was no use worrying, not until Julia saw her doctor. We had an appointment at Memorial Sloan Kettering on Monday. It had been years since I'd been there, since I'd gone with Julia to her annuals. I was going with her this time. They couldn't keep me away.

"Well, it was a good thing he was there," Jordan added.

I glared at her.

"That his *father* was there," she corrected, smoothing away her frown. "What happened, Frankie-boo?"

I turned to the darkness of the shaded window. "He wasn't who I thought he was." I wouldn't tell her how much I had hoped. It was stupid of me to have done so. To have thought that maybe with him, I could have found a place where I belonged.

We started the next movie and I rested my head against my sister's. Dark strands of my hair mixed with the light strands of hers.

As we were introduced to McClane's alcoholic despair, a flight attendant kneeled down to ask if we needed anything.

"No, thank you." I tried for a smile.

The woman, attractive with light brown skin and the hint of an accent that told me she spoke Spanish in addition to English, lingered, eyes trailing over us.

I lay my arm across Julia's back, spreading my fingers wide as if I could somehow shield her, shield us, from whatever the woman was about to say. My lip curled back. I would snarl if I had to.

The woman's magenta-stained mouth parted. "It's so sweet, the two of you. I used to be like that with my sister, too."

She moved down the aisle.

I almost called after her, to ask how she knew, to ask what she saw. Julia shifted against me, her breathing deep and even. I didn't want to wake her.

★ ★ ★ ★ ★

MY KINDA SORTA BADASS MOVE

By Karen Yin

I'm not sure how I became obsessed with trying out for the drill team.

Maybe it's because music gets me out of my head, which is caked with math formulas. Maybe being part of a squad is the kind of normal I dream about. Or maybe I want to prove I'm not trapped by my waipo's idea of femininity.

To fit my reflection into the long mirror tacked behind the bathroom door, I back into the hamper till the wicker squinches. I square my shoulders and rest my palms against the sides of my legs. In my mind, I hear the trill of a whistle, followed by tumbling drumbeats. I bring the thumb edge of my hand across my chest, the other arm parallel to my thigh, and practice the routine with tiny steps to avoid smacking into the mirror.

Waipo says I'm naturally graceful (insert colossal shrug). I just know that when I dance, my body no longer feels like a heavy suit. It's not anything I do consciously. When the music comes on, my thoughts shut off, and another part of me takes over. My mind breaks free of my head and radiates throughout my body, past the points where I end. I'm larger. I'm lighter. I'm in focus.

In the mirror, my expression fiercens with every step. Did my mother have such serious brows when she was fifteen? After I run through the routine for the dozenth time, I pause to stretch, and the marching band in my head fades. I reach for the ceiling, elongating the gentle curve from ribs to thigh. Then I perch my hands on my hips and roll them in fat figure eights, like the Engleman Angels do during drill practice.

Tryouts are tomorrow. Mel and I must both make the team, because sharing three classes isn't enough. We don't count Psych, because the seating chart is alphabetical, which means Jessy Wu (that's me) and Pamela Chen (that's Mel) are on opposite sides of the classroom. All April long, we marched, pivoted, and high-kicked in the gym with the other hopefuls. We're two of the best, but if neither of us makes it, I'll be forced to question everything I know about the world.

In the humming bathroom light, I reach for opposite walls like I own the space in between. Then I lean forward, till I can see every lash in the mirror, and make my warrior face. Time to level up and become Jessy 2.0.

The front door shuts with a bang, and heavy bags thump to the floor. Crap, I lost track of time. I fling the bathroom door open, and my reflection vanishes. "Waipo, let me get that for you."

I put the groceries away while she slices some pork belly for herself to supplement our vegetarian meal. Chores sound like, well, a chore, so I started calling them *achievements* so they sound fun. Before my waipo came home, I achieved soaking the dried shiitake, draining a block of tofu, and slicing the carrots, celery, and bell peppers for tonight's stir-fry. Then I separated the important mail from the junk. My progress report came—A's and A-minuses—so I replaced the old report on the fridge. I doubt Waipo cares. I've always done okay, so she assumes I'll keep doing okay. Does that bother me? Yeah. But also no, because I'll take whatever leeway I can get.

Waipo wedges a lime-green plastic colander by the cutting board. "Who died?" she asks. She points at my hair with her nose while her hands busy themselves pinching the ends off the string beans. I pat my head and blush when my hand touches the oversized zebra scrunchie. That's her way of telling me to take it off. I've been tying my hair back for the last two weeks so Waipo doesn't notice how long it's getting. Once it touches my shoulders—*snip!* If I could let my hair grow even half as long as Mel's, that would be, like, the epitome. But Waipo acts like we're living in China and my hair has to meet Chinese high school regulations.

"It only has a bit of white," I protest. "The rest is black."

"White means death. A bit of white means a bit of death."

I love my waipo, but lately, everything out of her mouth sounds like mosquitos buzzing. How can I be myself when adults won't stay out of my head? I dread telling Waipo about trying out for the drill team. Her first thought will be the cost, because that's her concern with everything. Can we have pizza? No, save money, eat at home. Can I have new shoes? No, save money, wear mine. Her second thought will be how I'm a massive embarrassment for wanting to show off. Because that's what dancing is to her—showing off. Why draw attention to yourself when you can be private and quiet, squished neatly inside your body-shaped box.

She can be super funny, though, to the point of being inappropriate. Like, the other day, she showed me a tomato shaped exactly like a butt. Normally, that would be hilarious, but as the frequent target of her character-building jokes, I felt bad for the tomato.

"Did you go to the library with your friend?" she asks. A slew of responses pop into my head, ranging from inert lies to highly flammable truths. After I told Waipo that I had a crush on a girl, neither of us brought it up again. That was three crushes ago, and I've been careful not to stress her out since. I opt for a blood pressure–friendly partial truth.

"We stayed after school to study," I say. *To study…drill routines.* Waipo nods as she smashes a handful of garlic cloves with the flat of her cleaver and lifts off the papery peels. Drill practice happens twice, sometimes three times a week. But she doesn't leave her job at the downtown fabric store till after six o'clock, so I'm on my own. She doesn't track me like some parents do. No money, no cell phone, no problem.

My waipo's brows arch like little caterpillars as she counts the remaining bundles of glass noodles, already planning a future meal. Meanwhile, I'm doing my own calculations. If I tell her my news tonight, I can push the extracurricular-activities-are-a-good-look-for-college angle. Or appeal to her sense of pity for my scrawny social life. Or her own need for a social life, which she'll feel less guilty about if I'm off practicing somewhere. But judging by the clatter of pots, she's about to shoo me from the kitchen. I wash down lingering words with a sip of Waipo's warm tea.

That night, I switch on the lamp to study the framed picture on my nightstand. My mama is frozen in time, enjoying an ice cream cone on Sepulveda while visibly pregnant. Her eyes smile at the man behind the camera, my father. Waipo tsk-tsked this photo, because according to Chinese medicine, eating cold anything was bad for a woman's system. But I love it. It's the only photo of us together. *Mama, if Waipo rejects regular American girl things, will she ever accept me?* I fall asleep before I get an answer.

The next morning, I make up some excuse about volunteering for my animal rights club and rush out before Waipo ensnares me with endless questions. Our apartment is two blocks from school, and I make it there in five by speed-walking. Mel's my source for Waipo-prohibited contraband, such as deodorant and lip gloss, so this pre-tryout pit stop is crucial to my mental health.

I was so excited about tryouts that I registered back in February. I signed the parental approval slip myself. I mean, I've been handling forms for Waipo since I was ten, so of course my handwriting would match the signature on file. This is one of the dubious perks of being her translator.

Once, I mentioned to Mel that I got my waipo's money back from this plumber who ripped her off, and she declared me a badass. I'm totally not. To me, being a badass requires an excruciating level of confidence. Like when Kara Wai takes down a circle of bad guys in *The Tigress of Shaolin*. Or when Patsy Mink became the first Asian American woman elected to Congress. Or I suppose, when you raise your dead daughter's only child as your own, like my waipo.

Plus, I so do not look badass, unless pink cat-eye glasses and hair as straight as a paintbrush are trending.

I wait for Mel inside the restroom, where a couple of girls have already planted themselves beside the tarnished mirror. Right on time, she saunters in.

"Hey, bei," Mel says, all fake-casual. *Bei* is short for *bao bei*, which pretty much means *bae* but in Mandarin. We think it's hilarious.

"Your hair!" I scream. Her beautiful locks are gone, or nearly. A few inches at the longest. I quickly recover with a smile, and she comes in for a kiss.

"Surprise! I haven't posted a selfie yet."

"I love it," I insist. "It's so Audrey Hepburn meets Sonic the Hedgehog. I just can't believe you did it." Yesterday, her hair was so long it tickled my forearms when we hugged.

Mel finds a square of mirror space and rakes her fingers through her hair to define the part. "I know, right? I got tired of talking about it."

"What did your parents say?" She has a mom and a dad. The

first time I met them, Mel introduced me as her girlfriend, so they claimed me as their other daughter. My heart hasn't returned to normal yet.

"My mom cut it! Dad was a little wistful but got over it." She steps closer to let someone pass through our now-crowded corner. "It's like ripping off a Band-Aid. A flick of the wrist and it's over."

The last time I removed a Band-Aid, it came off with skin.

"None of the girls on the team have hair this short, though," I say. I cover up my uncool comment by petting her spiky pixie hair.

"Then I'll be the first." Her earnestness outshines all signs of annoyance, if any. I'm too cautious to be bold like that. She's third generation, and from my second-gen perspective, her life is golden. Her parents have fewer rules, they don't worry about money, and they trust Mel with basic decisions. And they all speak the same language. It's as if we grew up in different countries—and my country has a population of two.

If we make the team, Mel and I won't be the only couple. The co-captains, Brenda and Yolanda, documented their sapphic drill team romance on social media—#DaDaLove, #EnglemanHigh—so the entire school knows.

A handful of students bring the noise outside with them, their chatter bouncing around the tiled room. I know Helen Hwang from AP Chem, but only enough to exchange awkward smiles and borrow a pencil. My sweats come off to reveal my mildly hairy legs in shorts. I was bummed when Waipo said no to shaving, but Mel convinced me that going au naturel was a power move, so neither of us bother scraping off our body hair. That's the best thing about being queer: the usual scripts are tossed out the window.

"You haven't told your grandma yet?" Mel asks, applying a purply tint to her lips. "She's your family, bei. How mad can she get?"

When she's done, she dangles the lipstick under my nose like a carrot. I reach for it, then pull back and shake my head.

"You sure? You'll eat it off before Psych."

In my lower belly, a dull gray cramp starts to billow. You've got to be kidding me. I was so preoccupied with tryouts that I wasn't prepared for this.

"Mel," I whisper. "I think my period started. I don't have any pads with me."

"I got you," she says, like a pro. "May I buy you a cylindrical menstrual product?" Mel gestures toward the tampon dispenser as if we were at a counter ordering milkshakes.

"No, I can't. I've never."

"Ask the nurse for a pad?"

I check the clock above her head. "The office isn't open yet."

"But it will be in a few minutes."

Helen comes up behind Mel with the smile of a benevolent god. "I overheard," she says simply. She holds up a lavender-wrapped tube as thick as my forefinger. After a beat, I gasp my thanks and grab it before my mind catches up. My waipo is anti-tampon because she thinks they'll stretch out my hymen—in which case, so what? My other option is to wear a crinkly pad with high potential to shift around during kicks. No way. I go inside a stall and mute Waipo buzzing in my head.

"Mel," I say in a serious tone. "Help me land this plane."

Comforted by her calm energy on the other side of the door, I take a deep breath. At first, the applicator won't go in. I try again, refusing to sweat. More girls come in—laughing, goofing around, banging the doors, oblivious to my plight a few steps away. After a few minutes of quietly freaking out, I nearly call it quits, but Mel suggests aiming the tampon toward the small of my back instead of sticking it straight in. Miraculously, it slides in like nothing.

When I emerge, I have a feeling of—I don't know—wild triumph? As far as tampon-ing goes, my first experience was borderline delightful compared to some stories. As I zip up my bag, I wonder how different I'd be if I checked in with myself once in a while instead of going along with what Waipo wants. I'm almost sixteen, and sixteen is almost an adult. The thought grows arms and legs until it pushes my mouth open.

"Where's your lipstick?" I ask. Mel drops it into my waiting hand.

About thirty of us line the gymnasium, pinning our numbers to our shirts and warming up with twists and kicks. I'm number eleven.

We have more than a few lookie-loos, but I don't mind. That was me last year. I pull my hair back in a gray knitted headscarf that trails past my shoulders like the locks I wish I had. Only seven spots are available on the squad. Mel squeezes my hand for good luck. The judges—Coach Kita, the co-caps, and a few officers—crowd two flimsy folding tables off midcourt. With steady eyes, they scan the room. My lipstick makes me feel twenty times more visible, like my face is continuously shouting hello.

"Whenever you're done gabbing, ladies." Coach Kita has this don't-mess-with-me vibe all the time. When we're sufficiently subdued, she launches into a generic welcome, with one hand clutching her silver whistle out of habit. Mel catches my eye and bats her eyelashes as she mouths the word *ladies*. When we first met, she pointed out how words for girls are often slurs when used for boys, and I've never been able to *not* think about how screwed up that is.

Mel is in the first group of six. As soon as the music punctures the silence, they work it. Their form is textbook—the snap of their arms, the timing of their kick combo. My bei is front and center, looking super charismatic in her new cut. When she spies me in the crowd, her face lights up. Even without literal cheers, they pump the energy way up. I can feel the air shimmer from the back of the bleachers. There's not a single flaw in anyone's performance, which makes me gnaw my bottom lip. I need to kill it. Five more groups to go.

By the time they call my number, my hands are trembling, and every inhale hits my heart like a rush of arctic air. All my tampon-inspired bravado has fizzled. I jump up and take a spot at the end of the line. Every second feels like three. Meanwhile, my nerves take my brain hostage, and I can't stop fiddling with the tail of my headscarf.

When the speakers blast the drum music, I miraculously come to, snapping my arms, pivoting cleanly, and hitting all the angles. I can do this! I *am* doing it! I'll never make fun of cheesy affirmations again, because this is working! I have no clue how I look on the outside, but all the pieces are sliding into place on the inside. Except—halfway through, I think of Waipo.

If I don't make it, then I won't have to tell her anything.

And life will go on as usual.

And I'll be absolutely miserable.

Mel's right. I need to rip off the Band-Aid. Making the team is my best chance of claiming my own identity, which is American and Chinese.

As quickly as it began, the song ends. I make my way over to Mel on the bleachers, who gives me a giant rocking hug. We sit shoulder to shoulder, waiting with hands clasped.

The judges thank us before lowering their voices and pointing at their clipboards. When Brenda and Yolanda raise their heads, I know the judges have decided. My heart floats half in, half out of my body. Say my number. Just say my number.

Yolanda drags the mic stand toward her. "Please come up if your number is called—nineteen, twenty-four, five, and eleven."

I wasn't aware that Mel had pulled away till my arm grows cold where she used to be. With a self-conscious smile, I clamber over the metal benches and join the other three in the middle of the gym. Why only four of us? Someone claps once, then lets it die. I find myself next to Helen, who keeps repeating, "O-M-G, O-M-G." Okay, like, so not helping.

"Because we're looking for that special Engleman Angel spark, please repeat your performance." Yolanda pops her *p*'s into the mic, and it's making my heart skip. So, do it again but better? Mel makes a half-hearted rah-rah gesture, and I smile to tell her I'm okay, even though I'm not.

On the floor again, I try to even out my halting breath. *Come on, Jessy, focus!* When the music starts, I search for that larger-than-my-skin sensation that helps me dance, and I hook into it, letting it cleanse me of anxiety. Time wobbles and I blur into the sound. My headscarf flutters to the floor, freeing my hair. I barely notice Helen laughing beside me. Every time she does, wholesome giggles ripple through the gym. The music carries me up, up, up till the applause brings me back around. Voices sharpen as my haze of concentration lifts, and I'm suddenly aware of the yeahs and whoos from the audience. Helen and I hug spontaneously, because thank goodness that is over.

Yolanda takes the mic. "Alright!" She gives me an encouraging look, so I sigh in relief and turn to go. But then I hear, "Number eleven, can you hold on, please." Coach Kita gives her a weird look and muzzles the mic with her hand before they huddle together.

Um, what?

As the judges gesture among themselves, the chasm between me and everyone else widens, like one of those camera shots where the background zooms out. I close my eyes to shut out the awfulness of the moment for a blissful second. When I re-open them, Coach Kita looks grumpy and Yolanda has a tiny curl of a smile.

Coach Kita's booming voice makes the mic redundant. "Let me make something clear to all of you. When you're an Engle-man Angel, smiling is your job. You smile first. You smile last. You smile when you're exhausted, when you're upset, when smiling is the last thing you want to do, because everybody looks to *you* to lift them up. We want personality, not perfection. So, against my advice, the judges are giving number eleven one more chance. Number eleven?"

Are you familiar with the expression *sucked the air out of the room*? I'm not sure what literally sucked more—Coach Kita with her sermon or the others with their synchronized gasp—but I assure you that every ounce of oxygen had been vacuumed up, because I couldn't get enough air.

No words come, so I bend over to retrieve my scarf and then adjust my glasses. I can't name what I'm feeling, but it rhymes emotionally with defeat. I did smile, didn't I? I usually smile too much. That's my problem. I'm always trying to make someone other than myself happy.

I brush my hair out of my face and notice that my hands are shaking. I don't want to take Coach Kita's words personally. She has a reputation for straight talk. Some kids trust her more because she doesn't BS, but today, her tough love was going all kinds of sideways with me.

A spasm of old anger bubbles to the surface. I don't want to be someone else's idea of perfect. I can't. Not anymore. All those times I was told what to do, how to be, who I am—by my waipo, my teachers, the other kids—flood my vision, making my eyes sting. No way am I going to cry. And as long as I don't look at Mel, I won't.

Yolanda clears her throat. "Jessy?" Both she and Brenda have apologetic expressions, and the other judges peek at me, unsure of what's about to happen. For once, I know exactly what's about to happen, and I've never possessed such clarity in my life. Because I am done.

I throw the judges a magnificent smile as I quietly unpin the eleven from my shirt. I crumple my number into a ball and, still smiling, extend my arm and drop it right in front of them. Then

I begin striding toward the double doors, my legs long and sure. The gym falls dead silent except for my footsteps.

"Jessy!" The breathy whisper came from my left, but I don't stop, not even when I hear Mel climbing down the benches. When they start chanting my name, stomping their feet, and rattling the bleachers, I reach the double doors and slam the handles with both hands, flinging both sides wide open. What was I doing in an airless room? There's a whole world out here where I can breathe. The sun holds me in its golden light, and I'm halfway to the gate when I feel my bei's warm hand slip into mine. That's when I lose it.

Mel and I dart across the street to the '50s ice cream parlor. We agree on strawberry, chocolate chip, and rocky road; caramel sauce, whipped cream, and nuts, no cherry. I tell her I'm fine, but she pays for everything, anyway. The spoonfuls of creamy sweetness cool my insides and remind me of my mama. If Mel becomes an Engleman Angel, we probably can't hang out as much, so we decide to sneak into the mall theater to be alone in the calming darkness. I no longer care what happens when I go home.

Waipo is in the throes of cooking by the time I step inside. The aroma of soy sauce and sesame oil clings to the air like worry. But I don't greet her. My obsidian heart sits heavy in my chest, ready to cut.

I can't be Chinese the way she wants. I try to hate her, but then I think of all she's done for me and I feel worse. It's way easier to hate myself, so I do. At my desk, I prop my textbook open and stare at my Trig assignment till it pixelates. I wish I could stay in my room forever and let my empty stomach gorge on rage and guilt.

But I really have to pee. I crack my door open.

"Xiao ya tou, have you eaten yet?" My waipo's voice rounds

the corner to find me. I can't tell if she's angry. Before I lose my nerve, I step into the light but not where she can see my face.

"I don't expect you to understand, but I had an awful day and want to be alone," I blurt out in my mediocre Mandarin. "I practiced my hardest for the 'dance' team, but I guess I'm not perfect enough, because they don't want me."

When I'm done, Waipo utters a small, "Oh." I lie about having eaten, and it barely makes a dent in my pride. Back in my room, I rest my head on my desk to feel the hardness against my skull.

Barely five minutes pass before she knocks. It's so tentative, so un-Waipo-like, that my anger cools. She comes in, preceded by a plate rounded with spinach and tomato, eggplant and tofu in garlic sauce, steamed egg, and a bowl of rice. I close my book so she can arrange the hot food before me. While I was busy being selfish, Waipo was making my favorite dishes because she sensed something was wrong. Before she places the chopsticks by my bowl, tears have already begun streaming down my face.

Waipo takes a seat on the corner of my twin bed and says, "Come, come, come." I close the gap between us and sink to my knees so I can hug her waist. She smells like home. She strokes my hair as I sob into her blouse.

"You remind me so much of your mother." She pats my back as I begin to hiccup. "Did you know she had a best friend till she married?" I shake my head. "They were so close. One could not sneeze without the other knowing. Your mother used to pick wildflowers before school for her friend. They had a really special relationship." Waipo hands me a tissue, and I blow my nose.

"What happened?" I ask.

Waipo doesn't answer right away. "I didn't think that being so close with another girl was healthy." She sighs, remembering. "I told her it was time she married, so she found a husband in Taipei, they came to America—"

"And then you came, and then Mama had me," I finish for

her. And then Waipo brought baby-me home from the hospital
without my mother. Or my father. Waipo never says anything
nice about him, and why should she. She'll always call him *her
husband*, because a man who ditches his daughter doesn't de-
serve the title of father.

I never made this connection before, but Waipo was abandoned, too. The difference is no one was around to take care
of her. I hug her tighter.

"What's your friend's name? The one you study with," she
asks, rubbing my back in circles.

I lift my head. "Mel?"

Waipo tries the name out on her tongue. "Mel. And you like
this Mel?"

I love this Mel. "Yes. She's Chinese, too." *She believes in me.*
"We like the same books and clubs."

"Was she with you today for the…" Waipo reaches for the
words in English.

I return to my chair and grip the edges so I don't keel over.
"Dance team. She…she tried out also. She's really good. I am,
too, but…"

Waipo's brow wrinkles, and I pause my breath. "If they didn't
choose you," she says, "then they are silly melons." We both
giggle, and blood returns to my heart.

"Invite Mel over for dinner," she says. "I'll make her favorite
Chinese food. What does she like?"

This I didn't expect. "Uh…"

"*Jessy.*" She uses my English name when she wants to lighten
the mood. "Don't *worry*. I just want to meet your *girlfriend*."

I gulp hard. I guess she never forgot about my crush. I stall
by using the chopsticks to shovel food from plate to bowl, then
from bowl to mouth. Waipo knows more than she lets on.

"My biggest regret is not listening to your mother when she
tried to tell me what her friend meant to her," says Waipo. "She

gave up on me. She gave up on her own happiness. I don't want the same thing to happen with you. Okay?"

In between bites of tofu cubes and greens, I nod. She pats my shoulder and rises to her feet. Before she disappears beyond the door, I rest my chopsticks across the bowl and take a breath. "Waipo," I call.

She peers back in, one hand holding the knob for balance.

"Mel likes to eat red-cooked pork belly."

Waipo nods once, like it's settled. "Then we will get along very well." She turns.

"Wait," I say. She arches one eyebrow, and I see myself in her more than ever. "Um, may I wear lipstick?"

"Not until you're seventeen." Waipo smiles. "But if you want, you can get your ears pierced this weekend. For all the A's on your report card."

The Monday after tryouts, high school was unreal.

"Jess!" screams this kid I don't know. He raises his palm. I say, "Hey," and reluctantly high-five him, because it's the law. This is the first of many moments where, in this parallel universe, I have a speaking role. So many people say hi that I walk right past my class. In the restroom, seniors compliment my glasses and share their mirror space. And believe it or not, the Goth kids make eye contact as they part around me. I even make plans with Helen to work on a Chem project together. It's weird how people see me now, though I've always been here. When the school day's finally over, I feel so warm and fuzzy about life that I accidentally flash Coach Kita a smile in the hall. And she smiles back. So I guess we're cool now?

Mel made the drill team, of course. And I didn't, of course. But someone else is a newly minted Angel—Helen! Mel said after my *mic drop*, Coach Kita made a big show of picking Helen because she smiled throughout, though her routine wasn't perfect. I'm convinced Helen will be one of the best Angels ever

and soon, a lieutenant. In the end, all we want is for our quirks
to be accepted, whether we smile a ton or never.

Now Mel comes over to the apartment a few times a week.
Waipo is thrilled to be cooking for someone who eats meat. I
explained to Mel that my waipo and I have a funny way of com-
municating, so even though it seems like she shrugged off my
confession, she relaxed a few rules, like letting me wear lip gloss
and my hair longer (to my bra clasp!). It turns out that gloppy
lip stuff isn't my thing, but I figured that out for myself. My
femininity, my queerness, my Americanness—they're jumbled
together. And my waipo being open to all of the above fills
me with hope. I do my part, too. I take on more *achievements*
at home, like hand-watering the herb garden and washing the
car, which gives her time to play cards with her friends. I may
not get her and she may not get me, but it's important that we
keep trying.

So, I have a new obsession! I borrowed a clarinet from the
music department, because the band has an opening. The band
plays at games, so Mel and I will be able to spend hours together
on the bus. I started tutoring this kid one floor down so I can
afford the band uniform, maybe even my own clarinet someday.
Ever since Waipo told me about my mom's girlfriend, I've been
sharing what's important to me and how hard I'm willing to
work for it. Waipo's pretty sure I'll be chosen for band because
I practice at least two hours a day in the music room at school.
Music lifts me out of my body, but *making* music feels like I'm
beaming tendrils of energy as big as the sound. Also, smiling is
not a requirement. I mean, it's hard to smile with a musical instrument in my face. The band director only cares about two
things—precision and musicality. And I'm pretty badass at those.

★ ★ ★ ★ ★

I LIKE TO BE IN AMERICA

By Anika Fajardo

From the moment Mrs. Manzo announces auditions for the eighth-grade spring concert, I am determined to land a solo. The spring concert is the most important event of the year at Applewood Middle School. Everyone gets dressed up. The boys wear ironed shirts and clean jeans. The girls get new dresses and heels—and the teachers don't say anything if you put on eyeliner and lipstick. End-of-the-year awards are given out for attendance, academics, and service. Students receive ribbons for best painting in art class, fastest runner in gym class, and best musician. The parents bring flowers for the performers—leis and corsages and big bouquets like the kind opera singers get.

"This year, the eighth grade will be performing selections from the classic Broadway musical *West Side Story.*" A groan rises from the class. "Maybe you've seen the movie? There's fighting and love scenes and dancing. Something for everyone." Mrs. Manzo sweeps her arms wide, gesturing to the whole class. "Tomorrow at lunch I'll hold auditions for anyone who wants to try out for a few solo parts."

"We're trying out, right?" I ask Danae and Zoe when class is over.

Ever since the three of us met in third grade, we've always done everything together. And our favorite thing is singing together. When we were little, we played dress-up·in gowns and tiaras, belting out princess songs for our parents, siblings, neighbors—basically anyone who was willing to watch us. Now that we're older, we've learned to sing harmonies and choreograph our own dance moves. We don't force anyone to watch us these days, but we post our best performances online, waiting for the thrill of a like or two.

"Of course!" Zoe and Danae say, and we link arms.

We do a little skip-hop-kick as we head down the hallway. I can't believe we only have six weeks left of being together at Applewood Middle School. Half the eighth graders will go to one high school—where Danae is going—and the other half go to another. Like me. A few kids, like Zoe, switch to the Catholic high school.

"We've practiced so much," I say. "I bet we'll all get solos."

From the outside, we couldn't be more different. I'm short and Danae is tall. Zoe has this wavy blond hair in an adorable pixie cut while Danae wears her hair in dozens of long black braids. My eyes are brown and Zoe's are as blue as the sky. In seventh grade, we each showed up on the first day of school in the same green sneakers—totally by coincidence. We laughed so hard that Zoe got the hiccups and Danae had to use her inhaler. Now we always wear matching shoes—on our different-sized feet. Mama calls us *three pieces in a pod*.

At our lockers, I study the list of songs Mrs. Manzo gave us. "This is my mom's favorite musical ever." Mama alternates between listening to Broadway musicals and Carlos Vives, an old Colombian rock star.

"I think my parents watched *West Side Story*," Zoe says, "but I don't know the songs."

"What? We need to fix that." I take out my phone and search

for my favorite song. "Listen, this is the best song in the whole movie." I hit play and my friends lean over my shoulder as we watch a clip of the song "America."

"Sofia," Zoe says as she watches, "this song was meant for you."

"See," I explain as the actors sing through the tinny phone speaker, "these characters are immigrants from Puerto Rico and half of them like where they're from and half of them are obsessed with the US. They're arguing about which side is better."

"Look at her," Danae says, pointing at the soloist.

"That's Anita," I tell her. I don't add that this is the part I'm already determined to get.

Zoe looks at me and then back at the screen. "She looks just like you!"

I don't look *exactly* like the character in the film, but I do have black hair and medium skin. I'm not as tan as Mama, but nowhere near as pale as Dad.

"You do!" agrees Danae.

I shrug, but I'm already thinking that this is a sign. I have to get Anita's solo. I can already imagine myself bowing at the end of my solo at the spring concert, Mama and Dad with a bouquet of pink dahlias for me.

"Listen," Danae adds. "She talks just like your mom, Sofia."

We all giggle because it's totally true. When I was little, I didn't know my mom had an accent—she just sounded like Mama. But when I got older, I realized she spoke differently than other people's parents. They sounded more like my dad, who's from Minnesota and has always lived here.

"I bet you'll get that solo, Sofia," Zoe says.

"I hope we *all* get solos."

That would be the *ice on the cake* as Mama would say.

That night while Mama cooks dinner, I tell her about the auditions.

"I really want the solo for 'America.'"

"Oh, my favorite!"

The song is already queued on her playlist—of course. She taps play and pretty soon, the bouncing beat shoots into the kitchen. Mama whistles and dances while I stir the arroz con pollo. Even though she sounds like the Anita character in the movie, Mama doesn't look anything like her—Mama's plump and darker skinned, and she wears her long hair in a bun most of the time.

She sways her hips and snaps her fingers. "*I like to be in America*," she sings.

I turn up the volume and join in. I use the goopy spoon as a microphone.

"What is going on in here?" my dad asks as he tries to get by. Mama sweeps him into a turn and then laughs when he bumps into the countertop. He's as bad a dancer as she's a good one. They're such a stereotype!

"She's going to be Anita from *West Side Story*," Mama gushes. She grabs me and it's my turn to twirl between the stove and the table. "She'll have a solo!"

"Well, I have to audition first."

"I know you'll be wonderful, mi amor," she says. "You can wear that skirt with the embroidery." I can tell that Mama is already envisioning the night of the concert as clearly as I am. "I knew there was a reason I bought that new purple sundress."

The song, on repeat, starts again. The chords bounce around us.

"Once is probably enough," Dad says, cutting off the music with a laugh. Music is the one thing my parents don't agree on. He's more of a classic rock kind of guy—ugh!

"Dad!" I complain.

"Don't put the cart before the horse, Sof," he says.

"What horse?" Mama protests. "There are no horses in *West Side Story*."

Dad laughs. "It's an expression, Julia. I just mean that Sofia might not get the part if she has to audition first."

"Who cares about cars and horses," Mama says. "Sofia is perfect for the solo."

Dad chuckles in that quiet way of his. "I'm not saying she won't get the part," he says. "But it might be too soon to justify that dress purchase, Julia."

Mama pretends to be shocked. She swats at him playfully and says, "Our daughter is graduating from middle school. That's enough of a reason for a new dress."

"Whether you get a solo or not, Sofia, you're still an amazing, talented kid."

He's so corny I'm forced to roll my eyes.

After dinner, I stand in front of the mirror in my room to practice. I keep my back straight, so my diaphragm has plenty of space for deep breaths. That's what Mrs. Manzo has been telling us since we were in sixth grade, dreaming about our final spring concert.

I inhale and begin with the vocal warm-ups we learned in music class.

"La, la, la. Fa, fa, fa," I sing. I love the feeling of music coming out of my body. We have an out-of-tune piano my dad inherited from his grandmother. I took piano lessons for six months but didn't like how my teacher made me play "Hot Cross Buns" over and over for weeks. With singing, you just open your mouth and music comes out.

"Tra, la, la. Tra, la, la." My reflection smiles back at me as I roll my r's the way Mama does. When you sing, it doesn't matter what language you speak.

Danae tried clarinet in fourth-grade band, but she quit. She said she sounded like a dead cow. Not that we'd ever heard a dead cow—or her clarinet. She was too embarrassed to play for me and Zoe. "Singing makes so much more sense," Danae said, and we totally agreed with her.

"Ooooooooh," I sing. The notes are a staircase going higher and higher. "Eeeeeee," I bring my voice down the slide as low as I can go.

Zoe's older brother tried to teach her a few chords on the guitar last summer, but she didn't like how much the strings hurt her fingers. When Zoe quit, she said, "Music shouldn't be painful, you know?" After the three of us abandoned our instruments, we went back to singing. The thing is, you don't have to struggle with strings or pay for tuning or get fancy lessons to sing.

"He, he, he." I put one hand on my belly and feel the short breaths. "Ha, ha, ha." Watching myself in the mirror, I see how much I look like the character of Anita in the movie. Doesn't that mean I'm going to get the solo? Besides, I practice all the time. Mama always says that you can't achieve your goals without hard work. "Practice makes *perfecto*," she says.

I search my phone and find a track of "America" that I can rehearse with. I tap my foot with the beat. "I like to be in America," I sing.

In the morning, my friends and I meet at our lockers.

"Look at you, Sofia! That headband is exactly right for your audition," Zoe says.

I reach up. It was Mama's idea for me to wear the headband. My abuela bought it for me when we visited my grandparents in Colombia. The red fabric band is embroidered with a few tiny butterflies.

Danae says, "It makes you look just like that Mexican girl in the movie."

"Anita is Puerto Rican," I correct.

"Close enough," Danae laughs. "You'll get the part for sure, Sof."

Even though my mom is Colombian—not Puerto Rican—it does seem like I will make the perfect Anita. I look like her, and I've worked hard. I must have sung the song at least twenty times last night. I feel a flutter as if the butterflies on my head-band have flown into my stomach.

When the bell rings, I head to Math class. I imagine me and my two best friends dressed up for the eighth-grade show in the matching black strappy sandals Zoe has been eyeing. All three of us with solos, together but ready to head out on our own. Our arms are filled with stunning bouquets of red roses, bright yellow tulips, deep purple irises—

"—Sofia? Can you tell us the reciprocal?"

I look blankly at Mr. Cooper.

"Reciprocal of…?"

"Pay attention," he snaps. My cheeks burn. Probably as red as those roses.

After Math, I meet up with Zoe and Danae again in English class. We're separated by Spencer Bixel on the one side and Donte Hopkins on the other. I lean around Spencer and call to Zoe, "I can't concentrate, I'm so excited."

"This year's spring concert is going to be epic," she says.

"We're going to rule auditions," Danae says from the other side of Donte.

Spencer and Donte smirk. "Hey, Donte," Spencer says. "We're going to be the best singers." Donte laughs. We ignore them both.

"Boys and girls," scolds Miss Gomez. "Eyes up here, please."

Fantasizing about our success at the spring concert will have to wait.

After class, Zoe, Danae, and I catapult toward the music room for auditions. Normally, we would be heading for the cafeteria, where we always sit together. We laugh and talk, swap food out of our lunches. Danae eats the pandebonos Mama packs in my lunch bag. I steal fries from Zoe's school lunch. And all of us finish off Danae's mom's chocolate chip cookies.

As we walk toward the auditions, Zoe talks nonstop about something her brother did yesterday; she becomes a chatterbox

when she's anxious. Beside me, Danae is hopping like a rabbit—
the only way she seems to be able to burn off nervous energy.
When I'm nervous, I get quiet and slouch until I am as small as
possible. We slink, chat, and hop our way into the music room.

"Singers." Mrs. Manzo claps her hands, and everyone shushes
each other. She plays a few bars on the piano. I recognize the
opening immediately. "Everyone will be singing a few lines
from 'America' for their audition."

I look around at my competition. There's Lucy Feldman, who
takes private voice lessons; and Kiki Arroyo, who had a solo at
the holiday concert; and Amaya Anderson, who can sing lower
than any girl in eighth grade. My headband digs into the sides
of my skull, but there's no way I'm taking the headband off. I
need Mrs. Manzo to see that I'm perfect for the role of Anita.

"I'll choose soloists based on what piece best fits each voice."
Mrs. Manzo points to a stack of paper on top of the piano.
"Can someone pass around the words?" Lucy—who is always
teacher's pet—jumps to hand them out. "Let's try it together
first. Everyone, on your feet."

She plays the opening again.

I hold the paper at eye level with my back straight the way
Mrs. Manzo taught us.

"I like to be in America," we sing in unison. I hear Zoe in
my right ear and Danae in my left. As I sing, I smile as I think
about how many of the words Mama gets wrong when she sings
at home. It doesn't really matter, though, because even without
the right look or the right words, Mama always sings the song
like it was meant for her.

After we're warmed up, Mrs. Manzo calls one student at a
time.

Zoe is first. Mrs. Manzo nods when it's time for her to come
in. She sings roughly at first and mixes up a couple words. But
once she gets going, Zoe is amazing. While she sings the first

bars, I close my eyes and picture her on Danae's backyard deck that we use for a stage sometimes. I'm so proud.

One by one, Mrs. Manzo auditions singers while the rest of us sit on the floor, waiting our turns, nibbling our lunches. Actually, the only thing I nibble is my fingernails.

When it's Danae's turn, she comes in early. Which makes her laugh, which gives her the giggles—in fact, it gets so bad that I jump up and give her a sip of water. After she gets herself under control, she sings strong and loud. She even adds a few of the dance moves we perfected during our sleepovers.

By the time it's my turn, I have no fingernails left. I gulp some water and then stand beside the piano. I can feel everyone's eyes on me as I fidget with the sheet of music in my hands. I shift my weight from one foot to the other. Even though I haven't had any lunch, my stomach churns.

As I inhale, my body fills with the need to sing this solo in the spring concert. This song is about the pull between the US and Anita's home of Puerto Rico. Listening to Mama sing this song in the kitchen makes me think about the small city in Colombia where she was born. The notes sound like the fresh mangos and tamales de pipían we eat when we visit my grandparents, and I can hear the rumble of small cars and horse-drawn carts in the rhythm. The song also makes me think about how glad we are to be back in the US again when we get back to Minnesota. Not only because we can drink the water from the kitchen faucet or because Dad doesn't have to try speaking Spanish or because I crave American Cheerios. We're also glad because it's home. It's where we live our lives. Where we belong. It's where we are us. My family likes to be in America, just like the lyrics say.

Mrs. Manzo nods at me. It's time for me to show her that not only do I *look* like Anita, I *am* Anita. My practicing, my singing, my vocal warm-ups are all going to pay off. She's going to see—just like Danae and Zoe did—that with my dark hair and my brown eyes, I look the part. She's going to be certain—just like Mama—that I *have* to be Anita. My hands are damp with sweat, and my mouth is dry. But I picture Mama dancing and whistling and snapping her fingers. This is *my* song. I know it.

"When will you find out if you got the part of Anita?" Mama asks when she gets home from work.

"Tomorrow morning. Mrs. Manzo assigns all the solos and there will be a couple ensembles." I help put away the groceries.

Mama fills a pot of water. "What's *ensemble*?"

"That means a small group of singers. Not the whole class, but not a soloist," I explain. I help chop tomatoes for our salad while Mama washes the head of lettuce.

"So you and Zoe and Danae are an ensemble?"

I nod.

"That sounds fun," she says.

But the three of us aren't going to be an ensemble anymore. Next year, we'll each be on our own—three separate solos. Normally, I wouldn't mind singing in a group, but I'm ready for a solo. Anita's solo. Just me, standing on the gym's stage in front of the eighth-grade choir singing, *I like to be in America.*

Later that night, I go take a shower. As the water warms up, I hear my parents in the living room, Dad trying to explain something about the Wi-Fi router to Mama, who keeps pronouncing it *weefee* and then giggling.

There are so many things that make it weird to have parents that are from two different countries and speak two different languages. At holidays with my aunts and cousins on Dad's side, I always feel out of place compared to the fair-haired and light-skinned Minnesotans. And my stumbling Spanish makes me stick out like a gringa when we visit Mama's relatives in Colombia. Sometimes I feel like I don't belong anywhere, like I'm those two sides in the song, fighting over which side is better.

As the bathroom fills with steam, I sing, "I like to be in America." I raise my arms and snap my fingers like a Broadway dancer, like Mama. The sound bounces off the tiles. I have never wanted anything as much as I want the part of Anita in the spring concert.

"Sofia!" Danae calls to me the next morning.

The eighth graders are crowded in the hallway outside of Mrs. Manzo's room.

"The cast list!" Zoe points to an orange piece of paper taped to the classroom door. My toes curl. This is it. I push through the crowd to reach my best friends.

"I got it!" shrieks Lucy Feldman. "I'm Anita!"

Zoe, Danae, and I stare at her and then exchange looks. It's true that she has the biggest voice in the eighth grade. And it's true that she was awesome in her audition. But Lucy Feldman doesn't look anything like Anita. She has red curly hair, freckles, and a turned-up nose.

"I'm so sorry," Zoe says to me. "We know how much you wanted that part."

"Maybe you got the other solo?" Danae says.

"Right." I nod. "Who's Rosalia?" We make our way through the crowd of kids toward the orange list. My knees wobble with nerves.

"You guys!" screams a voice before we've even reached the door. It's Amaya Anderson, shrieking. "Lucy! I got the Rosalia solo!"

Beside me, Danae whispers, "Uh-oh."

Amaya and Lucy join hands and jump up and down like they just won the lottery.

My heart flip-flops into my belly. "I can't believe it." Although, when I picture Amaya singing the second biggest solo in the song, I realize she's a great choice. Amaya has a sparkly voice and it blends perfectly with Lucy's. Even so, it just doesn't seem fair. Amaya and Lucy don't look anything like the Puerto Rican characters.

Not like me. I look just like Anita—Zoe and Danae said so. I think of the too-tight headband and the skirt with the embroidery that Mama suggested. And then I think of Mama singing *I like to be in America* around the kitchen. Mama doesn't look anything like Anita, either, I remind myself.

"Come on," Zoe says, grabbing my arm and pulling me toward the orange paper. Danae is right behind me. "Look!" Zoe gasps and points to the bottom of the paper where the names of the ensemble for "America" are listed. Danae and I elbow our way past Lucy and Amaya. I lean forward. There, under "America," are the names of the solos: Lucy and Amaya. And there is my name, under Girl Ensemble.

"I'm in the ensemble," I say.

"And so are we!" Danae cries.

I look again and there they are: Sofia, Danae, and Zoe. The three of us.

"We're all in the same song!" Danae shouts. She high-fives me and Zoe. Zoe shrieks and hugs us both.

"I wanted a solo," Zoe says, "but this is even better."

She's right. It's wonderful. It's perfect. The three of us. Singing in the same ensemble for the spring concert. "It's super cool," I say. But it doesn't feel like it. I wanted Anita's solo. I worked hard. I looked like the character. I know I shouldn't be disappointed, but I can't help it.

That afternoon in music class, Mrs. Manzo settles down the students. "Congratulations to the soloists. And if you didn't get a solo or a spot in the ensemble, it doesn't mean you're not an excellent singer. Soloists were chosen because their voices fit the parts. I'm so proud of all of my graduating eighth graders."

I try to smile back at Mrs. Manzo, but there's a lump in my throat. When we sing warm-ups, I can't quite hit the high "tra, la, la" notes, and the "ha, ha, ha" breath exercise turns into a cough.

"Let's try the solos and ensemble for 'America,'" Mrs. Manzo says. She invites Lucy and Amaya to the front of the room. "Ensemble, you stand on the side here." Mrs. Manzo points behind the piano. I shuffle toward our spot. We're basically in the corner.

Mrs. Manzo claps the beat and then it's Anita's solo. *My* solo, I can't help thinking.

Lucy Feldman beams as she sings the verse. She must have watched the movie, because she does the same motions as the actress. I feel my scowl soften as Lucy sings with just the right amount of sass. She doesn't look anything like Anita, but once she gets going, she seems to *become* Anita. Just like the way Mama becomes Anita even while cooking dinner.

Amaya comes in with the next verse. She doesn't have quite as much pizzazz as Lucy, but she belts out the words. Even though Amaya wears a hijab to school and doesn't look anything like a Puerto Rican, I can tell Mrs. Manzo was right: her voice is a perfect fit.

Suddenly it's our turn. Mrs. Manzo nods at me, Zoe, and Danae. "I like to be in America," the three of us sing.

At first, I'm nervous, wishing I could bite my nails. But then I glance at my friends. My *best* friends. Singing together. We sway our hips and do a little hand flip, the three of us coordinated from years of stuffed-animal shows and silly dance routines. This is better than any solo. In a few months, we'll be off to different schools, making different friends. There's plenty of time to show off, to get cast just because I look the part. For now, the three of us are together still. We fit.

Lucy and Amaya smile at us as we harmonize. Then they come in, taking turns with the next verse. Then it's the chorus again and all that matters is the music. I close my eyes and let my body become the instrument.

I picture us at the spring concert. We'll dress up and borrow each other's blush and eyeliner. Dad will get nervous and Mama will have to take his hand and tell him to "Cálmate."

Zoe, Danae, and I will perform for a real live audience—not teddy bears and stuffed unicorns. At the end, our parents will applaud, and the three of us will hold hands and take a bow. When the audience cheers for the soloists, I'll clap the loudest.

I open my mouth and let the song come out. I listen to my voice blending with Danae's and Zoe's.

"That was great," Mrs. Manzo says. "Let's try it again."

We stand tall with our backs straight and take a deep breath. We're ready.

★ ★ ★ ★ ★

MICHELLE AND YVETTE IN KAISERSLAUTERN

By Mélina Mangal

April 30, 1986

Six minutes until Landstuhl station.

I folded my map of Europe that Dad had given me months earlier, hoping the radioactive cloud from Chernobyl wouldn't reach this far. Images of Hiroshima burn victims I'd seen in textbooks filled my mind. Would the Chernobyl fallout be like that? There was so little information coming out of the USSR.

I grabbed my backpack and moved toward the exit, trying to look like I'd traveled to Germany by myself before. I didn't know how many others would be getting off and didn't want to miss the stop.

I was so excited to see Yvette and celebrate her twenty-first birthday with her. It had been four years since she'd left Dad, Mama, Monique, and me to join the Air Force. I'd only seen her once in that time, when she came home to visit right before moving to Germany. I had wanted to visit her when she was stationed in Delaware, but Dad had said, "Unless you're able to pay your way with your babysitting money, we can't all go."

I started to rethink my outfit when I stepped off the train. Landstuhl station was peppered with personnel in army green and Air Force blue. With my houndstooth mermaid skirt, lavender belt-cinched white blouse and black blazer, I blended right in—back across the French border in Vincennes. But here—I felt like a horse as I clopped onto the cobblestone with my vintage heeled Mary Janes.

I spotted Yvette right away, even though it had been so long. Wearing white stirrup pants and an off-the-shoulder pink sweatshirt, her hair was longer now. And pressed, or maybe it was a perm. After all, it didn't look the way it did when Aunty Ruth got to her with a hot comb that time Dad deposited us in Biloxi for a week. Her curls were gone.

She looked right at me and smiled, a more chiseled version of my own brown face. I actually hoped she wouldn't recognize me right away—that I looked more mature.

"Hey, little sis!" she greeted me with a hug. I planted *bisous* on each cheek.

"*Salut frangine!*" automatically came out of me. I had to turn on my English switch again. "Hey, Yvette!" I said, handing her a small bouquet of *muguet* I'd bought at the train station. "These are for you."

"Aww, thanks, Michelle." She sniffed them, then sneezed, just like Dad does. "Ooh, they do smell nice, though. Love me some lilies of the valley. They remind me of Mama and her patch next to the garage." With her newly straightened mushroom cut hair, Yvette now looked more like Mama.

"Smells like old lady perfume," came a voice nearby. I turned to see someone in fatigues and combat boots, a drab green cap pulled down low over her smooth brown face.

"Michelle, this is my friend Cassandra. Cassandra, this is my little sister, Michelle."

"Hi," I said, waving my hand.

"Hey," she said, looking me up and down.

"Everybody gives them for May Day in France," I explained.

"Don't you look all Parisian," Yvette said, grabbing my backpack.

"I can carry it." I smiled. "Actually, Tantine Bernadette and Tonton Maurice live just outside Paris, in Vincennes. They were so worried about me coming here after the explosion at Chernobyl. They said I'd be closer to the fallout, that a radioactive cloud was moving this way. We're safe here, right?"

"I got ya, Michelle," Yvette said, hoisting my backpack onto her back. "The Soviet Union's pretty far from here. I wouldn't worry about it."

I relaxed a bit and soaked in the views of the redbrick station and the street.

"The car's over there," Cassandra indicated with a wave of her chin.

Yvette looked over at me. "Can't believe Mom and Dad let you leave the country—by yourself, to live with people we've only seen in photos."

"You know, they are family, and they remember when you were born in Chateauroux. Mama's aunt and uncle are really pretty nice—just a little old-fashioned. Which reminds me, I have to call them later."

I thought of Tantine Bernadette's first impressions of me, as she touched my curly asymmetrical bob. *"T'es frisée comme un petit mouton."* She went on to say, *"Je n'attendais pas que tu serais si ronde. Mais comment ça se fait que tu parles si bien le français?"* Curly as a little lamb...wasn't expecting you to be so round. How is it that you speak French so well?

Being compared to a sheep? I didn't want to tell Yvette how humiliated I'd first felt. "We're American," she'd said when I asked her why *she* didn't try to speak French. "Besides, Mama speaks English perfectly—and Dad doesn't speak French, either."

I looked at Yvette, always cool, confident, popular. Maybe

I'd become like her someday. "You're the one who paved the way. I don't think they would have let me do it if you weren't stationed only four hours away."

"Shoot, it's only three and a half on the autobahn," she said, unlocking a shiny black car. "What do you think?"

"Cool!"

"It's really not a big deal. Mercedes are common here. Folks back in the States think, *oooh a Benz*!"

"Oh, yeah." I nodded, getting in the front seat. I didn't want to remind her that I didn't have my license yet. Dad constantly reminded me that Yvette had aced her driving test the first time and got hers at sixteen. She seemed to ace everything she tried. I still hadn't passed the driving test, and I would be eighteen in three months.

Yvette punched the stereo on, and Prince's voice sang "Purple Rain."

I pushed the image of radioactive clouds out of my mind. "I'm so happy the first of May is a school holiday so I could come celebrate your birthday with you."

"The first of May," Cassandra repeated from the back in a high mocking voice, "is a holiday!"

Anger flashed through me. Why was she imitating me? Then I realized I'd just translated *le premier mai* directly into English. Ugh. It was hard switching back and forth.

"Shush, Cassandra. You're bein' stupid," Yvette laughed. I took a deep breath and decided to ignore Cassandra.

"I'm so excited to finally see Germany—another stamp in my passport! Tonton Maurice said there's this castle nearby, and I also read that this area has really cool May Day celebrations."

"Toto? Did you say *Toto*?" Cassandra guffawed.

"Tonton," I repeated. "That means *uncle* in French. But he's actually our great-uncle, and that's kind of an affectionate title, like Aunty."

Yvette turned up the volume. Was she embarrassed? By Cassandra, or by me? And who was Cassandra, anyway? Yvette always had friends around, but I hoped to just hang out, alone, at least sometime during the visit. I wanted her to see the new *me*, not the little kid I used to be.

I thought it was a mix tape until I heard a radio announcer: something in German. Then, in perfect English: "This weekend only at K-Town's Redball Express Club, drop off your donations for our brothers and sisters in blue at Vlistock Air Base, affected by Chernobyl."

What? It was closer than I thought... "Did you hear that?" I asked.

"Yeah, sure did. In fact, that's where I want to take you later. That's one of my favorite places here in K-Town."

My heart flip-flopped. Did she hear what I heard? "Where?"

"Kaiserslautern. That's the big city here." She looked into the rearview mirror at Cassandra. "It's my BIRTH-day," she sang out. "Twenty-one, baby! Gonna hit the Redball tomorrow night!"

Excitement and fear fluttered through me at the same time. I was going to a dance club—for the first time!

"Man, it was hard when they closed the base after the disco bombing," Cassandra said, flexing her fingers.

"Where was that?" I asked.

"West Berlin. We were locked on base for a few weeks."

Great. Now I had to worry about disco bombings, too.

"You hungry?" Yvette asked. "We could stop and get a bite. I don't have much back at the dorm."

"Sure," I admitted, pushing the worry out of my mind. The thought of trying some German food right away appealed to me. It felt like hours since I'd eaten my jambon sandwich on the train.

Minutes later, Yvette pulled into a parking lot. The familiar red and white Kentucky Fried Chicken sign on the brick build-

ing surprised me. Here in Germany? I was hoping for schnit-
zel or strudel.

I thought the girls taking our orders in English were American until they turned to speak to each other in German. Yvette
paid in US dollars. We could have been back in Minneapolis.

"Oh, I almost forgot!" I said when we sat down with an order
of chicken and biscuits. "I brought you some goodies!" I pulled
the paper bag out of my backpack. "There are patisseries everywhere, even at the train station. I got you a croissant and *pain
au chocolat aussi*, I mean also. And Tantine Bernadette wanted
me to give this to you."

I handed her the small jar, tied with green ribbon. *"Confi-
ture de prunes!"*

"Oh, goody!" Cassandra said, mimicking my voice again.
"Prune jelly!"

I gave her a cold hard stare. Why wasn't Yvette cutting her off?

"It's plum preserves," I corrected her. "Made from the plums
in her garden. The word for plums in French is *prune*."

"Aww, thanks, Michelle," Yvette jumped in. "This should
be good." She opened the pastry bag and turned to Cassandra.
"You wanna try some?"

"Uh-uh. You know I'm watchin' my weight. Gotta fit in my
leather skirt for the Redball!" She sipped her iced tea as Yvette
took a big bite of *pain au chocolat.*

"Suit yourself," Yvette answered. "Missin' out. And you know
you won't be able to dance, IF you can get in that skirt!" She
burst out laughing.

Cassandra thwacked Yvette on the arm and rolled her eyes.
"Forget you."

"Ladies! Early dinner at the Colonel's?"

We all turned to see a tall, thin, baby-faced guy with a short fro.

"Oh, hey, T!" said Cassandra. "What you doin' here?"

"Same thing as you, grabbin' a bite."

"You see me eatin' anything here? I don't do the Colonel."

"Who's your friend?" he asked, eyeing me.

"This is my little sister, Michelle," Yvette offered. "She's visiting me from France." She turned back to me. "This is T."

"Terrance," he said smiling. "Wee, wee. *Parlez-vous français?*"

"*Oui, bien sur,*" I responded.

"Ooh—that's all I know." He turned to Yvette. "Let me hear you two speak French."

"I don't speak French," Yvette answered.

"You understand some, though," I volunteered.

She cut me a look that said, *I can speak for myself.*

Prince cut through the din again, this time with "When Doves Cry." My body wanted to groove.

"Oh, your brotha's singing, Yvette," Terrance said.

I looked at them. "We don't have a brother."

They all burst out laughing. I felt like I was back at Wilson High, being teased when selling candy bars for my trip to France. *You can't be French—you're Black.*

"Yvette's always tellin' me that she's Prince's sister," Terrance said.

"Well, I look like I could be his sister," Yvette laughed.

You look like my sister, I thought. The truth is, with her straightened hair, Yvette looked white, like Mama. *I* looked more like Prince. Actually, though he was darker than me, I looked just like Dad, with his widow's peak and dimpled chin.

Monique was ten years old, with sand-colored skin closer to Mama's beige complexion. I wondered how she'd look when she got older. I hoped she wouldn't have to deal with the same comments and questions I had to deal with.

"So what about little sister here, then?" asked Terrance.

Cassandra sipped more iced tea. "Prince's cousin." They all laughed, like it was the funniest thing ever.

Why was Yvette letting them make fun of me like that? She'd stood up for me before.

A memory flashed into my mind. When we were living

in Wisconsin, a gang of boys pelted us with rocks and names. Yvette wore her sharp-heeled lace-up platforms to school after that. The next time they started in on us, all she had to do was give a few swift kicks. They stopped messing with us after that.

Yvette finally stopped laughing. "We're going to the Redball tomorrow night. For my birthday."

"Cool. I'll see you there. You dance, little sis?"

Before I had a chance to reply, Cassandra butted in. "Let me guess—she probably dances like Jennifer Beals, 'cept she's all Miss FRENCH *Flashdance*."

I wanted to turn and run out of there. I braved potential nuclear fallout to visit my sister on her birthday. And see Germany. Instead, I was being tormented by Yvette's so-called friends.

They kept looking at me, waiting for a comeback. I steeled my emotions, like I'd had to do so often during my first weeks in France when people looked down on me, assuming I was Arab from North Africa. Then, when I opened my mouth and my American accent popped out, I was asked to explain everything from racism to gun violence and drug use—all American problems apparently.

"Of course, I dance," I said. "And not *Flashdance*."

What was I saying? I LOVED *Flashdance*, though I learned that Jennifer Beals hadn't actually done the dances. A dance double had.

Cassandra studied me closer. "Can you do the wop?"

I cut my eyes at her. "You'll see tomorrow night."

"Ooh, can't wait to see that!" she said.

See me embarrass myself in front of all of Ramstein Air Force Base? Why did I say that?

I couldn't admit I didn't actually know what the wop was. I loved to dance, but how was I supposed to know how to do all of them?

At a party that I'd been invited to through school in Vincennes, they couldn't believe I didn't know "le rock." Didn't all

Americans do this partner swing dance? Nobody in my world did it, at least not in real life. Only in movies from the 1950s.

Cassandra stood up. "Hey, T, give me a ride to the commissary, would you? I gotta pick up a couple things."

"Catch ya later, sistas," Terrance said, winking at me as they left.

"Bye, T," Yvette said to them both. "Catch ya at the Redball tomorrow night."

"You know it!" Cassandra said. "Auf wiedersehen, y'all!"

Yvette turned to me when they'd gone. "I've gotta get ready for work." She stood and pushed her chair in. "So what'd you think of my friends?"

"They were making fun of me."

"They're not making fun *of* you. They're having fun *with* you. You'll see—tomorrow night's gonna be the bomb."

If this was their idea of fun, I dreaded what was to come.

I didn't sleep well with all the lights and sounds of the base. It was quite warm, so Yvette left a noisy oscillating fan on. No air-conditioning, she said, like most places back in France. Though Yvette had a double room with two twin beds, she currently had no roommate.

Her room opened into a shared living room and kitchen area. There must have been a few other flight managers like Yvette, whose shifts changed depending on flight times. Several people popped in and out throughout the night. I heard Yvette's voice when she came back from work, talking with someone else. I wondered if this was how it would be when I went off to college.

I pretended to be asleep when she returned and changed from her fatigues into a T-shirt and shorts. When she got into her bed, I thought I'd finally get some sleep. I'd forgotten how loudly she snored.

When morning came, Yvette didn't even hear the phone ringing. I picked it up.

"Happy Birthday, Yvette!" said Mama. Hearing her voice

and seeing Yvette's framed photo of our whole family made me miss all of us together.

"It's Michelle," I explained. "I'm visiting Yvette for her birthday, remember?"

"*Eh, bien sur, ma petite,*" she switched into her native French. "*Ça va en Allemagne?*"

"*Oui, ça va. Attends, Yvette arrive.*"

I wanted to tell Mama about my trip, but I knew she must have stayed up late to call Yvette. We couldn't talk long. Long distance phone calls were expensive, and she'd just called the weekend before to check on me, when the Chernobyl disaster happened.

I stepped across the barracks room and shook Yvette. It felt quite satisfying. "Wake up! Mom's on the phone to wish you a happy birthday!"

She grumbled, but got up and spoke to Mom, in English.

I curled back onto the bed with my *Let's Go Europe* book to read more about the sites near Kaiserslautern. I wished I could get a local newspaper to find out more about Chernobyl. Was the wind blowing radioactive clouds closer? Would the base go on lockdown, leaving me stuck in the largest American community outside of the US (according to my book), unable to return to France? I still hadn't even seen much of Germany yet.

"Okay, Mom," Yvette replied, looking directly at me. "I promise, I will." She hung up and crawled back in bed. "Goin' back to sleep," she said, turning her back to me. "It's my birthday."

I opened my book again. She was right. It was her day. I came to celebrate and see her. And I was seeing her, alright—her whole backside.

According to *Let's Go,* we had probably already missed the May Day celebrations, but I wasn't going to complain. We were on our way to the castle.

"Stay straight after Vogelweh," Cassandra directed, this time in the front seat as navigator. I couldn't seem to shake her. But if it wasn't Cassandra, there would be someone else.

I stared out the window, soaking up as much as I could. We were now past the concrete block buildings of the base. Wood and stucco houses hugged the rolling hills.

Yvette slowed down at a stop sign. "Over there." Cassandra pointed. "Park near the cemetery."

Yvette looked at me through the rearview mirror. "You know I don't like cemeteries. This better be worth it."

I took a deep breath. I'd forgotten about Yvette's superstitions, just like Dad. Why couldn't we just have fun together?

It was a beautiful hike up the hill. Cassandra was suspiciously quiet the whole time, until we heard the bleating.

"Goats!" I shouted. Yvette smiled at me and shook her head.

"Keep them things away from me," Cassandra said. "You can smell 'em from here."

When we finally reached the site, Cassandra asked, "Where's the castle at?"

"It's the ruins of the castle," I explained.

"Got that right," she said. "I've driven by, but I've never come up here. I always thought there was more to see."

Yvette had wandered over to the farthest side. She stood, hands on her hips, gazing out over the countryside. Looking like a queen.

"Beautiful," she whispered when I approached. "Just beautiful."

The May sun was warm and bright. The surrounding forest was a lush emerald green, reminding me of Upper Michigan, where our family moved when I was much younger. During the long drive there, Mama and Dad told us stories of their childhoods, how they met when Dad was stationed in France with the Air Force, how they dealt with racist attacks against them in northern Minnesota and Wisconsin. I was about to ask Yvette her memories of that time when Cassandra cut in.

"Y'all ready? I need a nap. Gotta get my beauty rest for tonight."

"You sure do!" laughed Yvette.

I sighed. I could've stayed there all afternoon.

As we descended, I heard bleating again. "A goat is follow-ing me!" I laughed. I wanted to take it home.

"Oh, Lord," Cassandra said. "What next?"

"I should have time to get my hair touched up and my nails done," Yvette said as she pulled the car out back onto the road. I couldn't help bopping and swaying to Janet Jackson's "What Have You Done for Me Lately?" from the rear speaker.

"You make an appointment somewhere? 'Cause you know most places closed today," Cassandra reminded her.

All of a sudden, I felt the car start vibrating and wobbling.

"Ssshhh," Yvette said, turning down the music. "Something's wrong. Man, the car won't drive straight." Yvette pulled over and got out. Cassandra followed.

"Damn!" Yvette kicked at the gravel on the side of the road.

"Pop the trunk, and I'll put the spare on," Cassandra com-manded.

Yvette frowned. "I don't have a spare."

Cassandra shook her head.

"Can you call somebody?" I asked. They both glared at me.

"We're off base," Yvette said. She looked over at Cassandra. "Try calling T."

"With what? You see a phone booth around here?"

I looked around, as if somehow I'd be able to locate a phone booth that they'd overlooked. Across the road, I saw a small square and orange-suited street cleaners at work, probably from the May Day parade we'd missed.

"Let's head to the square. There should be a phone booth near there," Yvette said.

All the shops were closed. The street cleaners were packing up.

"Ask them if they know where we can make a call," Cas-sandra said.

"You know I don't speak German," Yvette replied.

"Everybody speaks English," Cassandra said.

The two older men, the same complexion as Yvette and I, continued loading the truck as we approached. It sounded like they were speaking Turkish. Two others, both darker, replaced bins.

None of them spoke English.

"*Verstehen sie?*" the youngest one asked us in German. We all shook our heads, no.

I thought of *les balayeurs* around Paris, cleaning the streets in their clean green suits. Some of them were from Benin, Togo, Chad...

"*Pourriez-vous nous aider?*" I tried.

"*Ah, oui! Vous parlez français. Vous venez d'où?*"

"*Je viens des États-Unis, de Minnesota.*"

His face lit up. "*C'est le pays de Prince!*"

I smiled back. "*Bien sûr!*"

Within minutes, I'd learned that his name was Ousmane, he was from Guinea, and his coworker from Zaire. He'd come to Germany by way of Belgium. He played guitar.

And, he offered to help.

Yvette and Cassandra silently watched while Ousmane and I spoke. I almost forgot they were there when Ousmane's coworker came back in his car with tools and a tire, and they worked together to replace Yvette's tire with a spare.

"That's all I got right now," Yvette said, handing me a couple of twenty-dollar bills. "Tell them thank you."

"*Vous nous avez sauvées,*" I said, handing him the money.

"*Quelqu'un m'a aidé une fois, et aujourd'hui c'était mon tour.*"

I wanted to remember that: someone helped me once, and today was my turn.

After the tire was changed and we were finally back in Yvette's room, I took out the present I'd been waiting to give her. "*Bon anniversaire,* Yvette!" I sat on the bed to watch her open it.

"Perfume!" She opened up the red box. "This is fancy!" She hugged me before sitting on her bed. "Thanks, Michelle. This ALMOST makes up for me missing out on getting my nails done."

"It's Nuage de Nuit. Tantine Bernadette brought me to a perfumerie in Paris and helped me pick it. I hope you like it."

Yvette sat on her bed, sprayed some of the perfume on her wrist and rubbed. She inhaled the scent. "Mmm, nice." She looked at me with a question in her eye. "You know what? This reminds me of Mississippi."

"Really?"

"Remember all those magnolias blooming? The air smelled so sweet. But this perfume also smells very French."

"Kind of like us." I smiled.

"Yeah," she agreed, nodding. "You know, the reason Dad wanted us to only speak English when we were little was because he worried we'd be picked on even more. Little brown-skinned kids with French accents."

"I had no idea," I said. "You can understand a bit, though, can't you?"

"Yeah, I can," Yvette responded. "I understand a lot of things," she said, looking deeply at me.

She put the bottle back in the box and placed it on top of her dresser. "You're gonna love the Redball," Yvette said.

The thought of Cassandra and T and Yvette's other friends watching how I danced filled me with dread. I wanted to just stay there and celebrate quietly with her. Watch a movie, eat popcorn, talk more.

"To be honest, I'm not really excited about going. Your friends are gonna make fun of me—the way I talk, the way I dance," I said.

"What? Look, Michelle. They hear the way you talk about French stuff and think you're acting white, like you don't want to be Black or something."

It felt like the breath was sucked out of me. "Is that what *you* think?"

Yvette gathered her shower cap, toiletries, and a towel.

"I think you need to stop worrying about being who you are."

I sat there, stunned. She pulled her outfit from the closet and laid it on the bed. "I'm gonna take a shower. We'll head out when you're ready, okay?"

I simply nodded. I was still trying to find my breath. I just wanted Yvette, and everyone, to see who I was. And to appreciate it.

A stream of friends had stopped by to wish Yvette a happy birthday before we headed out. Yvette punched on the music as soon as we got in the car. Billy Ocean sang about his "Caribbean Queen."

We drove past the commissary, then the main gate, and onto the autobahn to K-Town.

"It would be nice if you spoke up for me with your friends," I said over the music.

Yvette looked at me. "If I speak for you, folks will think you can't speak for yourself. I heard you hold your own in French. I know you can do it in English, too."

My anger froze, before swirling around with fear and excitement as we pulled into the parking lot of the Redball. It was now dark, but still warm outside. I stood and smoothed my short-sleeved yellow sweater dress. Yvette adjusted the belt on her off-the-shoulder lavender dress, then reapplied lipstick as she looked in her sideview mirror. We looked like tulips.

I felt the music before I heard it. It beat through me, as if competing with my heart.

Here we go—come on!

It was dark. I couldn't see individuals—only a pack of people moving in unison, like the lungs of a beautiful beast. In. Out. Arms swaying. Hips rolling.

I wanted to be part of it. *Allons-y!*

Cassandra and Terrance waved us over to their table. "Happy birthday, Yvette!" they shouted and hugged.

"Wanna dance, little sis?" It was Terrance, smiling down at me.

I hesitated. Here it was. Judgment time. They were going to make fun of me. Then Yvette's words hit me. *Stop worrying about being who you are.*

The music made me want to move. I looked over at Yvette, not sure if she wanted me to hang out at the table with her. The beat tugged at me.

"Have fun, Michelle!" She winked at me. "But not too much! T, make sure my little sister doesn't get lost out there," Yvette directed.

My heart fluttered again. I prayed for dance guidance.

The beat got me. Out on the dance floor, my body took over. I'd never heard music like this before, but it didn't seem to matter.

No one looked at me. Everyone danced.

I let it all go, the worry about Yvette's friends, the Chernobyl fallout, and trying to fit in everywhere—here, back home, in France. I just danced.

6 minutes...

Someone bumped me in the hip and I turned to see Yvette, all smiles. Cassandra, wearing a tight black skirt, was being led onto the dance floor by another guy. Yvette stood next to a guy about her height.

"My little sister." She pointed to me. "She's studying in France and speaks French. Saved the day today!"

"Word!" came Cassandra. "Wouldn'ta made it here tonight. Don't know about that dance, though."

"Hush up, Cassandra," Terrance said.

"Let her dance," Yvette shouted. "She's got her own thing goin' on."

"For real," Cassandra said, turning back to dance.

I smiled over at Yvette, happy to be there with her, for her. No English words came. No French words came. I let my body do the talking. For real.

★ ★ ★ ★ ★

IRISH SODA BREAD

By Eric Smith

It's not like Mrs. Esteves to be late for class. And when it comes to her World History course, no students are ever late for it, either. There're no books, no papers, no presentations. You just sit here and take notes while she lectures about the course of human history, that somehow, almost magically, she rattles off the top of her head, like a walking, talking encyclopedia.

And while that might sound boring to some, she makes it thrilling. It feels like more of a one-woman show you'd catch on Netflix.

None of us have any idea how she does it. Does she study up on her lectures at home? Are her speeches about the fall of Rome and other such monumental moments just so practiced over the decades of teaching here at Elizabeth High School that it's all just muscle memory at this point?

I can't even remember my best friend's cell phone number, never mind the storied history of Greek architecture.

"What do you think is going on?" Joel whispers, nudging my shoulder. I glance over at him, the same guy whose number I absolutely cannot recall and whose birthday I only manage to hold on to because he's notorious for celebrating his "birthday week," and shrug.

"I have no idea." I look around the classroom, and everyone else appears to be just as puzzled. I mean, it's fine if she's out for the day, or sick, or doing whatever it is teachers do when they're taking a personal day. Over the summer, I spotted one of our math teachers, Mrs. Nardello, at the same diner as me and my family, and I swear it was like seeing an alien. I know teachers have lives, but...it's still strange. And Mrs. Esteves being out, it's just so unlike her that it feels suspicious. She opened the first day of class telling all of us how she never gets sick, and to be ready to engage with the material every single day. To listen, discuss, take notes, and not to hope for a day like this. Joel drums his fingers on his desk, a thick notebook wedged under his forearm. I've got the same setup, a spiral notebook packed full of notes we've been dished over the course of the last few months, all meticulously typed into my laptop at home.

There's just one big test in this class at the end of the year, based on all the notes you've taken, and I'm not about to lose everything. She makes history feel so personal, like it belongs to me in a way my own history, as an adopted kid, really doesn't.

"Maybe she died?" Casey ventures, a girl who sits right across from me. Someone immediately throws a pen at her.

"Should one of us go down to the principal's office or something?" Vanessa asks everyone.

"Hell no."

"I'm enjoying this."

"Don't be a narc."

Suddenly, everyone is muttering their ideas and suggestions and possibilities over one another, a hum in the classroom not unlike the buzz on the bleachers during a football game. I sigh and look back over at Joel, who now has his phone out. This week we were going to dig into the Civil War, which I was

weirdly looking forward to. One of the last big trips me and my
dad took before I started high school was to Gettysburg, and I
brought the musket ball we found on the battlefield with me
to show Mrs. Esteves. The little iron weight sits in my pocket,
heavy and full of dark history.

"Hey, maybe—" I start.

The door to the classroom swings open, and someone hurries in. You can hear the audible shift in the air, as seemingly
everyone turns away from what they're doing or saying, to look
toward the front of the class.

"Sorry I'm late, kids," the...teacher, I guess, says. He drops
a bundle of notebooks and papers on Mrs. Esteves's desk. He's
dressed in jeans and some kind of band T-shirt, black combat
boots noisily hitting the floor. He sits down on the desk and it
takes everything in me not to gasp.

It's Mr. Brandt.

Fuck.

"He's *still* a teacher?" Joel mutters, and glances over at me.
I swallow. He looks weirdly exactly the same as he did when
we had him in second grade. Is he preserved somehow by his
terrible goatee? Do those band T-shirts of groups no one has
ever heard of and have no Wikipedia page keep him perpetu-
ally young? Maybe he has some kind of old hipster photograph,
taken with a Polaroid camera, sitting in his attic, like the worst
kind of Dorian Gray retelling.

"Alright, so I'm Mr. Brandt," he says, fussing with some of
the papers on the desk. "I'll be your sub, I'm sorry to say your
teacher Mrs. Esteves is—"

"She's dead, I knew it," Casey interrupts.

"No," Mr. Brandt says, laughing a little as more pens get
thrown at Casey. "But she's a bit under the weather, so I'll be
with you this week. Now, where did you all leave off?"

I look at Joel and he shrugs at me, and around the classroom
just about everyone is doing the same. It still worries me a bit,

her being sick. She's like the Wonder Woman of History teachers, seemingly impervious to anything.

"We, um…" Vanessa starts. "Don't use books? There's no *left off* anywhere. She just talks."

"No books," Mr. Brandt says, his tone flat.

"Nope." Joel shrugs.

"Huh." Mr. Brandt nods, but then looks over at Joel. Next, his eyes flit over to me. A wash of realization seems to course over him, and he smirks a little, and points at the two of us.

"Well, well, well." He crosses his arms. "If it isn't Sean and Joel. Still thick as thieves, I'm guessing?"

"You guessed right." I nod, talking through gritted teeth.

He snaps his fingers, pointing at us again, and paces the room a little by the desk.

"That gives me an idea," he says, nodding to himself. He rubs his hands over his stupid beard. "Alright. Forget the no-book lectures, because that's not my thing. We'll just let Mrs. Esteves take things over again when she gets back. My thing, though, my big thing is cooking."

Oh.

"My thing is food."

Oh, hell no.

"We used to do this project when I taught younger kids across town, before I opened my restaurant. Sean and Joel, I remember you two from that class, although… I think the assignment was a bit of a challenge for you, Sean." He smiles, shaking his fist in a little victory as my stomach tightens. "This is fantastic."

"Restaurant?" Joel grumbles, and looks at me. "He's here, so it must be doing *great*."

"Shh," I hush, urgently wanting to hear the rest of this, and absolutely fearing where it's all going. It all sounds so familiar, and it's rocketing me right back to second grade. To a memory I'd rather not revisit. To that "challenging" assignment.

"Since this is a History class, where you dive into culture

and background and all of that good stuff..." He walks back to his desk and sits behind it, kicking his feet up on it. The metal desk clangs again, and I scowl. That's Mrs. Esteves's desk. Who does he think he is? "And with this class being so close to lunch-time—"

Oh, no.

"I want to challenge all of you to bring something in tomorrow, to share with the class, from your culture's menu." He claps his hands and rubs them together. "Everyone can get up in front of the class, talk a bit about the dish, and then we'll just have a big ol' potluck before lunch. It'll be awesome, and you won't have to eat that garbage in the cafeteria for a day."

There are a few approving rumblings in the classroom, but for the most part, everyone is staring ahead at him like he's a little out of his mind.

"Um..." Rebecca speaks up, raising her hand from the back of the classroom. She's got blue hair and wears jackets covered in enamel pins and is frankly way too cool to hang out with someone like me, yet we have lunch together just about every single day. "What if no one in our family really cooks?" She glances at me with a smirk, and I get it. The two of us were rocking Lunchables way longer than we should have, our families both terrible at even making a peanut butter and jelly sandwich.

"Just google something." He shrugs, waving his hand in the air. "It doesn't have to be something fancy. We're not talking about bringing in a roast or a Thanksgiving turkey. Hell, bring in whatever you pick up at the supermarket on your way here. A snack of your peoples."

I glance over at Joel and he's just glaring ahead.

A snack. Of your *peoples*?

"Anyhow, it's not like this counts toward a grade, anyway," Mr. Brandt continues.

"Then why do it?" Rebecca asks.

"Because it's *fun*," he snaps back. "Doesn't Mrs. Esteves at least keep track of participation? I'll do that and report back to her, how's that? Now, why don't you all spend the rest of class discussing what you'll bring in tomorrow." He leans back in Mrs. Esteves's chair, the furniture squeaking, and pulls out his phone. And just like that, it's like we're alone in the classroom again, his focus on the little screen in front of him.

"Man, what am I supposed to bring in?" Joel grumbles, leaning back in his own seat. "My parents definitely don't use our kitchen to cook food so much as they use it to store leftover takeout. Ah, yes, here's my grandmother's traditional Cuban dish passed on from generation to generation, Frosted Mini-Wheats without milk because *Joel, we're out of milk.* Guy is acting like I'm just gonna roll in here with a flan."

I laugh a little and shake my head, anxiety just flowing through me. I pick at a groove in the desk, next to a number of other scratches, likely dug into the desk years ago by all the many people who have come through this room. A *Chris and Shannon 4 Evr* is dug in deep into the maybe-wood-maybe-plastic of the desk, and I wonder if they made it, and what their story is. Did they deal with the same challenges? Having names that didn't "match" their faces, staring down these impossibly personal assignments with other teachers?

"Hey, what is it?" Joel asks.

"Oh, nothing." I shrug, clearing my throat. "I don't know what to bring, either."

"Yeah, that's not it." He squints at me.

"I mean…" I sigh. "These kinds of assignments aren't easy for someone like me, dude. I show up with what my family cooks, and it doesn't match with what I look like. Bring your family's cultural dish to school is the worst kind of assignment. And besides, I've done this exact project before."

"What, really?" he asks.

"Years ago. Second grade. You and your family were in Miami that week."

I glance up at Mr. Brandt.

"And he was the teacher."

My memories of grade school are fairly vague as they are for most of my friends. And everyone, I guess. You remember the little things and the huge things, and seldom the moments in between. I can recall running around on the playground, being rejected from certain games, awkwardly making friends. The very first school play, if you can even call it that, where everyone sang about a different dinosaur...or was it about presidents? Who knows. The point is there are these small snapshots across my mind, of being carelessly happy and anxious, as most seven- or eight-year-olds are.

But there's one memory that stands out above all the rest.

The day I found out I was adopted.

I feel like most adopted kids have that memory seared into their brains. They must. I've only met a few, at adoptee meetups my parents used to take me to until I outgrew them, and everyone had a story. A quiet talk on a long awkward car ride. A tear-filled discussion at a TGI Fridays. Finding an adoption certificate by accident in a dresser drawer...

Mine began with one of these "bring your culture's food to school day" events when I brought in some Irish soda bread that I'd spent all afternoon baking with my mom. Carefully making our entire kitchen into a flour-dusted disaster, like snow covering the floor's tile and counter's marble. "The trick is to use baking soda instead of yeast," my mom explained.

"Yes, make sure you explain that," Dad chimed in, sipping his late-night dark-roast coffee nearby.

When it was time to stand in front of the class and talk about our dish, Mr. Brandt...

He *laughed*.

"Oh, Sean." He smiled from his desk, his feet up on it. "You clearly didn't understand the assignment, but that's okay. Tell us more."

I remember feeling confused, looking from him to the bread in my little hands to the students in front of me, their eyes all focused. Someone snickered, someone muttered, and I tried to keep going. We had pushpins, and we were supposed to put a pin in the large map of the world against the blackboard.

Where's My Family From? it read in big joyful letters.

I took the bright red pin and tacked it into Ireland.

Mr. Brandt laughed again.

"Sean, Sean," he said, walking over. "That's where the *food* you've brought in is from, yes. But you're supposed to put the tack where *you're* from. Your family. Are you sure it isn't…" He plucked the thumbtack out and moved it over toward the countries in Asia. "Or maybe…" He pointed at South America and handed me the tack. He stood there, looking at me expectantly.

I glared at him and took the tack back and stuck it right back in Ireland.

"Now, Sean…" He moved to take the tack out again.

"No, that's where I'm from," I pressed, putting my hand over it.

"No, but…this assignment was about where you're from. Not here, in New Jersey. But where you're *from* from."

"Here!" I shouted, pointing at the map.

"That's not…" He nudged my hand away and took the pin out again. "It's okay. You're just misunderstanding the project here. That's where your food is from. It's supposed to be where you are—"

I took the tack out of his hand.

And slammed it into Ireland.

The whole map ripped off the wall, a big tear down the middle. The entire classroom gasped.

"*Go sit down*," Mr. Brandt snarled, and I hustled back to my seat. "You're going to have to stay after class."

I got detention and had to stay after school. When my mom showed up to pick me up, and I explained what happened, we walked back home, mostly in silence. She held my hand, but in a lot of ways that day, thinking back, it felt like I was the one holding hers. The entire stroll to our house, she looked like she was going to fall to pieces, and my heart slammed in my small chest.

What had I done that was so terrible? Why was she so upset with me? I couldn't figure it out, and I had no idea why Mr. Brandt had made such a fuss over me being right. Why did he think I was from somewhere else?

After a quick whispered conversation with my father in our kitchen, the same place where we made that bread barely under a day ago, the two of them walked in. She fished for something in the bookshelves, high up, and brought down a picture book. There were two white parents on the cover, holding hands with two brown kids. *So, You're Adopted* was written in big bold letters on the front.

"Sean," my mom started. "We have to talk to you about something."

The book cover and the title sent my heart racing. And even now, thinking about that moment, frozen in my memory, I swear I can feel my pulse in my neck. That feeling of knowing that soon everything you thought you knew was about to change.

My dad took her hand, and she explained.

"All because of Irish fucking soda bread." I shrug and take a bite out of a French fry.

"That's...that's really messed up, man," Joel says, the two of us sitting at our standard lunch table in the cafeteria. We're surrounded by our usual crew, Yanis, Anna, Rosiee, and Rebecca. Lunches are spread out over the table in various states of being devoured, but all five of them are just staring right at me. Lunch is on pause, for now.

"Damn." Anna shakes her head. "How didn't I know this story?" She looks around at the rest of the table and is met with shrugs. "Did any of you know?"

"And how didn't you just spill all of this after it happened?"

Joel asks. "Like when I got back from Florida? I barely even re-member that trip."

"It's just…not an exciting story to tell?" I wince. "I mean, no one died. I didn't really want to relive it again, even then. Even telling it right now."

"Well, sure, but that doesn't mean it wasn't some kind of wildly traumatic experience." Rebecca leans on the table. "Do you need anything from us? Like, I imagine this is a pretty trig-gering thing for you right now."

"I don't know. Maybe?" I shrug. "It's not something we talk about a lot at home, and none of you have ever turned to me and asked, *So when did you know you were adopted?*" I laugh. "Which is good, 'cause that's super personal, and I'm good not talking about it, and would love to never discuss it again. It's not like I have a lot of experience unpacking all of this. We read that book and then I feel like we never really talked about it again."

"It's okay, man." Joel reaches out and squeezes my shoulder. "So, what's the plan?"

"What do you mean what's the plan?" I snort, and poke around at my lunch a little.

"Like…revenge?" he asks. "Are we going to put something in the food you make? Little bit of laxative?"

"Alright, cool it, Scorpio." I roll my eyes at him. "And be-sides, that's technically poisoning someone. Didn't we watch *American Vandal* together? I would love to not go to jail." I sigh and nudge at some ketchup with a fry. "I don't know, I'll prob-ably just skip school tomorrow, fake being sick. It's the easiest solution to avoid all that drama from him."

"Yeah, but is it cathartic?" Rosiee asks. "Will you get a sense of catharsis, a sense of closure, by just not confronting it?"

"Jesus, Rosiee, you take Mrs. Drummond's Intro to Shake-speare class and suddenly it's all catharsis this, catharsis that." Anna snorts, and Rosiee swats at her.

"Shut up, my point stands." Rosiee smirks and crosses her

arms. "I think confronting this will be good for you, is all I'm saying."

"Hmm." I glance over at Joel, who shrugs. "Maybe. I'm not even sure what I'd make, though. The best I do at home is reheat Hot Pockets, never mind cooking..." I squint, trying to think, and I look back to Joel. "What *would* I make?"

"Why would I know?" He laughs.

"I mean... I'm half Honduran so..." I wince.

"Because I'm Cuban I should know what Honduran food is?" He scowls at me, playfully.

"Oh, my God, I hate talking about this stuff. My parents didn't teach me anything about my background." I rub my hand over my face. "I mean, aren't Cuba and Honduras close to one another?"

"That's like saying New Jersey is close to Canada!" Joel laughs. "There's a whole *sea* right there."

"Ugh." I groan. "I guess I'm gonna have to google."

"I'm just busting your chops. I know it's a weird space for you." He smiles, patting my shoulder again. "I think it's a strange spot for all of us too, though, right?" He looks around at the table, everyone responding with various shrugs. "I mean, sure, I know I mostly talk about my Cuban side, but I'm half Portuguese, just like Mrs. Esteves. But whenever she talks about her family and their lives back home, it's all just foreign to me. My mom isn't really connected to her heritage, not the way my father is."

"And you'd never know how proud your dad is," Rosiee says. "He only has like five Cuban flags on his car."

"Wait, Sean, aren't you half Italian or something?" Rebecca asks me, and then looks over at Anna. "Can you just bring in pasta and call it a day?"

"Yeah, but is the easy route as *cathartic*?" Anna smirks, nudging Rosiee with her elbow.

"I hate you." Rosiee laughs. "I don't know, Sean, I don't think you should stress over this so much. I don't think any of us look like our family. And it doesn't matter."

"It kinda does, though." I shrug. "It's a hard thing to explain. The whole adoption thing. It's less about looking like someone and more of this...feeling. You carry it around in your chest, and it likes to spring up at inconvenient times to remind you that it's there. When someone in your family gets married or has a holiday party and you just stick out. No one says anything, but you just feel it."

Rosiee exhales. "Yeah, I guess I'm not really sure what that's like," she says. "But all of us are here for you, regardless. And Rebecca will totally make you a lasagna."

I groan and take my phone out to start looking up recipes.

"Hey, sweetheart!" Mom chimes as I walk in through the door, tossing my jacket onto the shoe rack that's less for shoes and more for anything you want to carelessly throw on it. I fling my backpack onto the couch and make my way through our living room and into the small kitchen, where she and Dad are both sitting across from each other on their laptops.

Dad reaches for a LaCroix can, and Mom swipes at his hand. He grabs a Sprite next to it and she gives him a thumbs-up, which I don't think he sees. They've been working remotely ever since the pandemic, and just never went back to the office. Which for them I think is a good thing. The two of them are like a sitcom family, always happy to fuss over one another and me, in ways that almost feel...not quite real. Like there's just too much love, and they aren't sure what to do with it all.

I'll admit, sometimes it makes me wonder how I fit in that puzzle. The two of them are so warm and so open, and I like to keep everything close to my chest. Better to avoid talking too much about my feelings or what's really going on.

Mom's a journalist and Dad... I don't know what he does. Something in human resources? He works one of those jobs where whenever I ask him what he's been up to, he shrugs and mutters, "Same old."

Which makes me want to make sure I never have a job like that. It's something he presses anytime conversations about college come up. *You don't want to end up like me, Sean.* Well, what do you do exactly, Dad? *Oh, don't worry about it. You just don't want to do it.*

Though I suppose in that way we do have something in common. Dancing around whatever truth is there. He doesn't have to say he's unhappy with what he does. The absence of saying it does it already.

"How was school?" Mom asks, typing away at something.

"Fine, I guess. Mrs. Esteves was out."

Dad nearly spits out his soda.

"What?" he asks, coughing. He looks away from his computer at me. "How is that even possible? Back when I was a student, she never missed a single day. The old battle-ax."

Mom reaches over and slaps at his hand.

"Hey!" He laughs.

"Don't talk like that." She huffs and gets back to typing.

"Well, I'd hate to have to fill her shoes," he says, shutting his laptop. He leans back in his chair, one of the two office chairs that are now somewhat permanent fixtures in our kitchen and grabs his seltzer. "Who was your sub?"

"Yeah...it's, um... Mr. Brandt," I say, carefully.

Mom's fingers stop typing.

Dad puts down his soda can with a soft plink against the table.

"That asshole is still a teacher!" Mom snaps, her eyes flitting over to me.

"Don't talk like that," Dad says, smirking.

"There's a difference between talking about a beloved icon of our local education system, who is also a Fulbright scholar, and that douchebag who scarred our child and drove that pub on Main Street into the ground," Mom snaps.

"I don't think I'm *scarred*," I grumble, crossing my arms.

"I'm gonna email the principal," Mom says, looking back at her computer, her fingers flying over the keys again.

"Hon—" Dad starts.

"What?" she asks, stopping and slamming her laptop shut. "How—how did they let him back in a classroom?" She groans with frustration and looks over at me. "What do you need right now? How can we support you? Do you need to take off for the week, maybe we could do another history trip or something? Boston?"

"No, it's okay. I think… I'm gonna deal with it." I nod. "It'll be cathartic."

Dad and Mom both sit back in their seats and look at one another.

Dad shrugs and opens his laptop again. "You get that vocabulary from your journalist mother, that's for sure."

After a full afternoon and evening of searching for a recipe that might be usable, I've stumbled on a few options that feel somewhat possible knowing my parents and what we tend to have in the house. Or, at least, what I might be able to pick up at the 24-hour CVS a few blocks away. I wait for Mom to finally shut her laptop long after Dad's gone to sleep and watch her, rubbing her eyes as she heads upstairs, the laptop under her arm.

"Don't stay up too late," she says, making her way up.

"I won't!" I call after her over the Netflix movie playing in front of me. Once I hear her door close, I hurry into the kitchen. I look through all our cabinets for something, anything. Just…a lone ingredient that resembles wherever the hell I come from.

I know I could make like, a pitcher of horchata if we have enough rice. I had it at that Mexican restaurant downtown a few weeks back, although it's made a little differently in Honduras. Or rice pudding, even. I don't think I've ever seen anything resembling a tortilla in our house, save for the nights when Dad attempts to make tacos, so the idea of whipping up a bunch of pupusas is impossible, I think. Will CVS have tortillas in the food section? Maybe?

Chefs, my parents are not. There's a wild amount of different pasta and various sauces, as my mom's go-to is any kind of dish that can be prepared the same way spaghetti is. We also have a whole bunch of soup, as Dad is eternally happy to eat a grilled cheese with bacon paired with any kind of bisque. Spices are everywhere for all the meats that are in the freezer. I take a whole bundle of spices out and set them on the counter, and behind them there are instant packets of rice...

Rice!

I take a bunch of the instant packets out. There are a couple dozen of them, which after ninety seconds in the microwave, basically help my parents hack whatever quick dinner they are whipping up. I line them up on the counter and look up a horchata recipe, thumbing through the differences between the drink in different countries and...it'll take eight hours. Twelve hours? Okay. Okay, this is impossible.

What about the rice pudding?

Okay. No. You have to use condensed milk? I scour our cabinets, but...we don't even have regular milk in the fridge. Is that something you can get at a CVS?

I don't have to show up with anything. I can just stay home. Catharsis and closure, I don't need it, I don't need to prove something to that guy. The guy who sent me and my mom walking home from our school, her hand shaking in mine, my mind reeling, my world unraveling at the revelation while wondering, questioning, all the things that I knew about myself. Questions I never thought to even ask. I've never even visited Honduras—what am I doing here? I've barely left New Jersey.

I lean against the marble countertop, and I just can't help myself.

I start crying.

I don't know anything. And this teacher is going to put me on the spot again. I'm not going. I don't have to. I'm not—

"Hey."

I look up, and it's Mom, leaning against the doorless frame that leads into the kitchen. She's in her bathrobe, her hair pinned up on the top of her head, and she looks...tired. She's got those blue-tinted reading glasses on that I usually see her wearing while writing at the kitchen table or in the living room.

"Working late?" I ask, wiping at the tears on my cheeks. I don't want her to see me like this, her or Dad for that matter, having a meltdown over adoption-related stuff. I try my best to avoid it entirely, just as they have all these years. Why bring something up that could potentially hurt all of us? "I thought you went to bed."

"Don't worry about that," she says, taking her glasses off. She walks over to me at the counter and looks at the mess of ingredients on the marble. "What's, um... What's all this, Sean?"

And I let it all out.

Mr. Brandt's return to that assignment. Talking about it with my friends. The idea that it might make me feel better to whip something up from where I'm "from" and show him. But how here, now, in the kitchen, I'm surrounded by evidence that I don't know anything about my background. I'm surrounded by questions and no answers.

"You know," my mom starts, and inches around me, grabbing some loose-leaf tea out of a canister. She taps some of it into one of those Keurig pods, in a gesture that would likely offend anyone really into tea or coffee. "When your father and I decided to adopt, there were all these classes we had to take. Can you imagine? Classes? You can have a baby the, um...well, old-fashioned way, I suppose, and there's no class requirement. You just sort of figure all that stuff out as you go. Your aunts sure did."

The Keurig sputters to life, pouring a stream of tea into an overly large mug. The kitchen goes from smelling like a dozen

different ingredients, all the spices I'd laid out on the countertop next to the unopened instant rice, to hibiscus and orange
peels. She pours a bit of tea into two smaller cups and hands
me one, motioning for me to join her at the kitchen-table-but-
usually-her-office.

"Go ahead." She gestures at the cup, and I take a sip. And
weirdly, it calms me down a bit.

"Thanks."

"Here's what I learned, Sean. From all of that, and from my
time as a journalist," she says, after taking a sip of her own.
"There are always going to be these people who expect you to
know all the answers right away. But that's not how life works,
is it? You take your time. You gather the facts that make a story
feel more…comfortable. Not necessarily comfortable to hold
or to tell, because often times some of the best stories are a *little*
uncomfortable, but comfortable in that you're a little more sure
of it every single step of the way.

"Your story isn't one that's going to be summed up nice and
neat with a single recipe." She smiles, and swipes at a tear on my
face. "It's just not, and that's okay. But I want you to know that
your father and I are here for you, when it comes to searching
for all of those ingredients."

She sniffles, and when I glance back up at her, I see that she's
crying.

"Mom, you don't have to—"

"I know what I signed up for, sweetheart," she says, reaching
out and hugging me tight. "Our search began when we started
looking for you, and you filled a broken place in our hearts
here. But that search only really ends for me, and for your father, when you feel as whole as we do."

"I don't even know what to say or what I want to look for,"
I blubber, talking into her shoulder.

"It's okay." She pats my back. "Few people ever do."

I let go, and take a step back, and look over at the countertop, sniffling.

My eyes settle on the baking soda.

I grab the little box and look up at my mom. A tear trickles
down her cheek and she wipes it away.

"Okay." She nods. "Let's get started."

My heart is pounding as I walk into my History class, and it's
mostly full already. A bunch of my classmates are milling about
each other's desks, some with what looks like whole casserole
trays in front of them. Did they carry around those things all
morning? Did they just...sit in a locker for the past four hours?
I make a mental note to maybe not try anything as I walk my
way over to Joel.

"Hey, man, you didn't text me." He nods at my backpack.
"Is there anything in there?"

"Yeah." I unzip my pack and pull out a little loaf of Irish soda
bread, and set in on my desk in front of me.

He snorts out a laugh.

"That...is not a traditional Honduran dish." His eyes flit up
and he grins at me. "Someone made a bold decision."

I shrug.

"What did you make?" I ask, noting his empty desk.

"Psh." He scoffs. "I'm not playing his game. You want my
grandmother's flan, you have to date one of my aunts or uncles,
just like everybody else. He's probably just using us for research
for his next failed restaurant."

I laugh and look around. Everyone's got a little something
from where they're "from" or whatever. I can't really recognize
much. It's all in Tupperware and glass trays covered with plastic wrap, paper plates and napkins strewn about nearby. I look
down at the little loaf of bread, definitely not enough for everyone in the class to have a piece, but that's not the point. There's
enough to show Mr. Brandt.

The classroom door swings open.

My heart pounds in my chest.

And…it's Mrs. Esteves.

"Hey, everyone," she says, peering in while lingering in the doorframe. She looks a little harried. Like she's in a rush to get someplace, but at the same time wildly tired. She glances around and her eyes settle on Joel. "Where's the substitute?"

"I dunno." He shrugs.

"Ugh," she grumbles, rubbing her forehead. She makes her way into the class and rummages around in her desk, pulling out a stack of papers and a notebook. "I'm sorry, I know it's a bit out of character for me to miss any days here, but I'll be out the rest of the week."

Whines of protest erupt from everyone.

"I know, I know." She smiles. "My, um… Well, I'll just say it. My husband and I adopted a little girl, and it all happened rather fast. Suddenly, after what's felt like years of waiting, there was this baby in our house, and I need some time to get things adjusted and figure out how sleep works again…"

I look down at the soda bread in my lap.

"No idea how to do any of this." She laughs and swipes at a tear. "But I'll be back, and we'll get started on…" She squints, like she's trying to remember. "Ah, yes. Civil War."

I don't think I've ever seen Mrs. Esteves struggle to remember anything.

"You all be good. And be extra nice to those parents of yours. Whew." And with that, she hustles out the door. The classroom erupts in muttering and talking, and I glance down at the soda bread, feeling this strange tug to get up out of my seat.

I grab the loaf and head toward the door.

"Dude, where are you going?" Joel shouts after me.

"I'll be right back!" I yell back and bound out of the classroom.

I see Mrs. Esteves down the hall, making her way toward the

stairs…and Mr. Brandt walking toward me. I hurry, walking as fast as I can before jogging a little.

"Sean, class begins in—" Mr. Brandt starts.

"Don't care!" I yell back, reaching Mrs. Esteves at the stairs.

"Mrs. Esteves, hey." I exhale, a little winded. An athlete, I am not.

"Oh, Sean." She smiles and looks down in my hands. "What is… Why do you have bread with you? In fact, why did all the students have food—"

"It's…not important." I laugh. "Substitute assignment thing. But, um…you know I'm adopted, right?"

"Yes, Sean." She smiles again, warmly.

"Well, it's just… I know it's not easy. For the kids, for the parents. 'Cause you know, I'm a kid, and my parents are parents, and… Well, it's just, if you wanted to talk about it, you know. I'm around. So are my parents. They'd probably like that."

"Oh." She lifts a hand to her chest. "Sean, that's…so wildly sweet. I'll… I'll have to take you up on that. Maybe find a way to talk to your mom without it being weird."

"It won't be." I smile. "I promise."

I look down at the little loaf of bread in my hand and offer it to her.

"Any chance you want this?" I ask. She takes it, staring at it quizzically. "It's Irish soda bread, this thing my parents and I do. Used to do. Maybe we will do it again, I don't know. New moms need to eat, right?"

"Don't you need this for your assignment?" she asks, handing it back to me.

"I don't." I laugh. "I really don't."

★ ★ ★ ★ ★

THE MORTIFICATION

By Shannon Gibney

Ann Arbor, Michigan, 1990

When Simone felt something moving down the inseam of her jeans, her whole body froze, so that she stopped mid-step and caused Kelly to bump into her. The object was halfway down her thigh when she realized with horror that it would soon fall out of her pant leg and onto the floor, her embarrassment clear for all the mall patrons to see.

"What the hell, Simone?" Kelly grumbled behind her.

When Simone still did not move, Kelly simply stepped around her and kept walking in the direction of JCPenney, the next store the girls had agreed to visit.

As the object ran down her calf, Simone wracked her brain for what it could possibly be. Had she forgotten to throw the toilet paper away at the bathroom and it had miraculously ended up in her underwear or just below it? Had some part of her jeans frayed and was now disintegrating from the inside out? The pos-

sibilities were endless, and she did not want to find out which
one was true.

Cate took her elbow. "What's wrong?" She peered into Simone's face. "Are you hurt?"

Cate was Simone's best friend, and also in the eighth grade at
Clague Middle School. Cate and Kelly were next-door neighbors
and had grown up doing everything together—particularly the
things girls were not supposed to do, like catching crayfish in
the creek and playing Dungeons & Dragons. Simone had come
into the picture in fifth grade when her family had moved from
Grand Rapids to Ann Arbor, and she appeared in one of Cate's
dance classes, cracking jokes and suddenly making tap, bal-
let, and creative movement fun. The two had been inseparable
ever since. Simone was sometimes invited to hikes and camping
trips with Cate and Kelly, and Kelly was sometimes invited to
sleepovers and mall excursions with Simone and Cate. It wasn't
that Simone and Kelly disliked each other *exactly*, it was more
like they just didn't *get* each other. And Cate seemed to have an
intrinsic comprehension of this dynamic. Still, Simone never felt
completely comfortable when hanging out with the two of them.

"I'm…" Simone tried to formulate words but was finding it
exceedingly difficult. Just then the object slid out the bottom
of her pant leg. It was the pad she had carefully tried to affix
to her underwear earlier that afternoon, but which had looked
precarious even then.

Cate followed Simone's eyes. "Oh, my God. Is that—"

"Nothing!" Simone reached down and snatched it off the
ground as fast as she could. She crushed it in her palm, and then
gingerly placed her hand in the pocket of her jacket. "It's nothing," she said, smiling awkwardly at Cate. Now her hand would
smell like blood and sweat and whatever else was down there
and made that part of her body smell so pungent. Disgusting.
She needed to find a trash can. And after that, another bathroom
to wash up in and stem the now open flow with toilet paper.
She started walking again and pulled Cate beside her with her

uncontaminated hand. A few feet ahead of her, Kelly's bright red winter coat stood out against a family in grays and browns.

Cate covered her mouth to mask her laughter, but Simone could feel her shaking.

"Stop!" Simone hissed. "It's not funny. I'm mortified."

This just made Cate laugh harder. "What does that mean?"

Simone was surprised to find a hiccup of laughter in her belly, too. The situation was dire...but also, she had to admit, at least a little comical. If it were happening to someone else, it would be much funnier. She looked around to see if anyone had taken notice of the incident. A mother was fighting with a toddler over a toy he did not want to hand over, and to their left, some high school boys were fiddling with shiny metal night vision binoculars just inside The Sharper Image. A middle-aged woman on their right laughed a little too loudly at a joke her smarmy boyfriend was telling. Simone sighed with relief—no one besides Cate had witnessed her catastrophic period failure.

"What does it mean?" Simone hissed in Cate's ear. "It means you will never *ever* mention this to anyone," she said. "*Especially* not Kelly."

In some ways, Kelly was as much of a misfit as Simone was at Clague Middle School. She was an unabashed jock who cared more about soccer and softball and field hockey than who was dating who this week or who had lost ten pounds or who had the cutest new Esprit top or who had flunked the pre-algebra test. She frequently interrupted conversations or made random inappropriate comments...and didn't even seem to notice it. As far as Simone could tell, the one thing Kelly had going for her was the same thing Cate had going for her: they were both white. This meant that, even though Shana Heim, Nicole Evans, and all the other *cool* white kids looked down on them, they still gave them a free pass, and didn't bother them in class or in the hallways. And the Black kids basically didn't see them at all, they blended in so well with all that white. Not so for Simone, who was mixed. The Black kids were fond of calling her *Oreo* and wondered why she was *always tryna act white* by getting good grades and pegging her pants. And the white kids stood askance at the commotion, some laughing, some ignoring the spectacle, others pitying it. Simone tried not to resent Cate and Kelly for their ability to blend in, despite being just as much of a nerd as she was, but it was hard. They also listened to Madonna's *True Blue* until the tape in the cassette wore thin, memorizing every word. They, too, could not have said why Janet Jackson's *Rhythm Nation* was such a big deal, while all the Black kids in the hallways at school were busy performing every step, belting out the chorus. To Simone, Cate and Kelly's whiteness was their superpower—one they didn't even know they had.

"That's not what mortification means," said Cate. She shook with laughter.

"See, you used a derivative of the word. You're familiar with it," Simone said dryly.

Cate eyed her sideways. "Doesn't mean I know what it means. Just that I heard my mom use it twice." She nudged her friend playfully. "And it also means that I should definitely tell Kelly about all of this. And everyone else in Mr. Gregory's class."

Simone felt her face go hot. Cate liked to tease her friends in order to show affection, but sometimes she took it too far. Like the time she made a zucchini chocolate cake for Simone's birthday party, tricked her into eating it in front of all their friends, and then pronounced that Simone had just enjoyed something she professed to hate.

Simone spotted a trash can at the entrance to JCPenney and headed straight for it. "You can't even joke about things like that, Cate," she said, imagining what Keisha Jackson and Jared Henry and the rest of the Black kids would say if they somehow got wind of this. She would never hear the end of it. It would probably follow her in infamy to high school next year. Simone thought that the Black kids hated her so much because she was mixed, and because they thought she put on airs, and because she was good in school...but she wasn't even sure. *You ready for next period, bitch?* she could almost hear Jared shouting at her down the hall as she headed to class. She smiled, despite herself. It would be a hurtful thing to say, but also very clever. Her superpower was constantly coming up with stories about things that hadn't happened, and probably never would, but were nevertheless immensely compelling.

"Just don't touch me with your right hand," Cate whispered to her. "And we're good."

They had never talked about the fact that Simone's dad was Black and her mom was white, and that sometimes people looked at their family strangely when they were out in public. Or that Simone felt more white than Black on the inside, but that she knew the world saw her as Black.

When they reached Kelly, she was looking at a navy knit pullover with a terrier on it at the front of the store. Simone had noticed that Kelly had an affinity for dogs on shirts...or dogs on anything, for that matter.

"But of course," Simone said, surreptitiously dropping the notorious pad in the trash can as they entered the store. "Find me a bathroom, and I will completely disinfect the offending member."

"Sorry," said Cate. "Wish I had something on me to give you as a replacement, but I used up the last one in my purse last week."

They strode over to Kelly. "That's cute, though," Cate said to Kelly as she put the pullover up to her chest. "You could definitely pull that off."

Kelly looked doubtful. "You think so? My mom is always telling me I need to *stop with the dog stuff.*"

Cate laughed, then shook her head. "No way. She's old and doesn't know what she's talking about."

Kelly's expression didn't change. "If you say so," she said.

"I say so."

Simone was relieved that Kelly had apparently forgotten all

about her freezing up in the middle of the mall for no apparent reason and bumping into her.

She backed away from her friends, scanning the store for any bathroom signs. "Be back in a sec... Gotta handle some business," she said softly.

Kelly wasn't paying attention to her at all, still immersed in examining the sweater.

"Of course, you might wanna get some shoulder *pads* to beef up the look..." Cate said to Kelly loudly, just as Simone was turning around.

Simone whipped around, and Cate winked at her.

Simone felt like her whole body was metal again. Heat rose in her cheeks and neck, and she checked to see if anyone was looking. The department store was bare; they were the only ones in their section. Lucky for Cate.

Kelly looked from Cate to Simone to Cate again. "What the hell?" she said.

Swear words. That was another thing Kelly spit out of her mouth like jawbreakers.

"What's going on with you two?"

Cate collapsed in laughter, and Simone narrowed her eyes. Plenty of embarrassing things happened to Cate, like Kevin Miller picking his nose in front of her in band and then telling her he liked her loud enough for everyone to hear, or her miniskirt ripping straight up the middle when she sat down in Social Studies—but nothing ever really seemed to *stick* on her. It was like every mishap was an aberration, whereas a pad dislodging from your underwear and falling down your pant leg in the middle of Briarwood was completely on brand for Simone, it seemed to her. She was just that kind of dork. She knew she was being melodramatic, but she didn't care. It wasn't her fault her mother hadn't shown her how to put a pad on properly.

Simone pivoted and walked briskly around the circuitous aisles that seemed to go nowhere, finally asking a salesperson where she might find the bathroom. The saleswoman was a smartly

dressed Black woman, presumably in her twenties, wearing wet
n wild peach lip gloss Simone had drooled over in the latest issue
of *Seventeen*. She was folding T-shirts when Simone approached
and gave her a conspicuous once-over as she neared.

Simone felt her face flush. She always felt inadequate around
most Black folks—something she could never talk about with
her father or brothers.

"It's over by jeans, then take a right," the woman told her,
her tone professional but also slightly cutting.

Simone nodded, thanked her, and turned toward the huge
Levi's jeans sign to her right.

"Hey, you're mixed, right?" she heard the woman say to her
back.

Simone stopped mid-stride, her entire body locked in place.
What the hell? She somehow managed to turn her head around
enough to meet the woman's eyes. They weren't cruel or mis-
chievous—just curious. Still, Simone could not shake the sensation of being a circus curiosity. "Yes," she said softly, and
shuffled away.

Once in the restroom, she debated what to do. A tampon dispenser hung on the wall. For ten cents, she could buy one. But
she didn't know how to put a tampon in. When her mother had
tried to show her how last summer, both of them visibly uncomfortable, she had balked. *You mean you put that* inside *you?*
she had asked incredulously. Her mother nodded, wordlessly. A
full minute passed as Simone imagined the logic and ramifica-
tions of sticking a bunch of cotton encased in cardboard up your
vagina. *No,* she said softly. Then, *No way.* That was when her
mother had handed her a box of pads, telling her that they were
easier to use anyway, and backed out of the room. She clearly
could not wait to get out of there and didn't even bother showing her how to stick the pad onto her underwear the right way.
Or maybe she just assumed it was obvious? Simone laughed now
at the memory. *Okay, so she's white, Leonard. But does she have to*

be that *white?* was the phrase that came to her in moments like these. She had overheard Aunt Jeanie, her father's older sister, say that to him once after her mother had been especially embarrassed over something very small.

"If only," she said, looking anxiously from the tampon dispenser to her face in the mirror. Her short frizzy, curly hair—another source of consternation among the Black kids—actually lay flat against her head today. Simone was pleased to see that she looked as cute as she imagined she would this morning when she had laid out her pink denim-wash jeans and baggy white sweatshirt for the trip to the mall. She sighed. But looking cute was not going to help her now.

She took a dime out of her purse and gingerly stepped toward the tampon dispenser. She would be fourteen in four months, had camped alone with her brothers in the Upper Peninsula last winter, still always got picked over boys for ball games in gym because she was so good. Simone Palmer was no pushover. She could handle a simple tampon. Her hand shaking, she deposited the coin into the machine and slowly turned the lever. The tampon came out at the bottom, maybe two inches long, and encased in a thin white plastic wrapper. She stared at it for a minute, trying to imagine herself confidently standing over the toilet, inserting the cotton into a part of her body she could only see with a mirror and had never wanted to. *Where does it go, exactly?* She knew from Health class that it went up the vagina, but what if she sat on it weird, or got bumped, or something...unforeseen...happened, and it got shoved into another part of her where it clearly shouldn't be?

Suddenly, the bathroom door opened. Simone yelped and dropped the tampon into the trash beside the sink. Then she ducked into one of the stalls, shut the door, and locked it. *I do not want to be here. I do not want to be here.* She shut her eyes tightly and thought about being in her big warm bed at home, her warm fuzzy blankets all around her. *Now what are you gonna do? You're still bleeding.* This thought forced her eyes open, and she watched someone with a scuffed-up pair of Nikes shuffle into the stall beside her. Probably a mom or a grandma or something. She realized that her feet were not in the position they would need to be in if she were, in fact, going to the bathroom. So, she backed up a little and sat on the toilet. She could see from the position of the woman's feet in the next stall that she was doing the same.

Why didn't I bring some extra pads along? She adjusted the strap of her purse, removed it from her shoulder, and hung it on the hook on the door. What else were purses for anyway, besides hiding contraband that you didn't want your parents, peers, or God to see? She usually had Now and Laters, Nerds, and Juicy Fruit gum wadded into the bottom right side of the purse, so that they wouldn't be immediately visible when she unzipped it but were nevertheless there and available if you wanted to surreptitiously dig deep enough. The problem was she didn't want any pads to accidentally fall out of her purse. That was why she never packed them when she wasn't on her period, and only packed one or two when she was. She was sure she had an extra one in the deep recesses of her purse when she had left the house earlier that afternoon. But alas, she was wrong.

Simone shifted her weight on the toilet and considered her predicament further. There was some (mostly) invisible rule that you were supposed to go to great lengths to hide that you were on your period when you were on your period. Two months ago, she had left a used pad in the bathroom trash, and her mother had caught up to her that night, shut the door to her room, and whispered that she needed to do a better job of disposing of them. Simone had looked up from her Spanish homework, blinking uncomprehendingly. How did one properly dispose of a pad, anyway? She had simply thrown it in the trash, which her mother told her was not acceptable. She needed to carefully wrap it up in toilet paper, and then *hide it* at the bottom of the trash. It had taken everything she had not to laugh out loud at that moment. *It's not fair to your brothers or your dad to have to see that*. To which Simone had replied, *Is it fair to me that I have to see Phillip's and Christian's pee everywhere on the toilet? Or see them scratch their balls?* Her mother hadn't answered, leaving the room soon after her "lesson" was finished. Simone had closed her textbook, musing on what had just transpired. Basically, what she took from her mother's speech and what she'd picked up from everyone else was that if anyone actually *knew* you were undergoing this monthly bodily ritual, which you had no control over but which half the people in the world went through too, your social capital would effectively be eviscerated. *Persona non grata, per period*. She laughed, despite herself. Human beings were ridiculous. None of it made any sense at all, but she played along, since she was one.

The toilet flushed in the stall beside her. Simone looked at her watch, an off-brand Swatch, and realized that her dad would be picking them up at the mall's east side in fifteen minutes. She was simultaneously grateful and also annoyed. She was hoping to find some decent hoop earrings at JCPenney, but there would not be time for that now. Swiping some toilet paper off the roll, she realized she was still mostly just grateful to get out of being in a public place *in my condition*. She cracked up for a second. If she could make it home without getting a stain on Dad's newly upholstered seats, she would count herself very, very lucky. She carefully folded the toilet paper into double squares four times. Then she stood up, pulled her pants down, and placed the toilet paper in the center of her underwear. If she had known a proper prayer to say for the occasion, she would have said it then.

"Simone, are you in there?" Cate's light still-childlike voice carried into the bathroom.

Simone cleared her throat. "Just a minute," she said as evenly as possible. Then she turned around in the stall to complete the ruse and flushed the toilet.

The mystery woman was drying her hands at the sink beside her. She was Asian American, very thin, and her hair was streaked with gray. She smiled at Simone for a minute before walking out.

Simone felt like they had been through a war together, each of them taking care of their personal business side by side in a bathroom stall, and even though they had never spoken. Simone smiled back. She wondered if the woman had ever had a catastrophic pad failure, and was suddenly seized with an irrational and slightly scary urge to ask her.

Simone stepped to the sink, rubbing the liquid soap between her hands, making sure to get all the fingers and every piece of skin, in order to kill all the nasty pad germs that were undoubtedly lurking there. "God, being a girl is such a mess," she said. She did not want to be a boy. She just wished, in times like these, that being a girl was a little bit easier.

She dried her hands and stepped out into the store again.

Cate and Kelly were seated in two big cushy chairs, Kelly clutching a JCPenney bag in her lap.

"So you got it, then?" Simone asked her.

Kelly looked at her blankly. "Huh?"

Simone pointed at the bag. "The navy pullover. You got it."

Kelly's eyes opened wider. "What? Oh, yeah. Cate convinced me."

On the green cushy chair, sitting kitty-corner, Cate smirked. "More like dragged her, kicking and screaming."

Simone smiled. "Just another day at the mall." Then she gestured to them both. "Come on, we gotta get moving. My dad's gonna pick us up in ten."

The girls acquiesced and soon they were out of the store, passing Claire's, where earrings cost a dollar, and the sweet, sugary aroma of Mrs. Fields freshly baked cookies. Everyone was so exhausted from the day's adventures that they barely spoke until they were moments from the double doors that led outside to the mall's east entrance. It was then that Kelly slipped something thin and plastic into her palm.

Simone looked down, surprised. "What... What's this?"

Kelly shrugged, the same uncomfortable look on her face as her mother's when she caught her with her first period. "It's a pad. For next time."

Simone's jaw dropped.

"Cate told me what happened. I wanted to give it to you while you were in there, but I figured you were handling your business alone."

Simone sent Cate a withering look. And to her credit, Cate cowered a bit.

"Look, it's no big deal," Kelly said to Simone. "I know that bathroom and the tampon machine inside it well myself. Something similar happened to me last month." She even smiled at the end of this revelation.

This turn of events stunned Simone into silence. She hadn't considered before that although Kelly was white, and a complication in her friendship with Cate, she was also a girl. There were things their bodies did and meant in the world that they couldn't control. The shape of a nipple showing through a thin shirt, and the lascivious grin it elicited from an older man. The way her hips were beginning to spread, and how this sudden tightness in her miniskirt both thrilled and terrified her. The pubic hairs they needed to make sure they diligently clipped around the edges of their bathing suits, so all would believe the fiction that they were hairless there. They were all attempting to understand their changing, heedless bodies. And this was something that connected them.

A gray Jeep Grand Cherokee wound its way around the parking lot, slowly making its way toward them. When her dad pulled up, he opened the door and asked, "Well, how'd it go, girls?"

Simone raised her eyebrows at her friends, who gave her two half smiles in response. They climbed into the seats, and Simone said, "It was fine, Dad."

★ ★ ★ ★ ★

BETWEEN LAYERS

By Tara Sim

I'm staring at the colorful display of burfi behind the display glass, practically salivating over the rose syrup–soaked gulab jamun, when a familiar word snags my ear in a lilting question:

"—beti?"

I glance at the cash register where my mom's chatting with the woman behind the counter. We're picking up our usual order of Indian sweets from the shop downtown. The red boxes are already stacked and bagged on the counter, ready to be brought to the café and arranged behind our own display glass.

I don't speak Punjabi, but I know what the woman said. *Beti. Daughter.*

That's your daughter?

My mom laughs lightly and replies that yes, I am her daughter. The woman's eyes go wide, though she's fascinated rather than scandalized. That's my cue to pick up the bag and walk outside to the car, a prickling sensation in my chest.

"She thought you were my daughter-in-law," Mom says with

amusement as we drive back to the café. "Apparently, they get a lot of those there."

I squeeze silent the little voice in me that wants to be offended. How could I be offended? Mom is brown, and I'm white. Or rather, white-passing. No one would know just from looking at me that I'm biracial, let alone Indian. There's no reason for me to be upset at the woman for assuming I'm not part of her culture. For assuming that I come from some middle-class white family where black pepper is the spiciest thing they can tolerate.

Whatever. Not like it hasn't happened before.

When we get back to the café, Arjun's wiping down the round tabletops and bopping to something that blasts through his earbuds. I recognize the faint tinny notes as a rap song my mom would *very* much prefer be kept in his earbuds and not played over the speaker system (which is usually reserved for peaceful, mystical-sounding music). Mom tries to get Arjun's attention, but the boy's too invested in his self vs. self lip sync battle. I'm still in a bad mood, so I slam my hand down on the table and he jolts.

"Jesus, what?" He pulls one earbud out. He notices Mom behind me and balks. "Ah, hi, Mrs. David."

"Hi, Arjun. Will we be ready to open in ten?"

"Yup."

"Perfect. Lydia, can you put the sweets out?"

"Sure."

Arjun goes back to his lip-synching while I open the display case and start taking out the sweets. Arjun's part-time—he goes to the same high school as me and was able to get a job here thanks to a friend of the family—and I can't help but be envious he doesn't have to spend more than four hours here at a time. My mom owns the place, which means I'm here *all* the time. I work here, I do homework here, and a couple times I've even slept here (Mom keeps a futon in her office).

Chai Time is Mom's crowning achievement, so I can't be

too mad. Though she'd worked in Indian restaurants nearly her whole life, she'd always wanted to open a tea and chaat café of her own. It wasn't until I was ten that she was able to finally get the finances together and grab a spot near the downtown bustle that was up for lease. Since then, I've been roped into waiting on customers after school and on weekends. Even Dad helps out sometimes if we're short-staffed, though Mom usually lets him rest on weekends, considering he has a nine-to-five as an accountant.

It's a cute place. The walls are painted light green, the tables made of rosewood. We put up some decorative art prints of Indian landmarks, as well as paintings from a local artist. It definitely says *Indian teahouse* without screaming it—aka, it's Westerner friendly.

I use tongs to place the burfi, ladoos, and halva on the stands in our display case while Arjun finishes up and switches the sign to Open. When I was younger, I used to beg Mom to let me do this: arrange the sweets just so, thinking presentation was of the utmost importance. Now I tend to just plop them down. Wherever they land, they land. And if one goes missing... Say, into my mouth...

"You going to Prisha's party next weekend?" Arjun asks as he finally pulls his earbuds out.

I freeze, the tongs nearly bisecting the burfi it's holding, and try not to swear because I'd *completely forgotten about it.*

"We are!" Mom answers for me, coming out of the back, wearing a red apron that clashes with the walls. "Should be fun. Her mom always goes above and beyond."

And now that Prisha's turning sixteen, no doubt they're going to go all out. Sweet Sixteen and all that. My own sixteenth birthday isn't for another couple months, and I live in perpetual dread of what Mom plans to do. I'm sure it'll involve smashing cake into my face. It *always* ends up with cake in my face. Why is that even a tradition? Who thought of that? Why would you *waste cake*?

But here's the thing: my family's mixed. Dad's a white full-blooded American, and Mom immigrated from India when she was a kid. They made a disturbingly pale child. Everything in my life has been put into three categories: American, Indian, and Blended. I never thought it was weird until I got older and realized most people didn't grow up eating roti and tea, or went to parties where their uncles and aunts indulged in intense dance-offs to heavy bhangra music.

I'm sure my own sixteenth birthday party will be Blended, but Prisha's will be one hundred percent Indian. Her family immigrated when she was two—she was born in India, she speaks fluent Punjabi, and her parents still have accents (unlike Mom, who mostly lost hers). This will be a full-on intense dance-off Indian party, complete with catered buffet and a veritable river of Sprite.

Which means it'll be uncomfortable, bordering on insufferable. When it comes to my family's parties, it's always awkward to be inundated with aunts and uncles who playfully ask, "Do you remember who I am? What's my name?" every time they see you, like some weird family tree pop quiz. There's also not much for me to do, since I hate dancing, and there aren't many people my age to hang out with.

But this isn't a family party, it's a *Prisha* party, which comes with its own unique obstacle course.

For one thing, I hate Prisha.

For another, Prisha hates me.

And, of course, it's right at that moment the problem herself walks in, a couple friends trailing behind her. She's dressed in white pants and a crop top, which seems like a weird choice considering the long baggy jacket she's thrown over it. Her long hair's straightened today, and when she tosses her head to throw some of it behind her shoulder, it sends a jasmine-scented breeze in my direction. I cough.

She doesn't look at me, though. She shuffles up to Arjun and kisses him, despite the fact that her boyfriend's supposed to be working. They've been dating for a few months, and he's the only reason she comes here. I have no doubt she'd rather go to a Starbucks or the cute café downtown with the ceramic teacups and amazing brownies.

Although now that I smell the food cooking in the back, that's up for debate. The best perk of Chai Time: free food. Free *good* food. Mom's samosas are delicious, and the other chef, Vijay, tends to make me a plate of masala poori if I'm having a bad day. Maybe I can ask for one on my break.

I'm just closing up the display case when Prisha and her friends appear at the counter, the only other two desi students at school. The three of them and Arjun make up a little friend group I've been deliberately excluded from, since I guess halves don't count. Prisha's wearing a little smirk in the corner of her mouth.

"We'll all take medium masala chais," Prisha says, and of course she has to order for her friends even though they're like, right there. "And three kaju katlis. Those are—"

"I know which ones they are," I say quickly, my smile more of a grimace.

She raises her eyebrows as she hands over a credit card. She's paying for her friends, too? What kind of power move is that? I refrain from shaking my head as I ring up her order, put the kaju katlis on a plate for them, and turn to the station behind me to start on the chai.

"Oh," Prisha says. "Um. Can your mom make the tea?"

I freeze. "What?"

"She makes it really good."

"She's busy in the back. I make it the exact way she does."

Prisha hesitates, then goes to sit down with her chattering friends. I try my best to ignore the anger trawling through me like a hot itch. Was she seriously implying I couldn't make tea? That my mom's is better just for the fact she's fully, *visibly* Indian and I'm not?

Is that your daughter?

I grit my teeth the entire time I make the tea. It shouldn't surprise me. Prisha always acts like this around me.

The party this weekend is going to suck so hard.

"I don't get it," Kristine says at lunch on Wednesday. The two of us are huddled with our third friend Becca on one of the outdoor school benches that's been marked up so many times the janitors have given up on saving it. "It's a *party.* Which means *cake.* What's not to like?"

I take a moment to sip my bubble tea and chew on the boba, thankful that Becca has her license and was willing to drive us to get it. "It's hard to explain."

"She doesn't like Prisha," Becca says sagely at my side, touching up her makeup in a tiny compact mirror. Her sideswept cornrows fall over one shoulder. "Some beef between them."

"I thought Indians didn't eat beef," Kristine says, blue eyes glinting with barely suppressed glee at her own joke.

"Oh, my *God.*" I kick her under the table and she yelps. "Not funny."

Kristine sniffs in mock offense. "You just don't have taste."

I shake my head but can't help a small smile. Kristine and Becca have actually gone to an Indian party with me before, and they loved it. I guess it's harder for me to explain my dread when the two of them think of my culture as something cool and unique. Which, I mean, it *is*, but it's also really hard to navigate when you're me.

Still, I felt a lot of pride at their wonder. Like I was showing them some other world through a door only I could access.

I trace my finger over a carving of a name on the table's surface—someone named Nick really wanted to leave his legacy here, I guess—and try to think about the upcoming party through my friends' eyes.

Then a small group walks by, laughing over something, and I nearly choke on my boba. Prisha is there, Arjun's arm slung over her shoulder, along with the two other desi students. They've always been tight-knit like this, like some weird South Asian clique I wasn't invited to.

Prisha must feel my stare, because she turns and sees me. She gives a small wave, and I turn back to my own friends with a scowl.

"Dang," Becca mutters. "What did she do, anyway?"

It's not really something she did. It's that she's so confident in her identity, never having to question herself or have others question her. It's that she constantly reminds me that I don't belong.

Like the door only I can access was built with locks on the other side.

There have been opposing forces within me for as long as I can remember. I am twins inhabiting the same body, two chemicals combined to form a unique reaction.

I notice it the most in my parents' shadow. When they walk arm in arm down the street, down a grocery store aisle, even sitting in a movie theater. It was never strange to me as a kid. It's not strange *now*, though now that I'm older I'm aware of the stares we get, people trying to do mental gymnastics to figure out how our family was formed. Like it's any of their business.

My mom was working at a restaurant when the head chef called out sick, so she stepped in. My dad happened to order something that was so ridiculously good—"The best damn curry I'd ever had," he says when he tells the story—that he simply had to give his compliments to the chef. When my mom stepped out, it was supposedly love at first sight.

Getting my maternal grandparents to approve of an interracial wedding, then going through with said wedding, wasn't simple and wasn't without struggle, but the falling in love part was. At least that's what Dad tells me.

Elementary school geography showed me just how far India is from America. But when you love someone, maybe the places you're from blend together, and suddenly your love for the other person becomes home. There are no cities, no countries. You rewrite maps and histories together.

That's always made me feel a little better when it comes to my identity. To me, *white-passing* has always been an adjective, the only term I know to describe what I am. But *passing* is a verb that goes hand in hand with privilege, like how I've been spared from face-to-face racism. But I don't *want* to pass. I don't want to give the impression I'm pushing something away when all I've wanted is to embrace it, when I'm given the chance.

Admittedly, it's something I hardly thought about until a couple years ago. Until Prisha started going to school with me. Until I realized I don't get many chances at embracing.

My stomach's in knots as we pull up to the hotel where the party's being held. There are lines of cars and people in suits and saris navigating through the parking lot. I don't recognize most of them; Prisha isn't related to us, since her family is just friends with mine, but there's some crossover here and there when it comes to cousins and marriages. I couldn't even begin to untangle the knot of our family tree.

I fiddle with the beaded design on my lehenga. They're all going to *stare* at me. Maybe I should have worn a Western-style dress, after all.

But no—that would have been more fodder for Prisha's smirk. And besides, I really like how I look in my lehenga. When I came downstairs, Dad had grinned and said, "Looking sharp!" Even he was wearing a nice sherwani suit my mom had commissioned for him a while back. He looks for any excuse to wear it—it's kinda cute.

The banquet hall is wide and crowded. The floor is that weird velvet carpet you only seem to find in hotels, and dozens of tables with purple tablecloths are filled with chatty aunts and uncles eating and drinking (I notice the obligatory liters of Sprite). There's the buffet against one wall—only appetizers, since dinner won't be brought out until 9:00 p.m. at the earliest—and a loud group of men are getting drinks at the bar.

Mom waves to a group of friends. "Lydia, can you put the gift over with the others?"

"Sure." But my dread escalates at the thought of being on my own surrounded by people I hardly know. I put the wrapped gift on the table with the others—I have no idea what it is, as Mom chose it—and turn around to sidle back to Mom's side, but I've already lost her in the crush.

Dammit. I stand there uselessly, letting the music overhead and the roar of voices wash over me as I silently panic. Just as I make the decision to find the nearest bathroom and hide, I hear a familiar laugh.

I look over and find Prisha and her friends huddled near a table with a large cake. The cake's a towering showstopper decorated with gold leaf, of all things; probably to make up for a substandard cake underneath. But I have no doubt her parents will smoosh some of it in her face all the same. Arjun stands beside her wearing a nice sherwani in dark silver that complements Prisha's gray-and-gold sari.

Her desi friends are here, as well as some other friends from school, who're mostly white. I know their names but I've never talked to them. A quick scan of the banquet hall tells me they're the only partygoers my age here, and I suddenly long for Kristine and Becca.

Hiding in the bathroom it is, then.

But as I'm halfway to the nearest door, Arjun calls out my name and beckons me over. Here we go.

Already Prisha's friends are assessing me. They're dressed in

Western-style outfits and are probably wondering why I'm not. I ignore them and force myself to smile.

"Happy birthday, Prisha."

Cue the smirk. "Thanks. It was actually yesterday, but whatever." Her eyes quickly scan my outfit. "Nice lehenga."

I honestly can't tell if she means it or it's some sort of jab. My pride leans toward the latter. "Thanks." I decide not to return the compliment.

"You work at Chai Time, right?" one of her white friends asks. I'm pretty sure I've seen her come in before.

"Yeah, it's my mom's café."

I can see the exact moment they reassess me. Even though I'm used to it, even though it doesn't usually bother me, something's been digging under my skin lately and wants to be let out.

That's your daughter?

I hate it. I hate the staring, the questions, the incredulity. I hate how even my *own family* will jokingly call me *the white one*, then turn around and be surprised when I don't want to go to their parties. Why would I want to participate in something they're unconsciously trying to push me out of? My mom even gave me a white girl name, like she *wants* me to pass.

I'm not Indian enough. Sometimes I don't even feel American enough. I'm not *enough*.

"You're so lucky," one of Prisha's other white friends says. "You get to eat Indian food whenever you want. It's *so* good."

It takes a lot of willpower not to laugh in her face. In elementary school, I was made fun of for bringing aloo parathas for lunch, and now those same people are so eager to fawn over tikka masala and korma. Those aren't even things I eat often, since Mom mostly makes simple stuff at home. And yeah, sometimes I get tired of it.

I should tell her she's lucky she gets to eat pasta all the time. Or, I don't know, grilled cheeses.

Prisha scowls at me. "What's your problem?"

It takes a moment to realize I said all that out loud. My face grows hot under their stares, some of them surprised (like Arjun) and others bemused.

My patience has been fraying. I didn't even notice when it snapped.

Mortified, I back up, intending to find that bathroom after all and hole up in a stall until Mom's ready to go home. I'll probably be there for hours, considering how much she loves to dance. Good thing I have some horror movies downloaded on my phone.

As I turn, something bumps into my lower back. A table. The whole thing wobbles, and I flail out an arm to catch myself.

I punch a hole right into Prisha's cake.

Although the bhangra music is still blasting, our little bubble is completely, utterly silent as we all stare at my arm. It's like playing Red Light, Green Light and we're all trying our best not to move after a call of red light. But I have to move. My fist is *buried in Prisha's cake.* Which is covered in an *excessive amount of gold leaf.*

Carefully, holding my breath, I extract my hand and wrist. They're covered in vanilla cake and frosting. There is a *crater* in the cake that thankfully doesn't threaten the structural integrity but absolutely threatens the visual appeal.

Mom's going to murder me.

My face is still flaming, my heart pounding like crazy. My mind scrambles for what to say, what to do, but there's nothing but static.

So I do the only thing I can, the one thing I've been trying to do all along: I run to the bathroom, weaving through the crowd as I go.

It's one of those fancy hotel bathrooms, the kind with red plush couches in a separate area. I go down the long line of sinks to the one at the very end, hoping no one comes in and sees me like this. I run the faucet and rub furiously at my hand, trying to get the icing and cake bits off but doing little better than smooshing them around.

That's when the dam in me breaks. It's been building since that trip to the sweets shop, and this was the final blow, as destructive as me swinging my hand into Prisha's cake.

When the door to the bathroom opens, I'm openly crying over my still messy hand. I don't bother to look up, hoping whoever it is will do their business and leave me to mine.

Instead, I hear Prisha say, "Seriously, *what* is your problem?"

I glower up at her. She has her arms crossed, her head tilted slightly to one side. She seems annoyed, but not furious. I suppose I should consider myself lucky for that.

No matter how much we dislike each other, I know full well that I'm in the wrong here. I swallow and try to add soap to the vanilla-scented disaster of my hand. "I'm sorry. I didn't mean to."

Prisha blows out an exasperated breath. "Of course, you didn't *mean* to. It was an accident."

I frown. That wasn't what I was expecting. I'd imagined her marching up to me and demanding me to pay her parents back for the damage, or… I don't know, something disparaging, embarrassing.

"It's just a cake," she drawls when she notices my confusion. "Jesus, look at you. It's not like you punched a baby or something."

I glance at my reflection in the mirror and flinch. My eyes are red, my cheeks flushed, my mouth drawn in a thin grim line.

"But you were rude as hell to my friends," Prisha goes on, leaning a hip against the counter. "I want you to apologize to them. Do that, and I won't tell my parents the truth. I'll say I did it."

I gape at her. "What?"

"Did you not hear me? I said—"

"I *know* what you said. I just can't believe you said it. It's my fault, so I should take the blame. Won't your parents be pissed?"

"Maybe for a minute, but it's whatever. It'll be less fuss if they think I did it, trust me. Then your parents don't have to get roped into it."

"But…" This can't be right. Surely, there's an ulterior motive here somewhere. Like she'll come up to me at school and demand free bubble tea when me and my friends go on boba runs.

She raises an eyebrow. I can't tell if they're naturally thick or if she styles them that way.

"You really think I'm a bitch, don't you?" she asks.

I mean, she's not wrong, but I can't admit to that. "That's not it."

"Then why do you have such a problem with me?"

I finally shut off the faucet. "*I* have a problem with *you?* I know you and your friends think I'm some sort of…joke, or something."

"What are you talking about?"

"Seriously?" I gesture to myself, getting water droplets on my lehenga. "I *am* a joke. No one believes I'm Indian. I get brushed off all the time. Excluded. You even wanted my mom to make you tea instead of me, even though she's the one who taught me how to make it."

She looks a little uncomfortable. "I didn't mean—"

"My mom didn't even bother to teach me Punjabi or give me an Indian name. Everyone assumes I'm only white until I have to *tell* them what I am, and then I get met with stupid questions and comments like, *Oh, you don't look it all*, like *yeah,* I *know* I don't look like it! That's why I have to *tell you!*"

I gasp for breath, my face flushed again in anger and shame. I shouldn't be complaining about this. There are a lot of areas I hold privilege in, and this is one of them: my skin isn't brown. I get to pass; I get to walk into white spaces without anyone knowing any different, without being *treated* different.

But I still mourn. I mourn for some missing piece that would tell me, fully and truly, that I belong with my family, my culture, my identity.

Prisha still has her arms crossed as she asks, "Are you done?"

I turn to rip a paper towel from the dispenser. "Yeah."

She blows out a long breath. "I'm sorry."

I pause in the middle of wiping down my wrist. "What?"

"That I made you feel that way. Like you're...excluded. Or weird or whatever. I'm sorry."

I wait to make sure she isn't joking. She stares at the tiled floor, lips slightly pursed. Slowly, I dry off the rest of my hand and ball up the towel.

"It's fine," I mumble. "Everyone does. You and your friends have your own dynamic. It makes sense you didn't want to include me."

Prisha wrinkles her nose. "We thought you didn't want to be included."

"Why would you think that?"

She scoffs. "Every time you see us, you have this constipated frown on your face. Like you're making right now." I quickly smooth my expression. "It seemed like you didn't want to be friends with us, so we left you alone."

I want to laugh, but if I did the sound wouldn't be amused at all. "You didn't even *ask*."

"Well." Prisha fidgets nervously. "I guess we both assumed things."

Am I seriously hearing this right? Prisha wants to be friends with me? She doesn't hate me?

I think about the door I held open for Kristine and Becca, letting them see a part of my life, a part of my culture. About how it came designed with locks to shut me out.

Maybe I'm the one who put some of them there.

"If you want to hang out with us, you can," Prisha says, her usual haughty tone back. "But we won't force you. Your choice." She turns, then pauses. "Oh, and about the cake."

I tense. I knew it—she's going to make me pay.

"My next five teas at the café are free," she says like a mandate. "And you apologize to my friends for being rude. Then we're even."

She leaves the bathroom, and I blink at her back. That's it? I stand there for a long time, wondering what just happened, what I'm supposed to do now.

I look down at my hand and realize a bit of gold leaf's stuck on my wrist. I peel it off and wonder about exteriors, about how easy it is to judge something based on first appearances. I'm not exempt from that. No one is.

Sighing, I put the gold leaf on my tongue and let it dissolve as I head back to the party. I make my awkward apology to Prisha's friends for my outburst, and it's clear that Prisha's told them to do the same because they rush over themselves to say sorry for generalizing. Later, we laugh together as Prisha's parents playfully shove cake into her face (after they turned the cake around to hide the hole). When I'm handed a slice, I'm surprised at how good it tastes.

As Prisha teases Arjun about something, I remember the woman at the sweets shop and her incredulous tone. There's a wide step between assumption and acceptance, between what you first see and what you later learn when you have to reconcile the two.

Looking over at the dance floor, I see my parents dancing together and smile. I have to remember that I was formed from love, of maps being rewritten, of histories being merged. It's all right to tell people what I am and remind them when I need to, because then it means I'm not passing—I'm embracing.

★ ★ ★ ★ ★

DIFFERENT

By Torrey Maldonado

Middle school sucks. It's been half a year and I thought since this school is close enough to my projects, it'd be lit. Wrong. Mad kids from my projects go here, but we can't link up during the day. My school is in a white neighborhood right on the other side of the highway from our projects, and the school keeps most of us Black, Puerto Rican, and Black Puerto Ricans separate from the white kids. Ask a school grown-up if they do that, and they'll say no. What a lie. If it's easy for us to be in classes with lots of white kids, then why did Ma need to come for a few days to argue with the guidance counselor, then assistant principal to get a meeting with the principal? For what? To show him my good grades and make him switch me into one of the mostly white classes. On the real? I wish I'd stayed in class with my people from the projects. It's not that my new class is too white—that's not the problem.

These white teachers are foul.

Lots of my classmates are foul.

They make me feel like I don't fit. White teachers' eyes don't light up when we Black and Puerto Rican kids walk in rooms. Also, they baby and worship white kids like white kids are God or something. And white teachers give us ZERO credit for saying the same exact stuff white kids say, and we say it BEFORE them. Just the other day, this cool white girl—Jess—defended me. "Mr. Kaplan." She raised her hand, then pointed at me. "Trevor was the first to say what Megan said. Trevor *actually* said it *twice* before she did. But you only told Megan, *Excellent point*, then you kept repeating Trevor's idea and complimenting Megan as if she came up with it."

My other white friend—Elliot—elbowed me. "Jess is feelin' you. Peep how she's calling Mr. Kaplan out for you." I ignored Elliot because Jess was being Jess. She fights anything she feels is racist or sexist. Anyway, wack white teachers are just one reason this class is trash.

Lots of kids who look like me or look like they come from where I'm from aren't. In our projects, mainly everyone is the same: Black, some Puerto Rican. Some families are mixed like mine: Black and Puerto Rican. Still, we the same. We got the same hood dramas, same dreams, same complexions, same features. How we kick it is the same. How we get each other without speaking? We the same. In our projects, a lot of us don't act different like, "Oh, I'm this…not that."

Ma doesn't let us play that game neither of "Oh, I'm this… not that." Just the other day, my older sister's boyfriend who is from a Manhattan projects and is straight African-American— no Puerto Rican family or friends—cracked a joke hating on Puerto Ricans. Ma wagged her finger, "Uh-uh," and told my sister, "He *has* to go." She kicked him out. Ma makes sure our family loves both sides of us. Ma doesn't play when people put down Black people or Puerto Ricans, and she doesn't want us hating either side of us.

But I got to admit, sometimes in this school and in this class, I don't want to be me, and I wish I could pick a side. I just want to fit in, but I know it won't happen because these kids keep re-minding me that we not on the same team. I thought maybe be-cause my classmates who aren't Black look like some family and that they have Puerto Rican–sounding last names that maybe we could be tight. But little by little—in History class and in-teractions—I kept seeing that they see themselves as different.

From jump, they *said* it—they said they different.

In Spanish class, Gisele answered a question, "I'm Cuban, and that's not a thing Cubans do."

Then Alberto—who asks us to call him "Al"—jumped in, "My family is Venezuelan, and we do things differently, too."

I give credit to Hector—the Puerto Rican kid from Staten Island—for saying, "Yeah, we might do some things differently but we're all Latino."

This girl—Valentina, who calls herself Costa Rican, and her family moved from Miami—killed it and corrected Al. "Well, you *could* say that *but* there are so many differences."

Props to our only Puerto Rican teacher for trying to do what Hector did and show how we might be the same. "Class," Mr. Rodriguez said, "there *are* experiences we Latinos share. Who can name some?"

Dumb me. I raise my hand. "Did anyone else have those or-ange blocks of cheese as big as bricks? They'd give them out in the community cent—"

Costa Rican Valentina interrupted me, "Trevor, that sounds like a projects thing."

All the other "Latino" students were dumb quick to nod with her. YO! Why the whole class felt together in one circle, and I was on the outside of it?

The Latino kids in my class didn't grow up how I did, and my Black classmates, too. They call themselves different things. For example, in Social Studies we did this go-around of where in the world our families are from.

Kingsley said, "I'm Jamaican."

Robert was all proud. "Trinidadian."

That African boy said, "I'm from Ghana."

Then they started sharing their experiences and none of them described themselves in voices that said, "We the same. Black people are one people."

When it came to me, I didn't share. Why would I talk about my Black life in the projects? When I did that before, the Latino kids reacted all stuck up. So what now? I mention my Black projects life, and Black kids who don't come from projects react like we not on the same team or they react stuck up how Latino classmates did?

From day one in this class and school, I been sick of all of these different names and labels to describe Latinoness and Blackness and all the stuck-uppitiness. All of that kills the vibe—it kills something in us and just splits us.

But the other day. With Jenny. It was too much.

Jenny was feeling me since day one of this Science class. Even Elliot peeped it. "Trevor, what you be saying to Jenny? She giggles even if you blink."

Jenny's the one who picked the seat in class next to me.

Jenny's the one who started writing notes to me on the DL in the margins of my loose-leaf paper.

Jenny's the one who kept whispering secrets to me.

Elliot kept noticing and kept yeasting me up. Like the other day when our class took a ten-minute break and Jenny pulled me to the window for jokes. Right after, Elliot bum-rushed me. "Why Jenny had her hand on your face, shaping your lips to make a kiss?"

I told him, "She was teaching me how to say what she is. She was squeezing my lips together for me to say *Peruvian*."

Elliot shook his head. "You dumb. She was making you pucker up for a kiss. You shoulda leaned in and boop." I won't lie, her fingers smelled like strawberry jam and I wanted to kiss them instead of pronouncing *Peruvian*. I would have kissed her if I had the heart.

Elliot noticing that and him saying she's crushing on me made me feel like that Fat Joe, Remy Ma, French Montana song-part, "Nothing can stop me. I'm all the way up!" I been crushing on her since we first met. It's everything about her.

Anyway, every day of us sitting next to each other in Science. All our joking. Our texts. It seemed we were flirting more and more, so the other day I built up the courage to tell her my feelings for her. We were in gym, and I opened my mouth to speak, and she interrupted me.

"Can I ask you a question?"

I was SOS—Stuck on Stupid. "No doubt."

She cocked her head. "Why do you look like Todd?" She pointed at my all African-American friend playing volleyball. "And him." She pointed at another all African-American friend. She caught me so off guard. I just blinked, trying to put words together. She kept on. "I've been meaning to ask you. Because your last name is Spanish, right? Are you not Spanish? Because you mostly be with Todd. And *them*. More than…" She named white-looking Latinos in our class.

Her questions. YO! She had me questioning my whole existence. And she killed it. It felt like she was killing something in me. I wondered if I was her "type."

So, bust it, I decided not to tell her my crush on her right then. *Be chill*, I told myself. *Flex back to regular with her and let her make a move if she's feeling you.*

Two days later, she OD's and made it dumb obvi who's her "type." I thought she was different than lots of Latinas in my class but nah. They might be "Cuban," "Venezuelan," "Costa Rican," "Peruvian," or whatevs, but they the same because they like the same "type" of guy: the heroes of the novela shows Ma watches on the Spanish channel Univision—they into white boys or white-looking Latinos.

Because I walked into the stairwell on a bathroom break and headed upstairs and, hiding in the stairwell on the second floor, Jenny was kissing Samuel. Yeah, I still would've been tight if she was tonguing someone like me—like Miles Morales, Black or Puerto Rican or both. But *this* herb, Samuel? He's a Colombian kid who is as white as Peter Parker.

Later in Science, when she tried to touch my hair, I jerked my head away so fast it shocked her. "Why you touching my hair?"

She shrugged. "I don't know. Just wanted to see what your type of hair felt like."

I got as serious as a heart attack and asked, "My type of hair?"

She nodded. "Nappy," she said and smiled all innocent. But everything that happened made her smile and her word *nappy* feel a thousand percent NOT innocent and so full of UGH and everything that's grimy about this class and school.

After dismissal, I crossed the highway, leaving the white neighborhood of my school behind me, and all the Black and brown people of my projects came into view.

As I got near the check cashing spot, a bunch of grown Black guys on the corner argued. One guy's accent was straight Brooklyn English, and the other was Brooklyn Rican. They keep getting heated as I get closer, so I started to cross to the other street to avoid them in case they threw hands or something popped off. That's when I heard the angry voice of the Black Brooklyn English–speaking guy turn sweet, "Papi, why we fightin'? Me and you *the same.*" And the Black Brooklyn Spanish–speaking guy calmed down and agreed, "True. True."

I eyed them. *The same.* Facts. If they stood side by side, they looked like family. Matter of fact, if we all stood side by side, outsiders might think we all belonged to the same family.

I kept walking, thinking about my messed-up middle school, Jenny, and about fitting in, being different, picking sides.

★ ★ ★ ★ ★

CONFESSION

By Erin Entrada Kelly

Yes, I did it. I confess.

There's no point in acting like I didn't. There were eleven witnesses, including—but not limited to—my best friend, Crosbie Oakland, who started the whole thing.

No.

Let me rephrase.

Crosbie didn't start anything. All she did was show up, being beautiful. And why shouldn't she? Crosbie *is* beautiful. And she looked beautiful in that sweater, the one that got the boys talking.

She says she's never wearing it again.

Tell me: where is the justice in that?

Anyway. It's not like I *murdered* someone. It's not like a person was *maimed*. Garrett Dixon's face will go back to normal in a few days, and so will his ego, probably—all while Crosbie's sweater sits in a ball in the corner of her closet, or maybe finds its way to a Goodwill donation bin. And maybe Crosbie will try on another sweater ten years from now, when we're twenty-five, and she'll look at her reflection and turn this way and that, and she'll remember that day in high school when her sweater caused so much conversation, and she'll feel uncomfortable in her own skin and confused about how she's supposed to feel about her body—Proud? Ashamed? Neither?—and then she doesn't buy the sweater even though it looks beautiful because it shows off all her curves, but she doesn't know if she's supposed to show off her curves or not, because what does it mean if you do?

That's why I did it, you know.

On behalf of Crosbie and all the sweaters she will never wear.

And on my behalf, too.

Or maybe that's just what I tell myself to feel better.

Maybe I just wanted to punch someone in the face.

I don't tell all this to my mother when she picks me up from the front office. She wouldn't understand. Besides, I can tell by her expression that she is in no mood to hear my side of the story. She doesn't even care that the nurse had to give me an ice pack for my hand. The ice pack is still resting on my swollen knuckles when she meets with the principal; I nearly drop it when my mother hustles me out and toward the car like a prison warden.

"Shouldn't we return this to the nurse's office?" I say, holding the mostly melted ice pack in my right hand as she pulls my left arm toward her car with its evenly placed bumper stickers. *Keep the Christ in Christmas. Choose Life. Jesus, I Trust in You.*

"Just get in the car, Emiliani," she says.

She only calls me Emiliani when I'm in trouble.

Whatever.

I get in the passenger seat, buckle up, and place my hands in my lap with the ice pack on top.

My hand hurts. Throbs. Like it has its own heartbeat.

Have you ever punched someone in the face?

It *hurts.*

After my mother whispers her usual pre-drive prayer to St.

Christopher—the patron saint of travelers—she starts the car and pulls away from Roosevelt High School, aka the scene of the crime. She mumbles something about sending me to St. Therese, which is the all-girls Catholic school in town, even though we both know we can't afford it. My mom works at the mall and my dad is a tax preparer. We aren't exactly making it rain.

"Don't you want to hear what happened?" I say, glaring at her profile. Sometimes it seems like I know her profile better than her face because she's always looking away from me in bitter disappointment. It's ironic, in a way, because my mother hates her profile. She says we were both cursed with a Pinoy nose, which means it's wide and flat. *Too bad you didn't get your father's nose,* she has said about five million times. She always follows it with *but at least your sister did.*

My sister Gloria—aka "Gee"—has the pointiness of my father's white nose and the fullness of my mother's Pinay lips. Apparently, Gee bested me in the world of lips and noses and in every other world, too, for that matter.

The only thing worse than being substandard in the eyes of your parents is having a direct comparison living in the same house.

Case in point:

"Gee has never given me trouble," my mother says, her eyebrows pinched. "Not one time has she ever been sent home from school by the principal. Not one time has she ever punched anyone in the face."

It's easy to be complacent when you don't care about anything but parties and makeup, I think. But I don't say it out loud. What's the point?

I look out the window. "Maybe I had a really good reason. Did you ever consider that?"

My mother sighs.

My mother is the patron saint of sighing.

"There is never a good reason to do what you did," she says. "Jesus says turn the other cheek."

"Well," I mutter, flexing my hand under the ice pack, "Jesus never met Garrett Dixon."

Mom thinks I don't love Jesus, but she's wrong. I love Jesus. And guess what? I think Jesus loves me. I'm not the same kind of Catholic she is—like, I'll never have those bumper stickers on *my* car, if I ever have one—but I go to church every Sunday. I even pay attention, unlike the Glorious Gee, who stares blankly ahead and is always a half second behind the responses because she's not really listening. I don't know what she's thinking in church, but it's probably like, *Prom is coming up—I should choose between the fifty-seven guys who asked me.* Or maybe like, *I wonder which superlative I'll get in the yearbook this year? Could be "Prettiest Senior Girl." Could be "Most Likely to Succeed." The waiting is so stressful!*

I'm not good at staring blankly ahead. When the priest gives an interesting homily, I lean forward. When the pew sticks to my thighs, I shift. When the kneeler digs into my knees, I waver. And every time I fidget, my mom pushes her knuckle into my thigh like I'm blaspheming the Lord. Maybe I shouldn't fidget, but the point is I'm *listening*. Gee may be sitting still, but she's not *listening*.

As we drive home, I wonder what Jesus would think about what I did. Would He reprimand me for punching Garrett Dixon in the face, or would He give me a reprieve? Would He understand? Jesus understands everything.

Allegedly.

I may get a chance to find out, because as we pull into the driveway at home, Mom tells me that I'm going to confession the next day to talk to Father Rogan.

"You're going to confession, and you will repent," she says.

I'm pretty sure you're not supposed to go to confession on demand, but whatever. Sure, I'll go. Like I said, I love Jesus. And confession is one part of the Catholic Church where you get to do the talking instead of the listening. I don't mind going. I'm just not sure what I'm going to confess. You're supposed to confess sins that you feel bad about, but I don't feel bad about punching Garrett in the face. Not even a little bit. The only part of me that feels bad is my hand, because it's *aching*.

When I walk into the house, I toss the watery ice pack into the sink and make a beeline toward my bedroom, where I plan to spend the rest of the evening, even though it's only two in the afternoon. I immediately shut the door, pull my phone from my back pocket, and collapse on the bed. It hurts to scroll, but so be it.

There are a zillion texts from Crosbie, asking if I'm okay. I tell her I'm fine—better than fine, I say, and send boxing glove and laughing emojis so she doesn't worry. There are other texts, too, from all kinds of randoms. They all want to know one thing: *What happened?*

First, I wanna tell you about Crosbie.

We have been best friends since second grade, when we both named lilac as our favorite colors. Not many second graders have "lilac" as a favorite color, which is why we immediately became BFFs. Crosbie's favorite color is still lilac. Mine is white. Not because it's "pure" or anything like that. Actually, the opposite. White is the absence of color. White isn't what people think it is. Sometimes, I feel like the color white.

Crosbie loves all the pastels.

Crosbie and I are interwoven, like the big soft blankets that her mother crochets. Crosbie's yarn is soft and delicate, and mine is rough and scratchy, but together, it makes something warm.

One reason we work so well together is because people think Crosbie is the sweetest person alive. Those same people think I'm a bitch.

Those people aren't wrong, by the way.

Another way we're different: Crosbie is absolutely beautiful. She has silky dark hair. Big blue eyes framed by long lashes. A small waist. (Not like mine. My mom likes to pinch my waist and ask if I'd heard of keto or paleo or Weight Watchers.) Crosbie is curvy in all the right places. I'm not sure who decides what the right places are, but whatever.

Crosbie is one of those people who doesn't know she's beautiful. But she's starting to figure it out, which is a good thing. Why shouldn't she be beautiful?

When she bought the sweater—lilac, her favorite color—she FaceTimed me to ask what I thought.

"What do you think?" she said.

"You look amazing," I said.

"And?"

"And it's your favorite color."

"And?"

"And you should wear it with your dark jeans."

She smiled. "Aaaand?"

I grinned and parroted: "And you bought it with your own money."

She'd said it a zillion times, via text and voice. *I can't believe I'm actually going to buy something with my own money.* I'd always add, your *hard-earned* money. Because her job sounds like it really sucks. On her third day on the job, a guy in the drive-through shook his receipt in her face and said, "I ordered large—*large*. Do you even know how to read?"

I would've spit in that guy's hamburger, given the chance. But Crosbie said he was probably having a bad day. Maybe he just got a divorce, she said. Or maybe he only has twenty minutes for lunch and he's always in a hurry. Or maybe this hamburger is the one highlight of his entire day.

She always has these narratives that excuse bad behavior. She and my dad have that in common. Except my dad uses the excuses for himself.

Personally, I don't care if the dude was having a bad day or if he got twenty divorces or if he had five *seconds* for lunch. You don't talk to people that way.

Like I said: Crosbie's money is hard-earned.

She'd had her eye on this sweater for two weeks, specifically because it was lilac. Her parents would have bought it for her if she asked, but she said she wanted to pay for it herself. If it were me, I would have let my parents buy it for me, then I'd buy *another* sweater, and then I'd have two for the price of one.

But like I said, Crosbie and I are different.

I wouldn't spend my paycheck on sweaters, anyway.

The sweater had a V-neck and quarter-length sleeves, and it was formfitting and the material looked soft, like a bed of freshly pulled cotton.

She confessed that it cost fifty dollars, which sounded like a fortune. But she was happy and proud, and I was happy for her.

While we were on FaceTime, she said, "Is it weird if I say that I think I look pretty?"

I smiled. "No. Not weird at all."

My dad knocks on my door softly, then pokes his head in while I'm on the bed, scrolling through my phone. I don't look up, but I can tell from my peripheral vision that he's holding the ice pack and it's full of fresh ice.

"Can I come in?" he says.

I shrug with one shoulder.

It's 3:00 p.m. When it's not tax season, my dad spends most of his afternoons at home, doing nothing but watching old reruns. He's made a narrative for himself, like I said, and his narrative goes like this: *I do enough work from February to April to last the entire year.* At one point, when bills were tight, my mom worked *two* retail jobs, all while my dad sat on the couch, complaining that he couldn't work because of his "bad back." That's another narrative he's provided himself: an injury that prevents him from doing more work. It'd be one thing if he actually *had* a "bad back." But it only seems to go "bad" when he's asked to do something he doesn't want to do.

Last year, one of my teachers at school, Ms. Belle, got into a car accident. The accident was minor, but it really messed her up. Something about her vertebrae. She had surgery, but it only made things worse. She'd have to stand up in the middle of class and walk around because it hurt to stay seated. But it also hurt to walk around. You could tell that she was in pain by the way her face pinched. One time, she stood up from her desk and stumbled. She almost fell. Suzanne Young, who sat nearby, caught her before she fell. Normally, the kids at school laugh at stuff like that. But this time, no one did.

Every time my dad complains about his bad back, I think of Ms. Belle.

I'm grateful for the ice pack, though. I put my phone down so I can lay the ice on my burning knuckles.

"I didn't know you had a right hook," my dad says, smiling.

"Only for sexist pricks."

"Well. Sounds like those boys don't hate women at all. If anything, they love girls a little *too* much." He chuckles.

My dad thinks he's funny.

That's another false narrative.

I pick up my phone with my left hand, but it's awkward because I'm right-handed. It slips out of my grasp. I pick it up. Drop it. Pick it up.

"You can't go around punching people in the face every time they hurt your feelings, you know," my dad says.

I focus on the screen. Earlier today, Crosbie posted a selfie in her new sweater. Now the photo is gone.

"I didn't punch that dude in the face because he *hurt my feelings*," I say. "I punched him in the face because he's a sexist prick. Like I said."

"Listen." He pauses. "Guys are like that sometimes. Especially at that age. You wouldn't believe the things that go on in their heads."

I'm pretty sure I would. But I don't say a word. I keep scrolling.

"Sometimes guys say stupid things," he says. His tone has more edge to it now. My parents can't stand it when I look at my phone when they're talking to me.

Maybe if they said things worth listening to, I'd put my phone down.

Here's what I want to say: *Clearly, yes, guys say stupid things. Because that's what's happening right now.* But I press my lips together as if someone has zipped them shut. I don't want to say something I'll regret.

"You can't let everything get to you," he says.

He's waiting for me to say something, but I don't. So he continues.

"The principal said the boys were giving Crosbie a hard time," he says. "I know she's your best friend, but you won't always be around to defend her. Girls like Crosbie...they have to get used to this sort of thing. That's just the way life is."

I put my phone down. "*Girls like Crosbie?* What does that mean?"

So much for my zipped mouth.

He clears his throat. "You know what I mean."

A warm sense of rage blooms in my chest and crawls up my neck. Yes, I know what he means. Girls like Crosbie. Beautiful girls with beautiful bodies. A thought worms its way into my brain: Was my dad one of these Garrett Dixon–types?

Since I've gone silent again, he starts a new sentence. "Your mom says—"

"What about the racist stuff?" I blurt out.

His eyebrows furrow. "What racist stuff?"

"The racist stuff Garrett and his idiot friends said."

"Why would they say racist stuff?"

He looks genuinely perplexed, like there's a thought bubble

over his head that says, *Crosbie is white. Garrett is white. Where's the racism?*

"They weren't saying it to Crosbie," I say. "They were saying it to *me.*"

His expression doesn't change. He is *still* perplexed.

This time, the thought bubble says, *But you're almost-white. Why would someone be racist toward you?*

Or maybe the thought bubble says, *But racism only happens to Black people, and we aren't Black.*

I wish I had a pin to pop those bubbles.

Or a knife.

He sighs. "The principal didn't mention any *racist stuff.*" He actually uses air quotes. "At least not that I heard of."

I pick up my phone again. The rage fire now blankets my entire body, down to the tips of my fingers and toes. "How convenient," I say.

I have an urge to throw my phone at my father's face.

This is not the first time I've had such an urge.

He stands. "You can't find offense in everything, Yani. That's what's wrong with people these days—everything's an issue, everything's a big deal." He walks toward my bedroom door. "Your mom says you're going to confession tomorrow. I think that's a good idea." Before he walks out, he says, "You can't punch *everyone* in the face."

So here's what happened.

Crosbie and I have only one class together: Art. It's the second-to-last class of the day, and it's usually pretty chill. The teacher, Mr. Dzieken, is laid-back for the most part. He tells us what to do and we do it. As long as we're working on our art, he gives us an A.

Garrett Dixon is in the class. He's always with this guy, Matt.

Garrett and Matt are your basic assholes. They aren't jocks or anything, but they're popular guys, mostly because they're good-looking and they have cars—trucks, actually—and they go to all the right parties.

Garrett is the loudmouth and Matt is his sidekick.

Garrett's greatest joy in life is making as many sexual comments as possible. If there's an innuendo dangling out there, he'll grab it and hold on for dear life. When Mr. Dzieken taught us stippling, for example, Garrett kept referring to it as *nippling*. Now that I think about it, the innuendo doesn't even have to dangle out there—he'll come up with his own.

So that's Garrett.

I'm sure you know guys like him.

You probably know *many* guys like him.

Usually, Garrett will make a passing comment or two to Crosbie, but we just shake it off. (I say *we* because I think of me and Crosbie as a team. A unit of one. Is that codependent? I don't know. Maybe.) On this day, his comment was about her sweater. It took him less than thirty seconds to comment on it.

He started with a one-word expletive, then said, "You are *really* filling out that sweater, Crosbie." He raked his eyes over her in that way. You know what I'm talking about. "In every possible way." Then he nudged Matt because guys like Garrett need an audience.

Matt did the same thing with his eyes, then said, "I didn't know you had all *that* going on."

Crosbie's cheeks turned a light shade of pink. She's very modest. She won't even change clothes in front of me and we've been best friends forever.

Crosbie and I sat silently at our table and I shot Garrett and Matt a death glare. Mr. Dzieken wasn't in the room yet. He usually didn't come in until the tardy bell rang.

Garrett continued, his eyes fixed on Crosbie's chest, "What do you think, Matt? Thirty-eight B? Thirty-eight C?"

Matt narrowed his eyes in the same direction and rubbed his chin. "Looks like C to me."

This is when my heart started pounding. Not in fear. In anger. Has that ever happened to you? Your blood rushes through your body, and it feels like you're on fire?

"Definitely more than a handful," Garrett said.

Crosbie shifted in her seat and crossed her arms. Hiding herself.

"Yani has something going on, too, but she hides it under those hoodies," Matt said.

I turned my head to face them. It felt like slow motion, like a scene in an action movie where some dumbass makes a wisecrack to the main character because he doesn't know who he's messing with and the action star turns and looks at him right before everything goes down.

"Naaah," Garrett said. He waved his hand dismissively. "Asian girls never have anything going on. That's probably why she wears the hoodies in the first place."

"But she's only a half-breed Asian," Matt said. "So..."

"Soooo, maybe half a handful?" Garrett said. Then he laughed. They both did, actually.

I should mention that there were other people in the classroom. But none of them were really paying attention. They had their own conversations going on—like Abbi Walker and Kenzie Rainer, for example, who sit between me and the boys. They were deep in some kind of gossip (which I usually eavesdrop on, not gonna lie), so they were confused and startled when I suddenly darted up from my chair. I stood up with such force that the chair shot backward and fell over. Everything got quiet.

Garrett and Matt weren't fazed. They've probably never been challenged in their entire lives, so why would it start now?

They didn't even flinch when I walked over to them.

The whole class was watching now.

Garrett's expression didn't change until I shoved his shoulder—hard. So hard that it shifted his chair at an angle and he was facing me directly. Then I saw a flash of anger in his eyes.

He was probably a bit confused, too, because who knew I could shove a person that hard? I didn't. I'm, like, five feet tall and I don't have much bulk, despite what my mother says.

He opened his mouth to say something, and out of nowhere—seriously, I didn't even think about it—I punched him in the face.

I didn't aim or anything.

I've never punched anyone, so I was kinda surprised that I actually hit him. But I did. Right on the cheekbone, just below the eye. He fell out of his chair. He was yelling about five million curse words—mostly the four-letter *C* word that Garrett-type guys love so much—and that's when Mr. Dzekien came in and I was shuttled to the front office. I didn't even have time to say anything to Crosbie, but I looked at her on my way out.

I think she was smiling.

After my father leaves my room, I scroll through social media, watch YouTube, and think about what happened. It feels weird, to be honest. Like it happened to someone else. But also? I don't feel bad. I don't think I do, anyway.

I wonder what I'll talk about in confession.

Should I confess that I don't feel bad?

Is that something to confess?

Usually, I *do* feel bad about things.

Last semester, I cheated on my Geometry test. Geometry is my worst subject, and I didn't want to get another bad grade. I don't really care about grades, but my mom does. When I get bad grades, she tells me how lazy I am, how I don't try hard enough. She talks about how immigrants work hard to come to this country to get a good education and look at me, just squandering mine away, not even trying.

I made an A.

I felt really bad about it. I'd planned to show my mom, all proud—*Look, Mom, I got one hundred percent!*—but I felt so bad that I didn't even tell her. And then I ratted myself out to my

Geometry teacher. She was really cool about it, though. She said I was showing integrity and good character by confessing, and she let me take a makeup test. I made a C, but at least I didn't feel ashamed of myself.

I wish I could tell my mom about how I showed *integrity* and *good character*, but she would only focus on the cheating part.

In seventh grade, I repeated a rumor I'd heard about Danika Klein—that she made out with boys behind the dumpster for five dollars apiece—and even as I said it, I knew it was wrong. I couldn't sleep all night. The next day, I retracted what I'd said and when I heard the rumor again, I stepped up and said it wasn't true.

During freshman year, a girl in my class dropped five dollars on her way out of the classroom and I took it and shoved it deep in my pocket, and then I bought some chips and a soda out of the vending machine and couldn't even eat it. A few days later, when I managed to scrounge up my own five dollars, I found the girl and gave it to her. *You dropped this,* I said.

I'm not saying I'm Mother Teresa or anything.

The point is: I *do* feel bad when I'm wrong.

I've confessed all this stuff to Father Rogan.

But at this moment, I don't feel bad about Garrett Dixon.

So what am I supposed to confess?

My sister knocks on my door around 7:00 p.m. and pops her head in.

"Can I come in?" she says.

Ugh.

The last thing I need is judgment from Glorious Gee.

I shrug.

She saunters in. She's wearing yoga pants and a fitted shirt that says Roosevelt High School Cheer. Her hair is in a perfect messy bun on top of her head. It's weird how we have the same parents and look nothing alike. If you saw her on the street, you'd assume she was white. You wouldn't even know she's a *half-breed Asian.*

She stands near the foot of my bed but doesn't sit down. She's not a regular visitor here.

"Everyone's talking about it," she says.

I'm not looking at her.

I'm looking at my phone.

Crosbie has posted a pic of us, one of my favorites. The caption says: BFFs.

"So," I say.

I'm waiting for her to render her judgment.

I try to imagine her punching someone in the face.

It's impossible to picture.

"So..." She pauses and plays with the hem of her shirt. "I guess you're kind of a badass."

I put my phone down and look up. "What?"

"Well." She lifts one shoulder. "You punched Garrett Dixon in the face."

"Yeah."

"If anyone needed to get punched in the face, it was Garrett Dixon." Pause. "He used to snap my bra in middle school. Like, all the time."

"Really?" It doesn't surprise me, but it's weird, how the Glorious Gee lives a whole separate life that I don't know about, with all her own experiences.

"Yeah," she says. "I even told Mom and Dad."

I raise my eyebrows. "What'd they say?"

"Dad said *he probably just likes you.*"

"And Mom?"

"She told me to pray for him."

I snort. "And did you?"

She laughs. "Hell no."

The room suddenly feels lighter. It's weird how that happens, isn't it?

She steps forward and gestures toward the ice pack, which is melted and sitting on the floor. She leans over and picks it up. I can smell her strawberry shampoo.

"Want me to fill this up for you?" she asks.

"Nah," I say. I stretch my hand. The swelling has gone down, but it still hurts.

She tosses the bag from hand to hand as she walks to the door. "Last week, Garrett grabbed my ass when I was drinking out of the water fountain."

I frown.

"Guys," she says, shrugging. As if to say, *Guys, oh well, what're you gonna do? That's how they are.*

"More like amoebas, in this case."

"Yeah. Or something that feeds on amoebas."

"You should tell someone at school about it. Like the principal or something."

"I already did. Today, actually." She fidgets with the hem of her shirt. "I went to the office this afternoon, right before cheer practice. I wanted them to know he probably deserved it. Some girls from your art class were already in there. McKenzie Rainer and Abbi Whatshername. Sticking up for you. Not that you need it." She chuckles lightly and motions toward my hand. "Looks like you can stick up for yourself just fine."

I think of Kenzie and Abbi in the office, speaking up in my defense. "I need it," I say, quietly.

"Garrett got suspended, too, by the way." Gee pauses, walks toward the door, rests her hand on the knob. "Do you think he'll stop being such an asshole after being publicly humiliated?"

"Probably not," I say. "But you know what else is disturbing?"

She opens the door. "What?"

"The fact that you drink out of that disgusting water fountain."

Her smile lights up in a big laugh. So does mine.

What can I say?

It's contagious.

★ ★ ★

On the way to church, I look at my mom's profile. I want to ask her what she thinks about what Garrett said. Not the *half-handful* part, but the racist part. I want to ask if anyone has ever said anything to her. I want to know how it made her feel. I want to tell her what my dad said, about people taking things too seriously, and I want to know her opinion.

I open my mouth. I'm about to ask something—I'm not even sure what—but she speaks first.

"I'm going to drop you off, then pick up Gee, and come back for you," she says. "Gee has practice today. See how she gets involved in school? Maybe if you got involved in school activities, you wouldn't get in trouble." Then she sighs and mutters, "How did I get such opposite daughters?"

I turn away and look out the window.

Have you ever been to confession?

Before you go in, you're supposed to pray for God's help and guidance, and examine your conscience. At our church—St. Margaret—they have small confessional rooms with a divider. You kneel on one side and then you say, "Bless me, Father, for I have sinned." Then you tell him how long it's been since your last confession.

When I open the door to St. Margaret, the distinctive smell of church washes over me. I hold the door open for a man behind me. He hurries up the steps and says thank you. He has a full beard, but his head is shaved.

An older woman with tired eyes and a rosary kneels in the nearest pew, waiting her turn for the confessional, which is currently occupied. The woman's head is bent, her eyes closed. The man and I kneel on the same pew, with distance between us. Usually, I clasp my hands together, but my right hand still hurts, so I press my palms together instead. Then I rest my forehead against my thumbs.

Normally, this is the part where I pray for guidance. And that's what I intend to do, but I don't feel like normal.

I think it's because I didn't *choose* to go to confession this time.

My mother basically *told* me I was going to confession. She assumes I'll confess the sin of busting Garrett Dixon's face. And maybe it *was* a sin. I mean, obviously—allegedly—we aren't supposed to resort to violence as a society. So, I know it's *bad*. In that sense.

But I don't *feel bad* about it.

I inhale.

I say a prayer.

I search my conscience.

Bless me, Father, for I have sinned. It's been four months since my last confession. This guy at school made some sexist and racist comments toward me and my friend, so I punched him in the face. But I don't feel bad about it, so I think I should confess that I don't feel remorse. But—I also don't feel remorse about not feeling remorse, so... what does that mean?

Bless me, Father, for I have sinned. It's been four months since my last confession. This guy at school made some sexist and racist comments toward me and my friend, so I punched him in the face. But that's not what I want to talk about. I want to talk about my dad. When I told him what happened, he acted like it was no big deal. I wanted to throw my phone at him. My mom always says that we're supposed to "honor thy parents." I'm pretty sure throwing a phone at my father's face is not honoring him. I didn't do it, though. But the thought crossed my mind. Is that a sin?

Bless me, Father, for I have sinned. It's been four months since my last confession. This guy at school made some sexist and racist comments toward me and my friend, so I punched him in the face. But I don't feel bad about it. I know I should, probably, but I don't. So can we talk

*about something else? Like the fact that my mother always compares me
to my sister and it really pisses me off? I don't know if that's a sin exactly, to be angry at my mother. Is it?*

*Bless me, Father, for I have sinned. It's been four months since my
last confession. This guy at school made some sexist and racist comments
toward me and my friend, so I punched him in the face. But let's talk
about my sister. She has nothing to do with it, really, but yesterday we
laughed together and it was really nice. If I'm being honest—and that's
what a confessional is for, right?—I've always thought she was kind of
an airhead. Like one of those beautiful girls who isn't very smart. But
now that I think about it, that's sexist, too, isn't it?*

*My mom says Gee inherited all my father's good white genes. My
mom is really proud of that, like she had something to do with it. She
says that I got her nose and her brown skin, and she says it like it's a
bad thing, and then again, everything she says to me she says like it's
a bad thing.*

*I don't know if there's a sin in there for me to confess, Father. Maybe
I'm just jealous of my sister.*

When I open my eyes again, the woman with the rosary isn't
there anymore. She's in the confessional. I get off my knees and
sit in the pew. I put my hands in my lap and stare at them.

I wonder what it'll be like at school next week.

I wonder how long the woman has been in there.

It'll be my turn, any minute.

To be honest, I don't feel like talking. I don't feel like "confessing."

I need to search my conscience more.

The door to the confessional opens. The woman steps out.
She doesn't make eye contact. She hurries off.

I stand. I stare and stare at the confessional.

My mom will be here any minute. She'll ask me if I confessed, but she won't ask me what I said—that's much too sacred to share, and she knows that. Maybe I'll just tell her that I did.

But that's lying. And it's a sin.

I can add it to my confessions for next time, I guess.

I stare for a few more seconds, then turn to the bearded man next to me. He's on his knees, but he's watching me curiously.

"You can go ahead," I say. I don't even whisper it. My voice booms through the empty chamber of the church.

Then I slip out of the pew and walk toward the wide heavy church doors.

I go outside, into the sun, to wait for my mother.

★ ★ ★ ★ ★

A HALFIE'S GUIDE
TO MEXICAN RESTAURANTS

By Rebecca Balcárcel

First of all, when the smiling, kind-of-cute host-guy says, "Two?" and picks up menus for you and your new white friend, don't respond with "Sí gracias," especially if you *don't* have an American accent and you've heard español every day of your life from your brown papa *and* your r is perfectly flipped rather than over-revved like a tourist's. Because if you start down that piñata-plastered runway, the host will lift off into wide Spanish skies and leave you sucking in jet exhaust and stumbling over that whole story of how you're only half Latina and your mom was born in white bread central, and how your Spanish is actually *worse* than a tourist's, etc. etc. Just say "thanks" for now.

If your new friend tries out her Spanish and she flattens the vowels, making gracias sound like it went under a potato masher, be happy because she seems sweet and doesn't mind sounding like a beginner. She wants to be polite, and it makes the midnight eyes of host-guy light up, which is a plus because he might lay extra chips and salsa on the table or give you free soft drink refills. Besides, you're keeping this Saturday lunch thing fun, and who wants to spend their work-the-drive-through money to nitpick about "ah" vs. "a." Ten to one, she knows more book-learned Spanish than you, anyway.

When the definitely-cute host-guy says, "Some-sing to drrink?" you know he was born *there*, and you congratulate yourself because the food in this place is going to be delicioso and not some over-hot-sauced Tex-Mex cowboy variety. *Now* you can say, "Water, por favor," and do your flippy *r* and smile like you're sharing a secret. Now he'll know that you have just enough Spanish to be interesting, but he'll stay in English as he says, "Be right back," and flashes a smile right into your eyes, like he knows you have one foot in his jet plane and might be interested in a ride.

Take in the red walls, the row of arches, and the giant metal suns smiling at you from every direction. Bask.

When your new friend says, "I love these little salsa bowls," hunching down to take a closer look at the three stout legs and flecks of white stone, go ahead and tell her that they are mini molcajetes, the traditional mortar and pestle of Latin America. But when she says, "Wow," and "Hey, I never really thought of you as Latina," hold back.

Don't say, *Well, I'm only half,* because you don't want to sound like you are dissing your father or actually yourself with that *only* crap, and don't say, *It's probably because my skin is light,* because it feels itchy to say that skin color doesn't matter and then it feels slimy to say that it does. So let's not say anything on that right now because you don't even know what you think about your permanent tan sometimes and why some people don't see it and some people do. And don't say, *I guess I should throw more Spanish into my sentences,* because, come on, that would be so fake, right, like code-switching is something you can't even contain because you're such a *Spanish chica, ai-yai-yai!* when you kind of wish you were, but you're just not. And especially don't say, *I'm hurt. How did you not see this entire half of myself, the half who sings* La Noche Buena *every Christmas and eats tamales for New Year's instead of black-eyed peas?* And definitely don't say, *I guess I hide my brown half when I'm getting to know people because what if I make them uncomfortable, or what if they don't like me, or what if I'm ashamed when I see my own father through their eyes as they ask, "Who is that construction worker?" when he's actually a professor who has read more books than our school librarian and our English teachers put together, I bet, and who they just might, you know, even accidentally, think cries and laughs freely but isn't capable of forming a complex thought? Or what if you love everything Latino and want me to teach you how to make tortillas and tell you all about my father crossing the raging waters of the Rio Grande, which he actually did in an airplane?*

So hold back.

Admit to the piece of perfection in your heart, that little light indivisible, that you don't know how to be half. How to be whole. How to show people who you are. How to know who you are in the first damn place. And ask the piece of perfection to show you how to merge your brown vision and white vision into one binocular whole, how to rub the mud off your two-part soul and shine.

When the tortilla chips are almost gone and the steaming enchiladas arrive, ask your new friend something real, like how her dad's recovery is going and if she misses her sister who used her waitress savings to hike the Appalachian Trail. She'll say her dad is more patient now and even took her to a hockey game, and while her parents are still freaking out about the sister's Appalachian thru-hike, they've decided it'll look good on a résumé. Your friend will say she's sending Clif Bars to her sister in the mail and that she watched an old movie with her parents last night, because she's that sweet. She'll ask how you are, and she'll mean it. Smile, because you're making a truly good friend.

But when the so-totally-cute host-guy asks if you all need anything and spends a second or two longer on your friend's face than yours and gestures to her empty glass first and offers a refill, it's okay to let that balloon in your throat deflate. When he asks her name, remind yourself that he has no jet and you were never in it. You're more of a motorcycle chick, anyway. Maybe. Today, at least.

And if your friend giggles as she says her name, you can't blame her for being flattered, though you wonder if this host-guy likes white girls better in general or just this one. Tell yourself, *Who would want to be with a guy who didn't like brown girls, anyway? Not me!* and notice that his eyes are a little too close together. Wonder if she feels exoticized with all this extra attention because she's the different one in this trio, or if she even knows that word and how it leaves you feeling like a posable mannequin. Wonder if this is what privilege looks like, getting all the attention automatically. Wonder if maybe you're just jealous, and hey, she *is* pretty—nice smile, cute figure. Any guy might ask her name. Pep talk yourself that you're pretty, too, though you don't believe it right now.

When the host-guy says to you in Spanish that he likes your friend and asks if you think she would give him her number, tell him in your best chancla-waving voice that he's too old and that she's a kid who just started high school and her father would whip his behind. Be proud that your Spanish actually *is* a little beyond tourist-level. When he puts his hands up defensively, know that you are saving your friend from a bad boy who thinks it never hurts to ask. And your friend, who is turning out to be truly sweet, would never know if he was being sincere or just playing her. Ignore the voice in your head that wonders if *you* would know, either, and the whisper that asks if maybe *you* wouldn't mind being played.

When your friend asks, "What did he say?" resist the urge to be mean and say something shruggy like, he flirts with everyone who comes in here. Instead, say, "He thinks you're nice."

"Let's eat here again sometime," she'll say, but take a silent vow to never come back. Plan to eat at an American chain restaurant next time. Plan to flirt with the white host-guy or the Black host-guy or even the host-*girl* so you can wonder if *you're* being exoticized.

Then shout down those hormones like a chorus of whistles and catcalls on the street and laugh at yourself. Don't let a guy come between you and your new friend. Split the bill and stubbornly speak English to the host-guy.

Step out into the parking lot, where it's been a great lunch and a great time, and hug your dear new friend. She'll say that this was the most authentic Mexican restaurant she's ever been to and then pronounce, "Adios," with three syllables. But don't get cocky. Remind yourself that your own pronunciation of the *s* would be smirked at in Spain where it's all about *th*'s, muchas grath-yas.

Drive the long way home in your mom's old car, which you're still paying for by picking up the littles at school, taking the youngest to karate, and driving Abuela to the check-cashing place because "¡No confío en los bancos!" she says and keeps her cash tucked in toes of shoes and pockets of coats since you never know when you might have to escape, take off in the night to another town or another country.

Drive past Fiesta, the Latin grocery; drive past Kroger, the regular grocery. Try to not feel divided, bifurcated, sliced down the middle. Imagine a rainbow arching over the streets, connecting the cursive *F* and the blocky *K*. At the red light, try not to obsess over the host-guy. Don't wonder if he would have liked you more if you could flirt in Spanish, if you could joke and drop puns and wield those words like swords dipped in gold.

As the red light turns green, tell yourself you're not a coconut—brown outside, white inside. You're not a mash-up or a crash-up or a mix-up. You're not parts. You're a whole. Not a spark, but a fire. You're not a piece of perfection, but the whole dang enchilada. You are one molten glow, girl, light indivisible.

★ ★ ★ ★ ★

EFFING NICO

By Randy Ribay

Overcast clouds hang heavy over our subdivision's dead–ass streets. Christmas lights shine into the quiet, and cold air seeps through the window frame. Hands clasped in prayer, I search the night sky for any sign of the fifteen to twenty-four inches of snow everyone's waiting for, but so far not a single flake has fallen.

I drop my hands and lean back in my chair. My World History II digital textbook is pulled up on my laptop, waiting for me to reread the chapter on imperialism since I completely zoned out when we went over it in class because…well, because it was mad boring.

But it's hard to care about a quiz that might not happen. It's also not helping that the rest of my family is downstairs with Nico watching the forecast on the local news with the TV on full blast. The meteorologist's nasally voice booms through the floor, punctuated by the occasional burst of laughter from my family. Probably because Nico said something funny.

Effing Nico.

Effing always saying something funny.

Betting on Father Winter to come through, I close out of the textbook, pull up Reddit, and start browsing /aww because that shit's cute as hell. I watch a video of a rotund cat climbing into a stroller. A puppy gazing at the falling rain as if it's the greatest thing he's ever seen. A pair of panda bear cubs engaged in the cutest battle of all time.

I'm in the middle of a video of a mountain lion playing three-cup shuffle when a messenger ping snags my attention.

It's Erika Jacobs.

I sit up.

hey, jerry, her message says.

I smile even as I cringe at the reminder that my family nickname has proliferated into the general public ever since Nico started at my school in the fall. Before that, everyone just called me by my actual name, Jericho.

Hi, Erika! I type, then immediately delete.

Good evening!

No. Too formal.

What's up, E!

Too extra.

She's no doubt seeing the ellipsis bubble and thinking I'm composing the world's longest greeting, so I finally just go with, hey, what's up, and hit Enter before overthinking it.

not much, she says.

cool, I say.

A few moments pass before her next message comes through.

your brother around?

I smack my forehead against the desk.

Effing Nico.

yeah, I reply. he's here.

oh, ok, Erika messages. it's just that we were supposed to meet online a few minutes ago.

school project or something? I ask.

or something ☺

There's so much wrong with this. So much. Nico moved in with us from the Philippines less than a year ago. Yet, he somehow aces all his classes, knows pretty much everyone at school, and apparently has a virtual date *or something* with the girl I've been crushing on since that day in the third grade when she peeled my orange for me.

I glance at his neatly made bed on the other side of our shared room and briefly consider sabotaging it. But before I can make up my mind as to how, another message from Erika Jacobs pings.

um can you get him please?

I roll my eyes.

sure.

I text Nico, but as soon as I hit send, his phone chimes from the desk on his side of the room. So then I cup my hands around my mouth and shout, "Nico!" through the open door, down the hallway. "Nicooooooo!"

There's no response. The meteorologist's droning must be creating some kind of sound or attention barrier.

Bah.

give me a min, I message Erika Jacobs, then get up and make my way downstairs.

Everyone's so hypnotized by the TV's promise of the winter storm that they don't even look up when I enter. They're all chilling around the couch in their softest pajamas, steaming mugs of hot chocolate cupped between their hands like this is a Swiss Miss commercial. It's way past Sarah's bedtime, but even she's down here, squished between Mom and Dad on one side of the couch, looking like the perfect blend of the two of them. Dad's black hair and round features, Mom's straight nose and hazel eyes, and light brown skin balanced between theirs—unlike mine, which is almost as pale as Mom's.

Then there's Nico, looking like the pictures I've seen of Dad when he was a teen. He has a different mom than Sarah and me, and I've never seen any photos of her, so I can't trace his features to hers. Anyway, he's stretched out along the other section of the couch, taking up as much space as the rest of my family combined. And he's using Mark Narwhalberg—the stuffed narwhal I bought my sister when she was a baby—as a pillow. I tried getting her to change the name after I learned that his namesake used to be a racist scumbag, but by then she was already attached to it.

Mom finally notices I'm down here and asks, "Done studying?"

"Yup," I say flatly. Then, "Nico—it's Erika."

"Kuya Nico," Dad corrects.

"Ano ba?" Nico says without taking his eyes off the screen. A list of school closures are scrolling past at the bottom of the screen, but it's mostly still private schools.

"Erika. Jacobs. She said you were supposed to meet her online?"

"Ah," he says as if suddenly remembering. "Right, right, right." But he doesn't move to get up.

Dad rattles off something in Tagalog. Nico responds in Tagalog. They go back and forth a couple more times before they both burst out laughing. I don't understand any of it, of course, since Dad never bothered teaching Sarah or me the language despite the fact we've been telling him for years we want to learn.

But they're laughing, so I chuckle a bit, too, so I'm not standing here like an idiot.

"Why are you laughing, Jerry?" Nico asks, finally turning to me. He's grinning his wide-ass smile that everyone loves for some reason. "You understand what we're saying?"

"I don't know, man," I say, squirming under the awkwardness of him calling me out like that. "Look, you going to go meet up with Erika?"

He turns back to the TV. "No."

"No?"

"No."

"Okay. Whatever." It strikes me—not for the first time—that Nico probably wouldn't even notice if someone peeled an orange for him because he'd probably have expected it. But, hey, what a cool smile he's got!

Nico gestures toward the screen. "It's my first snow, Jerry. It might start any minute, and I don't want to miss it."

"Um. Then what should I tell her?" As if I'm his messenger boy.

"Snowmageddon."

"Whatever."

I retreat upstairs. sorry, I message Erika. snowmageddon.

...so? she says.

I don't answer, knowing she'll probably forgive him.

About an hour later, Nico stomps upstairs and rushes into our room where I'm back at my desk. He chops my shoulders rapidly while bouncing up and down on his toes like a little kid. "Snow day! Snow day! Snow day!"

I lean away from him and peek out the window, but there's still nothing. "So they went ahead and called it, huh?"

"Yes, yes! Is it always this exciting?"

"Kind of." I close out of my digital History textbook, happy that I can now ignore imperialism guilt-free.

He tousles my hair, and I push his hands away. He grabs his phone from where it's charging on his desk. "Ugh. So many notifications." Without reading a single one, he clears them with a dismissive flick, then pockets the phone and disappears back downstairs.

I go back to watching this YouTube video about how the strange spelling of some 1980s children's cartoon is proof of alternate dimensions. Mom and Sarah come up a little while later, pop their heads in to say good-night, then start getting ready for bed. The muffled sounds of Dad and Nico conversing in Tagalog carries through the floor.

What are they even talking about all the time? Dad and I rarely talk. Like, really talk. After all, he's a sportsball kind of guy, and I'm a…well, an '80s-cartoon-conspiracy kind of guy. And when we do watch something together—mostly old martial arts films, the only place our interests intersect—his focus never wavers from the screen.

The video ends. The countdown begins for the next one to auto-play—which is apparently about how we're *actually* living in *The Matrix*. It's nearly eleven o'clock. A snowplow rumbles down our street, shovel raised, like a giant creature searching for its purpose.

I consider going downstairs. Even though the school cancellation's already been announced, it's still exciting to watch the live forecast leading up to a big storm, even if the storm itself is a letdown.

But then I think about how shitty it feels when Dad and Nico carry on in front of me like he's the son Dad actually wanted. The son Dad could have had all this time if he never emigrated, who would have understood him in a way I'll never be able to.

So I stay where I am and let the next video play.

It's nearing midnight, and there's not even a dusting. I slip off my headphones and listen for a few moments. The world's silent except for the muffled sound of the TV floating through the floor. No conversation. No laughter. Nico's still down there, but Dad must have gone to bed at some point when I wasn't paying attention. Figuring the coast is clear, I close my laptop and head downstairs to grab a snack.

In the living room, the lights are all off, the space lit only by the blue glow from the TV screen. I'm surprised to find Dad in the middle of the couch, passed out, hands clasped over his stomach, snoring softly. Nico's exactly where he was last time I came down, but now his attention's focused on his phone. His eyes don't even flick up as I walk past on my way to the kitchen.

I open the refrigerator, letting the yellow light spill out and interrupt the darkness only long enough to grab the stack of American cheese singles and the soy milk. I pour myself a glass then start to head back upstairs. But for whatever reason, I turn around and sit at the kitchen table facing the TV.

After unwrapping the first slice of cheese, I fold it in half, watching the cheese break along the crease. I then fold it in half again and again. I read somewhere that if you could fold a regular piece of paper in half forty-two times, it would be thick enough to reach the moon. Not sure if it's true, but it's always stuck with me, this idea that halving something could make it more instead of less.

I keep folding the cheese until I have a mini-tower of small orange squares. I pop the first one into my mouth as the meteorologist gestures in front of a green-screen map, indicating a purple and blue blob that covers the cities north, west, and south of us along the Front Range like a letter *C*. As they cut to a few audience-submitted videos of the snow heavily falling in driveways and backyards, she mentions that this is Denver's latest first snowfall on record. A quick glance out the tall windows that line the other side of our living room, though, confirms it still hasn't reached us.

"You think it will miss us?" Nico asks, his voice low enough so as not to wake Dad who's still sleeping between us on the couch. His tone's sad enough to make me feel sad.

"No way." I pop another cheese square into my mouth.

He sits up and turns to me. "I really hope to see snow."

"You will," I say. "Look at the map. It's a matter of time."

Nico lies back down. I take a swig of soy milk. Dad snores softly. The meteorologist cautions us to stay off the roads as they cut to a traffic cam's cloudy shot of late-night traffic already slowing to a crawl along I-25.

Eventually, it goes to commercials. Nico sits up, stretches, and makes his way over. He takes the seat across from me and watches, amused, as I finish my last cheese square and begin folding the next American single.

Spinning his phone around on the table, he points toward the fridge with his lips. "There's much better food in there you can eat, Jerry. There's still the caldereta I cooked."

"I'm good." I eat another cheese square, knowing full well Dad would be pissed if he opened the fridge tomorrow to find I finished off his favorite dish.

Nico laughs. "You're strange."

"So I've been told," I say.

But as he loses himself in his phone, what I want to say is that *this* is strange. Him. Here. Like a palm tree transplanted to the top of Pikes Peak.

Before Nico moved in with us, we didn't know much about him beyond that he existed. It was never a secret that Dad had—much to his Catholic family's shame—left his pregnant girlfriend in the Philippines after meeting Mom...and then got Mom pregnant right away. It's just not something anyone's ever really talked about much. So, Sarah and I have always known we had this half brother on the other side of the world who was less than a year older than me. We even have a few photographs of all of us together from the first and only time we traveled to the Philippines, back when Sarah was a toddler, though I only remember fragments from that trip, none of which include Nico.

Then, back in the spring, right after Easter, Dad and Mom sat us down and told us Nico's mom had passed away and that nobody else could take care of him so he'd be moving in with us. Dad made the arrangements, then a few days later we all piled in the car and drove to DIA. Suddenly, this kid who had only been a mythical presence at the edge of my life drifted into reality via the escalator in the International arrivals waiting area. Even then, he wore that huge smile, despite the reasons that had landed him in this country.

Pretty much everyone loved him instantly, and we went from a family of four to a family of five without batting an eye. He was polite and funny and sociable. He was good at sports. He slipped fluidly between languages. Dad was no longer stuck with only an anxious, socially awkward son.

So, yeah. *That's* strange.

When the commercials end and the news comes back on, Nico stays where he is, still lost in his phone. I finish my second cheese mini-tower, down the rest of my soy milk, then get up and put the glass in the sink. I start to leave, but Nico says, "Wait, Jerry."

I stop. "Yeah?"

He looks up from his phone. "Will you stay up with me? Until the snow starts?"

I hesitate, my stomach full of cheese and soy milk, my warm bed calling. "Yeah, I don't know, Nico. I'm tired, man."

"Please? Sarah promised she would, but Mom made her go to bed."

It's also still strange for him to call my mom "Mom." But whatever.

I rub my chin, shaking my head, as if this is a difficult decision. "Sorry, I really need to get some rest. But you do you."

"I understand." His smile fades, making me feel like I kicked a puppy.

Effing Nico.

"Fine," I cave. "I'll stay up."

Nico's face lights back up. "Really?"

"But as soon it starts, that's it. I'm off to bed. If you want to go out in the freezing-ass cold to make snow angels or something, that's up to you. But I'm not doing any of that shit."

"Cool, cool. Thank you, Jerry!" He rushes over and wraps his arms around me, rocking us back and forth as he shows his gratitude by trying to squeeze the life out of me.

I'm not sure why Nico wanted me to stay up with him. An hour later, we're back on either side of Dad on the couch, not even talking. He's glued to his phone—probably texting Erika—and I've just been watching this news about the winter storm hitting everywhere except for the little patch around our city. It's hard not to take everything personally.

I'm just about to announce that I'm throwing in the towel when the TV blinks off, plunging us into a hushed semi-darkness.

"Nico," I whisper, "you sit on the remote again?"

"It wasn't me, Jerry. It's not working." Then he says quietly so as not to wake Dad, "Catch."

The remote smacks me in the side of the head. I pick it up and press the power button, but he's right. Nothing happens. I glance over my shoulder at the unlit clock above the stove. "Power's out."

"But it's not even snowing here yet."

"The storm must be close enough that it took out a nearby transformer or something," I say, as if I know anything about power grids.

"Does the heat need electricity?"

I listen. The house is quiet, as if holding its breath. "It does."

"Hay nako."

"Oh, no, indeed. Hopefully it comes back before we freeze to death," I say with more than a touch of sarcasm.

"Could that really happen?"

"Anything's possible."

"My phone may die first—battery's low."

"Maybe it's a sign we should go to bed."

Nico abandons his phone on the coffee table and rubs his eyes. "No way. It will snow soon. I know it."

"How can you possibly know it?"

"The air. It smells different."

I sniff the air, then say nothing, not willing to admit he's right.

"Do you have any candles?" he asks.

"Only, like, for birthday cakes. But we have a lantern." I get up and dig out our camping lantern out from the hallway closet, hoping it still works. We haven't used it since Dad gave up on trying to pass his love of the outdoors down to my allergy-prone ass years ago. But when I switch it on, it casts a confident halo of white light. Returning to the living room, I set it on the coffee table and plop back down on the couch.

"See," Nico says. "No power, no problem. This happens all the time in the Philippines."

"Right. Dad always says that." We both stare at the lantern as if it's a campfire. "You ever miss your life back in Cavite?"

"Of course, Jerry," he says, face half in light, half in shadow.

"Then why don't you ever talk about it?"

He considers the question. "It's easier not to." There's something in his voice that's shifted. This isn't the smiling, people-pleasing Nico I'm talking to. This is another side of him.

We've never spoken about his mom's illness or anything before Colorado. He slipped so perfectly into his life here that it never seemed like he needed to. But now I wonder if that isn't the case. My therapist always says that when we don't speak our

feelings, we end up carrying them—and that shit gets heavy.
Of course, easier said than done.

"Is that what you're always talking about with my dad?" I
ask, realizing too late I said *my* dad, despite all of Mom's cautions to avoid language that might make Nico feel like he's not
really part of our family.

If Nico picks up on it, he doesn't let it show. Instead, he
shrugs. "Sometimes. Mostly it's normal conversation."

I glance over at Dad still snoring softly in the middle of the
couch.

"What's normal conversation?" I ask.

"I don't know. He asks about my day. School. Nuggets' games.
People back in the Philippines."

Hurt, I let out a sarcastic laugh. "When he talks to me, it's
usually a lecture about my grades, or my lack of interest in join-
ing teams or clubs or anything that would look impressive on
a college app."

"At least it must have been nice having him around when you
were growing up," Nico adds.

"Yeah, sure." Because what else am I supposed to say to the
son Dad left behind? Dad sent money every month, shipped
balikbayan boxes for Christmas and birthdays, and visited every
summer. But still. I change the subject. "What was your mom
like?" I ask, then quickly add, "If you don't want to talk about
her, that's cool."

There's the soft rustle of Nico grabbing a blanket from the
back of the couch and wrapping it around his shoulders. "When
I was younger, she had two jobs. After her first job, she would
walk me home from school, then go to her second job. Our
way home involved walking along this very busy street. No stop
signs or traffic lights. Just a rapid stream of cars, trucks, jeepneys,
trikes, motorcycles, people. No matter what time of day. Not
like here—" he gestures at the neighborhood out the window

"—where everyone's inside all the time and you can go hours without seeing another person."

I nod, remembering many busy narrow streets like that from our last trip to the Philippines, full of near-miss accidents. Whenever we needed to cross, I just held Dad's hand and he'd pull me through without flinching as if performing a magic trick while I was certain I was about to die.

"Anyways, thieves like these crowds. Sometimes, they drive by on a motorcycle, snatch someone's bag, then zoom off before the person knows what happened. And one day that happened near us—a man on a motorcycle slowed, grabbed this woman's phone right out of her hand, then started to drive off. But we were only a few feet away, and when he passed, Nanay snatched the phone from him. The thief tried to hold onto it but lost his balance and tipped over. Then he picked up his bike, scrambled back on, and sped away like a dog with its tail tucked between its legs. Nanay handed the woman her phone and then invited her back to our apartment for merienda." Nico laughs to himself quietly so as not to wake Dad. "That's what she was like."

I laugh quietly, too. "Sounds like she was pretty cool."

"Very cool," he says.

He sniffs, then rubs his eyes. It's too dark to see, but I think he's crying. As happy as his memories of his mom are, I suppose they'll always be laced with the pain of his loss. I should comfort him in some way, but I don't know what to do.

"Thank you for telling me about her," is all I can think to say. "I'm sorry she's gone."

He's quiet for a moment. "You ever wonder why Dad chose your mom over mine?" And there's a serious, practiced tone to his question that makes me think he's spent his entire life asking himself this question.

I glance at Dad still passed out between us on the couch.

"To be honest," I say, "no. Nothing against your mom. I just never have, I guess. I didn't know anything about her."

"That makes sense," he says.

And he sounds like he understands, like he doesn't hold anything against me. But I burn with shame at my self-centeredness laid bare. And I've carried a similar question with me my entire life, only mine never considered anyone else. Even now I can't help but bring it back to me.

"Why doesn't he like me?"

"He loves you, Jerry."

"I didn't say *love*. I said *like*."

"He likes you."

"He really doesn't."

"It's true that he's very strict with you. Much stricter than he is with me."

"At least I'm not the only one who's noticed."

Nico goes on. "It's because he cares. He wants you to succeed."

I don't respond. Genuine or not, I don't need Nico suddenly playing the part of concerned older brother with reassuring lies. I have clearer memories of Dad saying, "I'm disappointed in you," than I have of him saying, "I love you."

"Maybe he'd be happier if he stayed in the Philippines," I say. "With you."

We're quiet for a long time after that. It's as if we're both allowing space for the seed of this alternate reality to sprout, to grow, to bloom, to wither in the silence between us.

"Maybe," Nico says. "Maybe not. I think there are people forever trying to find something or someone or somewhere that will *make* them happy."

Dad's breath catches, startling both Nico and me. He coughs a couple times, his eyes blink open, and he glances around to get his bearings. "Hoy, is it snowing yet?"

"Not yet," I say. "But power's out."

He curses in Tagalog then says something to Nico who responds in Tagalog. Then Dad pushes off the couch, stretches, and lumbers away without saying good-night to either of us.

"You can go to sleep, too, Jerry," Nico says. "I'll be fine by myself."

"Nah, I've made it this far. I'm gonna see it through." I stand, stretch. "But I do need to piss."

I grope my way through the darkness to the first-floor bathroom. Out of habit, I flick the light switch, but it doesn't do anything. I go ahead and pee in the dark, using the sound of my urine splashing into the water to guide my aim as I think about Nico's words. As I'm washing my hands, the light comes on, and I'm startled to see myself in the mirror above the sink.

Tired.

Sad.

Tired of being sad.

Tired of being sad about being an unwanted son.

Fuck it, though. For real. I'm probably no better than Dad at figuring out this happiness thing, but I won't find it if I keep stressing about being a failed version of what he thinks I should be.

I splash cold water on my face and turn off the light.

When I return to the living room, the TV's back on but playing to an empty room. Nico's nowhere in sight. Outside, flakes of snow are falling fast and heavy like fat drops of slow-motion rain. I walk over to the sliding glass door and peer outside. Sure enough, there's Nico, standing in the backyard in the glow of the Christmas lights, arms out, neck craned upward, smiling.

He's out there barefoot in his T-shirt and pajama pants, so I grab his coat and boots and slide open the door. "Nico," I say, his name emerging into the cold as a puff of white. "Here." I toss him his coat and he catches it, then pulls it on, laughing. Then I throw his boots, but they smack onto the ground when he doesn't even try to catch them.

I go back inside, grateful I can finally sleep. But when I pass the closet, I hesitate. Instead of heading upstairs, I slip on my own boots and coat and go outside.

As soon as I do, a snowball hits me right between the eyes. As Nico cackles, I dive behind the grill, brush the ice from my face, and begin rapidly compiling my arsenal, ready to show no mercy.

We pelt each other with snowballs until our arms ache, until we're laughing so hard we're crying, until Dad slides open a second-story window and shouts at us to go to sleep.

"Truce! Truce!" Nico calls after that, hands up.

I launch one final snowball that hits him in the stomach, then meet him in the middle. We shake, our bare hands wet and stinging from the cold. Then he throws his arm around my shoulder and tries to pull me down so I do the same and we fall back together into the snow. So out of breath we can barely laugh anymore, we look up and watch the snow falling from darkness.

"This is amazing," Nico says.

"Yeah," I say, "but the best part of a snow day is actually watching the traffic report the next morning when all those suckers who still have to go to work are stuck on I-25."

He laughs. I laugh.

"Thank you for staying with me," he says.

"Sure, Kuya," I say.

I pull him closer.

Effing Nico.

★ ★ ★ ★ ★

SEARCHING

By Jasmine Warga

After her father died, one of the very first things Hiba Ahmed did was visit the Middle Eastern Grocery Mart. It wasn't that she was hungry. She actually had no appetite at all.

It was that she wanted to see if she was still recognized. Known. Not as a culinary tourist, but as someone whose people had made these recipes for years, their hands rinsing rice, quartering lamb, massaging mulukhiyah. Hiba had never really done any of these things. But she knew people in her bloodline had, and she figured that had to mean something.

She held a paltry bag of rice and approached the counter. She recognized the man sitting on the stool, chewing absently on a toothpick. When she'd come here with her father before, this man had spoken to her father. The exchange had been in Arabic, so Hiba hadn't been able to understand, but her ears recognized warmth and humor, and she knew the men had been friendly with one another. Once her father had put his hand on the small of her back and pushed her up to the counter, and announced in his lilting English, "This is my daughter."

"No Arabic?" the man had said.

Hiba had shook her head, and felt the judgment come down. The man smiled warmly at her anyway, but they both knew what the answer of no meant.

Now she held the bag of rice and held her breath. She wasn't sure exactly what she was trying to prove, but she wanted to be recognized. She wanted him to see her and know she was her father's daughter. Know that she belonged here among the faint smells of cumin and sumac, the sizzle of olive oil on the pan in the back getting ready to prepare to-go sandwiches for the day.

She held her breath. She waited for the man to look up and recognize her. Perhaps accidentally speak to her in Arabic. She would correct him, apologize for her English-only mouth. But then it would be an entryway to talk about her father. To see if he remembered him. He would remember him, she was sure of it.

"Rice? Only rice?"

Hiba's heart squeezed. She gave the man a long stare. She put the bag of rice on the counter. She pleaded with her eyes for him to say something.

"Rice, yeah?" the man repeated.

"Yes," Hiba said, her broad southern Ohio accent apparent even in the one-word response.

"Very good." The man typed quickly at the cash register and held out his hand for payment.

"My father used to bring me here," Hiba mumbled out.

The man raised his eyebrow. "Here?"

Hiba looked over her shoulder. There was no one behind her waiting. She could stay and talk, if he let her.

"Yes. Here. He was...my father. He died."

The man hung his head. He said something quick in Arabic, a mumbled prayer. Hiba was familiar with it. She'd heard it in the months that had followed her father's death, but she still couldn't quite make her own mouth say it right.

"He was Jordanian."

"Yes," the man said. She could tell he was growing impatient.

"I'm Jordanian," she offered.

"But you don't speak Arabic?" It was a question that was also a declaration.

Hiba shook her head.

"Your baba didn't teach you?"

Hiba shook her head again.

"Your mama——?"

"She's not Arab," Hiba explained. "She doesn't speak any Arabic."

"Ah, yes," the man said. He pointed at the bag of rice on the counter. "You make the rice for her?"

"Maybe," Hiba said, grabbed the rice, and left the store.

The Middle Eastern Grocery Mart was about twenty minutes from her home. She crawled into the driver's seat of her old Honda Civic. Her father had helped her pick out the car. He'd been so excited to teach her to drive. He'd cupped her cheeks in his hands and called her his American Dream. She wasn't sure what it meant to be someone else's dream. Especially if that someone was dead.

She leaned back the driver's seat, hugged the rice to her chest, and cried.

Months passed, and Hiba didn't return to the Middle Eastern Grocery Mart. Her mother slowly came out of her own grief fog. They were both able to pretend that things were mostly normal. Every once in a while, Hiba would catch her mom crying by the kitchen sink, but those moments became further and further apart. Hiba learned how to leave her mother alone. She went to school. She did her homework. She tried to be an American Dream.

"I want to go visit," Hiba said in the middle of dinner one night.

"Visit where?"

"Jordan."

Her mom put down her fork. "We went when you were little. Don't you remember? To see Jidu and Setti?"

"Yes. But they're gone now."

Hiba's mom's mouth tightened. "Yes."

"But Aunt Etaf is still there."

"Yes."

"And I want to visit her. Really, I just want to visit the country. I want to learn more about it. Half of me is from there."

Her mom took a gulp of water. "Well, technically, all of you is from *here*, honey. You were born here."

Hiba looked at her mom. "You know what I mean."

Her mom adjusted her glasses. "I don't know. We had plans for this summer. You have your SAT-prep class."

"I can do the workbooks in Jordan."

"I'm not sure I can get that much time off work."

"I—I want to go on my own."

A long silence filled up the kitchen. Dad had always been the loudest of the three of them, so they were used to silence now. But this one was different. It was a waiting silence. Hiba held her breath.

"Hiba," her mom started to say. "I'm not sure about that. You don't know Aunt Etaf that well. And you don't know…"

"How to speak Arabic?"

"Well, yeah."

"Or anything really about Jordan?"

She took another gulp of water. "I'm not sure that's true."

Hiba crossed her arms and put her elbows on the table. Her mom hated elbows on the table.

"Hiba," her mom said.

Hiba took her elbows off the table. But she wasn't going to concede the other point. "I want to go, Mom. I think it would be good for me."

Her mom wiped the corner of her eyes. There weren't any

tears there. Maybe there were no tears left. Maybe it was just a reflex. "You won't find your father there, sweetie. He's gone."

"I know that, Mom. I'm... I just want to know more about where he was from. About where I'm from."

"You're from here."

"I don't look like I'm from here."

"I'm not sure what that is supposed to mean."

Hiba got up from the table. She didn't want to fight with her mom. She didn't know how to explain to her what it was like not to look like she belonged in the place she was from. She knew there was something wrong with that. She knew she was supposed to be working to fix that. But she felt too tired to want to fix that. Instead, she wanted to go somewhere new. Somewhere that might have some answers.

Days passed, and Hiba didn't bring it up again. She watched as the calendar inched closer and closer to summer, filling up with things like SAT-prep classes, tennis lessons, and babysitting gigs.

Finally, she brought it up again.

"I messaged Aunt Etaf," Hiba said. Her mom had made baked chicken and rice. Hiba wasn't sure if she'd used the rice Hiba had bought from the Middle Eastern Grocery Mart. She closed her eyes and took a bite. She felt like she should know by the taste, but she didn't. She took this as a personal failing.

"Oh, yeah? How is she?" her mom answered.

"The rice is good."

"Thanks, sweetie."

"Aunt Etaf said I can come stay with her this summer. She said she'd even buy my plane ticket."

"She doesn't have to buy your plane ticket. We can pay for it."

"Does that mean I can go?"

"I said she doesn't have to buy it," Mom said. "Not that you can go."

"But can I go?"

"Hiba."

"Mom."

"I don't know what you're hoping to accomplish."

"Aren't you curious about where Dad grew up?"

"Of course I am, Hiba. And that's why we took a family trip there."

Hiba felt an unanticipated burst of anger bubble up in her chest. "You think one trip is good enough for 50 percent of my DNA? You think one trip is going to answer all those questions?" She paused, and shook her head. "I'm sorry, Mom. What I mean is—what I'm trying to say—" Hiba paused again. She didn't know how to say what she was trying to say. "One trip wasn't enough. Do you understand? Does that make sense?" Hiba's voice cracked a bit as she delivered the last question.

Her mom sighed. Hiba watched as the edges of her mother's mouth moved up and down. She was carefully weighing what she would say next.

"If it means that much to you, you can go. But only for three weeks. I don't want you to miss your whole summer here. You need to do—"

"American things?"

"Hiba, come on. That's not what I'm saying. It's not fair to make me into the enemy."

"I know, Mom." Hiba stood up from her chair and walked over to her mother. She draped her arms around her mom's shoulders. "But really? I can go?"

"Three weeks," her mom said.

Three weeks it was. Three weeks would have to be enough.

Hiba started making plans right away. She messaged with Aunt Etaf frequently through social media and email. Aunt Etaf didn't always respond. Sometimes she just sent a smiley face back. But Hiba felt comforted by that smiley face. She understood it. It meant her aunt was happy, that her aunt was looking forward to her visit.

The rest of the school year breezed by. The cold rains of

spring gave way to warmer and warmer days, mornings thick with sweaty fog and sparkly dew on the grass. She started to tell her friends about her summer plans. She apologized for her upcoming absence at pool parties and library SAT study sessions.

"Three weeks? Don't you think you'll be bored?" Priya said.

"No, but seriously, what about the SATs?" Madeline said.

"You sound like my mom," Hiba said, and then they let her be. But she could tell they all thought it was weird. Totally strange that Hiba wanted to pack up and leave for three weeks. To go to a country where she hardly knew anyone.

"I do know someone," Hiba said. "My aunt. I have lots of family there."

"Right," Priya and Madeline had said in unison.

Hiba's mom helped her to get ready for the trip. She made Hiba practice over and over again what she was supposed to do when she got to the airport.

"I'm not eight years old," Hiba said.

"You don't speak Arabic," her mother responded.

Hiba was quiet after that. She went back to meticulously packing her suitcase. She rolled her shirts, jeans, and dresses. She picked two practical pairs of shoes and one pair that wasn't so practical.

Finally, the day came. Her mom drove her to the airport. They rode mostly in silence. At the curb, her mom stepped out of the car to help Hiba with her suitcase. She gave her a long hug. "Your dad would be proud of you."

"Thanks, Mom."

"I hope—" her mom started but didn't finish.

"Me, too," Hiba said and hugged her mom again.

She ate a whole bag of potato chips while she waited for her flight to London. She ate two more while she waited in Heathrow Airport, jet-lagged and antsy. She also downed a bottle of orange juice, figuring she should have some kind of nutrient other than potato chips.

On the flight to Amman, she was seated next to a man in a suit. She never understood people who dressed up for airplane rides. It seemed like a relic of a long-lost time. Hiba herself was in sweatpants and an old hoodie. She'd aimed to be as close to pajamas as possible without actually wearing pajamas.

She and the man didn't talk for a long stretch of time. But when the meal service came, they accidentally bumped elbows, and the man turned to her to apologize, and then say hello. A backward order of things, the social dynamics of an airplane.

"You're going to Amman?" the man asked.

Hiba thought this was a strange question. She was on the plane, after all. "Yes."

The man chewed one of the lukewarm microwaved vegetables. Hiba stared down at her own tray and wished she had another bag of potato chips. When she looked up, the man was staring at her again.

"I'm visiting family," Hiba said, answering the question he hadn't asked.

"You're Jordanian?"

"Half," Hiba said. She hated this part. The dividing up of her identity into neat fractions, the quantifying of how much this and how much that.

"But you're American," the man pressed. It was not a question.

Hiba answered, anyway. "Yes. Jordanian American. My father was born in Amman."

"What's he do now?"

Hiba couldn't bring herself to answer that question honestly. "He's an engineer," she said. He had been an engineer. It wasn't a complete lie.

"Very nice." The man nodded his approval. "He must be very proud of you. Good for you to be interested in your culture."

The conversation trailed off after that. The airline attendant collected the trays. Both the man and Hiba pretended to sleep, uncomfortably squirming around in the confines of their small seats, Hiba occasionally sneaking a glance over her shoulder, straining to try and see out the window.

By the time the plane landed, Hiba really had to pee. She hadn't calculated how long the descent would be as they had to stay seated the entire time the plane was over Israeli airspace. She danced in place as she waited her turn to disembark and then rushed to the restroom. As she washed her hands, she stared at herself in the mirror and felt oddly pleased that at least she'd been able to find the bathroom. She imagined bragging about that to her dad, and then she started to laugh, which eventually gave way to tears. She splashed cold water on her face and headed to the carousel to pick up her suitcase.

Once she had her suitcase, she followed the directions to the entry point where they'd check her visa. This was easy enough, since the signs were in Arabic as well as English. There was probably something wrong about that—colonialism and all— but she didn't want to dwell on it too long because at this current moment, it was very opportune for her that the signs were, indeed, in English.

When it was her turn, she stepped up to the counter and handed over her passport. Her heart rattled in her chest as she replayed the instructions her mother gave her. She felt like she should be hearing her father's voice instead of her mother's right then—and the guilt and confusion of that only made her heart rattle more.

The man at the counter spoke to her in rapid Arabic.

"I'm sorry," Hiba said. "I don't understand. I only speak English."

"But your name is Hiba Ahmed."

"Yes."

"Hiba Ahmed does not speak Arabic?"

It's only after the man smiled that she realized he was joking. He stamped her passport and handed it back. Her hands trembled a little as she put the passport back into her bag.

"My dad never taught me," she said. She did not wait for the man's response. There was nothing he could possibly say.

When she came down the escalator and moved into the public atrium of the airport, she was relieved to see her aunt's face. The relief was more palpable than she'd anticipated. An anxiety she hadn't realized was there began to uncoil inside of her.

Her aunt smiled warmly as she caught sight of Hiba. She stretched her arms out wide in anticipation of a hug. When Hiba reached Aunt Etaf, she tumbled into the embrace. Aunt Etaf smelled like rosewater and sandalwood. She was dressed in nice dark jeans and a flowy blouse, her dark hair falling down her back in a braid.

"It's so good to see you, sweetheart," Aunt Etaf said, releasing Hiba from the hug and kissing the top of her head. "I'm so glad you came."

So was a word that Aunt Etaf kept using. On the drive to her apartment, she remarked that it had been so hot lately, that there had been so much traffic. That work was so busy. That the city of Amman was changing so much.

"You won't believe it," Aunt Etaf said. "We even have Dunkin' Donuts now." When Hiba didn't respond immediately, Aunt Etaf repeated, "Dunkin' Donuts," sounding out each syllable like it would unlock something. It didn't.

Aunt Etaf did not use the word *so* when it came to talking about Hiba's dad, though. She did not mention him at all. Hiba waited and waited. She waited during the car ride home from the airport, she waited during their first dinner together—a meal of carryout American pizza where Hiba awkwardly explained that she was happy to eat Arabic food and her aunt didn't need to cater to American tastes. Hiba waited during their second meal, and third, and so on—meals of carryout, of shawarma sandwiches, or once, when Aunt Etaf got off early, she grilled up a fish and it was one of the most delicious things Hiba had ever tasted, the lemon juice that had been squeezed on top lingering in her mouth for the rest of the night. Hiba waited in the early hours of the morning when Aunt Etaf made them both tea before she left for work at her job in the marketing department of a real estate development firm, and Hiba waited when they sat together in her apartment's garden and looked out over the twinkling hills of Amman.

"Why do you think my dad left?" Hiba finally said one evening when she was tired of waiting—waiting for the *so*, waiting for anything, for everything.

"Left?" Aunt Etaf took a long drag of her cigarette. They were both sitting on wrought-iron patio furniture. Hiba had a woven blanket wrapped around her shoulders. She still wasn't used to how cool it got at night.

"Left here. For America," Hiba clarified. She felt a hunger rumble inside of her. Asking the one very small question had revved the appetite of curiosity that she had tried to keep in check. She didn't want to be an annoying guest. She made her bed every day. She helped her aunt with the dishes. She entertained herself by walking the streets of her aunt's neighborhood, smiling at strangers, hoping they would recognize her as a local and also terrified that they would, and then she would be revealed to be an American who didn't speak a word of Arabic. She'd found comfort in seeing faces that looked like hers. Back home, she was a dot of brown in a sea of white.

But there hadn't been much to discover about her father in her aunt's neighborhood. Her father hadn't grown up in this fancy part of Amman. When her dad was little, the family had lived in a tiny apartment in downtown Amman on the east side of the city. Her aunt now lived on the fashionable west side. The buildings in this neighborhood made of slick white sandstone. The gardens curated, despite the lack of water. The streets freshly paved, new construction everywhere you turned. Street signs that no one local used but signified wealth and someone's idea of progress.

And no matter how many times Hiba took the same walk, no one ever talked to her. Part of her was relieved, of course, not to have to explain her lack of Arabic. But the other half couldn't stop wondering why. What marked her so clearly as an outsider? Could they tell from the shape of her lips that she didn't speak Arabic? Or was it her American sneakers? She kept walking, though, looking for an answer that she wasn't sure could be found.

When her aunt was in the apartment, Hiba studied what she could about her. Noticing the slow and steady way her aunt filled the teakettle each morning, the rhythmic way she wiped down the counter, the old Arabic song she hummed under her breath while pulling off her shoes that seemed both practical and stylish. Hiba wondered if her father had known that song. She couldn't remember him ever humming it. She tried to imagine it coming out of his mouth, and then, sometimes, she would try to imagine it coming out of her mouth—her lips curling around those Arabic words.

"Ah," Aunt Etaf said. She considered Hiba's question, the one about why her father had left Jordan for America. She twirled her cigarette between her fingers. Hiba had been subjected to a relentless education about the dangers of smoking and constantly resisted the urge to knock the cigarette out of her aunt's hands. "I guess he was drawn there. He was searching for something, I think."

"Searching?" Hiba's voice was soft. She could feel the explosion of questions erupting inside of her, a slight giddiness at getting close to something, and a fear of messing it all up by pushing her aunt too hard.

"Yes." Her aunt gestured at the air. "Searching. Looking? Isn't that the right English word?"

Aunt Etaf's English was nearly perfect, but she frequently asked Hiba if she was using the right word. Hiba always reassured her that her vocabulary choices were correct.

"Yes. I think it is. I was just wondering what he was searching for."

Her aunt smiled a little, traces of sadness in the corner of her eyes. "Ah. That's the question."

"Do you mean like...money?"

Aunt Etaf laughed, a sharp sound that made Hiba sit up straighter.

"Like success? In America?" Hiba tried to explain what she meant, but the more she talked, the more her face warmed.

"Do you think of America as success?"

Hiba felt her face warm some more. "No. That's not what I meant—I—"

"I'm only kidding," her aunt said, and laughed again, this time it was a more gentle sound. "It's just very American, right? To think of America as success?" Aunt Etaf tipped her head back and laughed again. "But it's also very Jordanian. We, too, think of America as success."

Hiba squirmed in her chair. "I just meant—my dad, it always seemed like he wanted, I don't know—"

"A big house?" Aunt Etaf offered. Another laugh.

"Yes. And—"

"He was searching, habibti. Like I said. Aren't we all searching?"

"But he's gone now. Do you think he found it?"

"Ah, ah, ah," Aunt Etaf said. She made a clicking sound with her tongue. She leaned over and cupped Hiba's face in her hands and kissed her forehead.

Hiba wasn't sure what to do. That didn't feel like an answer. But her aunt didn't say anything else. A silence settled around them. In the far distance, Hiba looked out over the hills of Amman, all the faint lights, twinkling in and out. She imagined all the people. She wondered about them, if they were searching for something, if they'd found it.

"Can we go?" Hiba finally said, breaking the silence. "Will you take me?"

"Where?"

"To here." Hiba pulled out an old faded photograph. She'd found it in a drawer in the kitchen of Aunt Etaf's apartment. She knew she should be embarrassed by her snooping, but her curiosity won out. "Here." She pointed at the picture. "Where you grew up. You and my dad."

"Ah." Aunt Etaf smiled faintly. "You found that photo?"

Hiba nodded sheepishly.

"It's the only one I have."

"I'll put it back."

"It's okay, habibti. You can have it."

Hiba swallowed. She wasn't sure what to say. She wanted to keep the photo, but she didn't know if that was okay. So instead, she asked the other question. Again. "Can we go?"

"To the old apartment?"

Hiba nodded.

There was a long pause. Hiba held the photograph gently, her fingers trembling.

"Sure. That can be arranged," Aunt Etaf finally said.

"Thank you," Hiba said. She felt her eyes watering and then felt the quick surge of embarrassment. She moved to wipe her eyes, but her aunt stopped her.

"You know your father isn't there, though? You know that, right? Habibti, let me know that you understand."

"You sound like my mom. She said the same thing when I said I wanted to come to Jordan."

"Your mama is a smart woman."

"I know my dad won't actually be there. I'm not delusional."

Aunt Etaf screwed up her face. "Delusional?" she repeated.

Hiba defined the word, even though she was pretty sure her aunt knew what it meant. Then she offered all the reasons she wanted to see the apartment. That her father had never taken her there on their previous family trip to Jordan. That she thought it was important to see where he had grown up. That maybe that would give her a better sense of who her father was.

Her aunt listened patiently to Hiba's rambling. But once Hiba was done talking, her aunt repeated, "Your father isn't there, though."

"I know. You've said that already. Everyone has said that," Hiba said defensively. She didn't want to be angry with her aunt, but she was starting to feel the itch of frustration. "I just want to go."

At this, her aunt smiled a little. "To search."

Hiba crossed her arms. "Maybe. I don't know—"

"It's okay to not know." Aunt Etaf reached out and put her hand over Hiba's. "It's okay."

Hiba cried a little when her aunt said that. She was too surprised by her tears this time to feel the same shame that she had felt before. Her aunt didn't cry, but she sat with Hiba and kept holding her hand.

The next morning when Hiba got out of bed, her aunt was waiting for her in the living room instead of moving steadily around the kitchen. Sun streamed in through the window, and Hiba had heard the singing of the muezzin hours ago, so she knew it was late in the morning.

"Shouldn't you be at work?" Hiba said. After she said it, she realized she sounded rude. She'd been in Jordan now more than a week and the newfound familiarity she felt toward her aunt was making her brash. She put her hand over her mouth. "Sorry."

Her aunt shook her head. "I should be. But I'm taking you today."

Hiba's pulse quickened. "To the apartment?"

"Yes. Come on."

Before heading out to the car, Hiba slid the photograph she'd found back into her aunt's drawer. She pressed her fingers to her lips and touched her dad's childhood face. Then she walked outside and squeezed into the front seat of her aunt's tiny old car. They rode in silence through the traffic-y curved streets of Amman, winding down the hills of the west side over to the hills of the east. Once they got to old Amman, the true downtown, the traffic was bumper to bumper. Lots of honking and shouting, but her aunt stayed calm. Hiba thought it was amazing that her aunt never consulted a GPS or any other kind of directions. Back home, Hiba could hardly make it anywhere without using her phone.

"Here," her aunt finally said, pulling in front of a five-story apartment building. The stone was more weathered than the buildings Hiba had seen in her aunt's current neighborhood. Pockmarked and stained. And it was situated near the ragged edge of the cliff, sandwiched between two other buildings that were in a similar condition to it. The land around it was dry and dusty. There was no manicured landscaping.

"We lived on the third floor. On the east side." Aunt Etaf pointed up.

Hiba stepped out of the car. She shaded her eyes with her hand and stared up at the building. The sky was a brilliant cloudless blue. The noises of downtown Amman swirled around her. Out of the building's front door, a mother exited, cradling a newborn. Hiba raised her hand into a wave, and then realized it might be an inappropriate gesture. The woman smiled at Hiba anyway, half wave and all.

"So?" Aunt Etaf called out from the car. "Did you find it?"

"I'm looking," Hiba said softly, still staring up at the building, still searching.

★ ★ ★ ★ ★

ABOUT THE EDITORS

REBECCA BALCÁRCEL loves to pet her cat, eat popcorn, and play in the sandbox of language. She authored *Shine On, Luz Véliz* (2022) about a bicultural Latina who codes, and *The Other Half of Happy* (2019), a Pura Belpré Honor Book, ALSC Notable Book, and silver medalist in the International Latino Book Awards, as well as the Américas Award. She serves the students of Tarrant County College as an Associate Professor of English, and her YouTube audience as the SixMinuteScholar.

ISMÉE WILLIAMS is the award-winning author of *Water in May* and *This Train Is Being Held*, a Junior Library Guild Gold Standard Selection and winner of the ILBA Gold Medal for best YA Romance. Ismée is a cofounder of the Latinx Kidlit Book Festival, as well as a pediatric cardiologist in New York City, where she lives with her family. She is the daughter of a Cuban immigrant and grew up listening to her abuelo's bedtime stories. Follow her on Twitter and IG @IsmeeWilliams, and her website ismeewilliams.com.

ABOUT THE AUTHORS

Born and raised in Mexico City, **ADI ALSAID** is the author of several YA novels including *Let's Get Lost, We Didn't Ask for This, North of Happy*, a Kirkus Best Book nominee, and *Before Takeoff.* He's also the editor of *Come On In: 15 Stories of Immigration and Finding Home.* He currently lives in Chicago with his wife and two cats, where he occasionally spills hot sauce on things (and cats).

AKEMI DAWN BOWMAN is a critically acclaimed author who writes across genres. Her novels have received multiple accolades and award nominations, and her debut novel, *Starfish*, was a William C. Morris Award Finalist. She has a BA in Social Sciences from the University of Nevada, Las Vegas, and currently lives in Scotland with her family. She overthinks everything, including this bio.

ERIN ENTRADA KELLY received the 2018 Newbery Medal for *Hello, Universe*; a 2021 Newbery Honor for *We Dream of Space*; and the 2016 APALA Award for *The Land of Forgotten Girls,* among other honors. Her books are *New York Times* bestsellers and have appeared on numerous Best Books lists. She serves on the faculty of Hamline University's MFAC program and lives in Delaware. Learn more at erinentradakelly.com.

ANIKA FAJARDO was born in Colombia and raised in Minnesota, and she is the author of *Magical Realism for Non-Believers: A Memoir of Finding Family*. Her books for young readers include *What If a Fish* and *Meet Me Halfway*, as well as *Encanto: A Tale of Three Sisters*, the middle-grade companion novel to the Disney film. She lives with her family in Minneapolis, where she teaches at Augsburg University's MFA program.

SHANNON GIBNEY is a writer, educator, activist, and the author of *See No Color* (Carolrhoda Lab, 2015) and *Dream Country* (Dutton, 2018), YA novels that won Minnesota Book Awards in 2016 and 2019. Gibney is faculty in English at Minneapolis College, where she teaches writing. A Bush Artist and McKnight Writing Fellow, her book *The Girl I Am, Was, and Never Will Be* explores themes of transracial adoption through speculative memoir (Dutton, 2023). She is also at work on *When We Become Ours: A YA Adoptee Anthology*, with writer Nicole Chung (Harper Teen, 2023).

I.W. GREGORIO is a practicing urologist by day, masked avenging YA writer by night. She is the author of the Schneider Award-winning *This Is My Brain in Love* (an Amazon Best Book, Bank Street Best Book, and NEIBA Windows & Mirrors Selection), and the Lambda Literary Finalist *None of the Above* (a Publishers Weekly Flying Start and ALA Rainbow List selection). As an ally, she is proud to be a board member of interACT: Advocates for Intersex Youth, and is a founding member of We Need Diverse Books. A recovering ice hockey player, she lives in Pennsylvania with her husband and two children. Find her online at iwgregorio.com and on Twitter/Instagram at @iwgregorio.

VEERA HIRANANDANI is the award-winning author of several books for young people. Her most recent middle-grade novel, *How to Find What You're Not Looking For*, recieved the 2022 Sydney Taylor Book Award, the 2022 Jane Addams Book Award, and was a finalist for the 2022 National Jewish Book Award. It was also named a Best Children's Book of the Year by *Amazon*, *Kirkus Reviews*, and *Bank Street College*, among other honors. The Newbery Honor–winning *The Night Diary* also received the 2019 Walter Dean Myers Honor Award, the 2018 Malka Penn Award for Human Rights in Children's Literature, and several other honors and state reading-list awards. Her first novel for young readers, *The Whole Story of Half a Girl*, was named a Sydney Taylor Notable Book and was a South Asia Book Award Highly Commended selection. She's also the author of the chapter book series *Phoebe G. Green*. She earned her MFA in Fiction Writing at Sarah Lawrence College. A former book editor at Simon & Schuster, she now teaches creative writing and is working on her next novel.

NASUĠRAQ RAINEY HOPSON is the author of the short story "The Cabin" in the award-winning collection *Rural Stories: 15 Authors Challenge Assumptions About Small-Town America* (2020), and the story "The Weight of a Name" in *Tasting Light: Ten Science Fiction Stories to Rewire Your Perceptions* (2022). Her debut novel *Eagle Drums* will be available in the fall of 2023. She is a tribally enrolled Inupiaq, an illustrator, and arctic gardener. She currently lives with her husband, two daughters, a small pack of dogs, a resident cat, and some chickens in Anaktuvuk Pass, Alaska, where she continues to explore the world and stories of being a modern Indigenous person. She can be found at nasugraqhopson.com.

When **EMIKO JEAN** isn't writing, she is reading. Before she became a writer, she was an entomologist, a candlemaker, a florist, and most recently, a teacher. She lives in Washington with her husband and children. She is the *New York Times* bestselling author of *Tokyo Dreaming*, *Tokyo Ever After* (a Reese Witherspoon-Hello Sunshine Summer YA Book Club pick), *Empress of all Seasons* (an Indie Next List selection), and *We'll Never Be Apart*.

TORREY MALDONADO was born and raised in Brooklyn, growing up in the Red Hook housing projects. He has taught for New York City public schools for over twenty-five years, and his fast-paced, compelling stories are inspired by his and his students' experiences. His popular novels for young readers include *What Lane?*, which garnered many starred reviews and was cited by *O, The Oprah Magazine* and the *New York Times* for being an essential book to discuss racism and allyship; *Tight*, which won the Christopher Award, was an ALA Notable Book, and an NPR and Washington Post Best Book of the Year; and his very first novel, *Secret Saturdays*, which has been in print for over ten years. His most recent middle-grade, *Hands*, published in 2023. He also has written picture books that will be on shelves soon. Learn more at torreymaldonado.com or connect on Instagram and Twitter @torreymaldonado.

Born in France, **MÉLINA MANGAL** grew up in the Midwest. Mélina's fiction appears in Milkweed's *Stories from Where We Live* series and in the anthology *All the Songs We Sing*. Mélina also authored a number of biographies for young readers, including the picture book *The Vast Wonder of the World: Biologist Ernest Everett Just,* winner of the Carter G. Woodson Book Award and named an NCSS/CBC Notable Social Studies Trade Book for Young People. Mélina works as a school librarian in Minnesota and enjoys spending time outdoors with her family, whether it's in her backyard or hiking in the woods. Mélina's first fictional picture book is *Jayden's Impossible Garden,* winner of the first annual Strive/Free Spirit Black Voices in Children's Literature contest. Visit her online at melinamangal.com.

GOLDY MOLDAVSKY is a Latina Jew from Lima, Peru (hey, that rhymes!). She is the *New York Times* bestselling author of *Kill the Boy Band, No Good Deed,* and *The Mary Shelley Club.* When she isn't writing thrillers, satires, and dark comedies, she is cooking up new stories in wildly disparate genres and spending time with her family in Brooklyn, New York.

RANDY RIBAY is an award-winning author of YA fiction, including *An Infinite Number of Parallel Universes, After the Shot Drops*, and, most recently, *Patron Saints of Nothing*—which received five-starred reviews, was selected as a Freeman Book Award winner, and was a finalist for the National Book Award, *LA Times* Book Prize, Walden Book Award, Edgar Award, International Thriller Writers Award, and the CILIP Carnegie Medal. Randy was born in the Philippines and raised in the United States. He earned his BA in English Literature from the University of Colorado at Boulder and his Ed.M. in Language and Literacy from Harvard Graduate School of Education. He currently lives in the San Francisco Bay Area with his wife, son, and cat-like dog.

LORIEL RYON has long held a passion for science and books. During her childhood, she was often found with her nose in a book, even at the dinner table. Now a writer of MG and YA fiction, she finds that her stories are often influenced by these two interests, as well as her upbringing in a bicultural family. Loriel is a registered nurse who holds bachelor's degrees in both nursing and biology. She currently lives in New Mexico with her husband and her two daughters who also share her love of reading. Her debut MG novel, *Into the Tall, Tall Grass,* was published by Margaret K. McElderry in spring 2020.

TARA SIM is the author of *The City of Dusk,* the *Scavenge the Stars* duology, and the *Timekeeper* trilogy, and can typically be found wandering the wilds of the Bay Area, California. When she's not chasing cats or lurking in bookstores, she writes books about magic, murder, and mayhem. Follow her on Twitter at @EachStarAWorld, and check out her website for fun extras at tarasim.com.

ERIC SMITH is a literary agent and YA author from Elizabeth, New Jersey. His recent books include *Don't Read the Comments*, *You Can Go Your Own Way*, and the anthology *Battle of the Bands*, co-edited with Lauren Gibaldi, and *Jagged Little Pill: The Novel*, written in collaboration with Alanis Morissette, Diablo Cody, and Glenn Ballard. He lives in Philadelphia with his wife and son, and enjoys pop-punk, video games, and crying over every movie.

JASMINE WARGA is the *New York Times* bestselling author of *Other Words for Home* (a John Newbery Honor book), *The Shape of Thunder* (a Junior Library Guild and Indie Next List selection), *A Rover's Story* (also a Junior Library Guild and Indie Next List selection), and YA books, *My Heart and Other Black Holes* and *Here We Are Now*, which have been translated into over twenty different languages. Originally from Cincinnati, Ohio, she now lives in the Chicago area with her family in a house filled with books.

KAREN YIN is a peace-loving, riot-inciting middle child with one eyebrow permanently arched. A second-generation American of Chinese descent, Karen is the author of multiple picture books, including *Whole Whale* (Barefoot Books) and *So Not Ghoul* (Page Street Kids). Recent accolades include a 2021 California Arts Council Individual Artist Fellowship, selection of her flash fiction by the Los Angeles Public Library for its permanent collection in 2020, and a 2015 Lambda Literary Fellowship. Winner of the 2017 ACES Robinson Prize for furthering the craft of editing, Karen founded several acclaimed digital resources for writers and editors, including *Conscious Style Guide*. Find her online at karenyin.com and her book recommendations at diversepicturebooks.com.